MW00437033

NO ONE DOES REVENGE LIKE A SPARTAN

GLITCHED

-BOOK ONE OF THE GLITCHED SERIES-

EISLEY ROSE

Majestic Pen
PUBLISHING

This is a work of fiction.

Names, characters, places, and incidents either are the product of the author's imagination or are used fictitiously. Any resemblance to actual persons, living or dead, events, or locales is entirely coincidental.

Copyright © 2024 Eisley Rose. All rights reserved.

No part of this book may be reproduced or used in any manner without written permission of the copyright owner except for the use of quotations in a book review. For more information, please contact:

info@majesticpenpublishing.com

Majestic Pen Publishing

312 SW Greenwich Dr, Suite 1643

Lee's Summit, MO 64082

www.majesticpenpublishing.com

The work was written by a human, and no AI was involved.

NO AI TRAINING: Without in any way limiting the author's [and publisher's] exclusive rights under copyright, any use of this publication to "train" generative artificial intelligence (AI) technologies to generate text is expressly prohibited. The author reserves all rights to license uses of this work for generative AI training and development of machine learning language models.

This book contains information intended to entertain the readers and is in no way meant to reflect actual medical advice. The beliefs presented in this novel are not the author's personal views, and you should consult your doctor for your individual needs. The purpose of this book is purely to entertain.

Cover art by Volodymyr Volianyuk

Cover design by Miblart

Edited by Jenna Adkins, Rebecca Prouse, and Amy Scott

The text of this book was set in Fanwood

Manufactured in the United States of America

ISBN 978-1-962686-00-6 (Paperback)

ISBN 978-1-962686-01-3 (Hardcover)

ISBN 978-1-962686-02-0 (Ebook)

Library of Congress Control Number: 2023951341

First edition February 2024

www.eisleyrosebooks.com

✳ Created with Vellum

This book is dedicated to anyone whose life has spiraled out of control.

It may not have been easy, but you fought to survive.

———

Inside you beats the heart of a Spartan.

- Glitched Inspiration Playlist -

Chapter 1:
"Sweet Dreams" by Marilyn Manson
"Where Is My Mind" by YOAV

Chapter 7:
"Poem" by Taproot

Chapter 10:
"Voices in My Head" by Falling in Reverse

Chapter 13:
"Coming Undone" by Korn

Chapter 15:
"Chandelier" (Sia cover) by Designer Disguise featuring
Alex of Osatia

Chapter 20:
"Click Click Boom" by Saliva

Chapter 23:
"Love Bites (So Do I)" by Halestorm

Chapter 25:
"I'm With You" by Avril Lavigne

Chapter 31:
"Paralyzer" by Finger Eleven
"Astronaut in the Ocean" by Our Last Night

Chapter 32:
"Believer" by Imagine Dragons

Chapter 33:
"Bodies" by Drowning Pool

Chapter 37:
"So Cold" by Breaking Benjamin

Chapter 40:
"I Get Off" by Halestorm

Chapter 44:
Bonnie Tyler "Total Eclipse of the Heart" cover by Our Last Night

Chapter 46:
"Echo" by Trapt
"Seize the Power" by Yonaka

Chapter 49:
"Hero" by Skillet
"Stay" by Rihanna featuring Mikky Ekko

Chapter 50:
"Grow As We Go" by Ben Platt
"In Case You Didn't Know Brett Young" by Boyce Avenue acoustic

Chapter 51:
Goo Goo Dolls "Iris" cover by Our Last Night
Britney Spears "Toxic" cover by Our Last Night

AN ANCIENT PROPHECY

"Fear not the one soul split in two, for they are destined to save this realm. Both bathed in blood and consumed by fire, absolution must be at the helm."

—The Oracle at Delphi (371 BCE)

CHAPTER ONE

Hovering above Alessa, her torturer growled in a thick Hispanic accent, "Where is it?"

Refusing to answer, she glared at the scarred man from the metallic chair she was tightly bound to, the silence stretching between their sweat-drenched bodies.

He spat on the ground, and his long, tanned arm flew forward. As his fist connected with Alessa's ear, her head jerked violently to the side.

The Spartan warrior squeezed her eyes shut, and a high-pitched ringing reverberated throughout her skull. Bending down in front of her face, the man exhaled his acrid breath, filling her nostrils with the nauseating scent of cigar smoke and tequila.

Bright red blood trailed down Alessa's jawline as she struggled to focus.

"Look, if she hasn't told us by now, it's not going to happen," a disembodied voice grumbled behind her attacker.

Another man gestured toward Alessa's broken body. "She's

not even healing anymore. How much longer can she hold out?"

Her torturers exchanged terse whispers while scarlet beads dripped down to the floor from Alessa's chin, diluting with the brown-tinged water trapped in the cracks.

Over the last day, the Spartan warrior's accelerated healing had ceased altogether, leaving her skin split open and her bones broken.

She hated to admit it, but they were right. As advanced as her mind and body may have been, thanks to the Spartans' betterment in medicine and science, Alessa couldn't survive much longer.

In a final act of defiance, she lifted her head and parted her pale lips into a psychotic grin, exposing the crimson-drenched cracks between her teeth.

Lashing out, the scarred man shattered Alessa's orbital bone with a sickening crunch.

Turning away, he rubbed his bruised knuckles. "Not so defiant now, are we, *mi hermosa?*"

The vision in Alessa's decimated eye vanished altogether, and she choked on thick, green bile as hot, salty tears streamed down her plum-colored cheek.

Disappearing behind one of the white brick walls, the scarred man stopped before a petite young blonde.

Her hazel eyes met his, and she stepped toward him, slapping a filled syringe into the palm of his hand. "Here it is, as promised."

Inspecting the burnt orange liquid, he rolled the glass container between his fingertips. "This'll do the job, *sí?*"

The blonde answered mechanically through tight lips, "I have no doubt it will erase her memory."

Flicking the side of the barrel, the tanned man smiled broadly. "Would you care to watch?"

Staring at his hands painted red with blood, the young woman clenched her jaw and pumped her fists. Struggling to maintain her composure, she shook her head and exited the room. "Just be done with it."

With a click of his tongue, he strolled back into the room. Glancing over at a nearby table cluttered with various tools of torture, his lips curled up in excitement. Before facing the bound Spartan, he set the syringe on the tray and grabbed a curved knife.

An uncontrollable shiver shot up Alessa's spine as he inched closer.

"We've given you more than enough time to cooperate. This is the last time I will ask you. Where ... did ... you ... hide ... the ... download?"

So, this is how I die. Not in some epic battle, not by my love's side, but instead, being tortured for information by Eric's thugs. I failed. I failed all of humanity. How did this happen? No one will know who's behind the attack. I definitely will not receive a warrior's funeral after this epic fuck up.

Alessa squeezed her eyes shut as the attacker waved the silver blade mere inches in front of her face.

I won't get to say goodbye. Gods, help me, somehow, some way. Hear my plea, Hades. I am not ready to spend eternity in your realm.

"Is your refusal to speak your final answer?" the man demanded through clenched teeth.

Alessa's wet eyelashes separated, and she sat as far forward as her restraints allowed before uttering five damning words.

"I'll see you in Hades."

Enraged, her attacker snatched the syringe from the table.

Who will take care of—

Alessa's thoughts were interrupted by a long needle being thrust into the base of her skull.

The chemicals in the orange liquid spread throughout her brain, rapidly frying her neural connections. With the vanishing of Alessa's memories, she was left with only her name.

"Oh, how I am going to enjoy this," her tormenter hissed, pressing the cold steel against her discolored skin.

Running the flat edge of the blade slowly up the Spartan's abdomen, he drew a jagged line from her navel to her breastbone.

A whimper escaped from between Alessa's trembling lips as he slammed his hand down on her shoulder.

"No, no, no." She writhed beneath the man's grasp.

His hot breath burned up the side of her neck. "I want you to know how much fun I've had with you." He licked the trail of sweat dripping down her throat. "But now, it must come to an end."

Thrusting his arm forward, he pierced Alessa's gut with the hooked end of the blade.

As he tore through flesh and muscle, she released an agonizing grunt, and upon withdrawal of the weapon, she fell unconscious.

Ugh ... this hurts so much. Where am I? What's happening?

She was lying on the floor of an older van; her body having been thrown haphazardly upon crinkly white plastic. Ridges in the metal frame dug into her broken ribs, but thanks to the arguing men, Alessa's quiet whimpers went unheard.

The disgusting taste of copper forced itself up the back of her throat, and every inhalation was more painful than the last.

One of the men nervously glanced back and forth between Alessa and the front window. "Guys, we gotta get her out of here. The plastic wrap under her is barely keeping the blood in place. Do you know how hard it is to get blood stains out of this floor?"

"Fine. This looks like as good a spot as any," the driver agreed.

The rackety old van screeched to a halt, and the side door closest to Alessa opened.

Unable to muster the energy to cry out loud, Alessa screamed internally as calloused hands grabbed her naked body and shoved her toward the exit. While dangling precariously over the edge, a stiff boot kicked her out and sped away.

Hitting the rough pavement, she stared at the bright morning sun.

What could I possibly have done to deserve this?

With the weakening of her pulse and the cessation of her beating heart, Alessa could no longer prolong her inevitable meeting with the king of the underworld.

And so, with one final breath, she lost her battle against death.

"Shock advised," declared the electronic voice from within the AED. "Everyone, stand clear."

"Clear!" a female paramedic yelled.

Beep ... Beep ... Beep ... Beep.

The second paramedic sighed in relief. "We've got a pulse. It's faint, but she's alive."

CHAPTER TWO

A distorted beeping echoed as Alessa's hearing was restored, and with the return of her remaining senses, the slow, steady rhythm of the heart rate monitor increased.

"Yeah, I know. All of this is insane," a muffled voice said from across the room.

"Right, Misty? No one should have been able to survive what this lady went through," a second voice agreed.

"This doesn't happen to just anyone," the first voice said.

"What are you saying?"

"I mean, do you think she's CIA or something?"

With the realization that a hard plastic tube was stuck down her throat, Alessa panicked. Her heart rate monitor went berserk as her hands flew up to her mouth.

"Wait! Hold on; let us help you," one of the gossiping voices urged, running to her bedside. "Don't touch it. I'll take it out." The person gloved up as Alessa's hands flew haphazardly.

Working together, they extracted the breathing tube.

Alessa's throat burned as cool air touched the flesh where the plastic tube had been lying in her trachea, and when she attempted to speak, all that came out was something that resembled a toad's croak.

"Oh, let me get you something to drink." One of the women rushed over to the sink.

As the cold liquid hit the back of her raw throat, Alessa hissed. It felt as though hundreds of tiny knives were stabbing her.

Uncomfortable with being in the same room as the newly awakened patient, the women nervously glanced at one another. "We need to notify the doctor you're awake," said one of the nurses before they both darted out of the room.

Confused about why she was hooked up to a breathing machine, Alessa wiggled her toes beneath the cream-colored sheet. Watching the covers dance, she exhaled. *I'm not paralyzed.*

Her toes rubbed against the underside of a thin, scratchy sheet, which had been pulled up to her waist and tucked between the raised side rails and mattress.

As she stretched her legs, Alessa was caught off guard by how excruciating the slight movement was, and with a sharp intake of breath, she inhaled a potent combination of cleaning supplies and illness. The oddly familiar scent stung her nostrils. *I think it's safe to assume I'm in a hospital.*

The fluorescent light above Alessa's head strobed brighter for a few seconds, and as she struggled to lift her hands to block the flickering light, her arm was pulled back by a connection of tubes burrowed deep into the back of her hand.

A single white wire was taped onto the end of her pointer finger, and the device's red light illuminated the tip of her fingernail.

Alessa's forehead furrowed in concern. *Why can't I remember anything that happened to me? How did I get here?*

7

As tears threatened to spill over, she noticed a fresh scar extending from her left wrist up to her elbow.

Placing her shaking fingertips on the puffy red line, she traced its path.

The heart rate monitor's beeping increased, and she covered her mouth. "What happened to me?"

Alessa's gaze drifted past her arm to the sheet covering her body, and she threw it off to the side.

A faded blue gown and yellow non-slip socks engulfed her petite, muscular frame.

Her abdominal muscles tensed with the jerky movement as she pushed a button on the bed to sit upright. "Ah!" Alessa exclaimed after suffering a sharp spasm in her midsection.

Gingerly inching the hospital gown up her legs, she wrinkled the fabric into a ball.

Her stomach lurched at the first sight of her skin's discoloration. The unsightly yellow-brown bruises covered the entirety of both of her lower legs.

Hot tears burned lines down her cheeks, and she frantically tugged at the remaining material. Alessa's lips parted in a silent scream as her additional injuries were exposed.

Not only were her legs a kaleidoscope of colors, but they were also littered with cuts, gunshot wounds with torn edges, what appeared to be human bite marks, cigar burns, and the outlines of several chemical burns.

Unable to catch her breath, Alessa eyed the white bandage draped across her left thigh, and her stomach dropped. *If the rest of my wounds aren't bad enough to need bandages, how bad is this one?*

She picked at the remaining tape from the corner of the white gauze and lifted the bandage, revealing a stitched gash at least six inches in length.

Alessa shuddered from head to toe, and the monitors beeped erratically. Her abdominal muscles seared in pain with every movement, and as she pressed her fingers into her stomach, she felt the outline of an even larger dressing.

Lifting her gown, she whimpered at the sight of the white rectangular covering taped to her midsection. "No, no, no..."

Alessa tore at the bandage, and as the edges stuck to themselves, a section of the raised, jagged wound was exposed.

Letting loose a wretched cry, she crumbled into hysteria.

Nurses and aides ran into the room, followed closely by an older doctor who was wide-eyed and barking orders.

Alessa's arms flailed as she scratched frantically at the tubes buried beneath her skin.

"Honey, don't do that." A nurse in purple scrubs held onto Alessa's arms. "Calm down; breathe."

"Twenty milligrams of Versed, stat!" the physician shouted amidst the chaos.

"Please, no. Don't do this," Alessa pleaded with the medical staff holding her down.

A strawberry-blonde nurse rushed toward Alessa and injected the IV line with the sedative.

"No!" Alessa shouted before aggressively shoving the woman away.

The young nurse flew ten feet back, hit the wall, and slid down it before landing in an unconscious heap on the floor.

Everyone in the room fell silent as they looked back and forth between the fallen nurse and Alessa.

The doctor stared at his patient in awe. "What are you?" he murmured.

As Alessa's sedative took effect, the room appeared to tilt, and she fell back, limp, onto the wrinkled sheets before drifting off into a dreamless sleep.

CHAPTER THREE

Alessa awakened, groggy and confused. She tried lifting her left hand, but it proved impossible, thanks to the handcuffs securing her to the bed's railing.

With the sound of clanging metal, she whined as she looked around the room. "Ugh, what now?"

Sunlight filtered through the foggy window, casting a ray of light onto an empty bedpan that teetered precariously on the edge of a red chair. Directly above it hung a flat-screen television, and a soft yellow glow from the bathroom's partially open door reflected off the metal IV pole near the head of her bed.

"Okay," Alessa exhaled. "I can't remember how I got into this mess, but what can I recall?"

She rubbed the skin on either side of the metal wrapped around her wrist. "My name? A ... Alessa. Alessa, what, though?" She bit her lower lip in frustration.

"How old am I? How tall am I? What's my favorite color?" Alessa grumbled as she tugged on the handcuffs. "Dammit! This is pointless. All I can remember is my first name."

"That's probably due to your head trauma." An older man in a white medical jacket and olive green scrubs entered the room cautiously, his hands held up in a gesture of peace. "I'm Dr. Reynolds, a physician at this hospital. I'm here to check on you."

Her body tensed as the unfamiliar man approached her bedside. "Head trauma?" Alessa narrowed her eyes. "Where am I? And why am I here?"

The doctor tucked a strand of dark hair behind his ear. "I'll get to that, but first, can you tell me your name?"

She nodded apprehensively. "Alessa."

"Good, that's good." The physician typed on his tablet. "Now we can stop referring to you as Jane Doe. And by chance, do you recall your last name?"

Pursing her lips, Alessa shook her head no.

"That's okay. You just woke up. We need to give your brain time to recover. Let's see if anything jogs your memory. How about your parents' names? Do you have any siblings? Where do you work?"

An overwhelming sense of dread swelled in the pit of Alessa's stomach as she shook her head in response to every question.

"Don't worry. You're doing great. After all you've been through, it's perfectly normal not to recall much initially. It's probably how your brain is coping with what happened."

"What happened?" Alessa asked. "And when do you think I'll start remembering more than just my first name?"

He tapped his tablet's screen. "Well, it's different for every person, and every situation is unique. In your case, after the extensive trauma you sustained, I would expect—"

"You keep mentioning the severity of my injuries," Alessa interrupted. "What happened to me?"

Dr. Reynolds scanned the room, searching for somewhere to sit. He moved the bedpan to the floor, and as he pulled the chair over to Alessa's bedside, the plastic on the bottom of the wooden legs squeaked against the tile.

He sat down and placed his tablet in his lap before continuing. "For lack of a better term, it appears as if you were ... tortured."

Unmoving, Alessa stared at the doctor.

"You've been a patient here at Pennsylvania Hospital for two days now after what can only be described as the most brutal attack any of our medical staff has ever seen."

Focusing on the black streaks scratched into the eggshell-colored wall behind the doctor's concerned face, Alessa disassociated, and as she stared past him, his features blurred. *Do not pass out. Do not pass out.*

The room appeared to tilt, and she closed her eyes. "Attack?"

"You arrived with multiple lacerations and contusions; your orbital socket was crushed, and your abdomen was, well..." He shook his head, ridding himself of the terrible memory. "Speaking of, can you see out of it? Your left eye, that is."

Digging deep into his coat pocket, the doctor emerged with a penlight. He leaned toward Alessa, darting it back and forth in front of her pupils.

"Shit, that's bright," she hissed. Attempting to block the light, she lifted her hands, but the metallic handcuffs on her wrist clanked against the railing. "Yeah, I can see fine. With both eyes. Turn it off."

An excited grin spread across his face as he sat back down. "Remarkable. That's great. It's wonderful news. What with the damage you..." He looked down at the floor, rubbing his hands together. "What I am trying to say is there is no medical explanation as to why you still have use of your left eye."

"Okay, I think I understand the severity of the damage," Alessa huffed.

"No, you don't. You couldn't possibly imagine." He scooted his chair forward a few inches. "Unless ... Are you a part of a government project? Perhaps one that is not public knowledge?"

Alessa's eyes widened in shock. "What are you talking about? You're kidding me, right?"

"I am most certainly not. Not even the longest-working provider at this hospital has seen anyone in your condition upon arrival, survive. Rumor is that the Mafia, the government, or perhaps some other organization, is targeting you. You arrived here just two days ago, covered head-to-toe in bruises, cuts, broken bones—practically every injury you could imagine —and yet you're here, alive. Except for a seemingly insignificant, tiny blur at the base of your brain, your scans all came back quite normal. And you're not barely holding on, you're damn near healed. Alessa, this isn't just highly improbable; it's physically impossible," he said in a hushed whisper.

Alessa shook her head back and forth in denial. "Doc, you clearly don't know the definition of impossible."

"We had to take you into surgery multiple times to reset your bones because they were healing so rapidly. Whatever you are," Dr. Reynolds glanced around the room, "you are no ordinary human."

Alessa stared at the man and laughed incredulously. "You are insane. Of course I'm a human!" She gestured from her head to her feet with her unsecured hand.

"I didn't say you weren't a human, but you have to be some form of an advanced—"

"This is ridiculous," Alessa interjected. "*You* are ridiculous. Can you please remove the handcuffs? I've really got to pee, and laughing is not helping. What is the deal with them, anyway? Am I a flight risk or something?"

"That, amongst other things," he responded, his tone serious. "You attacked one of the nurses."

"Oh, I'm sorry. I don't remember doing that. Is she okay?"

The doctor brushed away her concern with a flick of his wrist. "Just a mild concussion. She'll be back to normal in a few weeks."

"Weeks?" Alessa responded as Dr. Reynolds stepped out into the hallway.

After speaking with the guard, the doctor was handed a small grey key and returned to Alessa's bedside.

"You promise not to have any more violent outbursts?"

Alessa held up the palms of her hands in a peaceful gesture. "I swear it."

The doctor leaned in and unlocked the handcuffs. "That guard has the go-ahead to take you down if necessary."

Alessa rubbed the sore spots on the bony prominence on her wrist. "Wow. Understood. So, what does that make me, a patient or a prisoner?"

Dr. Reynolds gave a tight-lipped smile in response, ignoring her question.

Realizing she was nervously rubbing a pale line wrapped around her naked ring finger, she asked, "Did I have anything on me when I was brought here?"

He nodded toward her bedside table. "The only item was that piece of jewelry."

A band of bright white gems, alternating with transparent magenta and teal jewels, lay in a small metal bowl.

"You're lucky the finger you were wearing it on wasn't broken or swollen, or else we would've had to cut it off—the ring, that is," he chuckled.

When she extended her arm out toward the bedside table, a sharp pain in Alessa's abdomen took her breath away, and she fell back on the pillow.

"Oh, dear. You need to rest. I'll talk with the rest of the team and return later to do a full assessment. Does that work for you?"

Alessa nodded. "Hey, Doc? Thanks for, well, everything."

"No, thank you, Alessa. You've been incredible; absolutely incredible." He stared at her in awe. "Remember, a guard will always be stationed outside your door, so don't even think about trying to leave."

Dr. Reynolds' eyes narrowed as he forced a smile and exited the room.

Eyeing the ring, Alessa clenched her teeth and grabbed the piece of jewelry before falling back against her pillow with an audible grunt.

"Not human," Alessa scoffed, sliding the ring onto her finger. "What does he think I am? A cyborg? An alien? How ridiculous is that?"

A stabbing pain shot through her abdomen and side as she laughed to herself.

Lifting her gown to inspect the sharp pain in her side, Alessa noticed intricate black lines dancing up her right side.

"What is that? Wait. I have a tattoo?" she gasped.

The ink elegantly snaked down the side of her rib cage, extending past her hip bone.

Alessa hissed in agony and squeezed her eyes shut,

immediately regretting the jerky movement necessary to inspect the body art further.

A nurse stepped into the room from the hallway. "Would you like something for the pain?"

With pursed lips, Alessa adamantly shook her head.

"Okay, then. Let me know if you change your mind. My name is Charlise, and I'm your nurse for the day." She walked toward Alessa before inspecting the tubes connecting her hand to the machine. "That Dr. Reynolds has taken real good care of you since your attack."

Alessa grimaced. "Can we not call it that?"

"Well, what do you want to call it, then?"

"I don't know. Incident?" she said, knowing it sounded ridiculous.

"You look tired, baby girl. Your IV looks good, so I'll leave you alone and let you get some sleep. Here's the call button." Nurse Charlise picked up the rectangular remote and pointed to the button with the red cross. "Push that, and I'll get in here as soon as possible."

Alessa's eyelids grew exceedingly heavy.

"Sounds good," she drawled as she drifted off to sleep, completely oblivious that her subconscious was about to make her relive the day her entire world was turned upside down.

CHAPTER FOUR

"Wait up! Dad said we—ugh! Come on!" a seven-year-old Alessa complained, chasing a honey blonde, chubby-cheeked toddler through the thick foliage of the Colorado woods.

Running into the small cabin, the two girls passed a woman standing near the kitchen counter. The sunlight shone through the windows, illuminating her long, golden-yellow hair as she held a half-empty cardboard box.

"You two, play nice! I'm making dinner after we unpack," she called out after the girls as they ran past her into the back bedroom of the small cabin.

Alessa wrapped her fingers around the toddler's arm and shrieked, "Gotcha!"

Frustrated squeals echoed off the walls as the toddler pushed back. "Lessie, stop!"

In the bedroom, a tall, dark-haired man was sorting through a pile of clothes overflowing from an open suitcase. A smile tugged at his lips as he scolded the little brunette. "Alessa, be nice to—"

His words were cut short by the crack of a gunshot.

17

The loud noise echoed through the trees, and he pointed under the bed, demanding in a hushed whisper, "Hide. Now. And be quiet."

The scene skipped ahead as if her subconscious was fast-forwarding through a movie, and the next thing Alessa knew, the man who had instructed her to hide was lying on the floor with a fatal bullet wound to the head.

His dead, blank eyes bore through her as she held her hands over the toddler's open mouth, muffling the young girl's screams.

Alessa sprang upright. "Ah, shit!" she cursed with the painful stretching of her abdominal wound.

What was that? She pressed her fingertips into her throbbing temples.

A demanding knock on the door interrupted her crazed thoughts, and Dr. Reynolds stepped into the room. "Hello. Is now a good time to do my assessment?"

"Dr. Reynolds, I welcome the distraction." Alessa winced, massaging the sides of her forehead.

Reading her body language, he addressed her pain. "And how are you feeling? How is your pain, on a scale from one to ten?"

"Well, when I don't move, maybe a three. When I do, it's probably a six. And these damn headaches I've been getting, they can easily hit a nine."

Pressing a button on the side of his tablet, he held a stylus in front of the screen. "Can you describe these headaches?"

Alessa dropped her hands and absentmindedly spun the colorful ring around her finger. "Like a pulsating, stabbing sensation that makes my head feel like it's going to explode?"

Glancing down at the dancing violet and blue gems, she

tilted the crisscrossed band and admired its beauty. Depending on the angle of the light that shone onto the gems, the violets turned magenta, and the blues appeared green.

"What type of stones would you guess these are?" she asked the physician.

He leaned in to inspect the ring. "Um, diamonds alternating with, maybe, alexandrite?"

"Interesting. I wonder where I got it from."

Uninterested in Alessa's fascination with her ring, Dr. Reynolds continued his line of questioning. "How are you sleeping?"

"Fine, I guess." Alessa grimaced as the dead man's face flashed in her subconscious. "My dreams have been crazy and graphic. Is that normal for someone who has been through what I have?"

The doctor paused and looked up at Alessa from his tablet. "Are you remembering anything?"

Alessa rubbed the back of her neck. "No, not exactly."

"Well, tell me if you need pain medication, and we'll get you some."

Alessa stretched her stiff neck to the side. "Thanks. I'll let you know if it gets bad enough."

"Now," Dr. Reynolds set the tablet on the chair and held his hands out, "I need to touch you to assess your wounds. Do I have your permission?"

Alessa remained silent as she eyed the doctor.

"I'll tell you everything I'm going to do before I do it," he reassured her.

With a deep breath, Alessa conceded and lay down, swallowing the lump in the back of her throat.

Dr. Reynolds walked over to the counter and pressed a

button on a small circular device. "If you don't mind, I will say everything aloud to dictate my findings."

Alessa nodded and closed her eyes as her body unintentionally tensed.

"The IV is intact," he began. "The patient's wounds have healed quite well in an incredibly short time. It's like nothing I've ever seen before. Please open your eyes," he instructed Alessa.

Looking directly into a bright, pinpoint beam of light, Alessa jerked away. "Ah! You should warn a person before you do that."

Dr. Reynolds dropped his penlight. "Pupils are both equal and reactive."

Bobbing, bright dots invaded Alessa's vision, and she squeezed her eyelids shut tight before opening them wide. "Wow."

"I need to remove the bedsheet. Are you okay with that?"

"Go for it, Doc."

Grasping the cream-colored sheet, he pulled it away from Alessa, and she unintentionally froze as he pointed to her thigh.

"Can I remove the bandage and see how the stitches are healing?"

She nodded in silent approval.

Reaching above Alessa's head, Dr. Reynolds plucked a pair of purple gloves from the wall and tugged them on before tearing at the edges of the tape. He lifted the bandage. "Remarkable. I can't believe it's only been two days. Those stitches are more than ready to come out. I'll have the nurse remove them once I'm done. Next is the examination of your back. I need you to lie down, place your arms across your chest, and hug yourself. Let me know if any movement is too painful, and I will stop immediately."

As the doctor propped Alessa up on her right side, she stifled a scream, and her eyes rolled back into her head. The heart rate monitor beeped erratically in response to the excruciating amount of pain caused by the contraction of her abdominal muscles.

Alessa rolled onto her back, shakily exhaling.

The doctor patted the back of her hand. "I'll have the nurse bring you something to take the edge off."

Catching her breath, she nodded gratefully.

"Do you want me to continue, or would you like to take a break?"

"Get it over with," she said, clenching her teeth together.

"Alright, then. Please lift your gown for me. I need to see your stomach."

Alessa unintentionally shuddered, fearing what was beneath the dressing, but did as he instructed.

"Let's move down to the abdomen where the most grievous of her injuries is located." The doctor removed the bandage, and Alessa's eyes teared up as her jaw dropped in disbelief.

A red, jagged line started just below her breasts and extended down to her underwear. The raised, angry edges appeared to have been brutally ripped apart. Even the stitches that were placed were struggling to force the skin back together.

She cringed, and tears fell from her eyes. *I should be dead. What could I possibly have done to deserve this?*

Dr. Reynolds continued his assessment, his fingertips pressing into Alessa's flesh next to the wound, and she gagged and fell limp as the pain rendered her unconscious.

CHAPTER FIVE

In *Alessa's* dream, her heels clicked against the tiled floor as she strolled into the building to work the night shift.

She was wearing bright red pumps, a black pencil skirt, and a white silk button-up, and her auburn-dyed hair was curled into loose waves that fell halfway down her back.

Smiling, she strolled toward the day shift guard stationed at the front desk.

"Good evening, Jerry. How was your day?"

"Oh, you know, the usual," the older gentleman replied from behind the black-and-white monitor collection.

Alessa nervously ran her hands down the front of her shirt, smoothing its non-existent wrinkles. "Anything exciting happen?"

"Well, there was a raccoon that somehow got into the building. It took a good two hours to get the thing corralled." The older man chuckled, lifting a coffee mug to his lips.

"Did you end up shooting it or saving it?"

"The other workers wanted to kill it, but you know me and my big heart. I set it free once I got him back outside."

"And that, Jerry," she grinned, "is why I like you so much. You, sir, are one of the good guys." Alessa tapped the guard on the nose before scanning her ID badge.

"Identity confirmed. Welcome, Laura Newman," an electronic voice announced.

"Hey, Mike. Ready to take over?" Jerry addressed the night shift watchman as he stood up, holding his mug and a collection of magazines.

"You bet. Go on home and enjoy that wife of yours." Mike patted the man on the shoulder.

Jerry winked. "I'm hopin' she made meatloaf for dinner."

The last day shift workers exited the building as Jerry followed.

Sensing some pushback, Alessa eyed Mike. "Are you feeling alright?"

"Absolutely," the guard replied, his voice devoid of emotion. Plopping down in the chair, Mike peered at the camera monitors while typing several codes into the computer.

Enraged by her colleague's insubordinate attitude toward her, Alessa smiled at someone passing by before leaning into his ear. "Are we good to go?" she whispered so only he could hear her. "Because we only have one shot at this, and I'm sorry if you disagree with me being lead on this mission, but you need to pull your head out of your ass so we don't get caught."

One by one, every camera on the way to the vault was disabled and replaced by a segment of looped footage taken from another night.

Mike glanced up at Alessa with a cocky grin. "Yes, ma'am. The elders know best, so you being in charge must be the right call." He pressed enter on the keyboard. "Everything's a go."

With a nod, she stood up. "Okay, then. Glad to hear it." Plucking the ID badge from the front of her shirt, Alessa handed it over to Mike, exchanging it with a nearly identical badge secretly encoded for entry into Erebos Industries' vault.

Inhaling a jagged breath, Alessa clipped the new badge on and turned to walk away.

"Laura?" Mike called out to her.

Alessa froze and cautiously peered back over her shoulder.

"Don't screw this up."

Alessa nodded robotically before heading to the break room.

As she entered the small space, a group of gossiping co-workers stood by the counter, one of whom was her contact for the mission.

"Hey guys." She walked up behind them and grabbed a bagel from the counter.

A person with dyed ruby-red hair turned toward her. "Hey, Laura. How was your day?"

Alessa took a bite out of the bagel. "I slept. So completely uneventful. Yours?" she asked with a mouth full of stale bread.

"Forget how Rachel's day was," the brunette giggled excitedly. "We found out that Liz got knocked up by one of the researchers, and she hasn't told him yet."

"Wow. That, um ... sucks?" Alessa responded, feigning concern.

"I know. And she's afraid Bob will fire her if he finds out," said the redhead.

"Would you like some coffee?" Alessa's contact, Becca, interjected. "I've got this neat mug I've been meaning to try out. It's supposed to keep liquids hot for up to eight hours. I'll loan it to you if you want."

"That'd be great, Becca. I feel like it's going to be a long night."

Becca left the gossiping women to dig through her purse. She pulled out the mug and gave it to Alessa with an imperceptible nod.

Alessa pressed a button on the coffee machine and filled the mug with steaming hot liquid. "Ladies, I'd sure like to get caught up on the latest gossip, but I've gotta get going. I'll talk to you on break."

Passing by the trash can, Alessa tossed the remnants of her bagel into the bin and hurried out the door.

Stepping into the hall, she made a beeline for the women's restroom, where she swung the door open, headed straight for the sink, and tossed the coffee down the drain.

She stared into the white mug as the steam rose from the stainless-steel sink.

Earlier, when the hot liquid had touched the bottom of the ceramic mug, a heat-activated sequence of eight letters and fourteen numbers appeared.

Reading and memorizing the code, Alessa dashed toward the end stall and smashed the mug against the brick wall, effectively destroying the fact the sequence had been leaked. As the last shattered pieces fell into the waste bin, Alessa shut the door and secured the latch before reaching behind the toilet.

She then extracted a swiping card from behind the tank, pulled her skirt forward, and tucked the card in a small pocket stitched into the fabric.

With a nervous clearing of her throat, Alessa opened the stall door, and her heels clicked loudly on the tiled floor as she emerged from the women's restroom.

She paused before a closed door with the name 'Max' etched into the frosted glass. Turning the knob, she entered Max's small office and froze.

Max was sitting at his desk, as was the plan. However, sitting across from him was an unexpected guest.

Max eyed Alessa, telling her, nonverbally, to be very careful with her words. "Laura. Can I help you?"

"Uh, I'm sorry. I didn't realize you'd be here this late. I was ... coming in to grab those files for Mr. Tracy," *she lied.*

"Oh. Right." *Max rotated in his chair and leaned to the right before extending his arm toward a pile of papers on his filing cabinet.*

"Laura," *the man sitting across from Max said impassively.*

"Brett," *she responded in an equally rigid tone.*

Max handed the small stack of papers to her. "Here you are. The exact page you need is in the middle of all that."

Understanding his hidden meaning, she took the papers and hurried out of the office. Once she closed the door behind her, Alessa's stomach somersaulted as she side-eyed the security camera on the nearby wall.

Even though she knew the security guards could not see her sneaking around because the looped footage was playing, the pit of her stomach still ached.

Shuffling through the papers, Alessa found the plastic-wrapped set of fingerprints. "Gotcha."

Three sets of fingerprints were neatly laid out in three rows on the white page.

Reaching the vault door, she tossed the other loose pages in a nearby bin, pulled her ID away from her shirt, and inserted the card into the horizontal slit next to the door.

I never understood why their vault was in the middle of an open-access hallway, but it's pretty clever since there are always people around. Except for tonight, that is.

With a loud click, the locks shifted, and the door opened.

She fell into the darkness and exhaled, quickly closing the door behind her.

Reaching down in between her breasts, Alessa pulled out a

tiny black light, which she used to illuminate the side of the room before stepping down onto the bottom stair. She directed the blue beam of light up and down the left wall, searching for the user's box.

As the light hit the floor, the lasers glowed red, crisscrossing over one another.

Her eyebrows raised in excitement. "Things just got interesting," Alessa said before she lit up the small box on the wall. "Bingo."

Reaching down between her breasts once more, Alessa pulled out a tiny device filled with chemicals meant to illuminate lasers, such as these, when exposed to oxygen. Lifting her hand above her head, she slammed the device down to the floor, and it exploded in a cloud of dust, revealing ominous red lines stretched across the room.

With the floor illuminated neon red, Alessa secured the light between her breasts and clipped her fake ID badge onto the front of her shirt. Then she grabbed the small card from the lining of her skirt, kicked off her shoes, and set the paper on the floor.

Alessa bit onto the card and scaled the textured wall's crevices by the tips of her fingers, digging her toes in for support.

Hovering over the glowing floor, Alessa glanced at the lasers before stretching toward the target. Sweat dripped down from her hairline, and as the liquid hit the crimson lines, they made a hissing noise.

"Shit," Alessa cursed between clenched teeth.

The lasers weren't simply alarm lasers; they were meant to harm those who touched them.

She extended her arm even further but realized she'd never be able to reach the card insert within the user's box from her position. Shimmying her way back to the entrance, Alessa grunted as she jumped back to the safety of the entryway.

Standing upright, she plucked the card from her mouth and looked around the dimly lit room. The ceiling was painted black and was impossible to see without turning the lights on. Not wanting to draw any attention to the fact that someone was inside the secured room, Alessa squinted her eyes and triggered the implanted microchip's activation.

Her bright green irises glowed in the dark, enhancing her vision. Alessa could now easily see the exposed industrial ceiling.

"Okay, so, about ten meters up. That's nothing," she reassured herself, biting the card again.

Taking a deep breath, she lunged forward and kicked off the nearest wall. Propelling herself upward, Alessa bounced between the two connecting walls in the corner of the room toward the exposed ceiling.

Running ten meters straight up, Alessa grabbed onto one of the metal bars extending from wall to wall. Hanging from the beam, Alessa mentally calculated the distance between herself and the short decorative metal bar bolted into the wall directly above the user's box.

She could see the slot she needed to insert the card into and gave herself a pep talk. "That isn't too far of a drop. Nothing you haven't done before. You've got this."

Alessa swung her feet back and forth, let go, and flew forward. Grabbing the next bar, she continued using the metal beams as monkey bars until she dangled directly above the user's box.

She let go, and her red hair whipped into her face as she descended from the ceiling. As she fell closer to the decorative metal bar, Alessa prayed to the gods that it would support her weight.

She caught herself on the thin metal with an audible grunt

and grasped it tight. Dangling, she grabbed the card and extended her arm beneath her, stretching as far as possible.

As her fingertips slipped from the bar, Alessa dropped the trim card into the slot and fell to the floor.

The glowing red lasers flickered off in time for her bare toes to hit the cold tile.

Alessa breathed heavily, squatting on the ground in the dark room.

"There had to be an easier way than that." She plucked the flashlight from her bra.

With help from the blue light and her activated irises, she hurried across the dark room and pressed the first fingerprints onto the pad next to the door.

A green light glowed brightly with each set of prints she pressed onto the screen. Finally, she scanned the final set of fingerprints that belonged to the company's owner, Eric Lansing, and the door before her unlocked.

Unable to contain her excitement, Alessa barreled into the well-lit room, quickly closed the door, and plopped down in a black leather chair behind a desk. Sitting in front of a computer monitor, she entered the codes needed to access Eric's confidential files. Her access was granted as she entered the final sequence of letters and numbers.

Alessa clicked on the folder titled 'Red'.

A man donning a white medical coat appeared on the screen. Alessa's irises glowed bright green as she activated her implanted microchip's ability to download, enabling her to record the company's deadly secret.

"The golden-flaked serum will be marketed as the ultimate cure for smallpox, the vaccine and treatment all-in-one," the man began. "However, for the world to need either a vaccine or treatment, the disease has to be reintroduced to the world population. We plan on releasing the infected mist into the New York subway. A single mist spray on just one train will ensure everyone on board has the highly contagious disease."

Upon completion of her downloading the files incriminating Eric Lansing, Alessa rose from the chair and hurried toward the exit.

"Now, to get this information back home so the elders can—"

As she reached for the handle on the door, it burst open, and she was knocked sideways into a nearby wall.

Struggling to her feet, Alessa swayed back and forth before staggering in front of the desk. Peering into the bright smoke billowing into the room from the demolished door, a tear gas canister shot into her midsection, propelling Alessa backward.

The air was sucked from her lungs as the metal container pressed deep into her diaphragm, and Alessa's spine cracked as she smacked her back against the corner of the desk.

White, acrid smoke filled the room, and Alessa collapsed to the ground. Unable to breathe nor see, she was rendered helpless.

CHAPTER SIX

"Agh, my head," Alessa whimpered, squeezing her eyes shut against the intense, rushing blood pulsing throughout her skull.

She fumbled around the scratchy blanket for the bed's remote control. "Come on," she pleaded.

When she finally found it, Alessa urgently pressed the worn-down call button.

"Can I help you?" a voice bellowed from the crackling speaker.

"Yeah, could I get something for pain?" Alessa swallowed the bile that crept up the back of her throat. "My head is killing me."

"The nurse will be right in," the voice replied before disconnecting.

For the next several minutes, Alessa took slow, deep breaths as she tried to focus on anything but the pain.

Just as Alessa was nauseous, Nurse Charlise knocked on the doorframe. "May I come in?"

"Yes, please." Alessa looked out the door. "Is my babysitter still there?" she asked, referring to the security guard.

The nurse's sneakers squeaked with every step. "What do you think?" She handed Alessa four small pills. "In addition to your violent tendencies, the doctors don't want you goin' nowhere."

She filled a small paper cup with water and handed it to Alessa. "The police are coming by in the morning to ask you questions, and a few specialists are tagging along."

Alessa choked on the water. "Specialists? Wh-what? Why?"

"Baby girl, you should be dead." The nurse sat down in the red chair and patted the back of Alessa's hand. "But I choose to believe someone higher up healed you, and if that's the case, you must've earned it because you came in all kinds of messed up. You were meant to live."

Alessa laughed and smiled, unassured. "Or maybe I made a deal with Hades."

Ignoring her quip, Nurse Charlise continued talking. "Now, don't you go turning on the news." She pointed a finger at the black television screen. "Someone got a hold of your situation, and they runnin' with it, calling you robogirl."

Alessa's forehead scrunched up in a mixture of confusion and panic. "Wait, they're talking about me on the news?"

"Oh, yeah. But don't worry; they haven't gotten a shot of your face or nothin'. I mean, it is quite a story—you comin' back from the dead after being found near the river."

Alessa's eyes widened. "I haven't been told the whole story. Could you please fill in the gaps?"

"Maybe." The nurse shrugged. "What do you want to know?"

"Well, if you could tell me everything, from start to finish, that'd be great." Sensing the nurse's apprehension, Alessa smiled sweetly. "Please? I haven't talked to anyone except Dr.

Reynolds since waking up early this morning, and this is helping me feel better."

The nurse pressed her lips together before she caved. "Oh, alright. You sure you wanna know?"

Not trusting her voice, Alessa silently nodded.

"Okay, then. Three days ago, a couple jogging near the riverfront saw you get thrown out of a van and immediately called for help, which was nothing short of a miracle. But then there also happened to be an ambulance passing by not a minute later. I tell you, a higher being must've been with you that day. When the paramedics got there, you had no pulse for the AED to work with."

Mistaking her patient's silence for confusion, the nurse clarified her statement. "That means you were dead."

Alessa's stomach dropped, and she sank back into her pillows. "Huh."

"You want me to continue?"

"Yep," Alessa squeaked.

"Once the AED found the faintest of blips, it shocked your heart, and you were brought back to life. You had so many broken bones upon arrival—I think it was at least twenty."

"Twenty?" Alessa's breathing hitched as she fought the overwhelming urge to break down.

"During your surgeries, you lost a lot of blood. They gave you several blood transfusions, pumped you full of epinephrine, and shocked you several more times to keep you with us. At one point ... No, never mind."

"Please tell me. I want to know; I need to know," Alessa begged.

Hesitating briefly, the nurse continued. "At one point, me and the other staff did chest compressions on you for a good thirty minutes before your heart started beating again."

Alessa's entire body went numb as she forgot to breathe. "Wait. Are you saying I died, not once, but multiple times?"

Nurse Charlise nodded. "It's a miracle you're alive and talking to me. And that's why I believe God has special plans for you, honey. Ain't nobody going through all of that for nothin'. But to tell you the truth, I am a little worried."

Alessa's eyebrows furrowed. "Worried about what?"

The nurse looked out into the hallway before leaning in. "The doctors are obsessing over how quickly you healed. Don't get me wrong, in all my thirty years of being a nurse, I ain't ever seen nothin' like it, but I don't like the way they talk about you. And I don't agree with the *specialists* they are sending to talk to you along with the police tomorrow."

"What exactly have the doctors said?" Alessa bit her lower lip nervously, spinning the ring around her finger.

"They've been stuck on how the average fractured radius takes about six to eight weeks to heal, whereas yours practically healed in a day and a half; how you have no brain damage aside from the amnesia. You're sure you still don't remember anything besides your first name?"

"I-I don't know." As the headache continued tugging at her temples, Alessa closed her eyes.

"Oh, yeah, I forgot to mention, the day you arrived, we checked to see if anyone reported a missing person with your description," Alessa looked at the nurse with hope gripping her heart, "but no one had."

As the nurse continued talking, Alessa's eyes wandered from the nurse's face to a fly buzzing around the room. The tiny insect took refuge on the red circular clock beside the television. Staring at the black, buzzing speck, Alessa's eyes relaxed and followed the clock's second hand. The line moved slower with every passing second until it finally seemed to have stopped completely.

"Alessa? Alessa, are you okay?"

Alessa's eyes re-focused on the concerned woman. "I'm sorry. Could you please repeat that?"

"Like I said earlier, I don't feel good about those specialists they are sending to see you. I tried looking up their names online, but they don't exist." She leaned in. "Sorry to sound paranoid, but something just ain't right."

Overwhelmed, Alessa glanced back at the fly still perched on the clock.

The insect lifted its leg and cleaned behind its head before pushing off the red surface. Not realizing the window was closed, it hit the clean glass. Its tiny body bounced, and as the stunned insect fell to the windowsill, it twitched, clinging to its last moments of life.

The fly's interaction with the glass window just so happened to perfectly sum up how Alessa was feeling at that moment.

The nurse scooted her chair back, and it screeched across the floor. "If you need anything, please don't hesitate to ask."

Alessa blinked away tears and grabbed the nurse's hand. "Is there any way you could find me some clothes from the lost and found or something? I'm tired of wearing this gown and need to feel ... okay. Even though I'm here, in this hospital, I need to feel comfortable in my skin, and this thin piece of crap I'm wearing is not helping. Will you do this for me?"

The nurse's eyes narrowed briefly as she considered her patient's request. "You sure that's the only reason you want to wear civilian clothes?"

The atmosphere in the room became tense as Alessa slowly nodded without taking her eyes off Nurse Charlise.

"Okay, then. I'll be back after I check in on my other patients. You stay out of trouble, you hear?" She pointed her finger at Alessa before walking away.

Alessa watched the woman's white sneakers disappear around the corner before she snatched up the TV remote. Pressing the red power button, she searched the channels for the five o'clock news.

A female reporter wearing a blush pink blouse and a charcoal grey pencil skirt stood in the middle of the bright screen, directly in front of Pennsylvania Hospital.

"The unknown woman left for dead by the river is now in stable condition. The hospital spokesperson confirmed at three o'clock this afternoon that the young woman did indeed wake up from her coma. Doctors say she is confused yet alert and hopeful she'll fully recover.

"The police are growing impatient as there are still no suspects, and they are unable to question the victim until physicians clear her. We'll keep you updated on this story as more details emerge. Back to you, Todd."

Punching the power button, Alessa threw the television remote across the room. "I need to get out of here. I'm drawing too much attention."

Slowly and painfully, Alessa sat upright in bed. Then, she carefully stood upright with a deep breath in and out, holding onto the railing. Once she mastered standing from the seated position, she began pacing the floor, marching back and forth between the window and her door.

Satisfied with the steady increase in her stamina, she took a break from her cardio and escaped into the bathroom. Bending at the waist, she gripped the countertop and scowled at the unfamiliar red-haired woman staring back at her in the mirror.

For the briefest of moments, a majestic mountain range

flashed before her. But the memory faded as quickly as it had appeared, leaving a high-pitched squeal in its place. The migraine-inducing noise resonated throughout her skull.

"We have to get out of here *tonight*," Alessa said to her reflection.

CHAPTER SEVEN

Over the next hour, Alessa walked around the perimeter of her room, loosening her tight ligaments and stretching her sore muscles. The television blared in the background as the wheels turned in her mind regarding an escape plan.

"The reports from the CDC are sketchy at best," declared the male reporter on the television screen. "So far, within the past two weeks, there have been close to a thousand reported cases of individuals who have fallen ill with similar symptoms. Testing is currently being done on the infected to establish a diagnosis.

"Three days ago, we reported the first one hundred deaths caused by this unknown disease, and we are saddened to say that as of this morning, at least another two hundred more have succumbed to this mysterious virus. It seems to have originated in New York, and word is spreading that this may be an act of bioterrorism, but nothing has been officially declared.

"Common symptoms of the infected include headaches, fatigue, and muscle aches. Then, a high fever may be accompanied by a rash. Extreme vomiting or diarrhea is also considered a possible symptom. Please stay home and call your doctor immediately if you develop any of these symptoms."

Alessa stopped in place and forced herself to breathe through the pain as she stretched her hamstrings, one at a time.

"Inside sources claim the CDC is considering declaring the use of community centers as wards to contain the infected. Government officials are advising the public to purchase medical-grade face masks. This could be the beginning of a very dark road ahead. The disease appears highly contagious, and proper treatment isn't possible without a diagnosis."

Alessa's nurse cleared her throat from the hallway just outside the door. "Can I come in?"

"Of course you can."

Nurse Charlise shuffled toward Alessa with an armful of clothes.

"I think these'll fit." She dropped a pair of sweatpants that were two sizes too big, a T-shirt with a gaudy *5k run* label on the front, and a halfway decent light-grey sweatshirt onto the foot of Alessa's bed.

"Hey, this is great. Thank you so much." Alessa grinned, genuinely grateful for the nurse's help.

A code blue was declared on the overhead speaker, and the nurse whipped around to face the hallway.

"I need help in room five!" a resident bellowed from across the hall, opposite the nurses' station.

Nurse Charlise eyed her. "Now's your chance. Run."

Alessa was taken aback by the urgency in the woman's voice. "I'm sorry, what?"

The nurse took a step toward Alessa. "You think I was born yesterday? As if I didn't know why you wanted those clothes? Get outta here before they make a guinea pig outta you." She reached out and squeezed Alessa's shoulder. "God bless you and good luck."

As all available medical staff ran toward the emergency, Alessa's eyebrows rose in astonishment at the perfectly timed cardiac arrest. "Well, I guess it's now or never."

Pulling the curtain closed, she hid behind the hanging fabric, pried off the tape, and yanked the tubes out of her hand. She untied the thin hospital gown and kicked it away before sliding her legs into the sweatpants.

Carefully, Alessa pulled the T-shirt and sweatshirt on over her head, and before leaving her bedside, she shoved pillows, the gown, and blankets under the bedsheets so it appeared as though someone was lying in the bed.

"No, please, no!" a family member wailed as a staff member prevented them from entering room five.

"Security, a little help!" the worker yelled to Alessa's guard.

Without glancing back at his ward, the guard ran to help.

"Are you kidding me right now?" Alessa chuckled at the ease of her escape.

Peering out around her pulled curtain, she lifted the hood over her head, stepped around the hanging fabric, and exited the room.

Hurrying down the hallway, Alessa discovered an empty employee break room, where she dove into several lockers. She stole a pair of sneakers, a black backpack, and a wallet containing a decent amount of cash.

A bowl of healthy snacks, clearly meant for the hospital staff, was on one of the counters.

"Jackpot!" she celebrated before dumping the food bowl into her newly acquired bag. Slinging the backpack over her shoulder, Alessa rushed out of the break room and back into the chaotic hallway.

Across the hall, Alessa eyed a large supply closet, and, keeping her head down, she walked right in. She grabbed a fistful of sterile bandages, tape, gauze pads, and antibiotic salves before shoving the supplies on top of the food in her bag.

Following her raid on the hospital's supplies, she was ready to leave the ICU but was worried about how hard it would be to leave unnoticed.

Approaching the nurses' station, she was astonished to see the code blue was still active.

The medical staff were distracted by the coded patient and their upset family members gathering outside the glass doors.

Out of the corner of her eye, Alessa caught a glimpse of two men wearing silver suits, both of whom stood oddly erect at the nurse's station.

"Excuse me! I need to find a patient," one of the men bellowed toward the frantic workers.

Warning alarms sounded inside Alessa's mind, and her entire body tensed in response to the men. It took everything within her to keep walking steadily behind them as she made her way toward the ICU's exit.

Growing impatient, the taller of the two men yelled, "Hello?"

Chills ran down Alessa's spine, and she bit her lower lip, desperately fighting the urge to drop everything and run.

"Excuse me, sir. You can see we are a little busy right now. You're going to have to wait," Alessa's nurse addressed the men from room five's doorway.

Without hesitation, the shorter of the two men pulled out a gun and shot Nurse Charlise straight through her chest. Before her knees hit the floor, the same man shot three more staff in addition to the distracted security guard.

As the nurse's dead body collapsed to the ground, screams

echoed throughout the hospital's hallways, and Alessa flung herself against the nearest wall.

The taller assailant stepped behind the counter and glanced at the computer screen before pointing to Alessa's room.

Darting toward room three with weapons raised, they aimed at the bed and fired.

Alessa covered her mouth in shock and stifled a cry. *You've got to move! Move now!*

Re-directing her attention, she stood, shaking, and ran away from her room alongside patients and staff.

The shorter of the two silver suits entered the room, pulled back the curtain, tore off the bedsheets, and scowled.

The bed was empty.

As the other silver suit scanned the hallway for runners, Alessa turned back briefly, and the corners of the gunman's lips curled up in recognition.

He raised his firearm, aimed, and shot at Alessa at the exact moment she fell through the exit doors.

The bullet whizzed past her head and embedded itself in the white brick wall beside her ear.

Picking herself up off the ground, Alessa sprinted down the stairs.

Hitting the ground floor, she pushed open the door to the main entryway to the hospital, where she was enveloped by a sea of panicked patients and employees making a mad dash for the building's exit. By the time she made it outside, her midsection seared in pain, and her intake of air was reduced to tiny gasps.

Shuffling through the crowd, she stumbled down the sidewalk until the panicked bodies thinned. Exhausted and fighting to stay conscious, she leaned against a bench, blinking away the black dots invading her vision.

A large city bus pulled up noisily before her, and the doors opened with a mechanical whir.

"Shit," Alessa cursed and jumped back.

The older driver stared down at her and smacked his gum. "Got a ticket?"

Alessa looked around, dazed. "I-I'm sorry. I don't."

"Cash, then?"

"Uh, I have this." She pulled the wallet from the backpack and handed him a twenty-dollar bill. "Is it enough?"

The driver eyed Alessa. "Have you never taken the bus before? We don't have change."

"That's fine."

"Hey, what's going on back there?" He pointed back at the crowd.

"There are gunmen in the hospital." Alessa's voice broke.

"Seriously?" The man's eyes widened. "Get on up here, already, so we can get out of here."

"Thank you so much." Alessa hobbled up the stairs, wincing in pain each time she lifted her leg to the next step. She crossed her arms over her stomach and staggered down the aisle as the driver slammed the doors closed and pressed the gas pedal.

The backpack landed beside her with a thud, and as the bus lurched forward, Alessa's hand flew to her stomach as she succumbed to the pain and exhaustion.

CHAPTER EIGHT

In her dream, Alessa squealed as the man standing behind her playfully squeezed her sides.

"I've got something for you," he whispered seductively into her ear.

She grinned. "What is it?"

"You have to guess," the man teased.

"A new pair of sparring gloves?"

He leaned further into her. "Guess again."

"Oh! New arrows?"

"Wrong again."

Alessa rubbed her backside against the man's groin. "A whip?"

"Why didn't I think of that?" he growled, running his fingertips up and down Alessa's biceps.

Goosebumps appeared beneath his touch, and she shivered. "Just tell me already."

The man let go of Alessa and dug into the pocket of his pants. Then, snuggling into her neck, he reached his arms around Alessa's torso and held a small box before her.

Alessa grabbed his muscular forearms as he opened the lid.

Inside the box was the most beautiful band she had ever seen. It glittered with snow-white diamonds and magenta and blue-green alexandrite chips alternating throughout the thin black band.

Alessa gasped. "It's breathtaking."

He took the ring out of the box. "It was my mother's."

Alessa stared at the gift. "I can't accept this. Your mother, she meant everything to you."

"You can, and you will." He slid the ring onto her finger.

Alessa faced the man and wrapped her arms around his neck.

The bus driver's voice startled Alessa awake. "Last stop before heading out of the city!"

Her heart pounded against her chest as she fought the urge to vomit. Her head was a spinning mess, and her thoughts jumbled as her dream slipped back into the recesses of her mind.

"Again, this is the last stop in the city," the voice blared from the overhead speakers.

Since escaping from the hospital, Alessa had lived on buses for the past few days, and her resources were exhausted. She had spent all her money on bus fare, food, clothes, bleach and developer, and blonde hair dye.

As the bus's brakes squealed to a halt, she stood up with a grunt, her body sore from having sat for too long. With a swipe of her hand, Alessa brushed her ash-blonde hair out of her eyes and trudged down the aisle and off the bus.

Grey exhaust fumes encircled her as she stood on the side of the road, coughing the smoke out of her lungs.

Spinning the ring around her finger aimlessly, she strolled down the sidewalk.

An ever-changing electronic billboard ad hung on the building above her. 'Two shooters still at large. Please call the police if you have any information regarding the shooting at Pennsylvania Hospital,' the display read before flipping to 'Charles Chicken. The best chicken on the East Side.' A picture of a family grinning from ear to ear and smothered in chicken grease was plastered in a grotesque tribute to America's love of fast food.

Alessa laughed out loud while she dug in her pack for the last remaining granola bar. "Only in America."

Taking a bite, she glanced over at a nearby café. 'Louie's' was plastered above the entrance in elaborate metallic letters. The wooden door was painted a deep green, and the glass in the middle had thin, intricate swirls spanning from the top to bottom.

Hmm. I desperately need money, and I like the quaint café vibe.

"Why not?" she asked no one in particular. "What have I got to lose?"

A bell rang as she opened the front door, and Alessa dropped the strap from her shoulder, announcing her presence.

"Excuse me, are you hiring?" Alessa addressed the golden-haired man behind the counter.

The handsome man continued wiping down the counter. "Hey, Louie, are we looking for help?" he hollered into the back of the café.

A well-dressed man in his early forties sauntered through the swinging door, grasping a small stack of papers and a tablet. Thick-rimmed red glasses sat atop his salt-and-pepper hair. "Who's asking?"

The man behind the counter nodded toward Alessa.

"We are." The gentleman directed her to a nearby table and pulled up a chair. "My name is Louie, and I own this establishment. Please sit and tell me a little about yourself, if you don't mind."

Shit. She regretted not having prepared a backstory.

"My name is ... um ... Jane," she lied.

Having sensed her hesitation, Louie eyed her quizzically. "Your name is Um Jane?"

"No, I mean, yes. My name is Jane. Just Jane, no 'um.'"

Louie plucked the red glasses from the top of his head and placed them on the bridge of his nose. "Alright then, Jane. How'd you hear about us?"

He set his tablet on the white tablecloth with the headline, 'Over a third of the children attending a single New York middle school fall ill with a mysterious disease,' displayed on the screen.

While reading the article's title, a high-pitched ringing reverberated throughout Alessa's skull, and she closed her eyes, trying to block out the sound. "I didn't, exactly. Honestly—"

Louie's body language gave away that he thought she was lying. He intertwined his fingers behind his head and leaned back in his chair. If she couldn't tell the whole truth, it'd have to be a half-truth for him to give her a chance.

"—I just got out of a pretty bad situation. Truthfully, it was downright awful, and I'm looking for a bit of a hand-up to regain some semblance of control."

She twisted the truth enough to imply that she had been in an abusive situation rather than having been hunted down in a hospital. Hopefully, it sounded convincing enough for him to give her a paycheck.

Louie sat upright. "Other than your bullshit name, which I

can only assume you have adopted to escape the situation, I appreciate your honesty. As long as you don't bring whatever shit you left behind there, here, I'm willing to help you out."

Relieved, Alessa beamed. "Really? Oh, that's great. Thank you so much."

"Do you have any experience as a waitress?"

"Yes, sir," Alessa responded immediately, unsure if she did. It wasn't exactly lying if she couldn't remember if she had ever been a waitress.

"Have you ever broken the law?"

She dug her fingernails into her hands and shook her head. "What? Why would you think that?"

He held his hands up defensively. "It's nothing personal. These are the questions we ask all our prospective employees."

"I've never been arrested. Not that I can remember," she giggled nervously.

"Good answer. Do you live close, or will transportation be an issue for you?" Louie picked up his tablet and papers.

She played with her ring. "Well, that situation I just got myself out of left me homeless."

"I see ... It just so happens there's an apartment upstairs I rent out to my employees. You'd have two roommates if that's okay with you." Finished with the conversation, he stood up.

Alessa's eyes widened. "Seriously?"

He shrugged nonchalantly. "Of course."

She held up her hand to signal for him to stop. "Wait, why are you doing this? Why are you giving some stranger a job and a place to live?"

He sighed despairingly. "My sister needed my help a few years ago, and I didn't listen. Now, looking back," he shook the dazed look from his face,"I wish I would've."

Not knowing what to say, Alessa silently pushed her chair back from the table and trailed close behind as he walked toward the kitchen.

"If you can't afford a uniform yet, I'm sure the ladies have extra clothes you can borrow. We require black heels, a black knee-length skirt, and a white button-up blouse. If your shirt is see-through, which I find most are, please make sure you wear a tank underneath. Your hair must be pulled back at all times during your shift. The last thing I need is a customer suing me for hair in their food or drink. And I expect my employees to be on time every shift. Two strikes and you're out. Got it?"

"Got it."

They pushed through the swinging door into the kitchen, where two young women took condiment containers from the upper shelves.

"Ladies," Louie extended his hand toward Alessa, "I'd like to introduce you to Jane. She'll be working at the café and rooming with you, if that's alright."

The petite girl with golden brown curls bounced up and down. "Hey, I'm all about saving money on rent," she exclaimed in a Southern twang.

"Hi, I'm McKenzie." The tall platinum blonde flashed a pearly white smile. Her hair was pulled back in a tight ponytail, her eyebrows perfectly plucked, and a thin, sharp line of black eyeliner outlined her upper eyelids. McKenzie's bright pink lipstick matched the blush painted high on her cheekbones. "The Southern belle is Reagan," she tilted her head toward the other young woman.

Reagan grinned. "If you're wondering about my amazing accent, I'm from Arkansas—"

"Yeah, that's great and all," Louis interrupted, "but Reagan, you make sure to put your hair back before it gets all up in the customer's food."

"Oops. I'm on it, Louie." Reagan's freckled nose blushed a light pink, and she ran off to grab a hair tie.

"How about you start tomorrow?" Louie asked.

"Yes, absolutely. I mean, tomorrow sounds great," said Alessa, stumbling over her words.

"Ladies, I gotta get back. Please show Jane around the café and apartment before your shift starts."

Reagan grasped Alessa's upper arm and hollered back at Louie as he walked away. "Don't you worry, boss. You get on out of here. We'll take good care of her."

"We got this, Louie!" McKenzie said over her shoulder, trailing close behind.

The three women passed by two young Hispanic men cutting carrots as they headed toward the back of the kitchen.

Reagan pointed toward the men. "This is Tony and Jorge. They're our prep cooks."

Jorge had stopped chopping to wave his free hand, but Tony continued, and as he took his eye off the knife, the sharpened blade sliced through his finger.

As the chunk of the prep cook's severed finger hit the table, blood spurted from the open wound. Tony's eyes rolled into the back of his head, and his tanned face faded to white.

"Oh shit!" Alessa yelled before she dove behind the falling man. She groaned, her abdominal stitches pulling as she caught Tony under his arms.

Dropping his knife, Jorge bent down to help Alessa lay Tony on the floor while McKenzie and Reagan covered their mouths in disgust.

"Oh my!" Reagan swallowed.

"Does anyone know what to do?" McKenzie shrieked.

"Is he going to be okay? Is he dead?" Jorge panicked.

"He is going to be okay," said Alessa. "But I need you to get two quart-sized plastic bags and a gallon-sized plastic bag. Then fill the gallon bag with some ice."

Jorge sprang into action as Alessa turned her attention to McKenzie and Reagan. "McKenzie, I need a first aid kit, and Reagan, can you please get several clean towels?"

Both women took off in opposite directions to do what was asked of them.

"This is all I could find." McKenzie handed a red medical bag to Alessa.

She dug through the bag and pulled out a package of gloves, a bottle of sterile saline, gauze, and medical tape. "This is great."

Reagan arrived with the towels at the same time as Jorge.

"Okay, Jorge, I'll take the bags from you. Now, I need you to find a box or something to prop his feet up on. He looks like he's going into shock, and we need to get his blood pumping back to his heart." Alessa stood up at the counter. "Reagan, please pick up his arm and gently place it on the clean towels."

Reagan dropped the towels onto the floor and gingerly lifted the injured man's bloody hand before setting it down on the cloth.

"Got it." Jorge turned away and grabbed a small chair. He pulled it over before Tony sat on it and placed his friend's legs on his own.

"Great thinking," Alessa complimented. Gloving up, she grabbed the severed fingertip and brought it over to the sink, where she cleansed the appendage with the sterile saline before sticking it in one of the smaller bags. "McKenzie, it might be wise to call an ambulance."

Alessa placed the severed finger, now secured in three bags

and on ice, on the countertop before turning her attention to Tony. She knelt on the floor and felt the side of his neck. *His pulse is weak and thready; he's going into shock.*

"McKenzie, make sure the operator is aware it's urgent." Alessa poured the sterile saline over his exposed finger bone. Then, she wrapped the end of his finger in sterile gauze before securing it with medical tape.

Reagan ran to the front of the restaurant. "I can hear the sirens! They're coming around the corner."

Tony's eyes fluttered open as the sound of the sirens wailing reached the kitchen through the open front door.

"Hey, hey, shh. Don't move." Alessa placed her hand behind his neck. "You had an accident, but we've called an ambulance, and they're going to take you to the hospital. The doctors will fix you right up."

Tony licked his lips weakly. "If you say so."

As the paramedics entered through the kitchen door, Alessa stood up to move out of their way, and McKenzie gave the medical staff the rundown on what happened.

Reagan pulled Alessa to the side. "We are so lucky you walked in here today. We would have never known what to do without you. Did you used to work in a hospital or something?"

Alessa glanced at the paramedics lifting Tony onto the gurney. "Um..."

"And I'm not sure what you said to Jorge and Tony, but you took charge and made them feel better," Reagan added.

Alessa's face scrunched up in confusion. "What do you mean you don't know what I said? You were in the room with us the whole time."

Reagan rolled her eyes. "Not everyone speaks Spanish."

"But apparently, you do!" McKenzie exclaimed.

"I spoke Spanish?" Alessa mumbled under her breath.

"Now that we know that Tony's being taken care of, on with the tour!" McKenzie declared.

How did I know how to handle a severed finger? Or unknowingly speak Spanish?

CHAPTER NINE

The women turned left and filed up a skinny staircase. At the top was a bright yellow door, and McKenzie pulled a key out from her apron before slipping it into the lock. "Welcome home."

"It ain't much, but we've tried our best to glam the place up a bit," Reagan said as the three women crossed the threshold.

Alessa was taken by surprise. What they had done with the limited square footage was impressive. Anyone could point out the differences in the two women's styles, but somehow, they had made the place feel like an eclectic, cozy home.

To their left was the kitchen, decorated top to bottom in a rustic theme, with chickens and apples hand-painted on the backsplash. Straight ahead from the entryway, planted directly in front of three floor-to-ceiling windows, sat a large, shamrock-green sofa. To the left of the couch was a cream-colored oversized chair, and a carved wooden coffee table was centered in the middle of the room.

"Let me guess, McKenzie picked out the couch?" Alessa pointed toward the bright green fabric.

"Obviously. I'm the one with more fashion sense," McKenzie chuckled.

McKenzie pointed to a closed door to the right of the large television on the wall. "And here is the downfall of the place. The only bathroom."

Reagan opened the door, and they peered into the small space. "All of my stuff is on the right side of the sink, and on the left is Kenzie's. Lucky for you, we have another cabinet that hangs on the wall above the toilet." Reagan pointed at the closed cabinet doors. "We keep all of our extra supplies in here, but we can find somewhere else to stash that crap, so you have a place to put your hairbrush and whatnot."

Alessa shrugged. "I appreciate that, but at the moment, I don't have much of anything to put in there."

"That's okay, you will. And we'll still clear it out, so when you get stuff, you'll have somewhere to put it," said McKenzie.

"Oh, come look at our bedroom," Reagan squealed as she ran past the couch and swung open the door. Two twin beds were lined against opposite walls with a tall wooden dresser in between. "It's a tight fit, but it works surprisingly well. The biggest selling point about this place," Reagan paused for effect, "is the closet."

McKenzie flicked on the light. "See?"

Alessa peeked around the corner, and her jaw dropped in surprise. "You have got to be kidding me."

The walk-in closet was as big as the shared bedroom, and it was packed from floor to ceiling with clothes, shoes, and every accessory a person could ever dream of.

"I didn't know anyone could own this many clothes." Alessa caressed the textured fabrics hanging from varying heights.

McKenzie giggled. "That's because you hadn't met Rae yet."

Reagan huffed. "Oh, shut your mouth. You're acting like you're not just as bad."

Alessa admired the clothing as they bantered back and forth about who took up more of the space.

"So, where do I sleep? Is this going to be my room?" Alessa chuckled, only half kidding.

Reagan smiled. "No, goofball, I mean, if you want to sleep in here, go for it, but—"

"—you might prefer the couch. It's super comfy," McKenzie finished.

Alessa nodded in agreement. "That's fine with me. Anything is better than a bus seat."

Reagan's head tilted to the side. "Did you just say 'a bus seat'?"

"Uh, yes. Yes, I did." Alessa nervously shoved her hands deep into her pockets.

McKenzie's eyes narrowed. "Exactly where are you from?"

"Nowhere interesting," Alessa said dismissively. "Look, I don't want to talk about my past. I just got out of some dark stuff and would prefer to leave my past in the past."

Not expecting such an emotional response, both girls nodded mechanically before Reagan nervously cleared her throat.

"Well, as soon as we can think of something, we'll get you a better sleeping arrangement," Reagan reassured in her Southern twang.

"I'm thankful you both are letting me stay here."

"It's no problem," Reagan and McKenzie agreed simultaneously.

Exchanging a look of surprise, the two women dissolved into a giggling fit.

McKenzie walked toward the front door. "Alright, then. We need to get back downstairs to finish prepping for the morning rush. Customers will be arriving soon."

"If you need clothes to change into, you're more than welcome to help yourself to anything in the closet," Reagan offered as she followed close behind her friend.

"Thank you both so much. I know the boss said I'd be starting tomorrow, but since I don't know anyone around here and have no plans, do you mind if I tag along? It's been a minute since I last had a waitress gig, and it'd probably benefit me to shadow you two. After I take a shower, that is."

"Works for me," McKenzie agreed. "Let's go ahead and get an outfit together for you." McKenzie clasped her hands together and strolled down her side of the closet.

Grabbing a white button-up shirt and a black skirt, McKenzie eyed Alessa while holding them up before her. "Eh, these should fit well enough." McKenzie handed the clothes to Alessa. "The black skirt might look more appropriate on you since you're a good four inches shorter than me. Oh, I should grab you one of these." McKenzie pulled down a spaghetti-strapped undershirt from Reagan's side of the closet. "These white tops are known to be see-through."

Reagan stood in front of a tall rack of assorted shoes at the back of the closet. "What size shoes do you wear?"

Alessa wiggled her toes inside the sneakers she found at the hospital. They were a size eight and a bit too big. "I think maybe a seven?"

"Oh, I get it. My feet are different sizes depending on the type of shoe as well. And look at that, we have a size seven right here!" she exclaimed, handing Alessa a black pair of heels. "If you need any brushes, combs, extra hair ties, clips, bobby pins—anything at all—they'll be in one of the bathroom drawers. We have more than enough, so don't worry about it."

Alessa paused in front of the open bathroom door, her arms full of clothing.

"Oh, and we have new toothbrushes in your cabinet," McKenzie said as they made their way toward the front of the apartment. "We always have a few extra in case gentlemen callers stay the night." She wiggled her eyebrows. "You know."

Alessa laughed. "Wow. Okay, then."

"See you in a bit, Jane!" the women hollered as the front door slammed shut behind them.

"Jane," Alessa exhaled. *That will take some time to get used to, but it's not like I could go by my actual name when I have people coming after me. Alessa is not exactly a common name.*

Setting the shoes and clothing down next to the sink, she wiggled out of her backpack. It dropped with a thud onto the floor, and she peeled herself out of the convenience store-bought red plaid button-up and blue jeans.

After a much-needed warm shower, Alessa dried herself with a large towel, careful to dab both on and around the abdominal bandage.

Unzipping the backpack's large pocket, she grabbed the second to last bandage and a small tube of antibiotic ointment. As she pried off the old dressing, she bit her tongue to hold back the urge to cry, as she did every time she was forced to look at what had been done to her.

Even though the edges were less red and angry, it was evident the jagged lines would forever be etched upon her skin.

Placing her shaking right hand on the puffy tissue, Alessa traced its outline with the tips of her fingers. Suddenly, there was the sensation of a man's hands reaching from behind, and his arms felt as though they wrapped around her torso.

She jumped back but found the room empty except for her panic-ridden, foggy reflection staring back at her in the mirror.

"Jeez, get it together," she breathed, shaking away the feelings of unease.

Alessa squeezed a thick line of antibiotic ointment down her scarred stomach, applied the clean bandage, and secured the gauze with tape around its edges.

Alessa reached back to French braid her ash-blonde hair.

I need McKenzie to show me how to do my makeup. I look different with my hair dyed, but not different enough to not be recognized if those guys come after me.

She finished dressing and ran her hands down the front of the blouse self-consciously.

Even though her scars weren't visible through the shirt, she could feel the outline of the bandage, and it made her feel vulnerable.

Alessa stared at her reflection in the mirror. "As long as I don't get groped by a customer, I should be fine. I'll be fine ... Today is the start of your new life, Alessa. I mean, Jane. The past is the past, so breathe. Everything will be okay," she unsuccessfully attempted to convince herself before leaving the apartment.

CHAPTER TEN

One month later...

A disembodied, sinister whistling echoed in Alessa's dream.

Her head bobbed around as she struggled to sit upright, and as she blinked against the glow of the room's harsh lights, a tall figure surrounded by a yellow-white light strolled before her.

The whistling ceased, and the individual sucked on their teeth. "Well, hello there, beautiful. Enjoy your nap?" the voice spat venomously.

The shadow surrounded Alessa with its musky stench, and as it bent down, the black figure grabbed a fistful of her matted red hair before jerking her head back.

A man's scarred face came into focus, and she was forced to stare into his muddy brown eyes.

He took a long drag off his thick cigar and blew a circular puff of smoke between his thin lips. It bounced off her bloodied mouth before drifting up toward her nostrils.

Alessa's throat burned as she choked on the smoke, and as he

*seductively whispered her name, he released her hair, grabbed
her arms, and shook her violently.*

"Alessa!" he roared.

Alessa sprang upright on the couch, her hand pressed against
her chest as she hacked the imaginary smoke from her lungs.

"Fuck," she gasped. Looking around the room, she focused
on her breathing and orienting herself. "You're at the
apartment. You're safe. You're okay."

With an annoyed groan, she fell back into the couch
cushions and stared at the ceiling.

Reinforcing the fact that Alessa was indeed home, not
being tortured at some random building, Reagan's loud snores
penetrated the closed bedroom door and reverberated off the
apartment's walls.

As Alessa's morning migraine arrived on time, the room
appeared to tilt. Snatching up the nearly empty bottle of
painkillers, she poured four pills into her sweaty palm and
downed them before stumbling toward the three large glass
windows on the front of the building.

The sun's golden rays were barely rising behind the city's
tall buildings, which meant she was awake earlier than she
wanted to be.

Nightmares had plagued Alessa every night since she
escaped the hospital, and each morning, she suffered
excruciating headaches, which left her exhausted.

Blinking the sleep from her eyes, her memories muddled,
and her nightmare slipped away.

Left confused and annoyed, she snatched up the T-shirt
and shorts, splayed on the oversized chair, and dressed while
shuffling sleepily toward the front door.

She put on her blue sneakers before tiptoeing down the stairs, and after pulling her dyed-blonde hair back into a tight ponytail, Alessa exited via the building's back door.

Warming up, she twisted her spine left and right. The tightened skin on her abdomen where the scar remained tugged, once again reminding Alessa of her forgotten past.

With a loud exhale, Alessa shook her upper body before she took off running around the side of the café.

The stabbing sensation inside her skull turned into a full-on assault against her left eye, but rather than give in to the pain, she pushed herself to sprint.

Through blurred vision, Alessa located the familiar dark green dumpsters sitting against the far wall of a red-bricked building and charged toward it.

An older man teaching her to flip off a black wall appeared in her mind.

"You must imagine yourself as light as a feather so you may float up off the wall. If you do not believe you are capable, you will forever fight against the weight of your doubt," he instructed.

Alessa excessively blinked, and her vision cleared. Extending her arms, she propelled forward, hurdling the first of the two dumpsters, and as her feet hit the concrete, she jumped over the second large dumpster.

Another vision from her past materialized in which she was flying effortlessly between uneven bars.

Shaking the image from her mind, Alessa ran up the side of the building, grasped the metal bars on the fire escape's landing, and muscled her way onto the structure before continuing up the staircase.

Breathing heavily, she stepped onto the decked-out terrace, where she read an electronic billboard.

'Protect Yourself and Those You Love. Wear a Mask,' was written in bold letters directly below a woman's face covered by a pale violet medical mask.

She stared at the top of the building directly across from her, and the disembodied man's voice emerged from her subconscious once more.

"Run as fast as you believe you are able. And then push yourself to run even faster. The greater the speed, the greater your forward motion will be."

Alessa darted forward.

Gaining momentum, her irises flashed an intense emerald green as she reached the edge of the terrace, and as she stepped down, she pushed off, flying high into the air.

She felt weightless, soaring elegantly between the two buildings like a bird in flight.

But as gravity took hold, Alessa dropped, tucking her upper body into a graceful roll, and she completed her somersault onto the neighboring rooftop terrace.

Sticking the landing, Alessa blinked, and her irises returned to their typical blue hue.

Exhaling a shaky breath, she glanced back at the building she had just leaped from.

The sun immersed the city in its golden glow as she descended the fire escape and jogged toward Pat's apartment.

Pat was the only person Alessa truly trusted.

He was a retired army veteran who lost his vision due to ocular trauma while serving overseas.

As the sole survivor of an IED attack, which left him blind, Pat was declared useless by the army and given a shiny little medal before being sent home to deal with the ramifications of surviving his mates—insurmountable PTSD.

On Alessa's first day working at the café, she had Pat as a

customer, and they quickly became friends. It was as if their souls could sense the darkness within one another, and their unspoken trauma bonded them.

Alessa pressed the noisy buzzer on the front of Pat's apartment complex. His familiar, "What do you want?" bellowed through the speaker, and she couldn't help but chuckle at the grumpy, older man.

"It's Jane, let me in." She bent over and snatched up a few wildflowers growing in front of the building before the door unlocked with a click.

Sprinting up the staircase, she nearly collided with a couple of teenage boys listening to music on their large headphones.

"Oh shit, sorry," she apologized, tripping around them.

Shortly after knocking on Pat's blue door, he opened it and looked past Alessa with his typical blank stare.

She smirked. "Good morning, sir."

Even though the war had taken his eyesight years earlier, Alessa knew every one of his other senses was incredibly heightened.

Pat grimaced. "Is that flowers I smell?"

"Yep, I picked them myself. Can I stick them in a vase?" She marched toward the kitchen.

"Go ahead and use the vase from a few days ago. Just toss out the dead flowers that are probably still in there."

The cloudy glass vase full of crunchy dead flowers was in the middle of the kitchen table, surrounded by piles of mail and dirty dishes.

"Wasn't Jess supposed to swing by this week to clean up a bit?"

"She was, but her boy had some school function, so..." He shrugged. "If my kids don't want to come see me, I'm not gonna make 'em."

Alessa eyed Pat's overdue bills while collecting the pieces of paper into a single pile. With a silent shake of her head, she moved them to the corner of the counter.

"Have any more crazy dreams?" He strode toward the stairs of his private rooftop terrace.

Alessa finished filling the vase with cool water and stuck the fresh flowers in the glass. "Only every time I close my eyes."

She set the flowers in the center of the coffee table before following him up the stairs.

"I'm sure I sound like a broken record, but—" Pat pulled out his pistol and attached a specialized amplified silencer from his time in the United States Special Operations.

Alessa rolled her eyes. "I know, I know. They're just dreams. But Pat, if you knew what horrific images plague my mind ... and those are the few blips I remember. Most of them disappear within seconds of me waking up."

Pat aimed at the far wall, and as he pressed a button on the brick near the door, a target sprang out from a wall. A beeping device was in the center of the tall object, alerting Pat to where he needed to aim. His first shot went straight through the bullseye. "Well, I would know if you'd ever tell me."

Alessa picked up the bow and slung the quiver of arrows around her backside before she slid the chest plate into place.

"I'll tell you mine if you tell me yours," she quipped, wrapping the bracer around her arm.

He pressed another button, and as the next target broke free, Alessa released her arrow, striking it dead center.

"Touché." Pat laughed as they took turns moving around the terrace, firing at their fake enemies.

Alessa collapsed in a sweaty heap as the last of their foes was destroyed.

"I can't tell you how good it feels to be ... me. For you to not treat me like I can't do something because I..." Overtaken by emotion, Pat stopped talking. "What I'm trying to say is, thanks, kid."

"Oh, stop it. You help me as much as I help you. I would've lost my shit by now, but since you're crazier than me, you help me feel sane." Flashing an ornery grin, Alessa stood up.

Pat's cheeks reddened as he let out a hearty laugh. "You know just the right thing to say."

"I hate to cut our time short, but I've got to get to work. You want to stay out here or head back in?"

"Oh, I think I'll absorb the heat of the sunrise a few minutes longer. I'll see you later for lunch."

"You, old man, are insane." Alessa chuckled as she left the rooftop.

"Not the first nor the last time I'll be called that!"

An exhausted Alessa nearly fell in through her apartment's front door.

Reagan was swaying back and forth in the kitchen, singing to herself while making a hot cup of coffee. Beneath half-open eyelids, she stared into the steam rising from her mug and yawned. "Mornin', sunshine," she said to no one in particular.

"So, um, are you referring to me as the sunshine? Or are you trying to give yourself a little pep talk after your late-night festivities?"

"Shh. Your mouth speaks too much," Reagan slurred before sipping her caffeinated beverage.

Alessa laughed as she kicked off her sweaty shoes.

McKenzie whipped around the corner, peppy as ever, and snatched up the empty mug beside the metallic coffee machine. "Up early again, Jane?"

Alessa pursed her lips and opened a cabinet door for a clean glass. "Mm-hmm."

McKenzie leaned forward on the counter with her steaming mug in hand. "Could you stop being so selfish and send me some of that motivation? And Reagan, what the hell, girl? Are you even human? How do you not feel like complete and utter shit right now? You are the same girl who was out 'til three this morning with me, are you not?"

Reagan grinned smugly at her friend's annoyance, bringing the steaming mug to her lips. "I can't help that my liver is more effective than yours at filtering alcohol. And Jane, why do you run every day at the butt crack of dawn?"

Alessa stuck the glass beneath the kitchen faucet and filled it with cold water. "It helps alleviate my migraines. You know, endorphins and whatnot."

Parting her lips, McKenzie blew on the steam from her cup. "Were you in the army or something? Don't they run drills before the sun comes up?" She turned toward Reagan. "I can't even imagine."

A vision of herself kicking someone square in the face flashed before Alessa's eyes.

Purposefully ignoring the question, she walked away. "You two done in the bathroom?"

"Oh, I forgot. You don't talk about your past." McKenzie rolled her eyes.

"Don't start," Reagan warned. "Yeah, we're done, honey," she called out to Alessa.

Closing the door behind her, Alessa leaned back against the doorframe. *Maybe I was in a branch of our government and experimented on.*

Peeling the socks off her feet, she wiggled out of her shorts while heading toward the shower. Gripping the bottom of her sweat-soaked shirt, she pulled it off her torso before slapping the wet fabric onto the cold tile floor.

The hot water ran down her body, cleansing the sweat and dirt from her skin.

Apart from her abdominal scar, every single injury she had sustained one month prior had healed and disappeared entirely as though they had never existed. At least the physical injuries had healed. The psychological trauma from her ordeal seemed to be worsening every day.

Turning off the water, she reached for the green towel draped over the bar hanging on the wall, wrapped it around her torso, and knotted it above her breasts.

Standing before the fogged-up mirror, Alessa lifted her arm and wiped her hand through the condensation on the cold glass.

As her fingertips left a cleared path on the reflective surface, a handsome man's face stared back at her.

With a yelp, she jumped in surprise and spun around, expecting to find a man in the room with her.

But she was alone.

Bewildered, she turned to face the mirror and touched the slick surface.

What was that? Better yet, who *was that?*

The man had short, tousled, dark chestnut hair with a decent amount of stubble running along his jawline. His pink lips held the hint of a playful smile as his captivatingly dark blue eyes bore right through her.

Alessa chuckled. "That's it. It's official. I am losing my mind." She froze for a second before glancing up into the mirror. "But what if I'm not?"

CHAPTER ELEVEN

Her roommates bombarded Alessa as she pushed through the swinging kitchen door of the café.

"Morning!" McKenzie jumped at her.

"Shit!" She placed a hand over her heart. "Don't do that!"

"Your birthday is tomorrow. Whatcha wanna do?" McKenzie asked.

Alessa choked on her saliva. *Oh no, I forgot I told them my birthday was this month.* "I haven't thought about it."

She shuffled behind the counter and clocked in on the computer.

"But it's your birthday. We gotta do something," Reagan whined.

Alessa threw her hands in the air. "Like what?"

"Well, Rae and I have been talking, and we've decided if you don't have any ideas, we'd like to take you to a new nightclub."

"It's called Fantasia. Doesn't that sound fun?" Reagan beamed.

Marching toward her section of tables, Alessa scrunched her nose. "Fantasia?"

"My cousin's the bouncer, so he can get us in," McKenzie said. "Probably won't even have to wait in line."

"And we can dance and drink all night long!" Reagan's corkscrew curls bounced around in her ponytail as she clapped her hands together.

Alessa picked up a large black condiment bottle. "I don't know if I'm up for all that."

"You haven't been out of the house to have fun since you moved in like a month ago," McKenzie pointed out.

"We worry about you, hun. You don't have many friends, you don't seem interested in finding a cute guy, and you don't have a hobby outside of jogging," Reagan added.

Alessa rolled her eyes as she poured pepper from the large container. "Why are you so observant?"

McKenzie eyed Alessa. "Besides, you need to get laid."

Alessa's eyes nearly popped out of her head. "Kenzie! Why would you say that?"

"Because it's true." The blonde stared her down. "You are all wound up. I can tell the difference between a woman who's used to getting some and one who's not. And girl, your body tells a story."

Christopher strolled through the front door as the two women waited impatiently for Alessa to cave in.

In unison, all three girls turned their heads to admire their light-haired, tanned co-worker.

"Hey, Chris! You wanna go to Fantasia with us tomorrow night?" Reagan clapped her hands together in excitement.

Alessa glared at her obnoxious friend, who clearly couldn't take a hint and drop the whole nightclub idea.

Chris strolled behind the counter. "What's the occasion?"

"It's Jane's birthday."

"Oh, I didn't know that. How old will you be?" His forest green eyes bore into Alessa's.

She blushed before glancing down at her empty salt shaker. "Twenty ... four?" she mumbled. *That sounds about right.*

"Aren't you too young to forget your age?" he joked.

The edges of Alessa's lips lifted, and she pointed at him. "Shut it, you."

"Oh, you know I'm kidding. Mostly." He winked. "Would you like me to go?" He stepped toward Alessa.

Unable to form an answer as he inched closer, Alessa mumbled, "Um..."

As the space between them dwindled, a customer unexpectedly collided with the pair, spilling his hot coffee all over the side and front of her shirt.

Alessa's arms flailed out to the sides, and she screamed as the scalding brown liquid splashed up the side of her neck and down her arms.

"Ah!" Chris exclaimed and jumped back. Coffee cascaded down the front of his shirt and arms as he ran away.

"I am so sorry," the male customer murmured apologetically while grabbing napkins off the countertop.

Hearing Alessa's screams, McKenzie and Reagan whipped around to see the skin on their friend's neck already reddening.

Alessa's mouth hung open in shock, and she froze as the customer crouched in front of her with napkins in hand. Her arms dangled awkwardly as she stared at the blue baseball cap atop the man's head.

"I can't believe—I just—I'm so unbelievably sorry," the male customer stuttered while fumbling with the napkins and looking down at the ground.

As Alessa stood before the distraught man, Chris rushed behind the counter and unbuttoned his soaked shirt.

Peeling the wet fabric from his chest, he tossed it in the sink before turning the cool water on. "Ah!" Chris exclaimed as he threw his burned arms beneath the stream of cold liquid.

Hissing in pain, she jumped back as the customer pressed a handful of napkins against her chest. "Ah!" She blocked him from further attempts. "That's okay. I'm okay." She held her hands out in front of her. "Stop. Just stop!"

McKenzie ran up beside Alessa. "What happened?"

Reagan's hands covered her mouth. "Oh my! We need to get both of you to a hospital."

Chris cursed as he looked down at his right forearm. "Dammit. I got burned good." He turned around. "Jane, are you okay? You look like you got the worst of it."

Alessa panicked. "The hospital? Um, no, I don't think so. I don't exactly have health insurance." *Besides, I'll be healed in a few hours, and then I'll have some serious explaining to do.*

She tucked her left hand into the crook of her right arm before lifting her free hand to cover the side of her neck.

"I don't feel that burnt," her voice wavered as the blistered skin from one body part touched another.

Alessa's eyes darted from McKenzie to Reagan and then to Chris as she wished desperately to be left alone.

Amidst the chaos, the customer had pulled his baseball cap further down his forehead and snuck away.

Chris reached for Alessa. "Jane, let me see."

Digging her fingertips deep into the fresh wounds to keep her friends from seeing the marred flesh, she grunted, "I'm fine," between gritted teeth and took a step backward toward the kitchen.

"Seriously? There's no way. I hardly got any coffee on me,

and my arm looks like this." Chris pointed to the blisters popping up on his reddened arm. "Just let me—"

"No!" She jerked away.

Alessa eyed the male customer as he hurried out the front door. Passing in front of the restaurant's large front window, the man shoved his hands deep into his jacket pockets while lifting his gaze.

As their eyes met, his piercing blue eyes bore through her, and an overwhelming sense of familiarity punched Alessa in the gut.

"Jane?" Louie interrupted.

"Huh?" Snapping out of her trance, she turned around.

Her boss stood behind the front counter with concern etched across his face. "Go to the doctor and get checked out."

"I don't need—" she started.

"It's not a request. It's an order," he demanded, his voice stern.

"I'm at least going upstairs to change first," Alessa grumbled.

Louie nodded in agreement. "That's fine, but I expect to see a note from a physician clearing you for work."

"Okay, okay." Alessa scampered off toward the kitchen door.

McKenzie called out to Alessa. "We'll check on you in a little bit."

Louie pointed at Chris. "That goes for you, too. Urgent care or the hospital—your choice."

Chris grabbed his shirt from the sink basin and rung it out. "You don't have to tell me twice."

Alessa's stomach lurched, and she jogged up the back stairs with her arms still pressed into her blisters. As she reached the top step, she inhaled deeply, closed her eyes, and quickly extended her arms.

She shrieked aloud and nearly passed out from the pain.

Stumbling through the front door, she kicked off her black heels, untied her apron, and balled it up before tossing it next to her shoes. Unbuttoning her shirt, she hissed as she pulled the sodden, brown-stained fabric away from her raw chest.

With her shirt splayed open, she fell forward, barely catching herself on the counter, and leaned over the sink. Realizing the fabric still clung to her burnt arms, Alessa exhaled shakily in mental preparation for the agony she was about to put herself through. "Do it already," she growled.

Gripping the sleeves tight, she tore them off, and with a loud huff, Alessa dropped the shirt while fighting the urge to vomit.

The layers of skin on her arms matched the look of her collarbone, blistered and discolored, as was the side of her neck. However, the marks where the coffee had splattered onto her abdomen were already healing and barely light pink.

Shaking and exhausted, Alessa shuffled her way to the couch and plopped down with a loud groan before pulling the throw blanket up to her waist. Laying back, she looked out the windows at the overcast sky and replayed the incident.

Why did that guy look familiar? And why did the coffee being spilled on us feel almost ... intentional?

Alessa pictured the man's smoldering gaze as her eyes slowly blinked shut, and she fell into a deep, dreamless sleep.

CHAPTER TWELVE

"Jane?"

Alessa moaned. "Hmm?"

"Jane, wake up," McKenzie urged.

"No." Alessa moaned, stretching her arms up above her head.

Reagan touched Alessa's shoulder. "How ya feelin'?"

"Have you been sleeping all day?" questioned McKenzie.

Alessa sat up and examined her fully healed chest. "Uh, I guess?" she mumbled. "Honestly, I feel great. See? I told you it wasn't as bad as everyone thought. I guess I just needed a nap."

McKenzie punched Alessa's bicep on the way to the bedroom. "Whatever, slacker. I'm glad to hear you're doing better than Chris."

Alessa bundled the blanket around her waist as Reagan sat down on the arm of the couch. "Did he get checked out?" Alessa asked.

Reagan grimaced in disgust. "Yep. He has second-degree burns all up and down his one arm. Bleh."

McKenzie shouted from the closet, "Good thing it didn't land on his face. It would've been a damn shame."

"Kenzie Rae!" Reagan scolded.

"What?" She popped her head out of the closet. "It's true."

"Anyway," Reagan slid onto the cushions and wrapped her arm around Alessa's nearly naked torso, "I'm glad to see you're doin' alright. We were worried about you."

Pulling her legs onto the couch, Alessa wrapped her arms around her knees. "What are your plans for tonight? I was thinking about seeing a movie. You two wanna tag along?"

McKenzie emerged from the closet wearing a tight blue dress and black pumps. "Well, while you were sleeping the day away, two men sat down in my section, and after finishing their sandwiches, they hung around for a bit." She strolled down the hall and into the bathroom. "Thirty minutes into them sitting there, I got sick of the men taking up space and asked if there was anything else I could help them with." She jumped out, grasping a pair of dangly earrings. "One asked if I was single. I said yes. Then the other guy looked at Reagan across the restaurant and asked about her."

"We're goin' on a double date!" Reagan squealed.

Alessa faked enthusiasm. "Oh, that sounds fun."

McKenzie ran excitedly into the bedroom while Reagan clicked her heels to the kitchen.

"Oh, wait!" McKenzie shrieked. "You should come with us, and we could totally invite Chris!"

Alessa shook her head. "No, McKenzie. He won't want to go out after what happened today."

"Oh, nonsense. I'm sure they gave him the good pain meds at the hospital." Reagan picked up her phone.

"What are you doing?" Alessa eyed Reagan as she smacked her gum.

"Texting Chris when and where we'll meet up."

"Why do I even waste my breath? You guys never listen to me." Alessa rolled her eyes and sunk back into the couch.

"Stop getting in your way. If Chris doesn't want to come, he won't. It's as simple as that."

Reagan's phone chimed and lit up. "Look at that. He says he'll be there."

Alessa groaned in exasperation. "Ugh, fine. Where are we going?"

"The guys suggested we try this axe-throwing place, End Check."

"Wait. You're wearing that?" Alessa pointed at Reagan and giggled. "To throw sharp objects at a wall?"

"What's wrong with my dress?" Reagan turned around in her skin-tight dress and looked at her reflection in the stand-alone mirror.

Alessa chortled and picked the black tablet up off the coffee table. The top trending article, 'Entire Towns Quarantined,' was posted on the newspaper app's front page.

As the number of cases increases significantly by the day, the governor of New York is considering declaring a State of Emergency. Traffic has been decreased in and out of the state, and medical staff are practicing airborne precautions since the disease has not yet been identified.

The familiar ache of a migraine crept into the back of Alessa's skull, and she set the tablet back down on the table.

"Have you been keeping up with the news regarding the virus outbreak? It seems unreal." Alessa rubbed her temples.

McKenzie's laughter echoed from the bathroom. "Yeah, I don't believe any of that. It's a government conspiracy."

Alessa exhaled loudly before joining McKenzie in getting ready.

Rummaging through their clothes, Alessa chose a mint green sundress, white slingback heels, and a small white purse.

She hurriedly curled her dyed-blonde locks into waves, added a coat of mascara to her lashes, and a layer of bright fuchsia on her lips.

Less than ten minutes later, McKenzie impatiently hollered down the hall. "Are you two ready to go yet?"

Reagan grasped the doorframe and leaned out of their bedroom. "Oh, come on, we're not taking that long."

"Ladies, we're supposed to be there in twenty minutes, and it takes thirty minutes to get there," McKenzie whined.

Reagan set her hand on the back of the couch to balance as she slid her heels on one foot and then the other. "Did you call for a ride already?"

"Girl, I did that before we even clocked out."

A car honked from the front of their building.

"Our ride's here," McKenzie urged, grabbing a black clutch from the top shelf.

Reagan hooked an earring loop as they scrambled toward the front door. "Shoot! I forgot my purse."

"I'll get it," Alessa yelled, returning to the closet. "Which one do you want?"

"The yellow sequins with the flower on it."

Alessa balanced on her tiptoes and rifled through the bin on the top shelf as McKenzie's heels click-clacked down the stairs.

"Come on!" they shouted in unison at Alessa.

"Got it!" Alessa exclaimed, and she ran out the apartment door, trailing behind her friends.

. . .

At the club, the three friends were greeted by an employee standing behind a counter, wearing a light blue surgical mask.

"Welcome to End Check. Do you have reservations?"

Reagan addressed the employee. "Three lanes, under the name Reagan. We're meeting a few other people."

McKenzie pointed at their dates from across the room. "There. We're with them."

A tall, freckled, pale-skinned man wearing a green and white plaid flannel shirt with pale blue jeans was standing beside a muscular, mocha-skinned man whose hair and goatee had been dyed ice white, and he was dressed in an outfit nearly identical to his friend's, just a different color palette.

"Oh, okay. You're all set, then." The employee smiled. "If you'd like, you can grab a drink at the bar while you wait."

"Kay, thanks." Reagan bit her lower lip excitedly as they joined the two men standing at a high-top table. "Hi, Skylar, James. I hope you don't mind, but we brought a friend. This is Jane."

McKenzie's date wrapped himself around her waist while Reagan's date grabbed her side and licked his lips with a nod. "That's cool. Will she be with us the *entire* night?"

"Uh ... what?" Alessa scowled.

With the chime of the front door, Chris walked in. "Hey, Jane." He waved with his good hand, hurrying over to their group. "How you feelin'?"

"Oh, I'm fine," she breathed, reassured by Chris's presence. "Nothing to write home about. But I hear you got the brunt of it." She pointed to his bandaged arm.

"Eh, I'll survive. They gave me the good stuff." Chris winked. "That's why I couldn't drive here. Had to jog the three blocks from my house."

"That's what Reagan said they'd do," Alessa laughed.

"What happened to you?" McKenzie's date asked.

"Some guy spilled his hot drink on us."

"This way, please," an employee interrupted.

Reagan's date snickered. "Damn, dude, that sucks."

"Yeah. It wasn't the best day, but maybe it'll get better now." Chris winked at Alessa as they entered a narrow hallway resembling a shooting range with stalls separating the individual targets. A stocky man wearing a pale blue mask and a bright orange vest with his name tag labeling him their hatchet guide directed the group to their lanes.

"Good evening, and welcome to End Check. Has anyone ever done this before?" he asked.

The two flannel-shirted men both raised their hands high in the air with cocky smirks plastered on their faces.

"Welp. Looks like I'm about to be shown up by Dingus One and Dingus Two," Chris whispered.

A warm blush spread over Alessa's cheeks as she failed to contain her laughter and snorted.

"You two paying attention?" the hatchet guide addressed Chris and Alessa.

"Absolutely." She pressed her lips together and feigned seriousness as Chris saluted the man.

"Alright, then, back to my instructions. Now, your group gets these three stalls right here," he addressed. "I'm going to show you the proper way to handle the weapon before instructing you, individually, on how to safely and effectively throw it."

The instructor took a wide stance, placed one hand above the other, close together near the bottom of the handle, and raised the hatchet above his head. Stepping forward, he dragged his dominant foot and released the handle.

Striking the outer ring of the target, he extended his arm toward the bullseye. "Like so."

The group clapped before spreading out into their designated stalls.

"If this is your first time, don't be upset if you have difficulty throwing the axe hard enough to reach the target. This skill takes a lot of practice," the instructor reassured them.

Alessa's friends each took turns throwing the hatchet while everyone else watched.

When it was Reagan and McKenzie's dates' turn, they scowled in disappointment when they couldn't get any closer than the target's outer ring.

"Well, that's never happened before," Skylar spat.

"Yeah, the hatchet must be unbalanced," James complained.

Their guide eyed the men. "I assure you, that's not the case." He removed the weapon from the man's grasp.

Alessa and Chris glanced at one another, struggling to contain their laughter.

"Ma'am, I do believe it is your turn." The instructor handed Alessa the weapon, and she wrapped her fingers around the handle.

"You got this, Jane," Chris said.

Her friends whooped and hollered as she took her wide stance and raised the weapon.

Releasing the handle, she whined in despair as it bounced off the wooden target.

"Not bad. Try to release the hatchet as it becomes level with your eyes," the guide said before picking up the grounded weapon and handing it back to her.

Alessa bounced down into a near-squatting position.

Keeping her elbows bent, she lifted the hatchet overhead and closed her eyes.

Focus, she thought, exhaling slowly upon descent. She gave control over to a memory where a tall, muscular man was guiding her arm, and as she released the weapon, her eyes flickered green.

Thump! The hatchet was buried deep into the center of the bullseye.

"Whoa, Jane!" Chris threw his hands up in the air.

"That shit's rigged," James grumbled, and his friend shook his head in disbelief.

"Beginner's luck," Skylar scoffed.

"Fuck off," Alessa retorted.

Surprised by her aggressive reaction, she covered her mouth and snorted with laughter.

"Jane!" Reagan stared at her in shock.

"What I meant was," Alessa backtracked, "let me try that again to see if it was beginner's luck."

She positioned herself once more beside the table of hatchets, awaiting her weapon's return.

The guide grabbed the hatchet handle still wedged in the board and tried yanking it out. Beads of sweat dripped down his forehead as he continued to struggle, and after placing his left hand firmly on the board, he grunted upon finally extracting the axe.

"Wow. You really had that wedged in there." He handed it back to Alessa.

Readying herself, she bent her knees and exhaled, nice and slow, and with a blink of her eyes, Alessa's irises glimmered luminescent green.

Immediately after releasing the hatchet, she stepped to the

side, picking up two more. With a hatchet in each hand, she sent them flipping over themselves toward the first.

In quick succession, the blades struck the wooden board, one after the other, and splinters flew.

Alessa rubbed the burning sensation from her eyes with a satisfied chuckle, and they returned to their sky-blue hue.

As she turned around, everyone stood in silence, staring at her.

Suddenly self-conscious, she awkwardly cleared her throat and smoothed down the mid-section of her light green sundress.

"What the hell—" McKenzie began to ask.

"—was that?" Reagan finished as they all stared at her in awe.

Chris clapped, slow and dramatic. "Holy shit! That was amazing!" He laughed hysterically. "If we are ever in a zombie apocalypse, I call dibs on you being on my team."

Alessa laughed at the ridiculous notion. "You got it," she responded playfully before they all walked to the back of the building.

Thanks to the consumption of a large amount of alcohol, everyone grazed over the fact that Alessa had obliterated not only her friends' dates' egos but the target as well.

"Hey, so..." Reagan ran her tongue over her teeth. "We're going back to their place. Is it cool if you get your own ride home?"

"I'm not in grade school. I can make it home just fine." Alessa held both of her thumbs up.

"Great!" McKenzie shrieked. "We'll see you in the morning, babe!"

Her friends left the building, each with arms wrapped

around their dates, and Alessa stood up to leave. "That is my cue to exit."

Chris fell into step beside her. "Do you need me to come home with you?"

Alessa blushed.

"I didn't mean it ... like that. Would you like me to make sure you get home okay?"

Alessa held up her hand and shook her head. "I know what you meant, and thank you for the offer, but I'm good." She pulled out her phone. "I'm not sure if you noticed, but I didn't drink a drop of alcohol. I'm totally sober. I'll request a ride."

They stood on the street corner, facing one another.

"Well..." he stalled.

"Well..." Alessa mimicked, and their words hung in midair.

He stepped toward Alessa, and her breath faltered as she looked up at him.

Oh shit, is he going to—?

Chris's eyelids drooped, and he bent down with puckered lips.

This is happening.

As their lips touched, Alessa's reality blurred.

CHAPTER THIRTEEN

A man's muscular form pressed up against her hips, pushing Alessa back against the wall, and as his lips melted into hers, his calloused hands explored her body.

Her skin tingled in response to his touch, and after trailing his fingers alongside her neck, he reached his arm around her back.

Unhooking her black lacy bra, it fell to the ground, and he eagerly palmed her right breast.

The man bent down, taking her into his mouth, sucking and flicking her sensitive skin with the tip of his tongue.

She moaned as her body trembled beneath his, and she bit her bottom lip in anticipation as his lips inched down her inked side.

Gasping aloud, Alessa pulled away from Chris and dropped her purse onto the wet sidewalk.

"Are you okay?" Chris asked, confused.

"Yeah, no. I, um..." Alessa stammered. The loud squeal

resonating throughout her skull disrupted her ability to think clearly. "I think I have a migraine coming on. I need to get home."

"You sure you're okay?"

Alessa backed away from him. "Nope, nope. I'm sure. I'm good." She bent over to pick up her wet purse. "I'm going to head on out. Thanks for a—uh—lovely evening," she shouted back over her shoulder.

Alessa crossed her arms and marched further down the sidewalk, fingering where the man in her vision had touched her.

Turning back around, Alessa watched Chris disappear around the corner. "Well, that's not exactly how I saw our first kiss going," she huffed while digging her phone out of her tiny purse.

"—a good time?" slurred a deep voice from the dark.

Nearly dropping her phone, Alessa spun around to face the disembodied voice. She placed her hand over her heart and sucked in the cool night air. "I'm sorry. What was that?"

The figure moved out of the shadows and into the light cast from the streetlamp.

He repeated the question, but all Alessa could make out was, "—good time."

As the screeching noise in her head dulled, an uneasy feeling developed in the pit of her stomach. "I still can't understand you. I'm waiting for my boyfriend to pick me up," she lied.

Her eyes fell to the nearly empty bottle in the man's grasp.

With a cocky smirk, he lifted the glass to his thinly parted lips and took a swig. "I said, you lookin' for a good time?" He stumbled toward her.

Gripping tight onto her purse, Alessa stepped back toward the alley. At least if he came at her, she had an exit.

"N-no, de-definitely not."

"Aw, come on, sugar," the man pleaded.

Alessa swallowed nervously. "My boyfriend's almost here, so you'd better get lost."

The man rotated unsteadily and looked down at the next street. "Well, sweet thing, it looks to us like he's standing you up."

Alessa's heart skipped a beat, and her body stiffened. *Did he say 'us'?*

Chucking his bottle off to the side, he charged Alessa. As she spun around to run away, she was jerked back, and her purse dropped in a puddle in the middle of the street.

Alessa was held, dangling in midair, by the man's long arms wrapped tightly around her.

"Help! Please! Anybody!" she shrieked as a second man emerged from the darkness with another bottle of alcohol.

"Shut up, bitch!"

"Please don't do this." Alessa's lip quivered as she looked pleadingly from person to person.

The man standing directly in front of her bent forward and licked the side of her neck, leaving the scent of whiskey and tobacco upon her skin.

"Stop! Help!" She shrieked just before he punched the glass bottle upside her jaw.

"I said shut the fuck up." He grinned sadistically. "But whores never listen," he spat before placing the glass against his lips.

The world undulated before her as the men dragged her into the darkened alleyway.

Alessa dug her heels into the ground as she cried for help. The rough asphalt scuffed up the sides and broke the heel clear off from one of her shoes before they slid off altogether, leaving her barefoot.

A dark figure leaned up against the brick wall, awaiting their arrival. "Mmm," a third man sniffed her curled hair. "Don't you smell nice?"

Alessa squirmed and kicked her legs. "Somebody, please, help me!"

A fist punched deep in her gut, and as a rush of air escaped her lungs, she doubled over.

Her fallen body dangled as she struggled to breathe.

"Shh, my blue-eyed beauty." The man brushed her hair out of her face. "We're just going to have a little bit of fun."

Forcing her to her feet, the three men dragged Alessa's limp form to the side of the building and proceeded to slam her face-first into the alleyway's jagged wall.

Pressed against the brick, blood trickled down the side of Alessa's cheek, staining McKenzie's green dress. Her vision blurred as the men viciously tore at her clothes, ripping the thin fabric down Alessa's back.

A loud, drunken cackle echoed in the night before a large hand forcefully smacked Alessa's backside.

While the man held her in place, the others whistled and hollered their approval.

An electric charge filled the air as the men fought over who got their turn with her first.

"Come on, man, do it already. I want my chance," complained one attacker.

The man holding her let go as one of the other men pushed him aside. "No way. I got first dibs."

A whimper escaped between Alessa's trembling lips as one of the men's belts jostled, and his pants fell to the ground.

As adrenaline coursed through her veins, she was consumed by the rhythm of her increased heart rate.

Something primal and destructive was awakening within Alessa.

Closing her blue eyes, the immense feelings of fear subsided, and after blinking them open, her irises glowed fiery emerald green as her microchip activated.

The man's pants hit the ground with a thud as Alessa simultaneously pressed herself further into the wall in front of her. Then she darted to the right and pushed off the bricks, knocking the half-naked man off balance.

As the second attacker lunged for her, she sprinted up onto the brick wall before flipping over him. Landing behind the man, she kicked him in the backside and sent him head-first into the jagged stones.

Alessa sneered at her first attacker as he struggled to pull up his pants. "How pathetic," she growled before punching him upside his face, knocking him to the ground.

The largest in the group of men charged Alessa. Swinging a metal chain high in the air, he thrust it toward her with a deep grunt.

The chain narrowly missed her as she ducked and rolled out of the way.

Jumping up onto the balls of her feet, she crouched and stuck her foot out to the side. Swinging her leg around in a circle, she kicked the man's feet out from underneath him, knocking him flat onto his back.

The man with the bloodied face punched Alessa hard in the right kidney.

In between choking on bile and gasping for breath, she was forced down onto one knee.

As the man encircled Alessa, she grasped the metal chain dropped by the other assailant.

"Why won't you go down? Who the fuck are you?" the man demanded before picking a discarded bottle up from the side of the alley and smashing it against the bricks.

The man tried to intimidate her as Alessa wound the weapon around her knuckles. "I'm no one." Alessa's emerald green eyes bore into him as her voice dripped with disdain. "Just the one you chose to prey on tonight. And boy, was that a mistake." She smiled wickedly.

The attacking man's lip curled up in a snarl as he stomped toward her.

Thanks to the earlier punch to her kidney, another wave of nausea wracked her body, and she struggled to keep herself upright as he advanced. But as adrenaline pumped through her veins, she pivoted around and pushed off the asphalt.

Flying forward, she punched him square in the nose with the makeshift iron knuckles, and with a loud crack, the man collapsed in a large puddle of dirty water.

High-pitched, warrior-like cries sounded from behind Alessa as another of her attackers waved his arms in the air, wielding a small pocketknife.

Unable to take him seriously, Alessa chuckled as she watched his comical incoordination. *This guy*, she snickered to herself.

With a flick of her wrist, she propelled the end of the silver chain toward his neck. As it connected with his dark flesh, the metal coiled tightly around his trachea.

His panicked fingers dug at the metal in a clumsy attempt to pry it away from his airway, but as Alessa tugged on the link chain, it forced him down to his knees. The dark veins in his neck bulged, and lifting her foot, she slammed her bloodied heel down onto the chain. He jerked forward, and with a sickening crunch, his face smacked the concrete.

Winded, Alessa breathed heavily as she unwrapped the metal from her blanched knuckles and tossed the chain to the side.

Hearing one of the fallen men moan, she sprinted for the pocketknife on the ground, grasped it by the handle, and rushed the injured man.

Urine soaked through the denim as his jeans darkened and his eyes bulged in terror.

"You are right to fear me," she snarled between clenched teeth.

Flipping the knife up in the air, she caught the blade by its handle before thrusting the sharp edge toward his left eye.

As she was about to drive the blade through the man's pupil, her irises flashed back to their sky-blue hue, and she froze.

Bewildered, she dropped the knife and stood erect.

"Wha-what the—?" she stammered.

Stumbling backward, she found herself surrounded by a circle of broken bodies.

With shaking hands, Alessa scooped up each personal item she had dropped. Pausing momentarily, she thought about calling for help when, out of the darkness, a pair of silver eyes glowed, and she ran for her life.

CHAPTER FOURTEEN

In her dream, Alessa's classmates sat scattered throughout the large room, watching the new instructor's arms flail about during his demonstration.

"Damn, he's good," the blonde next to Alessa whispered.

Alessa huffed and rolled her eyes. "I guess he's not that bad."

The young blonde woman pointed at the man as he completed a backflip. "Oh, come on. I mean, look at him."

Landing crouched over, the instructor stood upright as the spectators sat in silent awe, and his muscles flexed. "Who would like to spar? I expect you to implement the techniques I demonstrated to you today."

Not a single person raised their hand.

"There's a rumor going around," whispered a young man sitting behind Alessa, "that he has a tiny dick."

"Anyone?" The tall man scanned the room.

"Seriously?" Alessa punched the guy sitting behind her in the arm. "Don't be stupid, Quade."

"You're disgusting," her blonde friend shook her head.

The instructor eyed Alessa and her laughing friends. "Quade, thank you for volunteering."

"Shit," Quade huffed. He jumped over the metallic bar onto the floor mat and shook his arms out to the side before the instructor.

Standing at the ready, still, and poised in front of his side of the line, the instructor raised an eyebrow. "You good?"

Quade answered with a silent nod.

"Then let's begin."

Rushing the instructor, Quade hollered aloud, chopping his hands through the air, left and right, up and down.

The instructor blocked every blow, and as the men glided across the floor, they kicked, hacked, and jabbed as if participating in a beautifully choreographed dance.

Intent on discovering just one of the instructor's weaknesses, Alessa bit her lower lip in concentration as she observed the fight.

A large bruise darkened beneath Quade's left eye after he took a fierce punch to the face. He then bent down and extended his legs before he swept them around, knocking the instructor off his feet.

With a loud thud, Quade's opponent fell flat on his backside.

"Ooh," the audience echoed.

Surprised, the instructor stalled briefly before springing up onto his feet. As his heels dug into the ground, he swung his arm forward, clocking Quade square in the nose.

As Quade wobbled back and forth, his hands flew to his face.

Taking advantage of his distracted opponent, the instructor dropped his leg and swept Quade's legs from underneath him.

Gravity took hold, and her friend's arms flailed out to the side, grasping nothing but air as the instructor slammed his fist down onto his chest.

A loud boom resonated throughout the room as Quade's body hit the floor. With a grunt, he threw his first two fingers into the air, admitting defeat.

"Ah!", "Ooh!" and "Wow!" echoed from the audience as they grimaced in time with the fight.

"Yield. I yield," Quade croaked.

The instructor's shoulders bounced up and down with each exaggerated breath as a grin spread across his face.

A swarm of women ran to the bar to congratulate the handsome instructor, and the crowd burst into cheers as he was declared champion.

The instructor's reaction to the ladies' attention gave Alessa an idea.

Interrupting the chorus of congratulations, Alessa strolled over to the metal bar.

"I'd like a turn." She smirked.

Alessa's phone vibrated, and her dream and its inhabitants disappeared as she became lucid. With an annoyed groan, she snatched her cellphone off the coffee table.

"Quade?" she garbled in a deep voice.

"Who's Quade? What? No, it's Louie."

"Oh shit. I'm sorry, Louie."

"I was calling to see if you wanted to take the day off since we don't have many customers this morning."

"Oh, sure. Not a problem."

"Okay, then. You have a good one, and I'll see you tomorrow." Louie hung up.

Alessa's vision swam as she struggled to keep her eyes open. "Ugh."

She dug her palms into her eyelids and pushed back against the building pressure inside her head.

Glancing over at the empty coffee pot, she remembered her friends had spent the night with their dates. "Shit."

She didn't feel up to making a pot, so she decided to grab some coffee from the café instead.

As per her usual morning routine, Alessa reached for the TV remote and turned it on.

"Wait a second." She looked down, expecting to find the ragged remains of McKenzie's dress, but instead eyed her filthy pink bra and panties. *What happened to my clothes?* Alessa whipped her head back and forth, searching the room for the ruined shoes and dress.

Alessa hissed at the pain induced by the movement and ran to the bathroom mirror to investigate further. She flicked on the light and discovered her face was covered in brownish-yellow bruises in the final stages of healing. Her blonde hair was a rat's nest, and her body was covered in a layer of dirt and dried blood.

Disgusted, she jumped in the shower, where clips of last night's events flashed before her as dirty water circled the drain.

Alessa drew in a sharp breath. "No, no, that wasn't me. I couldn't have possibly done that."

The water ran cold, and Alessa exited the shower. Wrapping the towel around her torso, she looked at herself in the mirror. While leaning forward to inspect her facial bruises, the image of her holding a knife up to a terrified man's eye materialized before her.

Coinciding with the spike in adrenaline, Alessa's eyes flashed green, and she jumped back, but with a single blink, her irises became sky blue once more.

"It's happening. I'm finally losing my mind."

"We apologize for interrupting the regularly scheduled broadcast, but we have breaking news. Last night, several men were viciously attacked outside of a local business," said the reporter. "Two of the men were pronounced dead at the scene, while one remains in critical condition."

Alessa darted out of the bathroom and stared at the television screen. "Oh, no. The knife, I dropped it."

"There are no suspects at this time, and no weapons were found at the scene," the reporter explained.

Her eyebrows scrunched up in confusion. "Wait, what?"

"If you have any information regarding the attack, please call the phone number at the bottom of the screen. We'll keep you updated as we learn more. Now, let's check out the weather..."

Alessa headed toward the closet. *Did I stash the knife? I only remember dropping it.*

Slipping into jeans and a T-shirt, she realized she had not simply defended herself last night. She had intentionally killed those men. She wanted to take their lives and even welcomed the fight.

Rage had been building inside of her for the past month, and the hate she had felt toward those perverts for thinking they could do whatever they wanted with no repercussions had pushed her over the edge.

How many victims had come before her?

After last night, I wouldn't be surprised if the one living man never looked at another person. Alessa smirked as she applied concealer to the darkened spots.

Picking up a pair of flats and her apartment keys, Alessa stopped by the café to grab two cups of hot coffee and a couple of freshly baked blueberry muffins.

She snuck out the back door and walked the few blocks to Pat's apartment building.

Thanks to the virus scare, there was less traffic, and the smog that once hid the sky no longer lingered. The few people she passed by on the sidewalk wore masks and didn't dare make eye contact.

Arriving at Pat's building, she pressed the button next to his apartment number.

"Who is it?" Pat demanded.

"It's Jane. Let me in. I've got nourishment."

The buzzer sounded, and she grabbed the door handle.

A sickly woman passed Alessa on her way up the stairs and coughed into the crook of her arm.

Darting the rest of the way, Alessa pounded on Pat's door. "Hey, Pat. It's me. Open up."

Pat greeted Alessa, wearing one of the most high-tech medical-grade masks she had ever seen. "What is that on your face?" she asked.

"Go ahead and laugh, but if you'd seen and lived through what I have, you wouldn't second guess my gear. What's happening in this country is not some simple virus like the news is reporting. It's biological warfare."

"Okay, Pat." Alessa rolled her eyes at his outrageous statement. "Take your coffee and sit. I'll grab some plates for the muffins."

"You think I'm joking, but I'm not. I've seen this before. Mind you, not these exact symptoms, but the whole situation is eerily similar."

The ceramic plates clanked together as Alessa took them down from the cabinet. "What is your take on all of this?" she inquired, genuinely interested in his theory.

"Well..." He took a sip of his hot drink. "Mmm. Thanks for

this." He held up his paper cup. "I think the United States is in for a ride, and unless we get our shit together, a lot of people are going to end up dead before this thing has run its course."

"You said warfare, so..." Alessa encouraged Pat to continue.

"Oh, yeah. Another country or an organization plans it. Someone out there is making this happen."

She exhaled. "It's not that I don't believe you, Pat. I don't want to believe anyone is capable of something that extreme."

"Well, believe me, people are capable of all kinds of terrible things. If you remember one thing, let it be this: no one is more dangerous than someone who believes they are doing the right thing, no matter the cost."

While holding the paper coffee cup, Alessa flinched as the image of a middle-aged man with a charismatic smile materialized before her eyes. She squeezed her eyes shut and successfully rid herself of the man's headshot.

Alessa's eyes grew heavy as they finished breakfast, and she yawned loudly.

"Up late?" Pat asked.

"Mm-hmm."

He walked Alessa to the door. "You better get on home. You don't need any help catchin' this thing." He put the mask back on his face before he gripped the door handle.

Alessa stopped in front of him. "Pat," she wrapped her arms around his shoulders and hugged him tight, "thanks for ... everything."

His body stiffened as he patted her back awkwardly. "Uh, yeah. You too."

"Hey Jane, will I see you tomorrow?" Pat asked as she stepped out into the hallway.

Alessa smiled and nodded. "Tomorrow."

By the time she made it home, she was exhausted, and after tossing her keys on the kitchen counter, she collapsed face-first onto the couch.

CHAPTER FIFTEEN

A young woman with beautifully rich, deep brown skin quizzed Alessa. "What is a virus?"

Alessa glanced up from her textbook. "Viruses are composed of either DNA or RNA and can reproduce once nestled safely inside a living host."

"Correct." The young doctor nodded, and her natural hair's kinkiness bounced up and down. "What surfaces can they survive on, and for how long?"

Alessa licked her dry lips. "This answer depends on the type of virus in question. Some can survive on anything from plastics, metal, and cardboard to cloth and blankets for minutes up to weeks after being deposited from their host."

"Well done."

Alessa tilted her head in concern toward the doctor. "They're considering this guy a serious threat, aren't they, Sera?"

"You wouldn't have been put on his case if they thought otherwise. But everyone here has a different person, organization, or group to monitor, and they usually amount to nothing," Sera reassured.

"Yes, I am well aware." Alessa turned the pages in her medical textbook. "That is typically the case, but I have a horrible feeling about this one."

"Are you suggesting your feelings are being sent by the gods as a warning?"

She looked into the doctor's eyes. "No, no. I'd never assume I was so important to be sent a message from the gods, but, Sera, I've got a terrible feeling about this corporation's leader."

Sera turned on the surgical simulation for the morning's scheduled procedure. "Alessa, I believe you will bring honor to us all, but I worry you'll forget to enjoy your life along the way."

The dream skipped ahead to a different day at a new location. A young blonde woman was looking into a microscope while Alessa talked excitedly.

"And his idea behind the possible use of biological warfare is certifiably insane! The microorganisms would have to be Group A type, easily disseminated and transmitted from person to person, resulting in high mortality rates. If I can find out where he is storing the information and successfully download the proof to my microchip, I can bring it back to the council, and we could prevent the outbreak altogether, or at least stop it before it gets too bad."

The blonde pursed her lips together. "Mm-hmm."

"What? What's the matter?" Alessa inquired, clearly annoyed.

The blonde sighed in exasperation. "We both know how involved you get with your assignments. Of course the elders think there's something to investigate, or else you would never have been given him as your assignment."

"So, what's with the attitude?"

"If they believe your fears to hold any truth, if they approve you going on site, this could be a dangerous position for you.

And we both know how determined you are to prove yourself worthy of being here."

Alessa scoffed. "Isn't that the point? Isn't that all our jobs here? To put our lives on the line for the sake of humanity?"

"Honestly, I'm not sure what my life is here."

Alessa placed her hand on the young woman's arm. "Don't let anyone hear you say that. You know I would change the past if I could."

The blonde held her hand up to silence Alessa. "Don't start in on that again. I know how sorry you are for what happened, but like I've told you repeatedly," she leaned in, "it is not your fault. You didn't ask for any of it."

Alessa was awakened from her nap by the *ding* of her phone announcing a text message.

"Ugh," she groaned as her pulse throbbed violently within her skull. Pinching the bridge of her nose, she pressed her fingertips deep into her eyelids.

Her eyes focused on the text.

HAPPY BIRTHDAY! CAN'T WAIT 4 TONITE. WEAR THE PRESENT WE GOT YOU. IT'S IN THE BOX ON THE KITCHEN COUNTER. LOVE YOU! KENZIE AND RAE.

Alessa tossed her phone and plopped down on the couch. "I hate migraines. Where is that bottle of painkillers?"

Begrudgingly, she tossed the blue throw off to the side, and with her eyes half open, she shuffled to the open bathroom door.

Leaving the light off, she filled the empty glass beside the sink with water and downed several pills before wandering into the kitchen, where she found a shiny purple box propped up on the counter's edge. A white ribbon was wrapped around it with a fancy bow slapped on top.

She remembered her friends' text. "Oh yeah, my gift."

Alessa picked up the card atop the box with her pseudo-name written in Kenzie's handwriting.

Wishing she could tell her friends her real name, but knowing she couldn't, Alessa huffed in frustration. She pulled on the satin ribbon and lifted the lid, revealing a stunning dress.

She picked her present up by its sparkly gem-covered, skinny silver straps and held it before her.

The cobalt-colored fabric cascaded from the top down in a crimped pattern, and the same silver gems used on the straps accented the bust line.

"Wow," she admired, twirling it around.

Alessa squealed and rushed to the bathroom, where she hastily undressed and slipped into the gorgeous gown.

By the time she was done curling her hair, her headache was replaced by an excited buzz. After she pinned half the loose spirals with bobby pins and applied her makeup, Alessa smiled at her reflection, pleased with the transformation.

"Hello!" McKenzie hollered from the entryway as Reagan exclaimed, "Hey, Birthday Girl!"

Alessa strutted out of the bathroom, and both women froze, their jaws dropping in unison.

"Oh my," Reagan drawled.

"Well, don't you clean up nice," McKenzie grinned.

The two layers of the dress contrasted beautifully against one another. The top thinner layer shimmered against the silkier one underneath, and the hem of the skirt stopped just above her knees, showing off Alessa's lean legs.

She wrapped her arms around her friends. "I can't thank you enough."

"Oh, Jane. Do you like it?" Reagan asked.

Alessa beamed. "Of course. I love it. How could I not?"

Reagan pointed at Alessa's ring. "Are you going to wear that to the club? I don't think it's exactly the part of town you wanna wear flashy jewelry in."

"Well, I had planned on it..." Alessa nervously rotated the ring around her finger.

"Here," Reagan ran into the bathroom and emerged holding a simple silver chain. "If you don't want to take it off, you can put it on this and tuck it between your boobs," she giggled.

"Great idea, Rae. I forgot about my boob pocket," Alessa laughed while sliding her ring onto the chain and clasped it around her neck. "Thank you."

"What's up with you and that ring, anyway? You, like, never take it off," McKenzie inquired.

Ignoring McKenzie, Alessa changed the subject. "So, when will you two be ready to head out?"

"Give us an hour." Reagan dashed toward their bedroom, and McKenzie laughed as she ran close behind. "Each!"

Their ride pulled up in front of the illuminated nightclub beside a long line of people extending past the street corner.

About half of them had on decorated medical masks as part of their clubbing attire, and an eerie glow was created by the neon lights bouncing off the bedazzled masks.

McKenzie hopped out of the cab and readjusted her skin-tight purple dress before stepping onto the curb.

Reagan followed in a high-low sequin dress. The shiny pink

fabric cascaded down to the floor, landing behind her beige strappy heels, and the bottom of her gown swayed back and forth as she sashayed toward the club's entrance.

"Have a good night," Alessa thanked the driver and rushed to catch up to her friends.

As McKenzie parted the crowd, she pushed toward the bouncer policing the front of the line. "Zane! Hey!" she bellowed over the music spilling out the front doors.

The large, muscular young man turned in their direction and nodded from behind his mask as he waved his hand for them to join him on the other side of the rope. He pulled down his medical mask and flashed a toothy grin. "Hey there, cuz."

McKenzie stood on her tiptoes and wrapped her arms around the bouncer's thick neck. "Are they making you wear that stupid thing?" she yelled into his ear, mid-hug.

"It's not so bad. Feels more like a fashion statement." He pointed at the crowd wearing their creative versions of decorated masks.

Reagan raised her eyes and bit her lower lip in a flirtatious gesture. "Yeah, well, you look like a creeper."

Zane chuckled. "I'll take that as a compliment."

"You know," Alessa couldn't help but interject, "as soon as you uncover your mouth and nose, it defeats the purpose of wearing a mask."

Why do I know that?

"Thanks for the lesson." The bouncer's eyes widened.

Suddenly, an argument erupted between two people standing in line, and fists flew.

"That's my cue. Have a good night, ladies." Zane replaced his mask before redirecting his attention toward the brawling men. "Hey, hey! Calm it down, boys."

As the three women strolled through the front doors, they were bombarded by blaring music and flashing strobe lights.

Alessa's heartbeat matched the rhythm of the bass as they made their way through the hallway and entered the club's main room.

At the bottom of the staircase, they stood, consumed by the sights and sounds of the building. Neon lights flashed between the white strobe lights, and multi-colored flames inside tall glass cylinders ignited throughout the dancefloor.

The nightclub had three distinct levels.

Its top floor was labeled with a VIP sign and roped off to the public, while the main level had tables spread throughout, making it more of a lounge-type atmosphere, and the dancefloor was down a flight of stairs.

They bent over the metal bar overlooking the dancefloor and watched in awe as the pulsating bodies gyrated to the music. The three friends threw their hands in the air and rocked back and forth, laughing ecstatically.

With the beginning of a new song, Reagan grabbed Alessa's hand and dragged her down the staircase to join the sea of bodies.

The women pushed through the mass of sweaty, gyrating people before they, themselves, jumped up and down with the increasing tempo. McKenzie bopped around like a madwoman while Alessa and Reagan fell into a giggling fit as their body parts bumped against one another.

A hand grabbed onto Alessa's elbow, and she screamed. "Chris! Shit, you scared me."

"I was invited, wasn't I? Wouldn't want to leave you hanging on your birthday," he yelled over the loud music.

He pressed his lips against Alessa's cheek, and her face grew hot.

"Happy birthday, Jane," Chris's lips parted in a flirtatious smile.

"Uh, thanks."

"Come on, let's dance." Chris pulled Alessa into him, and they swayed back and forth. Twirling her around, she spun into his chest and rested her hands atop his shoulders.

Unexpectedly, Chris dipped Alessa backward and bent over her. As their lips pressed against one another, the sensation of another man caressing her skin, leaving a fiery trail in the wake of his fingers, startled Alessa, and her eyes popped open.

Pushing Chris back, she broke out of his embrace. "Uh..." She breathed heavily. "I think I need a drink. I'll be right back," she hollered and bolted for the bar.

Feeling light-headed, she leaned onto the cool countertop and called out to the bartender. "Hey! Hey, can I get a shot of tequila?"

As the bartender blatantly ignored her, Alessa turned around to watch her friends dance and leaned back against the countertop.

Closing her eyes, she focused on the beat of the music and the hallucinated man's touch.

"Excuse me," a deep voice interrupted her thoughts.

"Oh!" she jumped.

"I'm sorry," the man yelled behind his face mask. "The bartender tried to get your attention, but you couldn't hear him." He held up a clear glass of liquid.

"Oh, thanks," she smiled in gratitude and threw her head back, downing its contents. "Whew!" she exclaimed with a shake of her head as it burned the back of her throat.

Slapping a twenty-dollar bill down on the bar, Alessa left the company of the silver-suited man and headed back out to the dancefloor. Ignoring her partially blurred vision, she tapped Chris on the shoulder and again fell into his arms.

Bouncing up and down with Chris and her friends, Alessa realized she wasn't feeling right. Her mouth was dry, but she couldn't stop sweating, and her heart was beating so hard she could feel it more than the bass.

The neon lights flashed against her ashen skin as she extended her hand toward Reagan's arm. "Rea ... I ... don't feel so—"

Bang! Bang! Two gunshots were fired in the club, and everyone screamed and hit the floor.

Scrambling about, half-naked bodies collided with one another as they fought to save themselves.

Chris held on tight to Alessa's hand and was pulling her toward an illuminated exit sign when a swarm of panicked club-goers violently ripped them apart. Chris desperately reached back for Alessa but was pushed onward by the fast-moving crowd.

"Jane! Jane, hold on!" he yelled amidst the chaos.

Alessa screamed, "Chris!"

From behind, large arms wrapped tightly around Alessa's midsection and pulled her back.

She kicked and flailed as the silver-suited man from the bar stepped before her.

The individual restraining Alessa stood her upright as the man before her balled his hand into a tight fist. As he punched toward her, hard and fast, adrenaline pumped through Alessa's veins, and her blue irises shimmered green.

Instinctively, she lifted both hands straight up in the air and pressed down with all her body weight. Alessa slipped through her captor's grip, and he was knocked unconscious by the silver suit.

Through her distorted vision, Alessa glared at her silver-suited attacker before she punched his groin.

As he fell forward, she kneed him in the nose, knocking the man back onto his rear.

Another silver suit charged from her right side, but Alessa jumped up and kicked him in the face.

The second she landed on her feet, a couple more men in matching silver suits attacked.

She blocked their kicks and jabs with ease, and as one of them chucked a blade in her direction, Alessa grabbed the other attacker's arm, twisted it behind his back, and used his body as a human shield.

With the knife plunged deep into the silver suit's torso, Alessa tossed the injured man aside while simultaneously yanking a small blade from his belt.

She then thrust it into the remaining man's left eye as if it were a dart.

Unable to fight the fatigue any longer, Alessa collapsed onto the floor as the entire room spun out of control.

What was in my drink?

Struggling to remain on her knees, her blinking slowed as additional men in suits surrounded her.

They found me.

Her eyelids grew heavy as she succumbed to the unknown drug's effects, and she fell onto her side.

As her senses failed one by one, the music became warped and twisted, and with one final blink, a dark figure jumped in between Alessa and the silver men.

Her eyes closed, and her breathing slowed dangerously as she gave in to the darkness.

CHAPTER SIXTEEN

In Alessa's dream, the older man raised a large wooden pole. "No, no, no! You are trying too hard," he commanded before bringing it down against the floor. "Again!"

A pre-teen Alessa dripped with sweat as she moved begrudgingly back to the starting line. Her tiny frame quivered as she bent over and bowed to her male opponent.

"Begin!" the older man commanded.

Alessa lifted her shin upward while the young man's legs flew toward her, and she deflected his attack. With a loud grunt, Alessa pressed in on the boy, swinging her arms and punching her fists, but her opponent blocked Alessa's every move.

She cried out in frustration, and the old man yelled with the bang of his pole, "Enough!"

Her feet were swept out from underneath her, and she fell hard onto her back.

"Do not think; simply do." The older man swung his wooden pole in front of Alessa's face, stopping an inch before striking her nose.

Breathing heavily, Alessa's eyes crossed as she looked at the pole.

"Do you see?" He pulled back on the piece of wood. "You overthink your next move. You over-analyze your partner, thus underestimating their strength."

Bending down, Alessa's elder extended his arm and wrapped his calloused fingers around her hand. "You need to spend less time in here," he pointed to her head before placing his hand on her heart, "and more time here. You must sense your opponent and trust yourself enough to know their next move before they do. You will be great someday, Alessa, but today is not yet that day."

Smell was the first of Alessa's senses to return as she inhaled the oddly familiar scent of musk and cinnamon. As her sense of touch awakened, she realized she was cradled in muscular arms. The side of her face was pressed up against the soft cotton of a T-shirt atop an impressive physique, and with every step the person cradling her took, her nausea increased.

With the increasing ability to feel her body, the pain intensified, and as she was lowered down onto a bed, a pathetic groan escaped from between her trembling lips. Curling up in a tight ball, she folded her arms in front of her stomach as nausea wracked her body.

The drugs burned their way through her, and every single one of her muscles felt as though they were lit on fire. Tears streaked down her face, and she opened her mouth in a silent scream.

"Shh ... it's alright. You're safe now," the stranger cooed, pressing a cold washcloth against her forehead.

Unnerved by the familiarity of the man's deep voice, Alessa

struggled to open her eyes but ended up clenching her teeth together in frustration, as she could not see clearly.

The man wrung out the washcloth before wiping away her fresh tears. "Alessa, you're safe. I'm here."

She suddenly stood behind a metal bar, staring at the handsome, bleeding instructor. A man stood frozen in place with his arm held in the air by another of her classmates.

He grinned sideways before pulling his hand from the classmate's grasp. "Alright, I'm game."

Alessa ducked under the bar and snatched a towel up off the floor. "You've got a little something right here." She threw the towel to the instructor and pointed to the corner of her mouth, mirroring his injury.

In amusement, he wiped the blood from his lips before tossing it off to the side.

Alessa positioned herself in front of the instructor on the opposite side of the line drawn on the floor. "Ready?"

Her eyes flickered bright green as his irises shifted from denim blue to silver. "Begin!" he commanded.

Alessa stepped first and jabbed to the right. Her fists flew as she aimed for his smug grin, but the instructor bobbed back and forth, dodging her every move.

The man grabbed Alessa's wrist, twisted her around, and pulled her back up against his chest. "Give?" he taunted, holding Alessa in a tight embrace.

Pressing her backside into the instructor's groin, she rocked back and forth. As his grip loosened in bewilderment, Alessa drove her elbow deep into his side.

He grunted as she jumped forward out of his reach.

"That was low," he growled between clenched teeth.

"I was taught to find my opponent's weakness." She smiled playfully and winked before sprinting to the room's far side.

His boots clomped close behind Alessa as she kicked the wall, climbed toward the ceiling, and pushed off the concrete before flipping up over him.

He screeched to a halt as she landed behind him and kicked the heel of her boot in the middle of his back. Her opponent grunted as the side of his face smacked up against a concrete wall.

Before she lunged forward, she punched her fist toward the back of his head.

Blocking her, the man whipped around and swung his arms up in front of his face, locking his hands around Alessa's extended arm.

She flipped sideways, loosening the instructor's grip before lunging forward.

Impressed by her agility, the handsome instructor arched his dark eyebrows.

Pressing hard through his grip, Alessa splayed her fingertips, nearly jabbing them into his windpipe.

He caught her forearm and jerked her forward, folding Alessa at the elbow. He panted, holding her body up against his own. "Do you give, now?"

"Do you?" she huffed. Maneuvering out of his grasp, Alessa rotated and slammed her elbow into his nose.

His head whipped backward, and he glared at her. Ignoring the blood trickling down his chin, her opponent forced Alessa back by throwing punches in quick succession.

The instructor grew increasingly irritated with every move she dodged until she finally bobbed the wrong way, allowing the instructor to grab her by the throat.

Lifting her in the air by her neck, he slammed Alessa down onto her back.

Her hands splayed to the side as she lay flat on the floor mat. "Give?" he challenged.

Alessa closed her eyes due to the lack of oxygen and her growing embarrassment.

The instructor's eyes faded to blue, and his grip lessened. His thumb stroked back and forth across her skin. "Are you—?" Several lines of concern furrowed between his eyebrows.

Extending her two fingers toward the heavens, Alessa croaked, "I give."

CHAPTER SEVENTEEN

As Alessa's dream faded into the background, she recognized the faint clicking of keys on a keyboard. After a minute or so of blinking the sleepiness from her eyes, she realized she was lying in a motel bed.

The walls were beige and bare, except for the single painting of an aging tree hung crooked beside a black television set. To the left of her bed, behind sheer white curtains, was a set of sliding glass doors leading out to a small balcony, and to her right, a man sat in front of a small wooden desk with his back to Alessa.

His dark, chestnut brown hair, short and messy, came into focus, and as the sedation loosened its grip, Alessa pushed herself upright. She hissed aloud as a migraine replaced the medicated stupor.

The man pivoted in his chair, and his eyes widened. Standing up, he plucked a glass of water from a nearby table and hurried toward her.

The tails of his pine green button-up shirt flapped open, exposing the deep grey T-shirt beneath. His faded blue jeans clung tight to his hips as he sat down on the bed beside Alessa. "I'm sorry, I didn't realize you were awake," he apologized while holding out the glass.

Feeling as though an ice pick were ramming itself into the side of her skull, she dry-heaved. Without missing a beat, he picked up a small trash can beside the bed and put it between Alessa's hands before holding back her dark hair in a makeshift ponytail.

"Is there anything I can get you?" he asked, placing his free hand between her shoulder blades.

Alessa jumped. "Don't!" she barked.

He removed his hand. "I'm sorry. I didn't mean—" The man let her hair fall loose around her shoulders and held his hands up defensively.

Alessa squinted and grabbed a chunk of her hair, holding it to her face. "Is my hair dark brown?"

"Oh. Uh, yeah. I couldn't stand you not looking like, well, you," he shrugged.

"So, you, what dyed my hair when I was unconscious? That's not creepy or anything." She side-eyed the man.

His lips curled in a lazy grin. "Good to see you still have your sense of humor."

Alessa looked slowly around the room. "Where exactly are we? And who are you?" She grabbed the back of her neck and squeezed it tightly. "And where can I get some painkillers?"

He walked over to the counter. "I've got some. How many do you want?"

"Four, please," Alessa mumbled. "For real, though, you dyed my hair when I was asleep?"

"When you say it like that, it does sound messed up," he laughed out loud. "I thought you looking like yourself might make you feel more like yourself."

Pouring the dark-colored pills from a bottle, he placed them in the middle of Alessa's palm, careful not to touch her skin.

She tossed them into her mouth, took a gulp of water, and tilted her head back.

"Thanks," Alessa managed as the handsome man knelt before her.

"So, you truly don't know who I am?" The man's stunning blue eyes looked up pleadingly.

Alessa eyed him with a blank stare. "Am I supposed to?"

"Okay..." He rubbed his hands up and down his thighs, shooting her a quizzical glance.

She pressed her hands into both sides of her skull. "Ugh. My head."

"It's probably a side effect from the sedatives," he explained.

She pressed her fingertips deep into her temples. "No, I don't think that's it. I mean, I'm sure they aren't helping with how shitty I'm feeling, but I get these wicked headaches every day. But, ugh, this one, by far, is the worst. They only seem to be worse when—"

"When?" he demanded.

Alessa shook her head and closed her eyes. "Never mind."

Opening her eyes, she focused on the man's face, particularly his full pink lips. "Wow. The drugs those douchebags gave me are messing with my mind because somehow you were just in my dream, and—wait. Why am I telling you any of this? And how did you know my natural hair color is dark brown?"

His head jerked upright. "Don't you recognize me?" Hope illuminated his features as he leaned into her. "Even the slightest bit? Alessa—"

She held up her hand. "How do you know my name? My *actual* name?"

He stood and rubbed the stubble on his chin. "In your dream, what were we doing?"

"Uh," she rubbed her eyelids. "We were, uh, I think we were.... fighting or something? Like, with our fists." She laughed to herself. "It's crazy, I know."

He crossed his arms in front of his chest. "What else do you remember?"

"Remember? No, I said it was a dream."

"Okay, then." He tilted his head to the side. "Tell me about two nights ago when you were attacked at the club."

"Hold up a second. Two nights ago? Are you telling me I've been unconscious for two whole days?"

He nodded. "I don't have time to keep repeating myself. Now, what do you recall about that night?"

Alessa took a sip of water. "Well, I was dancing at my birthday party with my friends McKenzie and Reagan. Chris was there. Then gunshots fired, and the next thing I knew, I was being attacked by these guys. They were wearing suits ... grey ... not dark grey, but like a light grey. Silver, I think. Yeah, I'd say they were silver."

"That's a start. What else?" The man stood alarmingly still, concern etched upon his face.

"Well, clearly, you saved me and brought me wherever we are."

He nodded and glanced away.

"Why would you save me?"

He waved the thought away. "Did anything seem out of place before you were attacked?"

Alessa grumbled. "Like what, exactly?"

"Were you being followed? Did you do anything unusual that day? Did you eat or drink anything at the club?"

"No. I ... Wait ... Yeah. Yeah, I ordered a shot of tequila. But I never saw the bartender make my drink. Some random guy handed it to me. Dammit." She put her hand over her mouth. "He was wearing a silver suit."

He clapped his hands together. "Well, at least now we know how they drugged you."

"Who is 'they'? And why—" she began to ask, but her thoughts were interrupted by the memory of two men dressed in silver suits shooting up the hospital searching for her one month prior.

She leaned over the bed and vomited into the trash can.

"Good aim," the man complimented.

She wiped the side of her mouth. "That's not the first time I've seen them."

"Do you remember who they are?" He slowly approached Alessa and stood in front of her. "Alessa, I will ask you one last time: do you remember who I am?"

Standing up, Alessa gazed deep into the man's stormy blue eyes until there was a flash of recognition. She covered her mouth and gasped. "Your eyes..."

He held his breath in anticipation.

"You're the guy from the coffee shop! The one who poured scalding hot coffee all over Chris and me. Why would you do that and then rescue me a few nights later?"

"Is that your first memory of me?" The handsome stranger reached for her hand, and as he touched her clammy skin, an electric shock passed back and forth between their fingertips.

She jerked her arm away. "Don't touch me!"

He marched back to the table and threw a chair across the room. Its legs broke off as it smashed against the far wall.

Splintered pieces flew, and as he glanced back at Alessa, his eyes flickered steel grey.

Her hair stood on the back of her neck as his two silver eyes watching her from the darkened alleyway appeared in her mind. "Were you watching me the night I was attacked outside of End Check?"

The man closed his eyes and slowed his breathing before nodding.

"Why didn't you stop them?" her voice cracked.

He brushed her concern away with a flick of his hand. "You had it handled. You wouldn't have even broken a sweat over those guys before—"

She eyed the six-foot-tall, dark-haired man. "Before?"

His jaw muscles tensed. "You truly don't recognize me at all, do you?"

Alessa thought back to her dream of them sparring, and sharp pains shot through the base of her skull. "I'm sorry, but I don't," Alessa apologized.

His face dropped, and he covered his mouth. With a shake of his head, he laughed to himself. "Okay, then. I guess I will be cautious with what I say." He breathed, running a hand through his hair. "Alright. So, I had my suspicions you were Alessa, but everyone kept calling you Jane at that café, and you looked so ... different."

She glowered. "If you thought I was Alessa, why did you throw scalding hot coffee all over me?"

His eyes darted away from her deadly glare. "Oh, um ... I had to devise a way to test your healing ability on the spot. To make sure you were who I thought you were."

"And the only thing you could think of was to burn the hell out of me?" she demanded.

He blushed in embarrassment. "You seem to have healed fine, but I apologize."

"Okay, clearly you think you know who I am, but who are you? What's your name? Who are you to me?"

"I don't think I should tell you just yet."

"What kind of bullshit is that? You want to know every single one of my memories, yet you won't tell me something as simple as your name?"

The man turned away, his fists clenching and unclenching. "That's fair. Okay, then." He cracked his knuckles. "Let's start with the basics. Yes, I knew you before your memory was erased."

"The doctors told me I was suffering from amnesia."

"I know amnesia, and this is not it. This couldn't be worms because their signature is erasing targeted moments in time, like people or certain events, not an entire lifetime. This is unlike anything I've ever seen before."

Alessa stared at the man, her eyebrows scrunched up in disbelief.

"Since this is uncharted territory, we must take this very slowly. First, I'm sorry, but I don't feel comfortable telling you my name, at least not yet. It's not that I don't trust you, because I do, but I need to make sure the information I tell you doesn't send your microchip into overdrive. I'm not even sure it's functioning at a hundred percent since we weren't notified you were still alive. However, since you could activate your chip multiple times, I assume it is still operational at some level."

"Uh, kay?" Alessa was completely confused.

He put his hand against his forehead. "I'm sorry. This is already too much for you. Just know I'm one of the good guys and I'm here to help. That's all that matters right now."

"Uh-huh," was all Alessa could muster. She was torn between wanting to run far away from the psychopath and wanting to believe every word that came out of his beautiful mouth.

He shuffled toward the kitchenette and pointed at a loaf of bread. "You hungry? I make one hell of a wicked PB and J."

She laughed at the ridiculous situation, but her stomach growled loudly in response. "I could eat."

"I'd be hungry, too, if I'd gone forty-eight hours without food." He opened the bread and spread peanut butter and jelly on a few slices. "They gave you the good stuff. I'm guessing wherever they had planned to take you was a bit of a drive."

She pushed away the terrifying possibilities of what the men had planned for her.

He handed Alessa a sandwich. "How's your head feeling?"

"Fine, thanks." She took a bite out of the sandwich. "I have an idea. What if you were to start talking about my past, and we see how I handle it?"

His eyebrows arched as he took a bite of his sandwich, waiting for her to continue her argument.

"Like, you give me a watered-down version?"

"Hmm. That idea isn't half bad. I'll have to leave out the emotional entanglements since whatever was done to you is more than likely attached to your limbic system, which affects both memory and emotions," he mumbled in deep thought before taking another bite. "But what if I say the wrong thing and it triggers too deep of a connection or emotion?"

"You know I'm sitting right here," Alessa pointed to herself. "This is ridiculous. I'm going home if you won't help me remember who I am." She swaggered toward the door, unsteady.

The man darted in front of her, blocking the exit. "You can't. It's too dangerous. They know who you are."

She stepped around him. "I don't care. I'm leaving. And who exactly are they, anyway? This whole thing is so—"

"Fucked? Yeah, I know." He wrapped his warm fingers around her upper arm. "But you cannot leave. I promise I will try to explain."

"Hold on. Will they look for me at my apartment? What about McKenzie and Reagan? I have to go back!" Alessa shoved him, but his fingers dug into her arms, holding her in place.

"Your friends are safer with you gone. Now, sit down," he ordered.

Alessa stood her ground.

The man laughed to himself. "Look, if you promise to let me know the second you feel funny or off, I will give you some back story. Deal?"

Alessa nodded in silent agreement before sitting back on the bed. She picked up her sandwich and took a bite as he rubbed his palms together.

With a reluctant sigh, he began.

CHAPTER EIGHTEEN

"It'll probably be safest to start with the basics. Your name is Alessa Custos. You are twenty-six years old and a member of a community in Colorado to which I also belong." Awaiting her reaction, he paused.

"Okay, then. Is that all I get? I think I can handle more than some of my statistics."

"So, let me ask you this: do you know much about the history of Sparta?"

A collection of images manifested in Alessa's mind but were gone before she could discern them. "Are you referring to the civilization of Sparta?"

The man nodded. "The one and only."

Flashes of bright colors coinciding with laughter and clanging metal reverberated within her mind. "I don't think so. Or at least I don't remember if I do." *Are my nightmares and visions actually memories?*

"Okay, then, I'll start with a history lesson. Sparta was founded by one of Zeus's sons, Lacedaemon, in 900 BC. It was a powerful city-state that took pride in the strength of its citizens and its entire community. Spartan men were as strong as demigods, the women were revered for their intelligence and courage, and their offspring were superior on a genetic level.

"The city thrived on its festivals and sense of community, and even though life was not perfect, everyone had their role to play in keeping the peace. As far as historians are aware, Sparta reigned for nearly one thousand years before its supposed demise, at which point the books declare they lost a war and their culture dissolved ... yadda yadda." He bit into his sandwich and pointed at her. "Which is complete bullshit."

Alessa slowly picked up her glass of water and stared at the man as he continued.

"The king of Sparta made the difficult decision to sacrifice some of his people so that his culture and descendants could survive the war. On the night the attack was carried out on Spartan soil, he declared himself the first king, king of the East, and his second in command became the second king, king of the West.

"After fleeing their homeland, they established new colonies in the Eastern and Western hemispheres. The first king stayed in the Eastern hemisphere, whereas the second ventured to the West. Oh ... Also, there were men within the community with more experience and training than the rest, and they were referred to as the society's elders."

Alessa refrained from gasping as the grey-haired man from her dreams came to mind.

The man rubbed his hands together excitedly. "You doing okay?"

"Mm-hmm," she nodded mechanically.

"Good. So, the surviving twenty-eight elders were instructed to go into hiding, along with their families and the enslaved people belonging to them. They each fled to their agreed-upon secret locations worldwide, known as compounds. At each compound, there were three elders. There is one compound on each continent, plus one extra compound in both the U.S. and Asia, totaling twenty-seven elders."

"Hold on," Alessa interrupted. "Twenty-seven? Didn't you say there were twenty-eight?"

He flashed a sideways grin. "Good catch; I did. One of the twenty-eight elders passed away on the boat heading to the new world, and his soul went into the ether. Out of respect, his entire bloodline and his workers threw themselves into the sea."

Alessa choked on her water. "Say what, now?"

He shrugged nonchalantly. "Spartans are a proud people and show their bloodline great respect. Anyway, three elders govern each compound, and together, they create the Council of Elders. However, every man who has fought valiantly is eventually rewarded with the title of Elder. But only those with blood ties to the originals will have a place on the High Council.

"Oh, I forgot to mention that the Spartan citizens who were doomed to remain within the city were given a powerful sedative on the night they were attacked, forcing them to sleep for days. Once they awoke, their lives were but a faded memory since their beloved king chose to abandon them, for lack of a better term.

"I can't say I fully agree with his actions, but since I don't have an entire civilization's fate in my hands, I don't have the right to an opinion. Not yet, anyway."

Her eyes wide, she stared at him, unmoving.

"Are you okay?" He slowly moved toward her with his hands held before him.

Pursing her lips, Alessa tilted her head to the side, and, unable to find the words, she made an unintelligible noise.

"Are you stroking out right now? What's happening?"

Alessa unfroze and shook her head in disbelief. "Why are you speaking about Spartans in the present tense?"

"Spartans still exist, and you're one of us. You are a Spartan."

"Mmm. Mm-kay. Yeah, because, I mean, why not?" Alessa stood upright and frantically paced back and forth. "Let's recap my week, shall we? You threw boiling coffee on me to test a theory. That very night, I was minding my own business when I was attacked in an alleyway ... while you watched. By the way, thanks for not helping me. Oh, and then, while celebrating my fake birthday, I was drugged, ambushed, and kidnapped. Then my kidnapper informs me that I am a descendent of one of the greatest warrior nations of all time—"

"I didn't say you were a descendent—"

"—which is not as dead a civilization as history would have the entire world believe," she continued, completely unphased by his interruption.

Scowling in disappointment, he stepped forward. "Does nothing I said to you sound familiar in the slightest?"

Alessa blinked her eyes shut, and a series of images flashed before her: the outline of a magnificent mountain range, a small cabin standing alone in the woods, her hugging a tall man, and finally, a terrifying memory of a clear plastic bag being slammed onto her head.

"How are you feeling? Should I continue?"

She jerked as his voice brought her back to reality. "Yes, yes, I'm good for now. Go ahead and rip it off like a band-aid." Alessa sat down and slapped her thighs.

"The second you feel sick—" he warned.

"I know, I know. Just get on with it."

He nervously rubbed his hands up and down his thighs

before continuing. "While living at the Spartan compound in Colorado, you were assigned to an intel position, retrieving secret files and information regarding the true intentions of Erebos Industries. Upon receiving intel about the release of a bioweapon, our elders had their suspicions as to who was behind its design, and the company you were assigned was one of many that were being investigated for suspicious activity. You were the head of the operation. We Spartans hide behind the front of a company, Vindico, when, in truth, we are a warrior society that has dedicated itself to saving the human race and has done so successfully, time and time again throughout history.

"The literal translation of Vindico is to liberate. Our kings decided to hide behind the fictitious name once they realized we had to start our lives anew to make the world believe Sparta had truly fallen. At this point, all Spartan citizens were recognized, even the enslaved, and everyone was officially referred to as Coepi.

"We started a new way of life, and at a certain age, members of our society are strategically placed into various roles outside of our compounds. We have members within every government, insiders in the stock market, hospitals, labs, research, etcetera. This is how we gain classified information."

He paused again and eyed Alessa.

"Please continue," she encouraged.

"In Spartan society, when a child turns nine, a microchip is implanted, and they are activated. This allows Spartans to tap into their full potential, enhancing their cognitive abilities to train better as soldiers. The microchip computerizes our brains, making our bodily functions faster and more effective. For example, when we are wounded, our microchips send a signal at the cellular level for a large amount of coagulants to be released. This action decreases both the time it takes for us to heal as well as the likelihood of us bleeding to death. The microchip also allows us access into our glamoured cities. At the age of twenty, Spartan men or women are either accepted as Coepi or deemed unfit. In other words, they are terminated."

"I'm sorry, what was that you said? Terminated. As in?"

"Their microchip painlessly ends their life."

Alessa's eyebrows arched in surprise. "Yeah, sure, because that's normal," she scoffed, her voice dripping with sarcasm.

"It doesn't happen that often, and in our culture, we can't exactly release a member into the world and blindly trust they won't speak of us. The act is for our safety and the entire human race. If the general population only knew how many disasters we've averted and how many plagues we've kept under control."

The dull ache originating near the base of her skull crept its way up the center of Alessa's head, threatening to encroach upon her temples, but she pushed through the pain and encouraged the man to continue telling his story. "I get it, you're amazing. Now, what does this lesson have to do with me? Where exactly do I come into play in all of this?"

He snatched his laptop off the table and fiddled with the keyboard before sitting beside her on the bed.

"You were trained as an agent, better known as a Custos. Its Latin translation means guardian or spy."

"Isn't that my last name?"

"Yes and no. Technically, you don't have one, so Custos became your last name once you accepted the title. But you were in dual training in the medical field. We typically choose a secondary position within our community."

"Mm-hmm," she said through pursed lips. "That could

explain why I knew all the medical jargon and happenings at the hospital. Speaking of which, how did I end up there?"

He exhaled loudly and rubbed the stubble on his chin. "About that ... Before I explain any further, I need to know how you're—"

"I'm fine," she barked through gritted teeth as she hid the pain.

"I'm not sure how any of this isn't hitting you on an emotional level, but if you say so," he shrugged. "You were under Sparta's orders to monitor Eric Lansing of Erebos Industries." He held up the laptop with a picture of Eric Lansing on its screen.

The company's logo flashed within Alessa's mind. "Are you referring to the pharmaceutical company?"

His face lit up, and he set the laptop atop the desk. "Yes. Yes, I am. Are you remembering something?"

She put her head down between her hands. "It's all a blur."

"Okay, well, Spartan elders believed Eric capable of biological warfare, and you were sent in to gather proof of his wrongdoings so he could be taken down. You were gone for nearly four months when we got the alert that your microchip had been disabled."

"And you all left me for dead? Because my microchip kicked it?" Alessa glared.

"You must understand, our microchip is only disabled when we..."

"When we what?" she urged.

He glanced up at Alessa, forlorn. "Die."

Her first reaction was to laugh maniacally. "*Of course* I died! If my nightmares are truly memories of what those sick fucks did to me, I died over and over again!"

The man placed both his hands over his mouth and closed his eyes.

The vision in Alessa's left eye dissipated with the increasing pressure inside her head. "But when my heart started to beat again, shouldn't my microprocessor thingy have rebooted? Perhaps updated you all that I was still alive?"

He swallowed. "That's one thing I'm confused about as well. You aren't wrong. We should've been notified."

She stilled as an idea dawned on her. "What about if an electric current were repeatedly used?"

"I guess if enough of an interruption occurs, it might be possible to corrupt the microchip," he agreed.

She pressed her fingertips into her chest, over her heart. "Continuously dying requires the repeated use of electric paddles..."

Alessa attempted to spin the non-existent ring around her finger, and she panicked. "Where is my—?" Pulling the bejeweled ring and chain out from in between her breasts, she exhaled a breath of relief.

The man's eyes opened wide as the alexandrite ring fell into the palm of her hand. He looked away, clearing his throat as she slipped the ring back onto her finger. "What's that?"

"Oh, I woke up with it at the hospital, and I can't explain my connection to it other than I feel incomplete without it." Alessa looked up at him, hopeful. "Do you know anything about it?"

Nodding mechanically, he replied. "Yes."

"Let me guess, you can't tell me?" Her eyes rolled into the back of her head with a sigh.

He smirked. "Excellent guess. Listen, you've learned enough for today. There's no way this isn't hitting you hard."

Her hands flailed about as she voiced her frustration. "Ah!

This is so annoying! I want to trust you for some inexplicable reason. I truly do. I want you to have been a part of my life. I want to give into my dreams that tell me to believe..."

The man's blue eyes bore into Alessa. "Then what's stopping you?"

"You are! You are what's stopping me. You refuse to give me enough of an explanation to help me make any sense of the major holes in my life, and I feel as though you just made up some fairy tale—"

"Alessa, I—"

"You know," she held her hand up to stop him from continuing, "I could've handled some sob story about what shitty parents I had. I would've even been okay with discovering I grew up on the streets. But no. The one person in this world I seem to have any connection with tells me I'm a freakin' underground Spartan, and I just ... can't!"

He slammed his fists down on the desk. "Alessa, you don't get it. If I say the wrong thing, one detail too emotional," his eyebrows scrunched together, "you need to dig deep and trust in me, please. This cannot be easy for you. I know this because I know how stubborn, strong-willed, and spirited you are. I know *you*, Alessa." The man stepped toward her. "You can't sit there and tell me everything I've said isn't making sense, that you don't feel any connection to what I have told you. Your memories, albeit buried deep, still exist inside you, and even though they're not at the surface right now, I truly believe they're not lost forever."

Alessa's eyes flickered over in his direction.

"You do feel it, don't you?"

Something violent and dark struggled beneath the surface, fighting to be set free. Coming undone, Alessa slammed the sliding glass doors open and stumbled onto the balcony, nearly falling into the iron railing.

"How long?" she demanded.

Following her, he stopped beside Alessa and leaned against the cool metal banister. "How long...?"

"How long have you been following me?"

Looking up at the clouds, the man exhaled. "Just before we ran into each other at the coffee shop."

Unable to hold back the pain any longer, Alessa screamed and grabbed the sides of her head.

The man dove forward, caught her mid-fall, and scooped her into his arms. "Dammit, I told you to tell me," he said through gritted teeth, carrying her back to bed. "Why do you have to be so damn headstrong?"

He stood up after setting her down on the bed. "You need to rest."

Alessa writhed in pain and grabbed his arm tight. "Don't leave me."

"I'm not going anywhere, but you've got to let your brain digest all of this."

Alessa's grip loosened as she fell fast asleep.

The handsome stranger pulled the thin sheet up to Alessa's chest and brushed several loose strands of hair away from her face. "I'll be right here when you wake."

CHAPTER NINETEEN

"What were you thinking, bringing children back with you? They cannot stay. I forbid it." An older woman in Alessa's dream scolded a middle-aged man dressed in a robe.

Alessa and the tiny toddler were standing in the next room, eating the ham sandwiches they had been given.

"What was I supposed to do, Anara? I saw the look in her eyes. That little girl will never recover from what she was forced to do. Her heart is that of a warrior now. The outside world will never understand what she's going through."

The woman glanced at the little girls; sympathy etched upon her face. "But what are we to do with them?"

"We will care for them and teach them our ways. I will train them to fight for our people, like we would if they were our children."

The woman caressed the side of his face. "You, my elder, are a fool."

The dream skipped forward in time, and Alessa was back in the white room, surrounded by her torturers. It had only been a few hours since she had discovered the evidence needed to take down Eric Lansing, and the men had been relentless in their search to find the stolen information.

They didn't realize she had stored all of it in her implanted microchip.

The heavy-set man strolled beside her and whispered something inaudible in her ear. With his hot breath caressing the side of her cheek, the hair on the back of Alessa's neck stood up as her stomach dropped.

He stroked his fingers through her scalp before grabbing a fistful of her red locks. Alessa's breathing hitched, and he yanked her head backward.

She went back years in time and was suddenly looking up at a blue sky full of white fluffy clouds while sitting atop a mountain. With her hands spread out, she welcomed the feel of the cool, itchy grass beneath her thin dress.

She was now a teenager, and a familiar blonde girl was beside her. "Do you think of them often?" the girl asked.

Alessa closed her eyes and inhaled the sweet scent of dandelions and wildflowers that surrounded them. "Mmm?" she responded, not fully listening.

The girl's silence concerned Alessa, and she opened her eyes to find the girl gone. In the blonde's place sat her handsome, blue-eyed, dark-haired kidnapper.

He fingered blades of grass. "What's the matter with you today? You seem distracted."

Confused and self-conscious, Alessa stumbled on her words, unsure how to respond. "I ... uh..."

He laughed. "Whoa, there. There's no need to stress yourself out. Here, take your bow and arrow and forget your troubles."

He placed her bow within the palm of her hand and held out her quiver, full of arrows.

Several randomly placed targets appeared before her, and

Alessa pressed her fingertips behind her right ear. Playing music only she could hear, Alessa drowned out the rest of the world.

Enya sang beautifully, slowing Alessa's heartbeat as she aimed at the targets. The man watched her perform her elaborate archery dance, and as Alessa reached back for another arrow, someone grabbed her forearms and twisted her around.

She was once more a small child being chastised by an adult male. "How did I end up here? Where am I?" Alessa cried.

The adult holding her arm painfully in his grasp laughed maniacally. "Don't you remember what happened at the cabin?"

The sound of a gunshot echoed within her dream, and she awakened.

With her heart pounding against her ribcage, Alessa sprang upright in bed. The painful pulsating within her skull matched the beat of her heart, and her eyes darted around the motel room as she searched the counter for painkillers.

Her rescuer was sprawled on the neighboring bed, asleep across his open laptop.

Alessa eyed the man while she tiptoed behind him toward the kitchen, and after downing the pills, she quietly turned on the TV.

"The most recent reports show that nearly ten thousand people have died in the United States since the first case was discovered. The mortality rate is rapidly increasing, and hospitals are overwhelmed. New York is shut down, and international flights are canceled indefinitely to reduce the spread of the mysterious disease outside the United States.

"A secret source claims the government is aware of the diagnosis but is holding back, hoping not to send the public into a panic.

"The president of a relatively new pharmaceutical company, Eric Lansing of Erebos Industries, claims to be in the final stages of production of an all-in-one cure and vaccine.

"The CDC has taken over hospitals, schools, and stadiums nationwide, establishing makeshift wards to quarantine the infected.

"Within the week, all states are expected to close their borders entirely."

"Eric Lansing," Alessa mumbled as a video of the middle-aged man waving and smiling appeared on the screen. "What are you hiding?"

A montage of pictures and formulas flashed before Alessa's eyes, and she shook her head to clear her vision.

With a loud exhale, she shuffled toward the bathroom, turned on the light, and shut the door. After a few minutes of much-needed release, Alessa turned on the shower and stripped the clothes from her body.

Stepping under the stream of cold water, she froze away any remaining sleepiness. As the temperature rose, her skin reddened, and the room filled with steam.

The water dripped down her body, sucking all the soap and grime along with it down the drain. Reluctantly, she turned the hot water off and stepped out of the shower.

Looking around the room, she realized she didn't have a towel to dry off with or clothes to change into. "Didn't think that one through."

While standing nude and dripping wet in front of the mirror, Alessa grabbed the hand towel and dried off as best she could with the small piece of cloth.

As she brushed her teeth with the toothbrush on the counter, Alessa eyed a man's dark purple button-up hanging on the back of the door. She shrugged the violet shirt over her shoulders before running her fingers through her brunette locks.

Alessa stepped into the room, and while fingering a button, her hand lingered between her breasts.

The dark-haired man glanced up at her. His eyes shifted from deep ocean blue to sterling grey, and he nearly choked on his mouth full of Raisin Bran, splashing milk as he dropped his spoon into the bowl.

She misunderstood his reaction and took it as him being annoyed with her wearing his clothes. "Oh, sorry, I had to borrow your shirt. It's not as if I could put my nasty dress back on."

The man coughed and attempted to regain his composure as he closed his eyes tight and shook his head back and forth.

Alessa took a step forward and tilted her head in curiosity. "Hey, were your eyes just grey—"

He interrupted with the clearing of his throat. "Are you feeling better?"

"Uh yeah, I guess so. A bit stiff, but nothing I can't handle." Alessa rubbed her hand on the back of her neck before peering down at her bare legs.

He shifted his hips as he focused intently on his cereal bowl.

"Um ... Do you, by chance, have any underwear for me?"

His eyes dropped to her exposed skin below his shirttails, and holding back a growl, he bit down on his lower lip. With an audible exhale, he answered, "Uh, yeah, I'm sure. Let me..." He dug through his backpack and held up a pair of black boxer briefs.

Alessa arched her right eyebrow questioningly.

"It's not like I carry women's underwear around with me. You want 'em or not?"

"I guess it's better than nothing." Alessa extended her arm.

He threw the briefs to Alessa, and she returned to the bathroom. "You never told me who my attempted abductors were," she hollered from the partially closed door.

"You sure you're ready for more?" he asked before taking another bite of cereal.

"Answer the question."

"Okay, then. The guys work for Erebos. Their official title is Bodyguard, but they aren't your typical run-of-the-mill bodyguards. They do much more than protect one person."

"Why exactly would a pharmaceutical company want to kidnap me?" She stumbled back to her bed. "Man, that shower wiped me out."

"While you were on a mission, we weren't in communication, so I'm not sure why they wanted to take you out. However, I think it's safe to assume whatever data you dug up was catastrophic to Eric Lansing and his company." He set his cereal bowl down in the sink.

"Listen, I am more than willing to keep filling the missing gaps in your memory, but you've got to tell me whenever you're having funny feelings or start to get those headaches. As superhuman as you may be with your microchip enhancing your fighting skills and healing, I'm afraid if you push yourself, your brain may be unable to handle it. Your body decides what it can handle. It has a defense mechanism built in, and the last thing we want is for it to overload and shut down."

Alessa swallowed a lump of fear. "Shut down ... That doesn't sound good." She hesitated momentarily before continuing. "You keep mentioning me activating my microchip. How do I know if I'm doing it?"

"Haven't you noticed your sudden change in eye color or a burning sensation behind your eyes?"

She stared blankly at him.

"I'm assuming that's a no," he chuckled. "You've probably reverted to your chip's activation being completely connected to your emotions rather than controlled by your will. Here," he sat down beside Alessa. "Watch my eyes."

Alessa leaned in toward him. Gazing into his denim blue eyes, she gasped and jumped back when they suddenly blazed gunmetal grey.

He blinked and laughed as his irises returned to their deep blue hue.

"That's my activation. Every Spartan has a different color, just like every person has a unique eye color." The man noticed Alessa staring at him questioningly out of the corner of his eye. "Yours is this intense green," he answered without her uttering a word.

Her eyebrows rose. "How did you—"

"I could tell you wanted to know."

Alessa recalled the brief moments she swore her reflection had changed throughout the past month. "Huh. I think I have seen it a time or two."

"Anyway, our irises change color when we activate our microchip, as I've explained. It can send an electrical pulse through our implanted chip, thus activating our genetic engineering. Have you ever heard of athletes' blood doping?"

"Isn't that when they get blood transfusions to increase their stamina?"

He nodded. "That is one way, yes. However, the kidneys secrete a hormone called erythropoietin or EPO. This hormone stimulates the bone marrow to produce more red blood cells. Increasing the amount of red blood cells circulating throughout our body also increases the amount of oxygen we can send to our organs.

"The moment we activate our microchip, it tells our kidneys to secrete EPO, which immediately pumps oxygen to every muscle in our body, including our brains. This allows us to think quicker, move faster, see the fight more clearly, and be stronger. It increases our athletic endurance, meaning we don't tire as easily, which makes us Custos."

He watched Alessa intently, waiting for her to drop with a migraine at any second.

Annoyed by his overprotectiveness, she rolled her eyes. "I feel fine. And since I'm feeling fine, please tell me your name."

The man ignored her and grinned sideways. "How'd you know what I was thinking?"

Alessa couldn't help but smile in embarrassment. "I don't know. I just did."

Their bodies stilled in response to the tense air surrounding them, but after a few moments, the man snapped out of it and cleared his throat while standing up. "It's good that you're feeling well because we gotta get moving." He gathered his belongings and slipped on his shoes.

"Where are we going?" Alessa hugged herself, not wanting to leave the illusion of safety the motel room had given her.

"Erebos has already proven themselves capable of tracking you down. It's only a matter of time before the Bodyguards find us here." Shrugging out of his green button-up, the man pulled his T-shirt over his head, revealing his ridiculously defined abs.

Alessa subconsciously bit her lower lip while she admired the black ink tattooed across the upper half of his chest and right bicep. "Wow," she murmured aloud.

"What was that?" He stopped and looked at her with his gorgeous blue eyes.

Embarrassed and blushing, she turned away and stammered, "Wh-where are we going?"

Grabbing a black fitted shirt from his backpack, he pulled it over his head as he hurried over to his laptop. "We need to find those responsible for putting you in the hospital."

Alessa startled. "Wait, no. Do you mean my killers? Why would I want to do that?"

With a click of his mouse, he opened a file. "It's the only way to get to Eric." He pointed to Eric Lansing's headshot.

Her eyes widened in horror. "No, no, no." Alessa waved her hands while backing away. "I am not giving those men another shot at killing me. No, thank you. They already succeeded once, which seems to be the only thing I cannot forget. What they did to me—" She crossed her arms in front of her chest and shivered.

He stood up and wrapped his fingers around her upper arms, locking her in place. "Alessa, I can't begin to tell you how sorry I am and how terrible I feel about not being there to help you when needed, but you need to find the strength to do this. Erebos is going to distribute its drug in less than one week, and only you know what it'll do to those who take it. This isn't just about your life or mine—"

"But I was caught. Didn't I fail the mission? I don't even know where I would have—wait..." She recalled a brief scene from a previous dream in which she stood before a computer and read the information displayed with the understanding she was downloading it to something, yet she held no device she could download anything to. "What does it mean if I downloaded the information?"

"It's where you download information and store it in your microchip. However, you would be the only one with the key to unlock the code to extract it, which is why it is imperative you get at least this part of your memory back. You need to remember how to do that and your chosen code. Look at the screen and tell me which men you recognize."

Looking at the third man's picture, Alessa flinched with the sensation of a phantom fist being thrust into her gut. "Him," she pointed.

The man clicked on the picture and moved his headshot into a separate folder.

He flipped through various peoples' mugshots until Alessa finally felt a cigar pressed into her arm. "And him."

As a Hispanic man appeared on the screen, Alessa's eyes burned emerald green. The older, tanned man was scarred up the right side of his face, and his lips were curled into a sadistic grin.

Rage welled up inside of her as an image of a knife dripping red with her blood manifested before her. With a shaking hand, she pointed at his image.

The man gestured at the screen containing all her torturers' faces and information. "These men took your life. They stole your memories. Aren't you the least bit angry? On some level, don't you crave revenge?"

Alessa's darkness festered inside, and her irises changed color. "Yes, I do."

"It's settled then." He grabbed a dark blue button-up and tossed it on over his T-shirt.

With a blink, Alessa's eyes transitioned from green back to blue. "And how am I supposed to do that? I don't know how to fight. I'm not even sure how to activate my microchip or control it when I do. It's like my basic nature takes over, and I do things without thinking about it."

"Don't worry. I'll help you," he offered.

"Wait a second. Did I miss something?" Alessa threw her

hands up in the air. "Weren't you the one who just told me there's no guarantee I'll get all of my memories back?"

He turned around and faced Alessa. "You are correct. There is no guarantee you will. However, you are already remembering more, and it seems to me if we take things slow enough, you have a real chance of recalling the dirt you had on Erebos. If you don't, Eric wins. And your killers win. The Alessa I know would never let that happen. So, you don't have a choice. You must remember the incriminating evidence against Eric."

"What if the old Alessa is gone?"

The man huffed as he shoved his laptop into his pack. "Trust me, the Alessa I know still exists. I see her every time I look into your eyes."

A shiver shot up Alessa's spine as his eyes bore into her.

Glancing away, he zipped up his bag. "I admit you're taking all this quite well. I mean, you haven't had a meltdown yet."

Alessa chuckled. "Well, as much as I'd like to say you're insane and go back home to my friends, too much of what you say feels like the truth." She paused in contemplative thought. "Do you think, by chance," she started slowly, "my subconscious is feeding my memories back to me in dream form to protect me from being—what did you call it? Overwhelmed or overloaded, was it?"

The man inched closer to Alessa. "What have you dreamt about?"

Shards of glass flew through the room as the sliding doors exploded from behind. Alessa hit the ground, and the man fell on top of her, covering her body with his own.

The Spartan sprang up and scowled, looking through the giant hole in the side of their motel room. "It's time to go."

CHAPTER TWENTY

The Spartan flung his backpack over his shoulder and pulled Alessa up to stand. Pushing her away from the explosion, he yelled, "Move!"

While they ran through the debris-filled room, several cans flew in through the broken glass doors, releasing acrid white smoke. He threw open the closet door before shoving himself and Alessa into the small space.

Using her indigo sleeve, Alessa covered her mouth and nose as the smoke billowed under the closed door. She blinked away the tears, blurring her vision, and coughed the smoke out of her burning lungs while the Spartan snatched up several small objects from the top shelf of the closet.

After twisting each of the tops, he placed the devices on the floor, surrounding them in a circle.

"What are you doing?" she panicked as he wrapped his arms protectively around her.

He braced himself. "Hold on!"

The walls vibrated, and as the circular objects exploded one after another, she squeezed her eyes shut.

Their legs buckled as the floor beneath them disintegrated, and grunting loudly, they fell into the room directly below, landing in front of an older couple lying in bed watching TV.

The Spartan picked Alessa up off the floor and looked her over. "Are you hurt?"

She brushed the dust from her shirt and bare legs, looking up at the hole in the ceiling they had just fallen through. "I think I'm good."

Stumbling through the debris, the Spartan dragged her toward the front door, apologizing profusely to the couple. "Sorry for interrupting your night. And sorry about the ceiling!"

The older man grinned and stared at Alessa, his eyes tracing up her exposed legs.

The Spartan placed himself between Alessa and the older man, blocking the man's view. "We've got to get you some clothes."

They spilled into the hallway before running out of the building, into the cool evening air, and down a side alley.

Approaching a small parking lot, he pointed at a black Z28 Camaro. "That one. Get in."

"Hold up. *This* is our getaway car?"

"Yeah. Why, what's wrong with it?" he asked defensively.

"Absolutely nothing," she responded, impressed.

"Alright, then. Stop wasting time and get in!" He jumped into the driver's side and put his keys in the ignition as Alessa slid into the passenger seat.

"Where'd you find her?" She ran her hand over the black leather interior.

The Spartan flashed a sideways grin and punched the car into drive. "Oh, she's all mine."

At the end of the alley, he whipped the car to the right and

GLITCHED

drifted around the corner. Shifting into second gear, they raced toward the highway. But as he glanced in the rearview mirror, he cursed in a language unknown to Alessa. "*Mhtrokoito!*"

"What? What does that mean?" Alessa panicked.

"Motherfucker," he growled as two silver SUVs with black tinted windows trailed behind.

Jerking the steering wheel hard to the right, the Camaro drifted, barely making the entrance ramp to Interstate 376W, and after shifting into third, their car reached eighty-five miles per hour.

The wind from the car's open window whipped Alessa's hair around, and as she tried to contain it, she watched a hand wielding a firearm extend out from one of the SUV's passenger side windows.

Pressing her back against the seat, she screamed, "He's got a gun!"

As gunshots fired, a bullet ricocheted off the Camaro's passenger side mirror.

"Shit." The Spartan held onto the steering while reaching into the back seat.

"What are you doing?" Alessa demanded through panicked breaths.

"I'm searching for—come on! Where is it?" He struggled to dig beneath a tarp draped across the back seat. With a frustrated grunt, he threw the cover off to the side, exposing a large arsenal of weapons.

"What in the hell?" Her eyes opened wide.

"Got it!" he exclaimed, finally finding the weapon he had been searching for. He tossed it to Alessa.

She jumped as the weapon landed in her lap. "What am I supposed to do with this?" she asked, holding it up awkwardly with two fingers.

Yanking the steering wheel to the left, he scoffed. "Try using it!"

Bullets struck the back of their car as they tried to outmaneuver the Bodyguards. Ducking and covering her head, Alessa shrieked and pressed the side of the gun against her ear.

Annoyed with Alessa's fearful reaction, the Spartan rolled his eyes and swore under his breath.

"But I've never shot a gun before!" Alessa yelled.

Turning around, he plunged back into the car's rear seat. "Like hell you haven't!" he barked back.

While bending down to avoid the flying bullets, Alessa caught a glimpse of a flickering red light on the side of her firearm. Curious, she pushed the button and heard a mechanical clinking sound within the barrel. "Exactly what type of gun is this?"

One of the silver SUVs sped up beside the passenger side of the Spartan's car while the other pulled up on the driver's side.

The driver of the vehicle next to Alessa pointed his firearm at her and pulled the trigger.

Instinctively, Alessa stretched her arm across the Spartan's chest and pressed him back against his seat.

Narrowly missing them both, the bullet flew out the other open window, striking the driver of the SUV.

The vehicle swerved and noisily smashed headfirst into the guardrail.

Enraged by the near hit, Alessa's eyes blazed a fiery green, and she aimed her firearm at the SUV directly beside her. Squeezing its trigger, several ninja stars shot out from the chamber before striking the driver's neck and then the passenger's.

The SUV spun out of control and flipped onto its side before skidding to a fiery halt.

Alessa's rescuer cursed as he looked back in the rearview mirror. There were multiple new silver SUVs in pursuit. "Ah, shit!"

Twisting around, Alessa squeezed out of her window before propping her left hip on the doorframe. With most of her upper body balanced precariously out of the speeding Camaro, she aimed her weapon and squeezed the trigger.

A bullet demolished the SUV's front right tire, and the entire vehicle screeched as it rotated in the middle of the highway.

While pressing the trigger flush against the handle, Alessa held the glowing red button simultaneously. A spinning ball of fire exploded from the top chamber and flew toward the additional trailing vehicles.

Upon impact, the leading SUV burst into flames. Unfortunately, the rest of the SUVs emerged unscathed through the fiery blaze.

Alessa's excited smile faded. "I need to surge!" she yelled into the Camaro.

The Spartan grabbed hold of a tricked-out grenade and turned it upside down. With his other hand, he entered a code into the bottom of the metallic cylinder as its timer counted down.

He dangled the weapon outside of the car before aiming the grenade at the side of the SUV. With a loud beep, the casing shot out of the mechanism, and hundreds of tiny, spiked pellets smashed through the SUV's window.

"How many of these fuckers are there?" he shouted.

Alessa fell back in through the window. "Dammit, Damon,

I said I needed to surge. What are you doing in here?" she scolded, throwing his weapons around in the backseat.

The Spartan stared at Alessa in shock as she continued rummaging through his supply of weapons, utterly oblivious to her remembering his name.

"Where is it? I know you always have it in case of—yes!" she exclaimed, finding the weapon. A fluorescent green line lit up both sides when she pressed the power button.

Several more SUVs sped up behind them and showered the Camaro with gunfire.

As her firearm beeped and the lines turned red, Alessa pushed herself out of the window. Dodging bullets, she dangled out of the car, and while facing the approaching vehicles, her body tensed as she squeezed the trigger.

The weapon bucked as the surge was sent forth, knocking Alessa off balance.

As the sound waves struck the road, the concrete before the trailing vehicles buckled. Their windows exploded as each of their noses smashed into the ground before they flipped upside down.

Alessa's feet slipped from their hold, and she shut her eyes, bracing for impact.

Lunging for her, the Spartan caught Alessa by the ankle, jerking her to a halt.

The dark purple button-up whipped around her torso, exposing her black underwear, and Alessa's eyes sprung open in surprise.

The road sped by mere inches below her face.

Flexing her abs, she sat upright, grabbed the top of the window frame, and swung her left leg through the window.

Immediately after falling into her seat, Alessa screamed in agony and grabbed the sides of her head.

. . .

The older gentleman from previous memories stood at the front of the classroom, introducing the new trainer. Alessa pushed her way through the crowded room while her friends playfully shoved one another back and forth, and for the first time, she set eyes on Damon.

His dark chestnut brown hair appeared clean-cut yet tousled. He stood six feet tall, and his fitted deep green T-shirt stretched across his broad shoulders while the shirt's short sleeves exposed his muscular arms.

Alessa's eyes dropped to his black athletic pants, which didn't exactly leave much to the imagination.

As the older man rambled about the new instructor's achievements, Damon stood with his hands clasped firmly behind his back.

Scanning the crowd, his gaze locked onto Alessa, and her breathing faltered as she met his intense dark blue eyes.

A hot shiver shot down Alessa's spine, and she inhaled shakily.

Alessa cried out, fighting the sensation of an ice pick being driven in between her eyes.

"Alessa, what's happening?" Damon panicked.

As the memory continued, Alessa was personally introduced to Damon.

The older gentleman held his hand out to her. "Damon, this is Alessa. She is one of our best trainees, and we anticipate her to be a top Custos."

Damon flashed a mischievous grin. "Is that so? She doesn't appear to be Wellborn..." He extended his hand. "Alessa, it's a pleasure to meet you."

She hesitantly placed her hand in his and shook firmly. "Likewise, even though you do appear to be Wellborn."

An invisible spark flew between Damon's hand and Alessa's.

His lips parted in a sideways grin. "I didn't mean anything by—"

"Oh, I know what you meant. You are no different than the rest of your people in believing that because I am not Wellborn, I won't amount to much."

Taken by surprise, he squinted. "That's not at all what I meant. And aren't you one of 'us people'?" Damon leaned in. "I'll tell you a secret: being Wellborn is not as great as one might think. It kind of fucking sucks."

"Huh..." Alessa glared up at the man in confusion. "You're unlike any other Wellborn I've ever met."

"You have no idea." He brought her fingers up to his mouth and pressed his lips against the back of her hand.

CHAPTER TWENTY-ONE

"Can you hear me? That's it. I'm pulling over." Damon veered into the right lane.

She whimpered aloud in response to her body being violently jerked.

"Alessa?" he asked, nervously awaiting her response.

She opened her green eyes. "Ugh. I think I just remembered the first time we met." Alessa pitched the weapon, still in her hands, into the back seat.

"Hey, be careful!" he yelled.

Alessa rubbed her eyelids. "Ugh. My eyes feel like they're burning out of their sockets. And my head feels like it's splitting in half."

"Your eyes burning is one of the temporary side effects of activating your chip. The more you get used to activating, the less it'll irritate you."

Once her vision cleared, Alessa focused on her exposed legs and gasped. Her black boxer briefs were exposed.

He laughed as she frantically tugged on the bottom of the

deep purple shirt. "I can assure you, your undergarments were the last thing on my mind during all that."

He nodded in her direction. "So, what's with all the violent shaking? Is that what happens when you relive a memory?"

Alessa arched an eyebrow. "Was I shaking?"

"Pretty bad."

She rubbed the back of her neck. "My head always feels like it will explode when I dream, remember, or whatever."

"And now, how are you feeling?"

"Not too bad. I feel like I ran a marathon. My muscles are sore, and my head..." Alessa remembered using the firearm, and she peeked into the back seat. "Firing that thing—whatever it was—it felt amazing."

His grip tightened on the wheel, and he turned right onto I-80. "Glad to see your Italian hasn't gotten rusty."

"Who, me? Speak Italian?"

"Yeah, you," he chuckled.

"When did I speak Italian?"

"Just now. You've always tended to break out in foreign languages when emotional. For some reason, you especially enjoy Italian."

Alessa recalled when she unknowingly yelled at the cooks in Spanish. "Huh. Well, I guess that explains the Spanish," she mumbled. "What languages can you speak?"

Damon licked his lips, and her heart fluttered. "Most Latin, Italian, Spanish, Russian, French, Greek, some Finnish..."

"Wow, I get it. Now you're showing off, Damon."

His dark denim blue eyes bore into her. "Say it again."

"Wh-what, your name?" Alessa stammered, taken aback.

"Say ... it ... again," he smoldered.

Without breaking eye contact, she repeated his name. "Damon."

Slowly blinking, he returned his attention to the road while inhaling a shaky breath.

Deep in thought, she stared past him. "I remember saying it back when I—"

"Activated," he finished for her.

"Right. When I activated, it was instinctual. Like how to work the weapons, my ability to calculate the trajectory of bullets, and even remembering your name felt like riding a bike. Why did it feel as though I, for lack of a better term, connected with the weapon?" Alessa asked.

"Vindico programmed its weapons so they can only be used by an individual implanted with a Vindico-specific microchip. The weapon is turned on when our fingers contact the trigger. At the same time, it reads our heat signature, and the technology inside the weapon searches for the exact type of microchip. Since it is directly connected to your brain, you automatically know how to use the weapon without conscious effort.

"Your being able to fire the weapon is great. It confirms your microchip is still somewhat connected to the database. It would've given you one hell of a shock if you weren't."

Alessa stared at him in disbelief. "How is any of this possible? Oh—your eyes, they're grey again."

Damon's lips curled up into a lazy smile. "Technology, baby. I activated for our fun back there. A lot of it is based on a surge of adrenaline. But you are also taught how to control it during your teenage years in the academy."

Alessa's leg bounced up and down, digesting everything Damon had told her over the past twenty-four hours.

Noticing Alessa's nervous habit, Damon snickered under his breath and placed a warm hand on her thigh. She jumped as an electric shock shot up her leg.

"Take a deep breath," he instructed.

Alessa closed her eyes and focused on breathing in and out, but with his hand sprawled out upon her bare skin, she couldn't concentrate on anything other than Damon's touch.

"Can you please answer some questions?" she begged.

Removing his hand, he flexed his fingers before wrapping them back around the steering wheel. "I don't think that's a good idea, given what you just went through."

"I promise I'll let you know if I even feel a twinge of a headache coming on," Alessa pressed.

Damon blinked, and his irises flickered from steel grey to deep blue. "You're not going to let this go, are you?"

Alessa's leg ached as the warmth from his touch dissipated. "Nope."

"Ugh," he sighed in defeat. "Then go on ahead."

"Okay, this might seem a little personal, but I've dreamt of you before, or remembered? I'm not sure at this point."

"So, what's your question?" Damon stared straight ahead, unflinching.

Suddenly nervous, she cleared her throat. "Um, from what I can tell, we were close, or at least, we were on good terms. So, why didn't you come to the hospital?"

A wave of guilt hit Damon, and he chose his words wisely. "Your last mission was to infiltrate Erebos Industries and download classified information."

Damon swallowed the newly-formed lump in his throat. "When your connection was severed, you were believed to be dead, and by the time I realized it could be you at the hospital, you were gone."

She tilted her head in surprise. "So, you did try to find me?"

"Against everyone's advice, yes, I did. They all thought I

was crazy, especially my father, but I knew you wouldn't go down without a fight."

She clasped her hands together and pressed her back into the seat. "Well, it's good I fled when I did since the Bodyguards showed up."

"I heard. This further confirmed my suspicions about the Jane Doe patient being you. Oh, I almost forgot," Damon smirked. "Happy belated birthday."

"Uh, thanks?" She giggled at the randomness of his comment. "When is my birthday?"

"September ninth."

"Interesting. And I'm older than I had assumed."

He chuckled aloud.

Alessa playfully punched him in the arm. "Well, how old are you?"

Damon rubbed his bicep where she had hit him and winked. "Thirty years young."

"Whew, you're old," she quipped.

"Hey, now, I'm not *that* old."

She smiled at him before looking out the windshield. "Does everyone at New Sparta, Vindico, or whatever, not have a last name? Like earlier, you mentioned my last name is Custos, but it's not really. And in my memory, just now, you mentioned me not being Wellborn. What's that all about?"

His face lit up as she spoke about her dream. "I'm glad to hear you're remembering more. Wellborn is the definition of a Spartan who is a direct descendent of a king or an elder.

"There are several social classes. The Custos, like you, are what aristocrats, who are top warriors, are labeled as. The aristocrats are those of us who have, at the age of twenty, passed the physical tests needed to be career warriors and are official citizens of Sparta. The Periodic are those who are not strong enough to be warriors, so they are inserted into normal human life to gain information for us, such as lawyers, stock market traders, government officials, etcetera. Helots are the titles given to those enslaved in the past, but they are no longer labeled as such since our elders realized they needed the Helots to thrive for our culture to survive, as I already explained. They are mainly our builders, maids, cooks, musicians, artists—"

"So, what you're saying is, I am a Spartan but not a Wellborn?"

"Correct. At the age of twenty, you passed the tests required to become an official citizen—quite impressively, I might add—and you earned your place as a member of the Spartan community. However, you were not born a Spartan."

"I'm sorry, what does that mean? Where did I come from if I wasn't born a Spartan?"

Caught off guard, Damon hesitated. "From your mom and dad, made the good old-fashioned way, I suppose." He wiggled his eyebrows. "In all seriousness, your elder found you in the mountains and brought you back to the compound when you were young."

A scene from her dreams came to mind: a cabin in the woods. Alessa's heart raced, and she pushed the visions away. "Is it common for your people to snatch up kids and make them Spartans?"

"No, not at all. As far as I'm aware, you are the exception to our rule of how we acquire outsiders. In other words, humans who are not of Spartan lineage. We have a rigorous process for how new blood is chosen. A candidate must be of age and prove themselves worthy. Typically, it's an individual serving in special ops, like a Navy Seal, or something to that effect.

They're the best of the best and always adults. Those chosen to join our cause cannot have any familial ties, so when we fake their deaths, their existence can be erased without question."

"Huh." Her jaw hung slack as she glanced away from Damon and stared out the passenger window.

"So, what memory did you relive? About me?" He side-eyed Alessa.

"A man was introducing us. I think he has also been in previous dreams."

Damon nodded. "That would be your elder."

The lights on the highway sped by as he accelerated.

"Whoa, there, speedy." She grabbed her seatbelt and buckled herself in.

"No use having this sexy car if I can't drive her hard." Damon's veins bulged on the back of his hand as he gripped the shifter.

Feeling her pulse increase, Alessa looked away from his hand and closed her eyes while she rotated the ring on her finger. "This elder guy, was he a big part of my life?"

Damon tilted his head to the side and chuckled. "He's the closest thing you have to a father figure, so I'd say so."

Caught up in her thoughts, Alessa stared out the windshield.

"What are you thinking?" Damon asked, interrupting the silence.

"And you don't know what happened to my actual dad?" Alessa's words dripped with vulnerability.

He pursed his lips before sighing. "You must know that is too emotional a subject to discuss."

Damon reached out to comfort Alessa as she turned away, but his fingertips stopped short, hovering before her arm.

With a shake of his head, Damon clenched his fist before bringing his hand back to his side. "Do you happen to recall anything about your final mission? Anything at all?"

Closing her eyes, she concentrated on the fragmented pieces of her memory that were haphazardly sewn together. Unable to discern fact from fiction, she sighed aloud in frustration. "There is one dream, or memory, from the night I was captured. It's more from the time I arrived at the worksite."

Damon's voice dropped an octave. "How did it happen?"

"I had these passcodes to get into a vault-like room with these crazy lasers I got past. Then there was this computer with secure files."

"Can you see the download?"

Alessa tried her best to recall the words written across the computer screen, but they appeared as a jumbled mess. The beginnings of an ache started in the far corner of her head. "I've got nothing."

"That's fine; don't worry about it. I'm sure it'll come back to you. We've got to give it time."

"How would I bring the information back to Vindico? It's not like I had a memory stick shoved in my bra or a camera hiding anywhere. How could I possibly have downloaded information to my microchip?"

The car tires squealed as Damon turned to the left.

"You were the camera."

She giggled incredulously. "Say what now?"

"Think of our eyes as a camera lens and our microchips the film. When we activate, our eyes take in the information we're reading and send it to our microchips to be sorted and stored within a specific area of our brains. We then download the information from our microchips into a document or video file, which we hand over to the Council of Elders as evidence."

"You're joking, right?" Alessa said in awe.

"Yes, because I have done nothing but lie to you," he drawled sarcastically.

"Sorry. This is a lot to take in. I feel like I'm doing a damn good job of not freaking out. Do we remember everything from every time we activate?"

"Hell no, we'd go crazy if we remembered every little detail of our lives. The microchip weeds out what we need to remember by sorting and distributing information to different areas of the brain. It works in conjunction with our long-term and short-term memory."

"Are there wireless capabilities involved? I mean, can't we download straight to Sparta?"

"Not yet. It hasn't been secure enough to do it without compromising the host. However, our developers are confident we'll have the capability soon. You know how websites can be hacked?"

"I guess so."

"If a host is directly connected to a server capable of being compromised, we can also be hacked if we don't have the proper firewalls in place."

The tires squealed again as Damon turned to the right, and Alessa's body leaned in the opposite direction as she gripped the leather seat. "Which means what, exactly?"

"Someone else could control us. Our minds, bodies, everything that makes us who we are, could be altered with the right technology."

"Isn't that ironic?" she snorted.

"How so?"

"It's the perfect way to describe how I feel right now. There's past Alessa fighting to break through, forcing all these memories and feelings upon the new Alessa; almost as if the two separate personalities are struggling to survive."

"You do realize there's a third option?" Damon suggested.

"What's that?"

"You could remember your past while embracing who you've been for the past month."

Alessa threw her hands up in the air. "When I was shooting at those men, I didn't even blink when knowing they could die. To be perfectly honest," she breathed, "I wanted them dead. Is that the kind of person I want to be? A cold, calculated killer?"

"Alessa," Damon's grip tightened around the steering wheel, "you've never been cold. Let's get that out of the way right now. You only felt good about killing those people because they are the bad guys. The Bodyguards are aiding Erebos Industries in what we can only assume will end with Eric killing millions of innocent people. That's why you were sent to investigate. You should want them dead. This is your job, and it's not always pleasant, but you matter, and what you do matters."

"Wasn't I trying to stop Eric Lansing from committing genocide? He was trying to kill anyone with a lethal genetic mutation. Am I right?"

"Yes, that is correct."

"From what I remember of Spartan history, didn't they used to leave babies for dead if there was the slightest imperfection? Why would an entire civilization that took pride in being superior care about saving humanity?"

Damon tilted his head in consideration and licked his lips before responding. "That was the way of our ancestors, but when Spartans were forced to flee our homes, our beliefs changed, and those practices stopped. Our kings declared the gods had forsaken us because of how we had treated our flesh and blood, and it was with this declaration we swore on our lives and those of our future generations that we would protect the human race in its entirety. Speaking of changing practices—what have you been up to this past month?"

She cringed at the thought of how mundane she was going to sound. "Working and hanging with a few friends. That's about it."

His eyebrows rose in surprise. "How very domestic of you."

"Hey, now. Reagan and McKenzie have been amazing, and Pat is probably the closest thing to a father figure I've ever had. Or, I guess, remember having."

"And what about that one guy?"

"What guy?"

His jaw flexed as he considered his response. "The one you were making out with on the dancefloor."

Perplexed by the jealous energy radiating off Damon, Alessa narrowed her eyes. "You must be talking about Chris. And he's just a friend."

"Do you grind up on all of your friends?" He smirked and cocked his head to the side.

Annoyed by his interrogation, she went on the defensive. "What if I do? Why does it matter to you?"

He cackled under his breath but chose not to respond.

Interrupting the awkward silence, she asked the question she'd been dying to know the answer to.

"Damon, how did I get caught during my last mission?"

He nervously rubbed the stubble on his chin. "We aren't one hundred percent positive."

"That's messed up," she huffed. "How does this all-powerful entity not know how I got taken down? Was I set up?"

Damon's knuckles blanched white as he squeezed the steering wheel. "Yeah, well, trust me, I swear to the gods, if I ever get my hands on whoever was behind your capture, they won't be alive once I let go."

"Alright. I need a break," she admitted as pain spread throughout her temples.

Laying back against the seat, Alessa looked out her window as Damon took another right turn onto I-79. She rested for the next half hour until her head no longer ached.

She broke the silence. "Can I ask where we're going?"

"You certainly can," Damon teased.

She rolled her eyes. "Okay, where are we going?"

He rubbed the dark stubble on his chin, and Alessa's eyes fell to his slightly parted pink lips. "We're going to the only place I know around here. Hades, at this point, she's our only option."

Alessa snorted. "Well, that's comforting."

Exiting the highway, Damon turned down a side street and headed into downtown Pittsburgh.

"No one knows you're alive except for me, and we need to keep it that way for as long as possible. We have no idea who the real enemy is, and we are less likely to get caught if we leave Sparta out of this," he explained. "I've worked with this woman on several occasions, and I believe her to be my closest ally—at least in this lovely state of Pennsylvania."

Alessa anxiously spun the ring on her finger. "You don't sound too sure about this."

"Listen, the only real problem with Brielle is that she's a double agent, meaning she works for whoever pays the highest for her services. She doesn't exactly care about how pure their motives are," Damon explained.

Alessa glared at him, hesitant to trust this woman with her life.

He pulled into the parking lot in front of The Pennsylvanian Luxury Apartments. "And she might be a bit on the crazy side, but you're going to have to trust me when I say she's our only option."

CHAPTER TWENTY-TWO

"Where are we, exactly?" Alessa asked as Damon parked the car.

"It's Brielle's apartment complex." He reached into the back seat and stuffed several weapons into his backpack.

Alessa opened her car door and stepped onto the cold concrete. "This place is fancy." She faced Damon, pointing at her severe lack of clothing and bare feet. "Is this gonna fly?"

"It'll be fine. Just let me do the talking when we get in there." He threw his backpack over his shoulder before heading toward the building.

Having no choice but to follow, she reluctantly trailed behind him.

They walked beneath a giant dome, and as Alessa tilted her head back, she discovered the most beautiful artwork painted across the stone ceiling.

"Wow. That's gorgeous," she mumbled, slowing to a stop.

Damon glanced over his shoulder at Alessa, and her eyes reflected the golden yellow lights cast from the stone.

"Alessa, we don't have time for this."

Her gaze fell from the ornate ceiling to the muscular man before her.

Clutching his shoulder strap, he continued toward the building in haste. "We have to keep moving."

Alessa caught up, and as they strolled through the front door, Damon walked right up to the front desk.

"Good evening. Please notify Brielle that Damon is here to see her."

The attendant picked up the receiver with a look of disdain and punched a sequence of numbers into the keypad. Eyeing Damon and Alessa, he tapped his right foot impatiently. As the phone rang, his eyes drifted from Alessa's naked feet up to her breasts hidden behind the dark purple button-up.

Uncomfortable with the man's lingering gaze, Alessa flattened the wrinkled fabric against her stomach before pulling down the bottom of the shirt in a vain attempt to cover her bare legs.

As she crossed her arms to shield herself, Damon straightened his back and stepped in protectively between the attendant and Alessa. "Is there a problem?" he asked.

"Nope, nope." The attendant nervously shook his head back and forth. "Just waiting for Miss Brielle to answer." He turned away from Alessa.

Finally allowed a reprieve from the stranger's gaze, her eyes wandered toward the ceiling.

It was decorated with extravagant glass windows, and the walls were lined with elaborately framed doors. Tiny rainbows reflected onto the woodwork by the strategically placed lights bouncing off the chandelier high above.

The desk attendant spoke to someone briefly on the phone before he permitted them to continue into the lobby. "She is expecting you. I assume you know what floor."

Damon touched Alessa's upper back and walked her through the double doors. "Yes, sir, I do."

They entered a grand hallway illuminated by the stars shining in through the skylight. The walls were a beautiful mixture of cream and gold, emphasizing the artwork painted on them.

As the metallic doors opened, Damon pressed the button next to the elevator, and Alessa hurried in. He hit the button for the fourth floor, and Alessa's stomach dropped.

With a *ding*, the doors opened, and they stepped out into the hallway, walking alongside one another down the hall lined with large floor-to-ceiling windows.

Damon hid his apprehension as they approached a dark wooden door and hit the doorbell. "Here we go."

The doorbell's chime played, and a woman's muffled voice called out from inside the apartment. "It's open!"

Before he opened the door, Damon turned to Alessa.

"Do not say a word, got it?"

Feeling like a scolded puppy, Alessa angrily tugged down the bottom of her shirt.

He grabbed the handle, pushed open the door, and stepped into the dimly lit entryway.

A modern kitchen filled with stainless steel appliances and dark granite countertops was on the right side of the hall, and an oversized living room was directly in front of them.

"Damon! What a wonderful surprise," a feminine voice purred. "You left so suddenly the last time; I wasn't sure when I'd see you again."

A gorgeous woman of Asian descent strolled toward them. Her hips bounced back and forth while she delicately balanced a glass of red wine between her fingertips.

The woman's skin-tight red dress barely covered her five-foot-eight-inch frame, and as she approached Damon, her black stiletto heels clicked loudly against the hardwood floors.

Her crimson lips separated into a seductive smile as Damon stepped out of the dark.

Who the fuck wears stilettos in their house?

Damon held his arms out and embraced the woman before kissing her on the cheek.

Anger surged through Alessa, and impulsively, she advanced out of the hallway and stepped into the light, interrupting their entanglement.

Brielle jerked back. "Who the hell are you?"

Damon grabbed Brielle's hand and pulled her back into him. "She's why we're here."

Disappointed, Brielle whimpered. "Oh."

She examined the half-naked woman standing barefoot in her apartment. "You look familiar..."

"She's a colleague, so I'm sure you've seen her before," Damon dismissed nonchalantly.

Brielle sneered in disdain. "She doesn't look like a Spartan."

Alessa's eyes flashed fiery green for a split second, and Brielle's eyes widened subtly.

Alessa turned her head to the side and furiously blinked away the fire behind her eyes.

Brielle returned her focus to Damon. "What is it you want from me?"

"I need you to use your connections to find information on several men. I'll take all the details you can get."

Brielle leaned into him and laid her hands on his chest. "And what do I get out of this transaction?" she whispered loudly into Damon's ear while glaring past him at Alessa.

He cleared his throat apprehensively.

"Excuse me," Alessa interrupted the room's growing sexual tension. "Do you, by chance, have anything I could borrow?" She gestured to her lack of clothing.

Brielle rolled her eyes toward Alessa and scowled. "Those stairs, over there, go up to my bedroom. There might be an outfit or two you can squeeze into."

Alessa glared. "Uh, thanks?"

She hurried past the couch and computer desk before scrambling up the stairs.

The bedroom's dark purple walls were decorated with sparkling candle holders, and two oversized chairs sat angled toward one another, facing a large mirror propped up against the left wall.

Alessa glared at Brielle's mattress as she passed the bed, wondering if Damon had ever been in it with the beautiful woman.

She kicked a small, dark object while stepping onto a shaggy rug and bent down to pick it up.

"Oh, uh..." Alessa grimaced as she realized it was a pair of black metallic handcuffs. Dropping them, she wiped her hands on her shirt. "Gross."

She opened the closet doors, and a bright light illuminated the highly adorned shelves and the short dresses hanging from the rods.

"Wow. McKenzie and Reagan would die if they could see this collection."

She pulled back the first dress and groaned. *Finding an appropriate outfit might be a problem.*

Damon leaned forward onto the back of Brielle's chair as she frantically typed and chewed her gum.

She stopped and turned around to face him. "What's your deal with the girl?"

He looked into her brown eyes, a few inches before his own. "I'm not sure what you're implying."

"Oh, come on, Damon." She shook her head. "Give me some credit."

"Why, Bri," he placed his fingertips underneath her chin, "are you jealous?"

Brielle huffed. "No."

Damon's lips turned into a seductive smirk before he dropped his hand and returned to the computer screen.

A few minutes went by as Damon tapped his foot impatiently. "How much longer do you think it'll be?"

She blew a bubble and popped it. "Probably a few minutes."

Damon rubbed the stubble on his chin and peered down at his torn shirt. "You don't happen to have any men's clothes up there, do you?"

"I may still have a pair of your pants. Maybe even a shirt or two." She looked him up and down. "They'd be in my bedroom closet, in the back, right."

Damon stood up. "Great, I'll be right back."

He jogged up the staircase, hit the second floor, and while placing his hand on the wooden doorframe, he lifted his eyes and froze. His fingertips gripped the wood as his gaze landed on a scantily clad Alessa.

She was facing away from him, wearing only a pair of pink panties and a matching bra.

Alessa bent over to pick a pair of blue jeans off the floor, and Damon's heart raced. His cock strained against his zipper as he watched her ass wiggle back and forth as she pulled on the pants, one leg at a time.

Her back arched and twisted as she seductively stretched her muscles. She buttoned her pants, grabbed a red shirt off the oversized chair, and pulled it over her head, working her way into the tight, lacy fabric.

Alessa turned to the left, facing the tall mirror, and ran her hands down her backside.

Damon's cheeks reddened as he imagined his hands in place of hers.

His eyes explored the curves of her body, working their way up to the lacy fabric barely covering her breasts.

The cap sleeves fell below her collarbone on either side, emphasizing her petite frame.

With his pants having grown uncomfortably tight, Damon shifted his hips, and he growled under his breath due to the friction of movement against his enlarged bulge.

Hearing Damon, Alessa's head jerked, and she jumped at the sight of him leaning up against the doorframe.

He glanced down at the floor with a seductive smile. "Sorry, didn't mean to scare you. I come in peace," Damon apologized with his hands held up before his chest.

She blushed. "How long were you standing there?"

"Not long," he shook his head. "Came up for a change of clothes."

"Oh," Alessa mumbled. "I'm just gonna grab a pair of shoes real quick."

She ran to the closet and reached for a pair of black-heeled boots as Damon's belt jingled.

Alessa's eyes widened, and she sprang upright. "What are you doing?"

He unbuttoned his pants and pulled the zipper down over his bulge. "I told you already," he grabbed his belt loop.

A scene played out before Alessa's eyes of a shirtless Damon pinning her up against a wall, his wet tongue licking up the side of her neck. She moaned as he bit just below her jawline.

Alessa turned back around, her eyes wide in shock. "I, uh ... I'll be downstairs," she stammered, rushing out of the room.

An electric shock shot up her spine with the sound of Damon's pants hitting the floor.

CHAPTER TWENTY-THREE

Rushing down the stairs, Alessa nearly fell as she hit the landing.

Brielle glanced at her curiously and pulled her cellphone away from her ear. "Are you okay?"

"Uh, yeah." Alessa plopped down on the couch in a daze.

Brielle ended the call while Alessa caught her breath.

"Who were you on the phone with?" Alessa asked.

Brielle scrunched her nose in contempt. "Are you always this nosy?"

Surprised by Brielle's defensive response, Alessa stared back at the woman. "I didn't mean to ... I was trying ... Never mind. Thanks for lending us the clothes."

"Well, you're taking my clothes. Damon's are being returned to him," Brielle glowered.

As Damon descended the stairs, Alessa's perplexed gaze landed on his shirtless frame. His eight-pack flexed as he reached back for the jet-black shirt, and as he pulled it up over his broad shoulders, he stepped down to the bottom stair with his shirt still unbuttoned.

Alessa inhaled a sharp, jagged breath as he moved toward her.

"Got it," Brielle announced.

He sprinted toward Brielle, sitting at the computer without acknowledging Alessa's presence.

Seeing the men's faces and information displayed on the monitor, Damon grabbed the sides of her face and pulled Brielle in for a kiss on the cheek. "Bri, you're incredible."

Alessa's cheeks burned with jealousy. *He's not yours, so why are you so hot and bothered?*

His eyes shone gunmetal grey as he scanned the files pulled up on the computer screen, committing the data to memory.

Suddenly, the apartment door burst open with a loud bang as it slammed against the wall.

An armed man rushed into the living room. "Get down!" He aimed his large gun at Damon and Brielle, who remained behind the computer monitor.

Ignoring the man, Damon focused on downloading the data. The man continued to yell as Damon remained unflinching in front of the monitor, downloading the data as quickly as possible.

Panicked, Alessa tried to run but was stopped mid-turn with her arm twisted behind her back. She screamed as a Bodyguard forced her to the ground.

Hearing her cry, Damon tore his gaze away from the monitor and saw Alessa being pinned down to the floor.

"Alessa!" He lunged for her but was attacked by several men wearing silver suits. He took down three of them, one right after the other, but as the fourth and fifth struck Damon, he was restrained and made to kneel with his arms clasped behind his back.

An unharmed, unrestrained Brielle strolled across the room toward a bald man who appeared to be the leader of the assault.

With his back arched, Damon glared up at Brielle. "Bri, what the fuck is going on?"

The men tightened their hold as his muscles strained against them.

The bald suit pulled a large stack of bills from his coat pocket and handed it to Brielle.

"Bri?" Damon pleaded.

Holding the cash, Brielle glared down at him. "Look, I'm sorry, Damon, but when you walked in with *her*, you left me no choice. I had to call them."

The veins in his neck bulged. "How could you do this to me?"

"You risked my life by bringing her here," she pointed at Alessa. "Had I not called Erebos's Bodyguards, and they found out I helped you, I would've been labeled an accessory. Damon, had I not told them, I could've been killed for seeing her and not reporting it!"

"Let me guess, your being paid didn't influence your decision? You stupid bitch. I trusted you!"

"And I trusted you!" Brielle bent down close to his lips. "So much for that."

Damon was caught off guard. "What the hell are you talking about?"

Brielle took a full syringe from the bald man before sauntering toward Damon. "I stupidly believed you cared for me, that we had become more. I was there for you. And how do you repay me? By bringing *her*," Brielle violently pointed her finger at Alessa, "into my home and making your choice painstakingly clear."

Confused, he squinted and asked, "My choice?"

Brielle glared down at him with a vicious stare. "Damon, darling, don't insult me. Maybe if you watch her die this time around, you'll know she can't be saved."

Damon's eyes flickered storm grey as he sprung from the men's grasp. Knocking them to the side, he growled and lunged for Brielle.

A Bodyguard rushed forward and cracked the back of his skull with the butt of his gun. Falling to his knees, a guard held him up on both sides.

"No!" Alessa cried out as she struggled against her captors.

A pained groan escaped from between Damon's unconscious lips.

"Stop it, please! You're hurting him," Alessa protested.

"You think that's pain? That's nothing." Brielle crouched over Damon and traced his lips with her fingertips. "Imagine loving a man so much that you would do anything for him, only to have him throw your love back in your face. Like it meant nothing—like you were nothing." Brielle chuckled humorlessly.

"I must admit, you nearly had me fooled." Brielle glared back at Alessa as she wiggled her finger. "But then your eyes changed to that awful puke green for one second, and I knew ... it had to be you."

"Did I do something to make you hate me? I'm sorry if I did, but I-I can't remember anything."

Brielle bent down beside Damon. "What didn't you do?"

His head bobbed, and his eyes blinked slowly as he struggled to regain consciousness.

"Let's calm those nerves," Brielle purred in his ear.

Damon's veins bulged as she stuck the needle into the side of his neck.

Alessa gasped. "What are you doing to him?"

Brielle pressed the serum into Damon's vein and retracted the needle before he collapsed to the floor.

"Damon!" Alessa yelled.

Brielle threw the empty syringe off to the side of the room. "Oh, shut up. It's just a neuron transfuse."

"A what?" Alessa's forehead scrunched in confusion.

"Wow. You really are going with the amnesia bit, aren't you? I'll play along. A neuron transfuse scrambles his microchip's data, temporarily reducing him to mush. So that way, I can do to you what I need to without him fighting me."

"I honestly have no idea what you're talking about, but please, let us go."

Brielle exhaled while she looked longingly at Damon. "I simply cannot do that."

Alessa tried for another angle. "If you truly cared about him, you wouldn't do this."

Brielle's eyes blazed. "Who are you to judge me?" She rushed toward Alessa with her hand raised, prepared to strike.

Bracing herself, Alessa closed her eyes tight and jerked her neck to the right.

Unexpectedly, Brielle stopped with her arm suspended above Alessa's head. "You know what? I have a better idea." She walked back toward the bald man and took a silver box out of his hands. While lightly caressing the lid, she confessed, "I was going to use this on you, but since Damon is lost to me, there's no reason to keep him around."

Brielle flipped the latch and opened the lid. Inside was a bright red pill in the middle of the container's black velvet lining.

"If you truly know everything about the Spartans, you know we have advanced healing."

Brielle laughed maniacally and wiped a tear away from her

eye. "Aw, shit. Honey, let me educate you. You may heal extremely quickly, but you can't cheat death, whether it be a bullet to the brain or a deadly disease. It's not like you need to wear a mask or anything with the outbreak, and your advanced healing may prevent you from developing cancer or allow you to heal quicker than a typical human being, but ultimately, you will die. Having the disease directly inserted into your body is the only sure way you Spartans will get it. He may be able to live a few hours longer than the average human but trust me, his heart will give out, which is what I'm counting on since I won't need it anymore."

Brielle picked up the pill and rolled it back and forth between her fingers, and as Alessa eyed the red pill, it triggered a memory.

CHAPTER TWENTY-FOUR

Alessa was sitting in front of a desk as the red pill appeared on the computer monitor, and as the image rotated, a man's raspy voice projected from the speakers.

"The golden-flaked serum will be marketed as the ultimate cure for smallpox, the vaccine and treatment all-in-one. However, for the world to need either a vaccine or treatment, the disease has to be reintroduced to the world population.

"We plan on releasing the infected mist into the New York subway. A single mist spray on just one train will ensure everyone on board has the highly contagious disease. The infection rate is approximately thirty people, meaning every infected individual can potentially infect thirty more.

"We have secured connections with the one lab within the United States capable of producing a cure and a vaccine. Erebos Industries will be the only company with the ability to make the much-needed medication, and the CDC will be so desperate for a cure that they won't stop to question us.

"No one will suspect the outbreak started with us. It will be

advertised as a wonder drug created to eradicate the smallpox virus.

"Once the liquid is ingested, the smallpox virus will successfully be eliminated. However, if there are any lethal genetic anomalies within their DNA, the individual will then contract an accelerated, mutated version of tuberculosis.

"This ensures our ability to control the future's genetic pool."

Eric's smiling face was plastered on the screen with the words 'future president of the world' displayed beneath his picture.

"The original strain of tuberculosis," the voice continued, "is only transmitted through droplets from an infected individual. Our scientists developed a new strain of tuberculosis in which, upon ingestion of the golden liquid, the weaponized disease will kill anyone with a lethal genetic mutation.

"The serum is encoded with the specialized ability to analyze the consumer's DNA. If a lethal genetic mutation is discovered, the individual will contract the bioengineered tuberculosis and be terminated within six days following ingestion.

"Furthermore, we also contained the bioengineered form of tuberculosis within a red pill as a prototype for targeted bioweaponry. The drug is still in the first stages of production, but we have high hopes for its specialized purpose.

"We will encourage government officials to consume this form of the advertised cure versus the serum, as it will put an end to their lives whether or not there is a lethal genetic anomaly present.

"For Eric Lansing to establish a new world regime, the current one must be completely dismantled.

"Either way, whether the red pill is ingested and the

individual is doomed to be infected, or whether a lethal genetic defect is discovered after the consumption of the serum, the genetically engineered strain of tuberculosis will cease all bodily functions within its consumer before the sixth day following ingestion. Report: one hundred percent effective."

Alessa screamed hysterically as Brielle grabbed a tuft of Damon's hair and yanked his head back. "No! Damon, please don't ... Damon, don't take it!"

"Oh, and don't worry about you being infected. Only the consumer comes down with tuberculosis in the pill form I've obtained." Brielle turned toward Alessa and glared. "And you can scream all you want. My apartment is soundproof."

Alessa pushed back against the men, holding her firmly in place.

"Don't hate me, sugar bear. This is the only way," Brielle mumbled in Damon's ear with tears in her eyes.

Alessa panted as her arms remained bound. "Wait, wait! If you truly love Damon—"

Brielle scowled and charged Alessa with her hand raised. "Don't you preach to me about love! I have loved him deeper than you ever could have."

"How can you possibly claim that when you're about to give him a death sentence?" Alessa demanded. "How can you justify killing Damon as an act of love?"

"I'd rather him be dead than be with you," Brielle spat before turning around and walking back to the unconscious man.

Panicking, Alessa looked into Damon's half-opened eyes. "Damon, listen to me. Do not swallow that pill!"

Pressing the red pill between his lips, Brielle coaxed his mouth open.

"No!" Alessa yelled as Damon's head tilted back. "Don't do this. Dammit, let me go!" Alessa begged the men holding her down.

She watched helplessly as the crimson pill fell between Damon's lips.

"No!" Alessa wailed, and her stomach flipped as another memory consumed her.

She was walking down a corridor next to the same blonde woman in previous memories when someone tugged on her arm. Mid-laugh, Alessa whipped around to find Damon clutching onto the crook of her right elbow.

Taken by surprise, she froze.

As he realized he was staring, Damon lessened his grip and nervously dipped his hands into his jean's pockets. "I was headin' out and ... well, I ... thought, maybe you'd like to join me."

Having never seen him like this, all anxious and jumpy, Alessa's eyebrows unintentionally rose. "You want me to leave with you?"

"Yep, that's what I said." He pressed his lips together before glancing behind Alessa and acknowledging the blonde. "Hey."

"Damon," her friend responded, her voice cold.

"You do know leaving without permission is frowned upon?" Alessa asked.

He shrugged nonchalantly. "What are they going to do? Kick me out?"

They stood in awkward silence as Alessa contemplated her response.

"I'm going to take your silence as a no. I'll go now," Damon mumbled, backing away.

Alessa tilted her head at the blonde, meeting her suspicious glare, and smirked before running after him. "No, Damon, wait."

Relieved, he relaxed and extended the crook of his arm. "It's about time. Come on. Let's get out of here."

Letting go of her insecurities, she wrapped her arm around his, and they hurried down the hall.

Heading outside, they left tracks in the freshly fallen snow as they walked toward the city's edge.

A snowflake landed on Damon's nose. "I see our elders are going for a festive vibe today."

Stepping through the protective, shimmering wall of light surrounding their hidden city, Damon and Alessa disappeared into the snow-covered trees.

She trailed close behind as they headed down the street and around the next corner. As the cold sliced through her ash-colored sweater, she instantly regretted not having grabbed a jacket.

She stared at the back of Damon's black combat boots with her head tucked down. The bottoms of his blue jeans were darkening, and as her eyes drifted up to his back pockets, her gaze lingered on his flexing buttocks.

Damon stopped abruptly, and Alessa collided with him. "Shit. Sorry."

He chuckled, opening the passenger door to his black Z28. "It's no big deal." He gestured for her to get in.

Alessa rubbed her freezing hands as Damon hurried to the car's driver's side.

He turned on the heated seats, and she moaned as the warmth radiated from the leather. "Oh, man."

A short drive later, they arrived at a quaint local coffee shop.

Killing the engine, Damon jumped out of the car, and as Alessa placed her foot on the wet ground, she looked up to find his hand extended toward her.

Surprised by his gentleman-like demeanor, she placed her hand within his, and he escorted her to the front of the small brick building.

Damon opened the door and stepped to the side. "Here we are."

A shivering Alessa ran through the entrance, rubbing her hands up and down her arms.

Several well-used wooden chairs were positioned around eight tables, closer to the bar, while two loveseats sat across from one another with a rectangular coffee table in between. In the far corner, a sliding ladder was propped up beside an oversized chair with an impressive collection of books extending from wall to wall.

Damon held up two fingers as he addressed the barista. "Hey, Jess. Two hot chocolates, please."

"You got it, love." The woman smiled sweetly.

Alessa clasped her shaking hands and held them to her mouth, blowing hot air onto her numb fingers.

Finally noticing her chattering teeth, Damon shrugged off his black leather jacket. "I'm such an idiot," he scolded himself before draping his heavily lined jacket over her shoulders.

Grasping Alessa's frigid hand, he pulled her over to the fireplace. "Come here."

Stopping before the warm fire, Damon sat Alessa down in an oversized brown leather chair before plopping in an identical chair directly in front of her.

He wrapped his warm hands around hers before lifting Alessa's fingers to his soft lips. Gazing into her eyes, he blew a breath of hot air, forcing feeling back into her, one sharp pinprick at a time.

Damon's lips turned up in a lazy smile. "That better?"

Unable to speak, Alessa nodded slowly, inhaling a jagged breath.

What was happening to her?

A server approached their chairs and handed them red and white mugs. "Two hot chocolates."

Alessa withdrew her hands from Damon's and graciously took one. "Thank you."

With a deep inhale, she breathed in the steam from the drink and leaned back into Damon's jacket. Snuggling further into the black leather, she was surrounded by Damon's enticing scent of cinnamon and musk.

Her insides warmed as liquid chocolate dripped down the back of her throat, and her muscles relaxed while she watched sparks fly out of the wood-burning fireplace.

Embers drifted through the air before landing on the floor, where the cool tiles snuffed them out.

"I've never seen you like this," Damon said.

"Hmm?" Alessa asked in a daze.

"You always seem so tense. As if you're always prepared for something bad to happen."

Alessa pressed her lips together, and her body stiffened.

"No, don't do that," he pleaded. "I'm just glad I'm not the only one who likes the vibe here."

"Where are we, exactly?"

"You don't get out much, do you?" Damon jested.

Alessa took another drink. "I won't leave unless I'm on assignment. No reason to."

Damon leaned onto his knees, grasping his mug between his hands. "This is my escape while stationed at this compound."

Her eyebrow arched unintentionally. "A coffee shop?"

"Yes, is that so hard to believe?" Damon sat up defensively.

"I never would've guessed this to be your scene. You seem more like all work and no play."

"Ouch."

"I mean, I didn't know you read books," Alessa responded without thinking.

Damon laughed and sat back in his chair. "Well, damn. This is just getting better."

"Shit!" Alessa blushed. "I'm going to stop talking now."

He held his hand up. "That's ok. I know I come off as a bit of a hard ass."

"A bit?" she asked, sarcasm dripping from her voice.

"I'm not going to apologize for the way I teach. It's how I was raised—to be a strong leader. And someday, I'll be expected to teach my children the same lessons I was taught, to ensure a strong future for our people."

His confession surprised Alessa. "You want kids?"

He took a drink of his hot chocolate rather than answering.

She breathed. "I don't mean to pry."

"But?" Damon urged her to continue.

"Are you not twenty-seven?"

A smile tugged at the corner of his lips. "I am."

"Isn't it an expectation for you to have chosen a suitable bloodline to marry or have announced an arranged marriage by now? I mean, especially since you are Wellborn."

"You certainly know your Spartan societal expectations," he replied.

"I'm sorry. I shouldn't have brought it up."

"I won't be thirty for a few years yet. And even though I am very much expected to find a strong woman to continue my bloodline, I have yet to find someone who doesn't just want me to have my children. It's annoying how women throw themselves at me without even knowing who I truly am—my hopes, my desires. I could be one hell of a shady guy for all they know, but they don't care, as long as I give them the power of mothering my offspring. I want to have a family, not simply procreate. Besides, what my father did to my mother left a bad taste in my mouth regarding the falsities of marriage. Are you aware of how my mother left this world?"

Alessa shook her head.

"My eldest brother and I were at training camp when my amazing, self-sacrificing mother died in the same plane crash as two of my older brothers and younger sister. Exactly one week to the day after her death, my father married his second wife." He closed his eyes. "My mother was the embodiment of love and light, and since losing her, I haven't found another woman who remotely comes close." Damon blinked tears from his eyes and cleared his throat. "But yeah, someday I'll be expected to pass on my lineage. What about you? When do you plan on popping out little Alessas?" He lifted his mug to his lips.

Alessa stared uncomfortably at the mug between her hands. "I don't want children."

Shocked, his lips fell slack. "Ever?"

She traced the rim of her coffee mug with a finger as her cheeks reddened. "All the reasons someone should be a mother don't pertain to me."

Damon's eyebrows scrunched together. "That can't be true."

Alessa stared at him incredulously. "How would you know?"

"I mean, I can't see you not being a good mother ... someday."

"Well, thank you, I guess." Alessa smiled politely. "But not being Wellborn limits my potential suitors, and not being a blood-born Spartan makes it damn near impossible. Honestly, I'm at peace with never having biological children. I make one hell of an aunt."

"Huh. I've never met a Spartan woman who didn't put having children first. It's refreshing."

Alessa laughed. "That's the first time I've heard it referred to as a positive."

Damon inhaled the steam from his mug. "What makes you think you won't find happiness with someone of your status?"

"If you must know, I've never given love the time of day. I'm not looking to fall head over heels for someone who is going to leave me or die someday. We're all alone in the end."

Damon whistled. "Damn, Alessa. That's deep. But also morbid."

She pointed a finger at him. "Morbid but true."

Damon stilled, and his deep sapphire blue eyes bore into her. "Ever think you just haven't found the right person yet?"

Alessa choked on her hot drink. "No, that's not possible. Everyone around me knows there's a darkness within my heart that cannot be tamed."

His eyes locked on hers. "Maybe your darkness shouldn't be tamed. Maybe it should be embraced."

Alessa's breathing hitched, and she broke away from his gaze. "Now who's deep?"

He tilted his head forward and laughed. "Not bad for a man who doesn't read. Now, enough of our existential discussion. You know what this drink needs?"

Damon placed his mug on the table before pressing his hand into the cushion beside her thigh. Leaning toward Alessa, he reached into his leather jacket, extracted a small bottle from the inner lining, and untwisted the cap. Keeping an eye on the barista, he discreetly poured the light brown liquid into Alessa's hot chocolate.

She grasped the mug between her hands, brought it to her nose, and smelled the sweet alcohol. "Irish cream?"

He confirmed Alessa's suspicion while pouring the liquid into his cup with a cheeky grin.

"Mmm," she moaned as the mixture of hot chocolate and alcohol burned down her throat.

Damon grinned devilishly as he tucked the bottle between the seat cushion and the arm of his chair. "I'm not one to partake in hard liquor, but this is not liquor; it is a liqueur."

Alessa cocked her head to the side. "Is this how you woo all the girls?"

Damon stared at her incredulously. "You, of all people, should know not to believe everything people say."

"You're right. I'm sorry."

Damon took a drink from his mug. "Especially since you're the first person I've brought here."

Embarrassed, Alessa swallowed the lump in her throat. "Oh."

He leaned forward, pressed himself in between her legs, and whispered breathily in her ear. "Besides, if I were trying to seduce you, I wouldn't need alcohol."

Slammed into the present, Alessa's stomach dropped, and as her emotions pushed her over the edge, she snapped.

CHAPTER TWENTY-FIVE

Alessa's eyes burned as they became a fierce emerald green, and she twisted down and around, pressing up into her captor's arms. Throwing the men off balance, they released their hold before she yanked a knife from the belt of one of the Bodyguards and hit him in the nose with its hilt.

Blood sprayed from the man's nostrils while she grabbed a handgun from another suit's jacket pocket.

Amidst the chaos, Brielle hit the floor and crawled to the side of the room.

A silver-suited man stood, stunned, to the left of Alessa as she shot him point-blank in the middle of his chest.

As his lifeless body flew backward, he took out another Bodyguard positioned directly behind him.

Alessa flipped the knife up in the air and caught it by the handle before she chucked it into the person restraining Damon's left arm.

As the man clutched his bleeding throat, he collapsed, and the remaining Bodyguard, still holding Damon, released him.

With a groan, Damon slumped down to the floor, and as

several guards pointed their weapons at Alessa, she grabbed the nearest silver suit and held him in front of her chest.

As the bullets struck his torso, he grunted, and his entire body vibrated back and forth.

The clicking of empty chambers echoed throughout the vaulted living room, and as she dropped her human shield, Alessa pulled two knives out from the man's belt loop.

She charged forward and was surprised by two men wielding large swords. Hitting the floor, Alessa rolled into a somersault and landed on her backside between them.

She drove one blade down into one man's right foot and another blade into the other one's left.

Both men howled in unison as they stumbled sideways.

Standing upright, Alessa jerked the knives out of the men's feet and extended her arms out to either side, sinking the blades deep into their stomachs.

Running toward the nearest silver suit, Alessa kicked off the wall, wrapped her thighs around the man's neck, and twisted his body as they fell to the ground. She landed on his chest and balanced, extracting two guns from his chest strap.

Alessa unloaded a round of bullets into three of the five remaining Bodyguards, bloodying their pristine silver suits.

Using the computer desk for support, Damon got up and leaned unsteadily against its tabletop. He forced himself to stand upright and remain conscious as the blurry room appeared to tilt.

Brielle dug into a fallen Bodyguard's jacket and emerged holding a gun. As she raised the weapon, Alessa punched Brielle hard in the jaw, knocking her down to the floor.

Ignoring the woman's cries, Alessa rushed over to Damon's backpack, slung it over her shoulder, and dipped underneath his arm. "Run!" she commanded.

With Damon draped over her shoulders, Alessa propelled them toward the open window with every ounce of strength she had left.

Within seconds, she calculated the distance from the window to the train tracks below and determined the velocity needed to survive the jump.

"Damon, jump now!" Alessa demanded.

Hitting the open air, they kicked off the windowsill and free-fell into the night before slamming onto the top of a moving train.

They continued sliding toward the edge of the car, and as Damon slipped off the far side, Alessa caught his hand at the last second.

Damon's body dangled precariously above the tracks, and as the cars trembled below their bodies, she struggled not to lose her grip.

"Damon!" she grunted as her fingers ached. "Damon, help me. I can't do this alone!" she yelled over the deafening wind.

Exhausting the remnants of his strength, Damon reached up for the ladder and took hold of the metal bar. As he clung to the side of the moving train, Alessa guided him into the nearest car.

She pushed him inside just in time for his knees to buckle and give way. Her grip tightened as his body went limp, and she helped him down to the ground as gracefully as possible before wiggling out of the backpack.

Alessa's adrenaline decreased as the thrill of the escape subsided, and as she deactivated, her irises returned to their original sky-blue.

Alessa sat beside Damon and lifted his head, placing it in her lap before she leaned back against the rear of the empty passenger car. She was drained, both emotionally and physically.

His eyebrows wrinkled up in angst as his eyes darted frantically back and forth behind closed eyelids.

Alessa's fingers hovered above his face for a moment before she ran her fingers through his soft brown hair, and as she gently massaged his scalp, Damon's features relaxed.

Tears welled up in her eyes while she mindlessly stroked his hair and thought back to the red pill he was forced to swallow. Tears spilled over onto her cheeks as she choked back the urge to scream.

For the first time in what seemed like forever, Alessa felt alive. She was finally recalling bits and pieces of her former life, including who Damon was.

He was the only one who came back for her. That had to mean something. At least, she hoped it did.

The weight of their current situation settled deep in the pit of her stomach. How was she supposed to tell Damon he only had a few days to live?

The familiar ache of a migraine snuck in behind her eyes, and as the pain spread, Alessa's eyelids grew heavy, and she slumped over, unconscious.

As Damon and Alessa slept, the train jolted them back and forth.

Alessa remained propped up against the wall until a short time later when Damon's violent shaking awoke her.

"Damon?" she squeaked, struggling to blink the sleep from her eyes. "Shh," she stroked his cheek.

Out of the corner of her eye, Alessa spied a bunched-up wool blanket left behind on a bench. She gently set Damon's head on the ground, stood up, and stretched her stiff back. Picking up the scratchy blanket, she stumbled back over to his unconscious form, draped the blanket over him, and curled up into his side.

Damon's muscles relaxed, and a few minutes later, his shivering stopped altogether.

"Mmm," Damon moaned, and he unexpectedly wrapped his arms around Alessa's waist, pulling her in close. She gasped as every muscle stiffened in response to his touch.

Over the next hour, Alessa tried to remember her dreams from the past month. Somewhere in the recesses of her mind, there had to be a clue to saving Damon. She hoped to replay her memories like scenes from a movie but was instead gifted disjointed images and blurry figures. Blips of information came to her—such as a blonde girl's face, random mountains, Eric Lansing's cocky grin, an older man standing in the rain, a wood cabin in the woods, and then, finally, the bang of a gunshot.

She jumped at the sound of the disembodied noise.

Another hour passed by before Damon whimpered her name. "Alessa ... Alessa ... It's so hot." He threw the warm blanket off to the side as his forehead furrowed in distress.

Alessa touched his rosy cheeks and was alarmed at the intense heat radiating from his skin.

"Shit," Alessa hissed, scanning the room for a way to cool him down.

"Alessa..." he moaned again.

Her stomach clenched as she realized the quickest way to reduce Damon's body temperature was to remove his clothing. Alessa's cheeks blushed as she unbuttoned his shirt and peeled the fabric from his sweltering torso.

Flipping the shirt's fabric to the side, she exposed his well-defined abs and burly chest. His soft, dark brown chest hair curled around his two pink nipples, and she felt the burn behind her eyes.

Unable to block the onslaught of emotions that bombarded her, Alessa chastised herself. "Stop it." She licked her lips and exhaled loudly as she glanced at his belt. "Seriously, Alessa, get over yourself and out of your head. It's not like this is a turn-on," she cocked her head to the side and swallowed, "for him."

Grabbing his belt, she loosened its hold before unbuttoning his pants, and after crawling toward his feet, she tugged on each leg until the jeans pooled around his ankles, revealing his navy boxer briefs.

Tearing her gaze away from Damon, Alessa tossed his jeans to the side of the car, and as his muscular body trembled with fever, he reached across Alessa's lap, coiling himself tightly around her thighs.

While nuzzling into her stomach, his hot breath caressed the inside of her thighs and groin. She gasped in surprise as she moistened, and her body tensed within his embrace. "Oh, come on..."

Staring at his beautiful pink lips and full eyelashes, she gave up resisting the urge not to touch Damon and trailed his cheekbone with her fingertips, caressing the stubble on his face.

As Damon's shaking reduced to a subtle tremor, Alessa relaxed into him, and after what seemed like hours, her eyelids grew heavy before finally closing.

CHAPTER TWENTY-SIX

Damon swayed back and forth, blinking the fog from his eyes. "Where the...?" he mumbled, disoriented. Tilting his head back, he saw Alessa propped up against the back of the train car, asleep, and after he uncurled his arm from around her, Damon sat upright and groaned.

His body felt as though it had been through a meat grinder.

While rubbing his sore arms, Damon realized he had been stripped of his clothing. "What in the...?"

In Alessa's dream, she lay naked on a crumpled-up blanket in the middle of a field. Her fingers intertwined with another's fingers while gazing at the bright stars above.

The man lifted their joined hands and pointed at a collection of stars. "That is the Big Dipper. It comprises seven stars, and the two pointer stars on the end form a diagonal line across the sky, pointing to Polaris, the North Star."

"Mmm." Alessa sleepily blinked as the man pressed her fingertips against his lips, gently kissing each one.

"Alessa. Alessa, wake up," Damon interrupted her dream.

"Hmm?" she moaned.

"Why am I naked?" he demanded.

"What?" Alessa's eyes burst open.

"I said, why am I naked?" He pointed at himself.

"Oh. You were feverish before, so I cooled you down the only way I knew how." She rushed over to Damon's pile of clothes and tossed them in his direction before crossing her arms over her chest defensively. "And you're not naked. I left your underwear on."

Damon tugged his pants on with a crooked grin. "You sure you weren't taking advantage of me?"

Mortified, Alessa's eyes fell to the ground, her face flushing a fiery red as Damon buttoned his pants.

"Where are we?" he asked.

Maintaining her distance, Alessa responded. "On a train."

"A train..." He stilled for a moment before continuing to dress himself. "And how did we end up on this train?"

She grimaced, realizing she'd have to explain the ordeal to Damon. "You don't remember?"

Damon's eyebrows rose while awaiting her response. "What exactly are you referring to?"

"Damn, that drug did a number on you," Alessa replied.

He stared at her, astonished. "You drugged me?"

"No, I didn't drug you. Shut up and let me explain. Jeez." Alessa ran her fingers through her hair. "When we went to your psychotic girlfriend's house—"

Damon held up his hand to interject. "Brielle is *not* my girlfriend."

Alessa rolled her eyes and threw her hands up. "Ex-girlfriend, whatever-the-fuck she is." She breathed heavily. "Anyway, shortly after we got there, that bitch called the Bodyguards to report us. Then, they arrived, and she shot you up with a ... um ... a neuron transfuse. Yeah, that's what she called it. And you became a lump of hot mess."

Damon stared at her, unmoving.

"Oh, and while you took a little nap, I activated and kicked everyone's ass before we jumped out of her apartment window and landed on top of a moving train."

He shook his head in disbelief. "There's no way Brielle used a neuron transfuse on me."

"Come again?" Alessa leaned in toward Damon and blinked for dramatic effect.

"She wouldn't do that to me."

"Then don't fucking believe me. I don't care." Alessa angrily plopped down on the floor. "It's not like I fought every person at her apartment to save your life or anything."

He looked at Alessa, pained. "Look, I'm sorry. It's not that I don't believe you; it's that I don't want to. Is that everything that happened? She called the Bodyguards, drugged me with a neuron transfuse, and you got us the hell out?"

Unsure of how to tell Damon he was dying, Alessa turned away, bit her lower lip, and jaggedly nodded. "Pretty much," she lied.

He exhaled loudly while rubbing his forehead. "Okay, so where are we going?"

"I think I heard them mention D.C. over the intercom. Hey, what's with the sword fighting? I thought we were all about technology, but when I had to fight those guys back there, they broke out swords and knives."

Damon chuckled and rubbed his hands together. "You know how I said we can connect to certain weapons created by our company?"

"Yeah. And?"

"All the Bodyguards know is we can connect with technology. They don't know to what extent. As a failsafe, they rely on hand-to-hand combat. That way, they have another way to fight if we ever connect to their weapons and control them. Besides, if a gun runs out of bullets, it's useless, but if they know how to fight with their hands, it gives them a better chance of winning. At least against those in the general population," he winked.

Alessa stared ahead, contemplating the new information. "Oh. Do they have implants, like us?"

"Some do. Did you notice any of their eyes change color?"

She shook her head. "I didn't."

He pointed at Alessa while continuing his explanation. "Then those were generic Bodyguards. There are different levels. However, instead of their microchips being individualized like ours are, theirs are more of an all-for-one deal.

"Spartan chips enhance the abilities we already have or specialize in, while theirs give them a certain set of skills that every Elite Bodyguard can access with their implant. Then, they can individually pick and choose which skill to improve upon. Also, they can be controlled. Spartans cannot."

Deep in thought, she squinted. "If these Elite Bodyguards have a microchip like we do, can't Bodyguards download things like we can?"

"Not that I'm aware of." Damon stretched his neck to the

side and rubbed his sore muscles. "Even though they have microchips, they don't have the technology we do. It's similar but is used for a different purpose.

"Ugh. I feel like someone kicked the living shit out of me. When we landed on the train, I must've pulled a muscle or ten."

Alessa nearly choked on her saliva. "Hmm, yeah. I mean, you were dangling off the side when I grabbed your arm and kept you from falling to your death."

"Thanks for that, by the way." Damon flashed a handsome smile.

Alessa waved her hand in the air dismissively. "You saved me at the club; I saved you from being crushed by a train. I'd say we're even now."

Damon chortled as he buttoned his raven black shirt. "Of all the trains passing by, we happen to land on the one going to Washington, D.C."

"Is that a good thing?"

"It just so happens Washington, D.C. was intended to be our first stop."

Alessa scrunched up her nose. "First stop of?"

"Before I blacked out, I finished downloading the information Brielle had pulled from her sources."

Alessa stared at him blankly, waiting for him to explain himself.

"I downloaded the information she had displayed on the monitor to my chip and stored it."

Alessa froze. "You know how to get to Eric and his men?"

"Eric Lansing's details were a bit sketchy. He owns several houses throughout the world and a yacht. I'm hoping one of the men we interrogate will know where to find him."

Alessa dropped her head and rubbed her eyes. "Alright, then. Who's first?"

"Craig Neuhauser. This man is one sick fuck. He's been known to test the drugs on the homeless to demonstrate the side effects for his clients. He's like how public relations is if they were to forgo all human rights."

Alessa covered her mouth in disgust. "That's horrible."

Damon extended his wrist, whipped his hand around, and popped a cellphone projection from his black watch.

"Uh, what is that about?" Alessa's eyebrow arched in confusion. "Where did that come from?"

Ignoring her, he snapped his fingers, and a small rectangle manifested before his eyes. "Call Steve," he commanded.

"Wait, how are we going to get Craig to talk?" Alessa questioned Damon. He held up his finger, signaling her to give him a minute.

"Hey, Steve, it's Damon ... Yeah, business is good. Look, I need to ask a favor. Can you take Neuhauser out for breakfast this morning? I can't say why ... I don't know, make something up." Damon's voice dropped an octave. "I don't want to hear it. You follow orders your superiors give, and I happen to be one of those. You are in this position to be his colleague. Do your job and tell him whatever you need to, to get him to meet with you ... Yeah, yeah ... We're still working on the case. We found a new way in ... Yes. I need him distracted until ten a.m. ... I don't care where; text me the address." He disconnected the call and flicked his wrist again until the phone disappeared into his watch.

Alessa stared at Damon, awaiting an explanation.

"Oh, you wanted to know what that was. That's the phone I use when I'm not in the presence of the general pop. They'd lose their minds if they saw me using that versus a physical cellphone. You know you have one, too. On your watch, back home."

Alessa stared at her naked wrist as a woman's voice blasted from the overhead speakers. "We are currently approaching Washington, D.C. Please gather your belongings."

"Look, Alessa, with what little time we have left, I need to teach you how to activate your microchip intentionally."

Skeptical, she arched her right eyebrow. "I thought you mentioned my activation was purely linked to my emotions and uncontrolled."

"Don't give me that look," Damon scolded. "You need to listen to what I'm telling you. Our ability to activate is tied to our deepest emotions: fear, love, hate ... But once you re-learn how to control your emotions and use them to turn on your programming, you can activate on command."

"And what if my trying to activate triggers an attack on my limbic system again?"

He pressed his lips together in contemplation before answering. "That's a risk we have to take."

Alessa's breathing faltered, and she looked away from Damon. It was the first time she had felt the weight of her responsibilities as a Spartan, a protector of humankind.

Damon instructed Alessa on the hows and whys of activating their microchips and then demonstrated his activation until they heard the train's brakes screech against the tracks.

He placed his hand on the door, getting ready to exit. "You ready?"

Alessa struggled to keep her panic beneath the surface and inhaled a shaky breath. "And if I'm not?"

Damon shrugged and said, "Then a lot of innocent people are going to die."

CHAPTER TWENTY-SEVEN

Damon hopped down to the tracks below before turning around and catching Alessa.

Together, they sprang onto the platform and blended in with the small crowd heading toward the train station.

The patrons ranged from those adorned from head to toe in protective gear to others walking around completely unprotected, without even a mask.

Even though a highly contagious disease was being passed around, the train station was surprisingly busy. Trains whistled loudly, and announcements were made over the intercom.

Passing the women's restroom, Alessa's anxiety got the best of her, and her heart beat out of control as she panicked. "I-I'll be right back."

She stumbled to the bathroom counter after falling in through the swinging door. The tips of her trembling fingers gripped the cold, sharp edge, and her lips tingled as she peered at her pale reflection in the mirror.

It was no surprise she was breaking down. Alessa leaned

into the glass and inspected the pronounced red veins invading the whites of her eyes.

Exhaling shakily, she splashed cold water on her face, and as the cool liquid dripped down her cheeks, she replayed Damon's coaching inside her mind.

"Our ability to activate is tied to our deepest emotions: fear, love, hate ... But once you re-learn how to control your emotions and use them to turn on your programming, you can activate on command. At first, you may only be able to activate your microchip when you're emotionally charged. Try to relax, take slow, deep breaths, and feel. Feel an emotion so deep that it triggers you. Only then can you regain control of your true self."

As much as she hated the thought of remembering more details of her torture, Alessa closed her eyes and focused her energy on recalling who the pharmaceutical rep was. She concentrated on his name, Craig, his picture, and breathed in and out, relaxing her mind well enough to relive their horrible moments together.

The impact of Craig's hand punching deep into her gut jerked Alessa backward, and before hitting Alessa's right cheek, he cracked his knuckles and balled his hand into a tight fist.

With the impact, her head whipped violently to the left. As she glared up into the man's eyes, she spat out the blood pooling in the side of her mouth onto the concrete floor.

Another person in the far corner spoke out from behind their lit cigar. "Let's take a break, gentlemen. Looks like she's going to be noncompliant for the time being."

Craig scowled and spat next to Alessa. "I'll see you later," he promised before opening the exit door.

It slammed shut, and she was bombarded by an onslaught of violence, all of which she had endured at Craig's hand.

Alessa's irises flashed bright green, and she convulsed as hatred for the man burned throughout her entire being. Every fiber of her body pulsated with the need to seek revenge as adrenaline coursed through her veins.

With her memory of the demented drug rep restored, Alessa was no longer conflicted about obtaining information through any means necessary. Now, she looked forward to their encounter.

Finding comfort in spinning the bejeweled band around her finger, Alessa focused on slowing her breathing.

"You're in the present. You're not in the white room. You're safe," she reassured herself. Regaining control, her blue-eyed reflection returned.

"Huh. And just like that..." Alessa exited the restroom.

Damon stalked a nicely dressed man in the train station's main hall. As he came to a halt, Damon continued walking forward and dipped his hand deep into the man's coat pocket. "Oh! I am so sorry, sir, that was my fault. I really should pay more attention to where I'm going," Damon apologized while hurrying away with the man's wallet.

Eyeing Alessa, Damon motioned for her to meet him by the front doors, and as they matched pace on the busy sidewalk, his watch vibrated and buzzed. He whipped his wrist around and held projected glasses in his hand. Placing the pair of blue-outlined frames on the bridge of his nose, he looked at an illuminated screen in one lens.

"Where in the hell did those come from?" Alessa demanded. "And what was that about, back there? With you and that guy?"

Damon held up the wallet. "We need money. Anyone who dresses that nice always has cash on them."

She scolded him silently with a glance.

"What?" He removed his glasses and flicked his wrist to make them disappear again. "It's not like we have another option. I can't exactly take money out without alerting our elders about where I am."

She hurried behind Damon as he walked quickly away. "Why were you so nonchalant with using your technology just then, but earlier—"

He waved his hand in dismissal. "No one will question me putting on a pair of sunglasses. They'll justify me pulling them out of nowhere, as they didn't see me pull them out of my pocket. It's amazing what people can create with their imagination to make sense of something."

Damon lifted his hand high in the air and stepped onto the curb. "It's already after nine o'clock, and I only know where Neuhauser is until ten. We've gotta get moving."

Alessa stepped beside him as a taxi pulled up. "Where are we going?"

"Come on." Damon opened the door and waved for Alessa to get in first.

She slid across the back seat before he plopped in next to her, placing his backpack on the floor between his legs.

"Delizioso, please," Damon instructed the driver before returning his direction to Alessa. "You know that guy I called this morning?"

"Yeah?"

"He's one of us and has been working undercover with Erebos Industries for quite some time. I ordered him to distract Craig this morning, so we have a place with limited security. They're eating breakfast at a local restaurant, and that is where we're heading."

After a brief fifteen-minute drive, the yellow taxi pulled up next to an upscale restaurant.

Alessa fingered her sexy lace top and tight pants. "Uh, Damon, I am not dressed for this place."

Damon paid the driver. "Don't worry about it. We're not going inside," he reassured her while stepping onto the sidewalk.

Alessa stood upright and nervously clasped her hands together. She played with her ring as Damon touched her arm and escorted her into the café next to the upscale restaurant.

"Good morning," Damon greeted the hostess. "We'd like the patio, please."

As the young woman glanced up from her podium, her eyes nearly popped out of her head as her lips fell into a seductive smile behind her transparent mask. She stood tall, pushing her breasts up and out.

"This way," she directed while her hips bounced dramatically from left to right.

Unable to hide her annoyance, Alessa's face scrunched up as they made their way through the building.

The hostess directed them onto the enclosed sidewalk in front of the café. "Your waitress's name is Holly, and she'll be right with you," she informed Alessa. "And I'm Becky. Please don't hesitate if you need anything, anything at all," she directed at Damon.

He flashed a charming smile while rubbing the stubble on his cheek. "Thanks."

"There are a few things I need to get." Damon set Alessa down in the chair. "I'll be back soon."

As he turned to leave, she reached out, grabbing his hand tight.

He paused and looked down at her. Touching the back of her hand, he leaned in. "I'm coming back. I promise."

She nodded and exhaled a sigh of relief, reluctantly loosening her grip, and Damon disappeared back inside the café.

The masked waitress approached Alessa's table. "Hello, Miss. Do you know what you'd like to order?"

"Uh, sure. I want a hot chocolate, please."

"That'll be one hot chocolate. Anything else?" the waitress asked.

"Um..." Alessa pointed to a neighboring table's order. "I guess one of those pastries as well."

"And one blueberry scone," the waitress nodded. "I'll be right back."

As the waitress walked away, Alessa leaned back in the chair made of twisted iron as her mind wandered. She contemplated her and Craig's future encounter—everything from what she would say to the man to how they would keep him from telling Erebos her location played in her imagination. As Alessa fantasized about shooting the man in the head, the waitress startled her back to reality.

"Here you are." The waitress set the drink and pastry on the table.

Alessa jumped. "Wow, that was fast."

"If I can't get a scone and a hot chocolate to you within

three minutes, I'd be fired by now," the waitress smirked. "Are you sure there's nothing else I can get you?"

Alessa brought the steaming drink to her lips. "No, this is great. Thank you."

Grasping the hot mug, Alessa scrunched her legs up in the chair, and as the chilly morning air seeped in through her thin lace shirt, her fingertips soaked in the drink's warmth.

A group of teenagers laughed across the street. While the boys playfully hit one other on the arm, the girls giggled next to them. Alessa focused on the shorter girl with light blonde hair, and her eyes flickered green.

CHAPTER TWENTY-EIGHT

In her memory, she was standing in a room full of assorted gymnastics equipment, and the walls were covered, floor to ceiling, with weapons. The room was painted a deep red, and the lights above her were dim.

She jumped up and kicked, twisting mid-air before landing on the black floor mat. Sprinting across the room, she propelled into a cartwheel, two forward round-offs, and a forward flip. When she stuck the landing, her lungs burned, and her muscles ached.

Eyeing the pseudo walls, she darted toward them before landing on the first level. Alessa then jumped to the second and third before skipping the fourth, landing on the fifth level. Pulling herself up, she balanced across the beam and flipped onto another structure hanging just above the floor. She then rolled forward before gracefully diving off the platform.

Alessa landed safely back down on the floor mat, and a young woman with golden hair applauded from the corner of the room.

She held her hands on either side of her pink lips and hollered, "Well done, Lessie!"

As the scene dissipated, Alessa leaned over the side of the table and dry heaved. Her vision swam, and she fought back the urge to black out. Focusing on her breathing, she inhaled slowly to the count of six before exhaling to ten. "I've seen her before," she mumbled aloud. *And every time I get this sick, I remember someone I was more connected to. Who is she? It's not like if I ask Damon, he'll tell me. I guess I'll wait for my subconscious to reveal her identity.*

She looked down at the remnants of her scone. "I wonder if Damon's eaten yet." She flagged down the waitress.

"Is everything okay?"

"Yeah, could I get two more of these to go, please?"

The young waitress nodded, placing her red pad in the front of her apron. "Two blueberry scones coming right up."

As she waited for the masked woman to return with the pastries, Alessa watched a man and woman lean against the far brick building. Their arms were wrapped around one another in a tight embrace.

As their lips touched, Alessa activated once more.

Alessa was being pushed back up against a smooth wall as a pair of large masculine hands explored her body.

The man pressed his hips into her own, and as Alessa's head tilted to the side, he nipped and licked up the side of her neck. His thumb was stroking her jawline before his mouth continued moving further down, kissing along her collarbone.

The man's fingers reached around her backside, pulling her off the wall.

As she slammed up against his hard body, she gasped and moaned.

Their lips melted into one another as he placed his free hand beneath her chin, demanding she give up control.

Her strength dwindled, leaving Alessa gasping for breath as her body begged for her to give in to his touch.

"Alessa?" Damon placed his hand on Alessa's shoulder.

"Mmm?" She jumped at his touch, spilling the rest of her drink all over the table. "Shit!"

"Whoa." Damon's lips parted in a sideways grin. "What are you daydreaming about?"

"Um, nothing."

"Are you okay?" Damon asked.

Alessa blushed with embarrassment. "Yep, no, I'm good." She rubbed her burning eyes. "Let's just—let's get out of here."

Unconvinced, he squinted. "You sure you're alright? Was your chip activated?" He stepped toward her.

Alessa glanced up at Damon's hardened jawline and licked her lips, still feeling the physical effects of the memory.

"Here you go," the waitress interrupted them. While handing Alessa the scones, she saw the brown liquid spilled all over the table.

"I'm sorry. I, uh—" Alessa started.

"Can we have the check?" Damon put a stop to her rambling.

"Yep, I got it right here." The waitress took out her black flip book and tore off the bill. "Don't worry, hun. I'll clean this right up."

Damon whipped cash out of his pocket and counted it while Alessa stood awkwardly off to the side. He flashed a charming smile as he handed the waitress a small stack of bills. "Keep the change."

As the waitress counted the money, she beamed. "Are you sure?"

Damon nodded and reached back for Alessa to join him. "Yes, I'm sure."

As Alessa's hand slipped into Damon's, he jogged while hollering back at the waitress. "Have a good one!"

Dashing through the restaurant and out the front, Alessa reluctantly pulled her hand from his grasp. "I got these for you." She held up the bag containing two blueberry scones.

Damon beamed as he took the pastries. "Hell, yeah! I'm starving, thank you."

He took a bite from the first pastry and hurried toward a side alley. Finishing breakfast in record time, Damon set his backpack on the ground.

She finally noticed the plastic bag he was carrying. "What's in there?"

He reached into the bag and pulled out a pile of clothes before handing Alessa a short black dress and fuchsia-colored heels.

"What's this for?"

"Put it on," Damon instructed.

"Why am I—?"

"Do as I ask, Alessa," he demanded.

Alessa huffed and marched behind the nearby dumpster.

She stripped off her jeans, shirt, and boots and shimmied into the tight dress. "How did you know my shoe size?"

Damon stammered, taken aback by the intimacy of the question, "D-don't all women wear a seven?"

Confused, she stepped out behind the dumpster and faced Damon while tugging her skirt. "Yeah, sure, Damon. Why did we need to change, and why do I need to wear this short skirt?"

He buttoned his pants, his eyebrows arching as he looked her up and down. The fabric clung to Alessa's womanly curves as she stood before him with her hands on her hips.

"I could tell you hated being in Brielle's clothes." His lips relaxed into a seductive smile. "And because I wanted to see you in it."

Caught off guard by his response, Alessa felt exposed and pulled the white jacket out of the bag.

Chuckling to himself, he stripped off his shirt as she tugged on the long coat.

Alessa pulled the coat tight around her. "Before I went missing—"

Damon's eyes unintentionally darted over in her direction. "Yeah?"

"Was I seeing anyone?"

Damon's jaw flexed as he looked to the ground while slipping on his shoes.

"As in a boyfriend?" Alessa pressed.

His head darted up as he tied his shoes. "Why would you think that? Do you remember something? Is that what was going on back there at the restaurant?"

Too embarrassed to confess her sex-filled daydreams, Alessa shook her head back and forth fervently. "Nope, no. I was just wondering. I mean, I have this ring I feel very connected to, but I am unsure who gave it to me. Whether it was a friend or someone who meant more, I don't know. I'm trying to figure things out."

He huffed. "I'm sorry, but I can't tell you. But if you had a boyfriend, I'm sure he would have meant a great deal to you.

You know, if I were to tell you that information instead of you remembering on your own, your limbic system could become overloaded thanks to whatever concoction you were given.

"Besides, now isn't the time for this. You need to focus on what you're about to do. Things could go bad if—anyway, there's a switchblade and a few other toys in your pockets."

Alessa happily tossed Brielle's clothes and shoes into the trash before reaching into her right coat pocket. She anxiously fingered the blade. "I guess so."

Damon finished his look by placing a limo driver's hat atop his head.

"Well, don't you look distinguished?" Alessa giggled.

He shrugged the backpack over his right shoulder before handing Alessa a pair of oversized sunglasses.

Damon peeked around the side of the building, and she slid the glasses on in time for Craig's limo to pull up to the curb in front of the fancy restaurant.

"What's the plan?" Alessa inquired.

While looking around for inspiration, Damon smirked.

A pre-teen walked down the street, swinging a baseball bat around in circles.

"I'm workin' on it," he responded.

As the kid strolled by, Damon grabbed his arm and pulled him into the alleyway.

"Hey!" the kid yelled.

Damon gripped his upper arm tightly. "You wanna make some money?"

The kid glared suspiciously at Damon. "How much money we talkin' about?"

"Let's say two hundred dollars."

"For doing what, exactly?" He leaned away from Damon, his eyes full of distrust.

Damon pointed over to the black limo. "For smashing in that windshield."

The kid shook his head. "Yeah, I don't know. I could get in a lot of trouble for that."

"What if I make it four hundred?" Damon counted the cash in front of the boy.

The kid held out his hand. "Pay upfront, and you got a deal."

Damon narrowed his eyes at the boy. "I highly advise you not to take the money and run."

Craig exited the restaurant's front doors and walked toward the limo.

"Damon..." urged Alessa.

Handing the boy his payment, Damon nudged him forward. "Go get 'em."

CHAPTER TWENTY-NINE

As Craig sat in the limo's back seat, the kid ran up to the vehicle's windshield and smashed the bat hard onto the glass. The windshield cracked, branching out like an elaborate spider web.

The limo's driver swung his door open. "What in the hell do you think you're doing?" His face reddened in anger as he glared at the teenager snickering at him. "You little shit!" he yelled.

Laughing hysterically, the kid ran away while clutching his wooden bat.

"Get back here!" The driver bolted after him.

Damon sprinted for the open driver's side door and slid into the seat while Alessa darted for the vehicle's rear. Grasping the handle with her shaking hand, she opened the door and plopped beside the drug rep.

Craig glanced up at her in surprise. "Who are you?"

The limo jerked forward, and she slammed the door shut. After taking a deep breath, Alessa stared into his eyes. "You mean you don't recognize me?"

"Is this some kind of joke?" the drug rep demanded with a confused smile. "Is this one of those stripper-grams?"

Alessa's anger festered as her eyes began to burn.

Looking away from Alessa, he lowered the partition. "Driver, where are you taking me? This is not the right direction."

"I guess I do look a little different since the last time we were together," she interjected.

Annoyed, his attention returned to Alessa. "What are you saying? Seriously, you need to get out of here right now." He pointed at the car door.

Her eyes flickered green behind her darkened sunglasses as her rage intensified.

"Stop the car!" Craig shouted through the lowered partition.

Grabbing the side of her sunglasses, Alessa removed them slowly. "I'm stupid to have thought you would remember me. I mean, look at all those innocent lives you've taken. What's one more?"

The drug rep stared at her, and his anger melted into fear as recognition flashed across his face. "No ... no, this can't be."

Alessa cocked her head in amusement.

"You're dead. You ... I watched you die," Craig panicked. "Driver, stop this car immediately!"

Damon turned around and pulled his sunglasses low enough for Craig to see his eyes flash silver.

"This is impossible," Craig mumbled under his breath, his arms stretched across the back of the seat.

"No, this is not impossible, just very, very improbable. And you're correct in saying that you watched me die. My heart did stop. In fact, it stopped multiple times."

Alessa reached into her pocket for the switchblade. She

twisted the metal blade repeatedly for dramatic effect while secretly hoping not to have to use it. "Let's just say I made a deal with Hades."

Craig noticed her shaking hand. "Something's different about you." He analyzed her subtle movements through squinted eyes. "You're nervous."

"No, I'm not," she retorted defensively.

"Yes, yes you are." Craig relaxed back into his seat. "You are not the same girl I remember. Do you even know how to use that thing?"

Alessa swallowed the lump in her throat as she leaned forward, trying to appear confident. "Of course I do. Would you like a demonstration?"

"You'd better leave before I put you back in the ground," Craig sneered.

Alessa's eyes flared bright green, and she raised the blade in the air before slamming it down into his left thigh.

Craig screamed as his muscles split, and as he reached down to pull the cold steel from his leg, Alessa darted into her left pocket and pulled out a second knife. The drug rep's hand touched the blade's handle protruding from his thigh just as Alessa pressed her other weapon against his throat.

"You'll want to leave that in for now," Alessa suggested.

With the sharp dagger held against his trachea, Craig removed his hand from the handle. "What do you want from me?" his voice quivered.

"I'm going to be perfectly honest with you, Craig; I don't remember much about my past. However, I'm not too happy with the flashbacks I am having. I realize we can't go back in time and take back what you did to me. However, I will give you a chance to somewhat redeem yourself. All you need to do is tell me about the red pill's components and how to get to Eric Lansing."

"I have no idea what you're—"

"Uh, uh, uh. No lying," she interrupted, wagging her finger back and forth in front of his face.

Alessa grabbed the handgun, weighing down her jacket pocket, and yanked it out before jabbing it into his groin. "I don't have any qualms about firing a bullet into your buddies, so let's try this again. What are the components of the red pills, the pills Erebos Industries created?"

Craig grunted while nervously eyeing the gun. "Oh, you mean that pill."

She grinned sarcastically. "I thought this might help jog your memory."

"The pill's a genetically enhanced form of tuberculosis that, if ingested, causes liquidation of the individual's lungs within five, maybe six days—if you're lucky."

"But there has to be a cure."

"Not necessarily," he disagreed.

Alessa dug the gun further into his groin. "But there *is* a cure."

He whimpered. "You sound desperate. Someone you know take the damn thing?"

In one swift movement, Alessa scooted back, extended her arm, pointed the gun at his right shoulder, and squeezed the trigger.

Craig shrieked as the bullet ripped through his flesh and muscle before shattering bone.

She redirected the gun at his groin. "I'm asking the questions. Is there a way to reverse its effects?"

The man scowled and spat onto the floor near her fuchsia-colored shoe. "There is a cure. It's an oral serum," he grunted.

"It repairs any damage the red pill will have caused, but it has to be taken before one's death, or it won't be effective."

"So, what you're telling me is that as long as an infected person takes this cure before they die, all of the damage will be repaired?"

"That's what I just said," Craig spat through gritted teeth.

"Where can I find it?" she demanded.

"The only one with access to the cure would be the company's president."

"Eric Lansing..."

"The one and only. He's your guy, not me," Craig hissed in pain.

Alessa stared daggers at the drug rep.

Recognizing the homicidal look in her green eyes, Craig panicked. "Wait! Now that I think about it, Henry should also know something about the cure."

Alessa stared at Craig in silence, awaiting an explanation.

"You know, Henry Penway—the chemist who developed the drug? He'll probably know how to get to Eric since there wouldn't be enough time to make a new batch of the cure before they expired."

"Henry," Alessa repeated while Craig frantically nodded.

As the limo came to a stop, Craig anxiously glanced at the door. "Are we done?"

"Yes, Craig. You are." Alessa dropped her gun down in the man's lap and stabbed the knife through his right hand, down into the fabric of the seat, before yanking the switchblade out of his leg. Thrusting the cold steel in through his free hand, she pinned him to the leather.

As she shoved the barrel of the gun up beneath his chin, she growled, "Give Hades my regards."

"No!" Craig yelled as Alessa squeezed the trigger.

Bone fragments and brain matter exploded onto the seat and ceiling as his body fell limp.

She stared transfixed at Craig's lifeless body as blood dripped from his skull.

I just did that.

She cringed, and her stomach rolled.

Damon remained in the front seat, feeling weak and feverish. "Come on, man. Pull yourself together," he scolded himself, gripping the steering wheel. With a shake of his head, he took a slow, deep breath before grabbing his pack and exiting the car.

As he stepped onto the street, Alessa leaned out of the limo and vomited onto the concrete.

"You alright?" he asked, helping her out of the back seat.

"I killed him," she mumbled in shock.

Damon helped a forlorn Alessa steady herself. "There was no other way this was going to play out. Had you let Craig go, he would've gone straight to Eric, and then he would've known you were coming for him. Besides, Craig was the scum of the earth. The world's a better place without him in it."

Alessa shuddered. "I know what he did was horrible, but I just brutally executed the man. He had no way of defending himself."

Damon held onto her trembling shoulders. "You can't think like that. You're protecting the innocent by taking out the bad guys. This is what we do. This is your life's work."

A tear fell from Alessa's eye. "I had no idea ending a man's life would be so easy. I mean, I didn't even flinch when I—"

"It'll get easier, Alessa, I promise," Damon interjected.

She shook her head. "I'm not sure I want it to. I'm scared I'll lose myself."

Damon pulled her away from the bloody scene. "Come on, let's get out of here."

Alessa stumbled along as if in a trance. "He said we should talk to Henry Penway."

"Sounds like a plan. He was one of the men on our list, so I guess that makes our next stop Florida."

Pausing in front of the nearest dumpster, Damon stood behind Alessa. Helping her shrug out of the blood-stained coat, Damon turned it inside out and then used the soft lining to clean the splattered red spots off her skin.

Emotionally exhausted, Alessa stared silently into Damon's eyes as he intimately wiped the blood off her cheek.

Damon tossed the red-stained coat and hat into the dumpster before shrugging off his jacket. He then draped it across Alessa's bare shoulders and threw his backpack over his shoulder. She clung to the warm fabric and pulled it tighter while Damon stretched his arm behind her, guiding her toward a taxi.

By the time they reached the train station, Alessa was fighting to keep her eyes open, and after buying two tickets, they boarded the train to Fort Lauderdale.

Damon held Alessa's hand within his own and pulled her close as they made their way down the aisle.

Finally, he sat down next to the window and dropped his backpack onto the floor while Alessa collapsed into the seat next to him.

Damon threw his arms out to catch Alessa from falling over. "Whoa, there."

"Why am I so tired?" she whined.

Damon let go of her, and she leaned back against the seat.

"We use a decent amount of energy when we activate, but since you are mainly activating due to your emotional state, it takes about double the effort." He unzipped his backpack and pulled out his laptop. "Don't worry, you have plenty of time to rest. Plus, the more you activate, the easier it'll be to recover. Think of it as exercise."

"Mmm." She slumped down in the seat.

"And Alessa, you did it. You were able to activate your chip on command, even if it was emotionally driven. You did well."

"Mm-hmm."

From the moment Alessa's eyelids closed, she dreamt.

The familiar blonde sat beside Alessa and her friend, Quade, bouncing up and down excitedly. Alessa tried listening to the young woman as she talked about that morning's lesson, but found herself unable to pay attention.

Alessa glared at the women huddled together, surrounding Damon.

As the females squealed, he stood erect with his arms crossed and a polite smile plastered on his face.

He looks uneasy, Alessa reassured herself.

She rolled her eyes and took a bite of her red apple. "Ugh. Can you believe those stupid girls hanging all over him? It's disgusting. I mean, they should go for someone that could at least somewhat be in the same league."

After swallowing the fruit, she glanced back at Damon, and their eyes locked.

The blonde stopped talking as she followed Alessa's gaze across the room. "I'm sorry?"

The corners of Damon's mouth lifted in a faint smile, and Alessa broke eye contact with him, focusing intently on the table before her. Feeling embarrassed and confused, Alessa took a steadying breath before shoving the apple back into her mouth.

"Have you heard a single word I've said?" the blonde demanded.

Alessa's head jerked upright apologetically as she bit off a large chunk of the apple's flesh. "I'm sorry. I didn't mean to ignore you. He's just so—"

"Devilishly handsome?" Damon interrupted. Alessa's friends grew silent as she choked, nearly inhaling the piece of fruit. "I hope you weren't talking about me," Damon laughed.

Quade grinned. "I assure you she was."

Alessa shot daggers at her friend while she mentally yelled at him to shut the fuck up.

Damon arched an eyebrow while addressing Alessa. "I see. Well, then, I hope you bring your A-game today. I've got quite the lesson for you."

"How does it feel to be the Elvis Presley of our compound?" Alessa gestured toward the group of women.

Damon laughed in amusement. "There's a thought. I mean, I do play the guitar ... and sing." He bent down and whispered in Alessa's ear. "I wonder what your hidden talents might be."

The image faded as Damon walked away.

"Alessa." Damon gently stroked the side of Alessa's face with the tips of his fingers. "Alessa, it's time to wake up."

As her eyes opened, she discovered she had snuggled up to Damon's arm.

She jerked away and sat upright, wiping drool from her bottom lip. "Well, that's embarrassing."

He smiled as her cheeks reddened.

Chasing away the familiar ache of a migraine, she rubbed the back of her neck. "How long have I been out?"

"You've been asleep for the better part of a day."

Yawning, Alessa stretched her arms up in the air and twisted her stiff spine back and forth. "I can't remember the last time I slept that well."

Directing her attention toward the window, Damon pointed at the changed landscape. "Well, I'm glad you're all rested because you'll need your energy for what's coming. Welcome to sunny Fort Lauderdale, Florida."

CHAPTER THIRTY

While catching a ride to Henry Penway's lab, Alessa rubbed her temples, urging the persistent headache to go away.

Upon their arrival, Damon and Alessa were greeted by two guards stationed on either side of the entrance. Each wore a light blue medical mask, and as they stood tall, the guards folded their arms in front of their chests.

"It's a bit ironic, don't you think?" Alessa snickered.

"What is?"

She discreetly pointed at the guards. "They look like poster boys for the infection, yet they're guarding the lab it was made in."

Damon tilted his head in appreciation of the irony. Extending his arm, he directed Alessa to walk in first.

They were greeted by a young secretary wearing a decorative mask sitting behind a large desk.

"Oh, good morning," the secretary purred from behind her face garment. "My name's Wendy. What time is your appointment scheduled for?"

Damon's face relaxed into a seductive pout. "Why, hello,

beautiful. My name is Matt Jones, and this is my assistant, Debbie Hughes. Unfortunately, I cannot give you an appointment time as I did not make one."

The secretary's nose scrunched up in confusion.

Damon continued his spiel. "See, Henry and I, we go way back. We're old friends, and when we last spoke, he told me to stop by the next time I'm in town, so here I am."

The secretary blushed as she fell into Damon's deep ocean blue eyes. "Oh, good. For a moment there, I thought I'd made a scheduling error. I'm sorry, but Mr. Penway is out of the office."

"Is there any way for me to get a hold of him?" Damon leaned over the desk.

"Actually, no. He's deep-sea fishing, which I'm sure you already know is one of his favorite things to do. He likes to take a few friends and head out to sea with Charlie's fishing crew— they do business together.

"Anyway, it's about this time every year, they go out on the ocean for at least a day or two every week. I don't see how bobbing up and down on a boat while waiting for a giant fish to bite a line is considered fun," she shrugged.

"Charlie, huh?" He stood erect. "Maybe I can catch him out on the water today. Fishing is one of my favorite things to do as well." He winked.

Alessa turned around and headed for the front door as Damon followed close behind.

The secretary pointed her finger in the air and stood up. "If you're serious about finding them on the water, it shouldn't be too hard. They typically fish around the same spot, and Charlie's boat is white and gold, with *Queen Victoria* written on its sides."

Damon flashed a smile. "Thanks, doll. Have a good one."

"Doll?" Alessa questioned with an amused smirk. "You are being misogynistic."

"Only when I can tell it'll give me the necessary information. Let's hit up the nearest jet ski rental to get our hands on this bastard." He scowled, jogging ahead of her toward their cab.

While grabbing the door handle, Damon took a raspy breath before suffering from a coughing fit. As he fell to his knees, Alessa rushed to his side.

Dropping to the ground, she rubbed his back while comforting him. "Breathe, Damon; just breathe."

He swore aloud while placing his hand on the side of their ride.

The driver got out of the car wearing a white medical mask and glared wearily down at them. "You don't got that killer disease now, do ya?"

"No, he's fine," Alessa barked.

Hesitantly, the driver opened the rear door as Alessa helped Damon sit in the back seat.

Seeing the driver staring at them in the rearview mirror, Alessa snapped. "I'm not lying. You can look up the symptoms. Coughing isn't one of them."

Her face blanched white as she questioned how long she could keep Damon in the dark and leaned back into the seat. "Take us to the closest marina."

After a short drive, the man pulled up to a sandy beach, and Damon handed him the fare. "Keep the change."

Surprised, Alessa peered over at Damon as they exited the car. "Where do you keep coming up with all this money? The guy back in D.C. couldn't have had that much on him."

Damon shrugged nonchalantly. "You slept for quite a while on the way here, and I had time to kill, so I went pocket shopping. It's amazing how many people still carry cash on them."

Alessa shook her head in disapproval as they walked in through the door of the small marina.

An older man sat in a chair with his feet propped up on the counter. His thin, floral Hawaiian shirt blew in the wind, and his tanned pants matched the sand scattered across the floor.

He peered up from his fishing magazine. "Can I help you?"

"I sure hope so." Damon approached the counter. "My fiancée and I want to rent some jet skis."

The man leaned forward and placed the feet of his chair back on solid ground. "For the two of you, it'll be one hundred and twenty bucks for the rest of the day." He walked around to the register.

"Great." Damon grabbed the money from his wallet and handed it over. "A few buddies told me to look up a deep-sea fishing company. I think it was ... Charlie's. You know anything about them?"

The man scowled. "Yeah, I know of him. Biggest piece of shit there is."

Damon chuckled in response to the man's unexpected disdain. "I take it you do not recommend his services?"

The man planted his palms firmly on the counter. "No, I do not. He's a prick. The only good thing I have to say about his business is that his boat can get out on the water in just about any weather. The further out from land you go, the rougher the ocean, and with all that boat's gadgets, it can handle the rockin' real well. But, if you're looking for deep sea fish, I have a few other recommendations."

Alessa smiled. "That sounds great. When we return from cruising around, we'll get those names from you."

"About how far from here do they take people out?" Damon inquired.

"Maybe five miles east of here, and I'd say about twenty minutes out from the shoreline."

"Good to know." Damon nodded toward Alessa.

"Now, will you two need life jackets?" the shop owner asked.

"Oh, I guess we will," she replied.

"That'll be twenty-five apiece."

Alessa turned to walk out the door. "Is there a place around here we can buy swimsuits?"

"Sure is. It's just a short walk down the beach that way," the man pointed out the door. "Here are your keys. You'll get your life jackets down by the watercraft. My grandson, Gus, should be down there. I'll call him and let him know you're headin' down that way. He'll be near the water, right in front of the building you're going to."

"Thanks." Alessa waved to the shop owner.

Before walking out the door, Damon stopped. "Dammit. I gotta stash my backpack."

He shouted back to the store owner. "Is it possible to leave my pack here?"

The man sat back in his chair and picked up the fishing magazine. "I don't see a problem with that. I don't have any plans for the day."

Damon returned to the counter and tucked his bag beneath the older man's desk. "Thanks, I appreciate it."

"Have fun, you two," he yelled, flipping the page.

Leaving the shop, they trudged alongside one another through the sand.

"So..." Alessa smiled awkwardly while tripping over her

feet. "First, I'm your assistant, and now I'm your fiancée. We have quite the relationship," she said with a chuckle.

Damon looked off into the distance and grew serious as he slowed behind Alessa. "If you only knew," he mumbled.

Their feet sunk into the sand as they strolled toward the swim shop.

After entering the store, Damon handed Alessa a couple hundred dollars before heading to the men's racks.

Wasting no time, she grabbed a charcoal-colored one-piece swimsuit off the nearest rack.

Alessa cringed as she walked toward the dressing room. *No one needs to see my nasty abdominal scar.*

Skipping over all the tacky, brightly colored shorts, Damon decided on a pair of plain navy swim trunks and dark sunglasses.

He disappeared inside a dressing room stall and listened to Alessa talk to the girls at the front desk about which sunglasses looked better on her.

"Women..." Damon muttered under his breath before opening the curtain.

As Damon emerged from the dressing room, Alessa was standing at the counter wearing the dark grey swimsuit.

The suit's strings were tied behind her neck and in the middle of her back, and the patterned mesh fabric stretched over her toned stomach. Its sides were slashed open, revealing the intricate tattoo that danced up her right side.

Alessa's brunette hair was pulled back in a partial French braid while the rest was pulled into a messy bun.

Damon's irises glimmered steel grey as his gaze fell upon the bottoms clinging tightly to Alessa's firm backside, and he squeezed his eyes shut, imploring their return to blue.

After paying the cashier, Alessa slipped the new sunglasses

on her head and turned around. Her eyes landed on Damon's chiseled abs and quickly scanned down to his navy blue shorts.

Alessa playfully called out to him with a grin, "Come on, baby. Let's get going."

Damon pressed his fingertips into his eyelids, demanding his eyes stay blue as he marched up to the counter to pay for his merchandise. He tried his best not to glance at Alessa's exposed skin but was losing the battle.

After exiting the store, Damon and Alessa quickly spotted the man leaning against two watercraft near the shore.

"Are you Gus?" Damon hollered from a distance.

"That'd be me. Go ahead and grab a life jacket." The young man pointed toward a small collection. "Have either of you driven one of these before?"

Damon climbed over a red jet ski, sporting a huge grin. "A time or two, yes."

Alessa clipped her life jacket into place. "Uh, yep," she agreed, unsure if she had.

"Alright, then. Will you need instructions?" the young man asked.

"Thank you, but we're good." Damon clipped the buckle on his life jacket.

Gus looked into the distance and yelled, "Hey, Joe! Wait up, I gotta talk to you!" and shouted back to Damon while he jogged away, "Okay, then. Have fun!"

Damon pulled up the bottom of his swim trunks. "Well, that worked out well."

"What are you doing?" Alessa asked as she stretched her leg up and over the seat of the second jet ski.

Unclipping a gun holster from around his thigh, he handed it to Alessa. "Do you need help putting this on?"

She took the holster and gun. "I think I can figure it out."

She tightened the strap before wrapping it around her right thigh.

He leaned in. "Do you remember how to drive one of these?"

"Honestly, Damon, how hard can it be?" Alessa started her engine, squeezed the handlebars, and shot out onto the water.

Damon laughed and sped after her as the salty ocean water splashed onto his face.

CHAPTER THIRTY-ONE

Darting back and forth behind boats, Alessa stood up and squealed.

Jumping the wakes, she flew high in the air, and as Damon hit the same wake, he flipped up and over, landing a barrel roll. He splashed back down in the water and hollered out in success before he cut across Alessa and raced toward the open ocean.

Following his lead, Alessa jerked her jet ski to the left, and as they looked for the fishing boat, the warm wind pressed into their bodies, leaving a layer of salt caked on their skin.

In the distance, Damon spied a larger boat and flicked his wrist. From out of his wristband, a high-tech pair of goggles appeared. Holding them up, he read *Queen Victoria* on the side of the white and gold boat.

"Get ready!" he yelled over at Alessa.

Alessa unsnapped her gun holster and withdrew her firearm.

As Damon veered to the right, Alessa directed her jet ski to the boat's left.

Her pupils dilated, and her irises flickered green, triggered by the adrenaline coursing through her veins.

One man on the back of the boat stood up and raised his weapon at the incoming couple, but Alessa aimed and shot first.

As the bullet struck the intended target in the chest, he jerked backward and fell, alerting the additional passengers of their imminent arrival.

The people scrambled about, grabbing for any means to fight back.

Alessa gunned down two of the men as they were in mid-arm extension, and on the opposite side of the boat, Damon shot three more.

Pulling beside the boat, she grabbed the ladder and dangled off the side before climbing the metal bars. Alessa jumped onto the deck and pistol-whipped the individual who blocked her from continuing the attack.

Damon joined her on deck and handled two men while Alessa followed Henry, who was stumbling over fallen bodies, running toward the front of the ship.

Eyeing a loaded crossbow propped up against a nearby wall, Alessa lifted the heavy weapon, aimed, and released the arrow just as Henry leaped high onto the railing.

The barbed tip caught the man in the shoulder, and Alessa jerked backward on the bow. As she yanked the rope between him and her, she slammed him down, hard, onto his backside.

He choked as the air escaped his lungs.

"What exactly was your plan, Henry? Were you going to try to swim back to shore?" Alessa taunted.

Writhing in agony, Henry moaned and arched his back.

Damon twisted his uninjured arm unapologetically and yanked him up onto his knees.

Alessa glared down at Henry while bringing forth the

memory of him pressing a lit cigar deep into her skin: the sizzling flesh, the smell of her burning arm hair, the sadistic grin on his face.

Alessa rubbed at the phantom pain on her forearm.

The chemist stared at Alessa in astonishment.

She cocked her head. "Oh good, you remember me."

"H-how can this be?" Henry stammered.

"You know, there are people in the world who are medical professionals who save peoples' lives rather than take them. Didn't you take the Hippocratic Oath?"

Henry glared at Alessa, looking her up and down as she encircled him. "I see you're wearing a one-piece."

Her jade eyes flared, silencing him, and Henry screamed as Damon pressed into his wound.

"I'm not here to relive the past, Henry." She paused in front of the men. "I have some questions that need answering."

"As do I." Henry sneered. "I see you fared well after what was done to you, but how did your final affliction heal? There has to be some scarring."

Enraged, Alessa's entire body trembled, and Damon struck the man's cheek, forcing the chemist down on all fours.

Henry shook the colorful spots from his vision with a sadistic laugh. "What can I say? As a scientist, I am intrigued by how our interaction has affected you."

Alessa turned away from him and marched toward a collection of spears propped up against a storage rack.

Placing her finger on the sharp spearhead, she pressed and startled as the blade pricked through her skin. Her fingertip dripped blood onto the wooden floorboards.

"Any horrific images keeping you up at night?" Henry taunted.

Damon tightened his grip on the chemist and sat him upright.

Henry howled before continuing. "How about the memory loss serum? Has any of it started coming back? I am honestly surprised you survived. It was supposed to erase your memory just before it took your life. The stupid bitch must've fucked up in her calculations. Or maybe she purposefully led us astray—"

Alessa wrapped her hand around the pole and glared at him, unspeaking. Grasping the weapon, she discovered an assortment of deep-sea fishing accessories on the table beside her. Alessa beamed maliciously as she picked up a hooked weapon and sauntered back toward Henry.

Damon sucked in an uneven breath as the Alessa he knew appeared before him, and he shifted his hips, trying to hide his excitement.

"We're going to play a little game." Alessa bent down just a few inches before the chemist's face. "I'm going to ask you a question, and if you don't answer truthfully, I'm going to see just how sharp this blade truly is."

Alessa stared into his hazel eyes and watched the sweat dripping off his nose. "Why did you agree to help spread the smallpox virus? How could you even think to make it in spray form?"

"That answer is simple. I did it because it had never been done before. I was the first person ever to change its form of transmission. I revolutionized biological warfare by containing the live virus in a new form," explained the chemist.

"You are quite proud of yourself, aren't you?" Alessa growled.

"Why, yes, I am. My name will be written in textbooks. I will be advised on every medical research project. I am the revolutionary forefront of medical technology in the new world."

"The new world?" Alessa spat.

Refusing to answer, Henry pursed his lips.

She lashed out and sliced the blade across the chemist's cheek.

He cried out as blood poured from his cut, and he struggled against Damon's hold.

Dropping the blade, Alessa hiked back to the rack of spears. "I explained the rules to you. Damon, place him on the wall."

Lifting the chemist off his knees, Damon slammed him up against the wall outside the boat's cabin.

Henry was forced to stand upright with the arrow still protruding from his arm. "Please, no. I'll tell you. I'll tell you!"

While wielding a spear, Alessa stopped before the chemist. "Go ahead, then."

Damon set Henry down and stepped back a few feet to give Alessa her space to interrogate the man.

"When I first accepted the position, Mr. Lansing explained his plan to weed out the weak. He proposed that humanity had grown evolutionarily stagnant. You see, thanks to today's modern medicine and technology, the world is now plagued with genetic anomalies and diseases that were once a death sentence. By allowing these people to live, they can pass these conditions onto their children, which weakens the human species as a whole."

"But by releasing the smallpox virus, aren't you exterminating all humankind?" Alessa asked.

Henry's eyes shifted nervously from side to side as his fingers twisted a nail out from the wall behind him. "Not exactly. I'm sure you already know there's a cure."

Alessa nodded. "I am aware."

"The virus was spread through the mist we released, and then the chemicals mixed with the smallpox virus highlights all the human host's inadequacies. Once the infected individual receives the supposed cure, their DNA will be searched for all known lethal genetic defects. If any are found, they will contract a deadly form of tuberculosis and will be eliminated. Mr. Lansing is working relentlessly to secure a future for the best of humanity."

Alessa gasped. "What you're talking about is genocide."

"Sacrifices must be made," Henry said without remorse. "You can blame me all you want, but the truth is, without my invention, humans would've continued down a path of self-sabotage, eventually leading to our species' destruction."

Successfully pulling the nail out from the wall, Henry charged Alessa.

Damon dove in front of Alessa and extended his forearm to block Henry's attack. The chemist dragged the nail across his meaty flesh, and scarlet red ran from Damon's arm.

Infuriated, Alessa pointed the spear and drove the tip through the chemist's left bicep, impaling him to the wall. She screamed savagely, rotated the rod, and stepped back while panting.

"Are the smallpox pills being manufactured at the same place as the cure?" she demanded as Henry bellowed in anguish.

"Yes!"

She twisted the spear. "Where are they being made?"

The chemist cried out. "Texas! Texas! What's with all these questions about the disease?" he grunted. "I can't believe you haven't mentioned *her* once."

"Who?" Alessa stilled, perplexed.

Henry's eyebrows arched. "You truly have no idea who I'm referring to?"

"Shut the fuck up!" Damon demanded.

Alessa glanced over at Damon and then at the chemist, awaiting his answer.

Henry scrutinized Damon. "Well, isn't this interesting? You haven't told her, have you?"

Damon punched the man hard in the jaw.

"Damon, stop!" Alessa yelled before returning her attention to Henry. "Who are you talking about? Who should I remember?"

Damon held his hand over his bloodied arm and stood with his lips parted in a silent apology.

Henry spat, and his blood splattered across the floorboards as he glowered up at Alessa.

She grasped the pole and violently yanked the spear from his flesh and muscle.

As the chemist collapsed, she thrust the weapon deep into his gut and pressed him back toward the bow.

Henry's body stiffened as he grasped the pole sticking out of his belly.

Reaching the edge, Alessa pushed the chemist off and dangled his body precariously over the side of the boat.

As the barbed edges caught on his insides, Henry screamed and struggled to hold on to the stick jutting out from his abdomen, his feet sliding against the boat's floor.

"Fuck! Stop, please, stop!" the chemist wailed. The ocean was stained crimson with Henry's blood, and his face paled as several dark figures swam just below the surface.

"Tell me who!" Alessa shouted.

"Kai!" Henry cried. "Your sister, Kai!"

Nearly losing her grip, Alessa stumbled. "You're lying."

"What could I gain by lying to you at this point?" the chemist whimpered. Slipping further down the spear, blood bubbled from the corners of his mouth. "Who do you think gave us the information to capture you?"

Alessa's head throbbed as she thought back to the blonde girl's appearance in nearly every one of her memories.

"If you can't even remember your sister, who else are you forgetting?" the chemist laughed, frenzied.

Kicking Henry off the end of the spear, Alessa screamed, "Fuck you!"

Falling off the boat's edge, he plunged into the cold ocean. Henry's arms flailed, and his torso bobbed up and down as he cried out one last time before disappearing beneath the choppy water's surface.

As the sea turned red with the chemist's blood, Alessa shuffled away as if in a trance while Damon trailed close behind, begging her to listen to him.

Bellowing out in agony, Alessa sank down, hard, onto the floorboards as she was swallowed by heart-wrenching memories of her sister.

CHAPTER THIRTY-TWO

"Kai, you're doing it all wrong," Alessa explained in her memory. "You keep leading with the wrong foot. If you'd pay attention..."

"Ugh!" Kai grunted. "I'll never get this stupid move down."

Alessa looked up into her sister's translucent green eyes and retook the beginning stance. "Stop complaining and just pay attention to what I'm doing."

"Can't we take a break and do something fun?" Kai whined.

Alessa rolled her eyes at her sister. "Not until you can do this move in your sleep."

"Come on, Lessie. I'm tired, and my ceremony isn't for another ten years," a ten-year-old Kai complained.

"And within those ten years, you need to be better than your opponent, or else," Alessa huffed.

Kai's shoulders dropped. "Yeah, yeah, I know what the alternative is."

Alessa grabbed her sister's hands. "Then why don't you take it seriously? I can't lose you. I won't lose you."

Kai dropped her head and stared at the floor.

"You're the only one standing in your way. I believe in you, but you also need to believe in yourself. Besides, you must win against your opponent at your ceremony to stay. But then, if you choose a trade in which fighting isn't required, you'll never need to fight again. You're brilliant. They could use you in research."

The memory faded into Alessa looking up at the blue sky full of white fluffy clouds while she stood atop a mountain. Her hands spread out, welcoming the cool, itchy grass beneath her thin dress.

The blonde girl was beside her once more but was a little older. "Do you think about them often?" she asked.

Alessa closed her eyes and took a deep breath, filling her lungs with the scent of dandelions and wildflowers. "Mmm?"

"Mom and Dad," Kai answered.

Her heart racing, Alessa's eyes darted to the blonde teenager, but instead of her sister's face, the dark-haired, bearded man from her dreams at the cabin stared blankly back at her with a bullet hole in between his eyes as he lay on the floor, his head tilted unnaturally from the fall onto the hardwood.

With a loud gasp, Alessa awakened.

"Shit!" Damon swerved the vehicle as she erratically flailed about.

Their car screeched back onto the road while the surrounding vehicles honked their horns.

"Dammit, woman, would you watch where you're throwing those things?"

Sinking back into the passenger seat, Alessa rubbed her temples and leaned forward, placing her head between her knees.

"You feelin' alright?"

"I think I'm going to be sick," she grumbled.

"Please don't. I don't exactly have anything for you to vomit in right now," he pleaded.

With her eyes closed tight, Alessa forced herself to slowly breathe in through her nose before forcing out the air through pursed lips.

"Better?" Damon asked.

She rubbed the back of her sore neck. "I think so?"

"Good, that's good. You had me thinking you might not wake up this time, but I couldn't exactly take you to a hospital, so I did the only thing I knew to do."

"Which was?" Alessa asked.

He laughed nervously. "Let you sleep it off. I could tell you were breathing, so there wasn't much else I could do but wait until you woke up. But this time, you were out for quite a long time."

"How long are we talking?"

"We're almost to Texas."

Alessa rubbed her eyes. "Texas? You weren't kidding. I forgot, why are we going to Texas? And why are we driving and not flying?"

"Galveston, to be exact. Remember, it's where Erebos's manufacturing plant is. At least that's the building's main use," Damon explained. "And as far as flying is concerned, it's out for two reasons. First, all planes have been grounded until further notice, and second, due to personal reasons, I don't fly unless I have no other choice."

"Okay, then." Alessa's eyes examined his healed forearm. "Huh. I could've sworn Henry cut you."

"He did." Damon turned the steering wheel.

"Oh, right." Alessa nodded slowly, remembering their advanced ability to heal.

She looked down and noticed Damon was no longer wearing his swim trunks but was instead in jeans, a teal shirt, and a black leather jacket.

Alessa fingered the yellow sundress she was wearing over her swimsuit. "Where'd you get the clothes?" She touched the newly acquired necklace around her neck. "And the jewelry? What's this?" She held up the small gemstone in the middle.

"I bought everything while you were taking your fifteen-hour nap, and that is a moonstone," Damon explained.

"You have a habit of doing odd things while I'm unconscious, but thanks. It's gorgeous." Alessa lifted her foot and admired the brand-new black combat boots. "These are nice."

Alessa rotated, preparing to confront him. "You knew I had a sister, didn't you?"

Damon sighed as he turned the steering wheel to the left. "Yes."

Alessa glared at him. "You told me I had no family, Damon. You lied to me."

"I couldn't tell you about Kai. You had to remember her on your own." Damon glanced over at her apologetically.

"Why's that? You told me about Sparta, my abilities..."

Damon shook his head. "That's different. Your brain handles receiving non-emotional information differently."

"I don't understand." Alessa threw her hands up in the air in defeat. "How is my entire back story not emotional, but remembering my sister nearly kills me?"

Damon's shoulders stiffened. "I have to be very careful with what I tell you."

"You've already said that, but—"

"But nothing. Certain aspects of your life affect you more than others. For example, when we discuss Erebos

Pharmaceuticals, you get a headache. But when you finally remembered your sister, you fell unconscious for hours. You weren't simply sleeping off an activation event. I couldn't wake you. I tried."

Alessa bit her lower lip. "So, if you tell me something I can't cope with or that I'm not ready to hear?"

"Best case scenario? You get a bad headache or go into shock," Damon said.

"And worse case?" she asked reluctantly.

Damon hesitated and swallowed before reluctantly answering. "You die."

"Oh," Alessa replied under her breath.

"I'm trying my best to avoid the latter."

She ran her hands down her legs, smoothing out her bright skirt. "My subconscious kept reminding me of Kai; I just couldn't connect the dots quite yet. Oh, Damon, I cannot wait to see her!"

He pursed his lips and gripped the steering wheel. "Um ... Alessa..."

"Yeah?"

After a deep breath, he continued. "At the same time you failed to report back, she was declared missing."

Alessa's lips remained slightly parted as she stared out the windshield. "I don't understand. What are you saying?"

His head tilted. "Who knew you were being sent to Erebos Industries?"

"No, no, no ... Damon," Alessa interjected, adamantly shaking her head to the left and right. "Kai would never—"

He exhaled. "Two days before your disconnection from our database—"

"You mean before I died?"

He nodded. "Yes, two days before you died, Kai left for a

supply pickup and never returned. Her connection was lost within hours. It's believed it was Kai who outed your involvement—"

"That's not possible, Damon!"

"—and gave away your position," he continued. "Then was possibly terminated immediately after."

"No, no ... Damon, she's not dead. I mean, look at me," she pointed at herself. "I'm alive, and my connection was lost. Besides, she would never. She couldn't have known what they were doing to me."

"Do you honestly think she could've survived what you went through?" Damon demanded.

Alessa's stomach flipped at the thought of her sister being tortured.

"She can't be dead," she muttered. "Kai's out there, somewhere, waiting for me."

As he focused on the road ahead, Alessa anxiously spun the alexandrite ring around her finger. "After all this is settled, you and I will find her and bring her home."

Unable to force Alessa to come to terms with the death of the sister she had only just remembered, Damon slowly nodded his head.

"Hey, Damon?" Alessa asked.

"Mmm?"

"Thanks for, you know, well, everything."

He licked his lips and looked out the driver-side window, preparing to get over a lane. "You would've done the same for me."

Alessa relaxed back into her seat. "I'd like to think so."

Damon turned his head toward her, and his eyes bore into her soul. "I know so."

For the rest of the drive, Alessa closed her eyes and played back the once-lost images of her sister while, in the background, various rock ballads blasted from the speakers.

She recalled the curve of her sister's smile, the warmth of her hugs, their playful banter, back and forth. Then, unexpectedly, the terrifying image of Alessa hiding with the little girl underneath a bed popped into Alessa's mind, and her eyes sprang open as the sound of a phantom gunshot echoed.

Just before pulling up to a tall, elaborate gate in front of a large building, Damon turned to look at Alessa from head to toe. Examining her appearance, he made a *tsk* sound with his tongue. "This isn't going to work." He shook his head and reached into the backseat.

"What's wrong? What are you looking for?"

He held up a zip tie and an assist opening blade. "Props."

Alessa leaned away from him. "Whoa, there. What are you planning to do with those?"

"You know how I said the manufacturing plant has multiple uses?"

"Yeah?"

Reaching for Alessa's leg, Damon grabbed a hold of her skirt and ripped up the side of the fabric.

She struggled against him. "What the hell are you doing?"

Leaning into Alessa, Damon's eyes flickered gunmetal grey.

As he tore at the fabric covering her torso, exposing the top of her breasts, Alessa's breathing faltered.

Then he extended his arm toward her, holding a small knife. "Here, put this in your shoe."

As instructed, she slid the folded blade down into the side of her black combat boot.

Damon eyed Alessa once more. "And rough your hair up a bit."

"Are you serious?" She eyed him suspiciously.

"We don't have time for you to question every little thing I ask of you. Don't you trust me by now?"

With a loud groan, she conceded and ran her fingers through her hair, tossing it about.

He gestured for Alessa to hold her arms out before her, and as she intertwined her fingers, Damon wrapped the black tie around her wrists before pulling it tight. "They need to believe that I've captured you."

Alessa's eyes squinted. "Okay."

"I need you to lie back as though you've been knocked unconscious. Can you do that?"

Alessa fell limp in the seat and closed her eyes obediently.

Driving to the guarded fence, Damon rolled his window down and addressed the armed man. "Name's Curtis. I'm here to see Miguel about some business."

The guard raised his firearm. "What business would that be?"

Damon pointed at Alessa. "Found this bitch trying to escape. I got it out of her that she was planning on snitchin'. I figured Miguel would like to break this one himself."

Staring at Alessa's exposed thigh, the guard licked his lips.

Breaking the man's concentration, Damon cleared his throat. "Well?" he pressed, directing the guard's attention back to the closed gate.

"Oh, yeah." The guard flipped the switch, and Damon hit the gas.

Damon's lips hardly moved as he calmly instructed Alessa. "When we get inside, you may see some things. Remember that these people are the lowest of the low and capable of anything.

I need you to keep your shit together, you got it? I can't have you break down during the mission. This is life or death."

He parked the car at the side of the building as Alessa nodded her head in silence.

After grabbing several small guns from his backpack and hiding them on various body parts, Damon exited the car and marched to the passenger side. He swung the door open, pulled on Alessa's arm, and yanked her out of her seat before flinging her petite frame over his muscular shoulder.

As her body thumped atop his arm, Alessa grunted aloud with the force of air being expelled from her lungs.

Her limp body swayed side to side as Damon strolled toward the entrance.

Well, damn. That was hot. Wait, seriously, Alessa? She chastised herself for becoming wet while draped atop Damon's shoulder. *Now is not the time.*

Damon approached the three men stationed at the front doors. "Where do you want her?"

One of the men snickered. "Is she here for business or pleasure?"

Damon smacked Alessa's ass. "Both, I guess."

She held in a gasp as her right cheek absorbed the intense tingling.

"You'll want to take the elevator up to the third floor and put her in the room down the hall and to the left," the man instructed.

Damon stepped forward. "Got it."

"Hey," a young, pale-skinned individual extended their hand, reaching for Alessa's skirt. "What's she look like underneath?"

Alessa held her breath as she felt a hand on the back of her leg.

Damon jerked away and growled. "She's mine."

They dropped their hand. "Didn't mean anything by it. I-I get it, man."

Damon shot a death glare at the guards before walking away.

As the elevator doors opened, he stepped in with Alessa draped over his shoulder.

She opened her eyes but remained silent while listening to Damon noisily breathe in and out.

Once the doors closed, he set Alessa down and placed his hands on either side of her face. "Are you okay?"

"Yeah, I'm good," she nodded slowly while unintentionally licking her lips.

Bending down before her, Damon pressed his hand against Alessa's calf while reaching into her boot. "Took all I had not to punch them in their fucking faces."

Grabbing hold of the knife, Damon hesitated. His warm hand lingered on her smooth skin as he smelled her sweet scent, and closing his eyes tight, he fought hard against the urge to activate.

Alessa's breathing hitched as he ran his fingertips up the inside of her leg while standing erect.

Damon placed the blade between her wrists and pulled upward, cutting the plastic tie in half.

She rubbed the indents out of her skin. "Thanks," she said breathily.

With a loud gasp, Damon winced and pressed the palm of his hand into his chest.

Alessa jumped forward. "Damon, what's wrong?"

"I don't know. I just got this sharp pain." He brushed her hand aside. "It's nothing, I'm sure I'm fine."

"Damon—"

The elevator dinged, and the doors opened wide.

Ignoring Alessa's concern, Damon exited the elevator. "Get ready."

She jogged to keep up with him as he rushed forward.

"Where are you going? Isn't that the room over there?" Alessa pointed to a closed door at the end of the hallway.

"That's where I told them I was taking you. We need to get to the fifth floor. That's where the plant is."

She glanced back. "So, what's in that room?"

"It's probably the interrogation room."

"It's where they torture people, isn't it?"

Ignoring her question, Damon stopped before the stairwell's door and stretched his neck to see through the glass. "Looks clear." He pulled a gun from his belt and handed it to Alessa.

"If we need to be on the fifth floor, why did we get off on the third?"

Damon grabbed a gun for himself. "The elevator's location is displayed on every floor atop the doors. See?" He pointed.

Alessa saw the number three illuminated in yellow.

"The guys on the first floor would've been able to see if we had gotten off on a different floor." Damon pushed the door open and extended his arm. "Ladies first."

CHAPTER THIRTY-THREE

The heat from the stairwell slapped Alessa in the face, and after slipping the blade into the side of her boot, she bolted up the stairs with her gun raised.

By the time they reached the fifth floor, Damon was hunched over, huffing and grunting.

Alessa glanced back, concern etched on her face. "Are you well enough to do this?"

"Why do you keep acting like I'm sick? I'm fine." Standing straight with his weapon raised, Damon's eyes flashed silver. "Open the damn door."

Alessa bit her lower lip hard, consumed by guilt while she peered in through the small glass window. After pushing open the steel door, they stayed low to the ground and entered the enormous room.

"Wow," Alessa muttered as the door closed quietly behind them. They crouched over, towering above the workers, and stared at the facility's sheer size.

The shiny, metal machinery extended from floor to ceiling,

and loud noises echoed throughout the room as mechanisms whined and whistled. A small group of factory workers stood in a circle, clearly in the middle of a serious discussion.

Ducking down, Damon tapped Alessa's shoulder and pointed out three guards stationed at one of the factory floor's exits. In addition to each guard holding a P90 firearm, an arsenal of weapons was propped up against the far wall.

Alessa continued further into the room, onto a metal catwalk, as Damon stayed put and assessed the amount and types of weapons they had to compete with.

"Who the hell is this?" a man yelled in a thick Spanish accent down below. His long black hair was slicked back, his shirt stained yellow, and a pair of brown suspenders held up his tanned slacks. "Who are you?" he spat at another worker.

A male Bodyguard in a shiny silver suit approached the man. "This is Ezekiel."

The Hispanic man's leathery face scrunched up in annoyance. "Where's Camden?"

"He was compromised," the Bodyguard responded.

"That's bullshit! Who the hell told you that? He's like *mi familia*," he proclaimed, throwing his arms in the air.

"Sir—"

"I'll talk to him myself," the Hispanic man interrupted, pulling a handkerchief out of his pocket. Panting angrily, he wiped the sweat from his forehead.

The Bodyguard stood erect and clasped his hands behind his back. "Camden's being held in the interrogation room."

"Shit. Is he *muerta*?"

"He's not dead yet, but he will be very soon. He defied orders," the silver suit informed the man.

The man in charge wiggled his right pointer finger. "No,

no, that's impossible. They reassured me a Bodyguard can't go against orders. That's just not possible."

"Clearly, that's not the case for every Bodyguard. He's different. Camden must be terminated."

Damon squatted down beside Alessa and rested his hand on her shoulder. She jumped, and he held a finger to his lips, signaling her to keep quiet.

The tanned man mumbled under his breath. "*Dios maldita sea.* He was one of our best. Don't drag it out. Just take care of him quick."

Looking back, Damon realized the guard stationed on the right wall was missing. "Where did he—?"

The sound of footsteps echoed behind Damon and Alessa.

"Who are you?" the armed Bodyguard demanded as they sprang upright.

Alessa froze in place as Damon closed his eyes and slowly exhaled.

The silver suit raised his weapon. "I said, who are—?"

Whipping around, Damon's irises shone granite, and he shot the bodyguard in the arm.

As the guard dropped his gun, Damon pushed forward into a somersault. Completing the roll, he propped himself onto one foot and shot the guard again.

The bullet embedded itself between the man's eyes. His limp body fell backward and hit the catwalk with a loud thud.

The arguing men instantly hushed as they redirected their attention toward the commotion.

"Fuck," Damon growled. "Well, they know we're here now."

As Alessa peered at the individuals below, she recognized the scarred Hispanic man and gasped. "Miguel!"

"We need backup on the factory floor!" an additional guard bellowed into his handheld radio.

Alessa sprinted over. "We gotta go now."

Dragging Alessa toward the dead guard, Damon yanked grenades from the man's belt. "Here, take these." He handed them to her. "But don't drop them yet."

Juggling them between her hands, Alessa tilted her head and inched toward the fallen man after glimpsing a shiny object tied into the guard's boot strings. Upon closer inspection, Alessa discovered a silver key.

She set the grenades down between the metal bars on the floor and unlatched her necklace.

Hearing the clang of live grenades against the metallic floor, Damon cursed. "What the hell are you doing?"

Alessa slipped the key around the chain on her neck. "If he was guarding this key, it has to be important."

Damon shook his head in disbelief. "You have got to be kidding me."

In the meantime, two additional guards went missing from their stations.

Alessa glanced over. "Uh, Damon?"

He looked up just in time to see a guard aiming at them. "Move!" He shoved Alessa out of the way onto the connecting catwalk.

As bullets flew past, Alessa and Damon sprinted toward the other side of the room.

About a third of the way across, Damon yelled, "Now!"

Pulling the pin from their grenades, Alessa and Damon dropped them on either side of the railing, and they fell as if in slow motion.

A Bodyguard extracted a large blade from its sheath strapped to his back and blocked the exit.

Another silver suit roared from behind Damon, swinging a double-edged sword.

"Is this guy for real?" Damon quipped.

As Alessa's attacker whipped their blade around, she leaped back and fell into a backward cartwheel before completing a backflip.

The guard's blade narrowly missed Damon's head as he dodged to the right. The blade sliced through the air, and Damon squatted down and pushed up off the metal bars before jumping high. His feet landed on the two opposing railings, and Damon stood in front of the man briefly before kicking off and flipping over his attacker.

Landing behind the guard, Damon kicked the man square in the back and sent him flying forward.

Alessa dropped onto the catwalk before running toward her attacker. The person lunged for her, and she leaped to her left. As the sword swung toward Alessa, it struck the floor, ringing metallically.

Wrapping her fingers around the handrail, she twisted and propelled herself to the outside of the catwalk. Mid-air, she rotated her hands on the bar and thrust herself over the railing.

"Activate, already," Alessa demanded of herself.

The Bodyguard stood upright, unmoving and confused, as Alessa gained momentum, and her feet slammed into his side, kicking him over the edge.

As Damon's attacker fell in front of Alessa, his double-edged sword wedged itself into the catwalk's floor, and it stood erect.

His body continued forward, and with a sickening crunch, the man was impaled up into his lower jaw and out the top of his head.

Alessa covered her mouth in disgust. "Oh!" she gasped.

Damon stepped around the gruesome scene. "Well, that's unfortunate."

Two Bodyguards charged from either side of Damon and Alessa immediately before the first grenades exploded. Damon dodged to the left as Alessa sprinted back to her right, and each confronted their attackers.

Just before Damon reached his opponent, he hit the floor, grabbed the vertical rod connected to the handrail, and pulled himself outside the walkway. He swung and held onto the metal flooring, dangling beneath his attacker's feet.

Alessa jumped onto the railing. She then hurtled toward the first of the two Bodyguards, and as she dropped down, Alessa pulled a knife from the guard's belt and drove it into the middle of his back.

Stabbing through his spine, Alessa rotated the knife and severed his spinal cord.

She then launched headfirst, sliding before the second guard, and grasped the metal railing as she flew outside the walkway. Pushing off the metal, she lunged to the far catwalk and glared back at the second guard.

The Bodyguard whipped out a handgun, aimed at Alessa, and fired.

Thrusting his hips under the floor, Damon swung his legs and midsection forward, wrapping himself around the flooring. Pushing himself onto the catwalk, belly down, he stood up behind his attacker.

Damon kicked one of the guard's knees in a single fluid motion, folding the man in half. As the Bodyguard collapsed, Damon wrapped his fingers around the Bodyguard's throat, crushing his windpipe.

Running toward Damon, the other Bodyguard grabbed two firearms from inside the fallen man's jacket.

Damon eyed the weapons and pushed up and off the handrail. He fell through the air before sticking the landing and rolled forward onto the angled catwalk fifteen feet below Alessa.

Losing her fight, Alessa yelled for help. "Damon!"

CHAPTER THIRTY-FOUR

A feral growl escaped Damon as he glared at the guard shooting at Alessa. He sprinted across the catwalk and hit the far wall, scaling it up to the connecting beam, and jumped up onto the side of the railing. Grabbing the man's boot, Damon snatched his foot out from underneath him.

The guard lost balance and crashed down to the metal floor.

"Throw yourself to the crows," Damon snarled in Greek, tearing the gun from the man's hand. Grabbing the Bodyguard's leg, he jerked him backward, propelling him over the catwalk's edge.

Bullets ricocheted off the metal bars as another Bodyguard closed in.

Damon hung onto the catwalk with one hand, aimed the gun at the Bodyguard, and squeezed the trigger.

Two bullets sunk into the guard's skull with a sickening thud, and with an audible grunt, Damon dragged himself over the side of the walkway.

Alessa cried out as she dangled precariously from a silver rod.

Sprinting toward Alessa, he hit the floor and stretched his arm toward her. "Grab my hand!"

Alessa's grip weakened, and her hands slipped. "I can't!"

He stretched as far as he could. "Reach out and take my hand!"

The heat from the fire licked up Alessa's legs. "But I'll fall!"

"Alessa," Damon urged. "Trust me, I've got you. Now, reach out and take my hand!"

She closed her eyes and took a steadying breath. Gritting her teeth, she launched herself upward and stretched her arm toward Damon. As their fingertips touched, he pulled her up and over the railing.

Stepping back, he placed two fingertips beneath her chin, and they stared at one another in silence with their chests heaving.

As another explosion erupted, Damon grabbed Alessa's hand. "Let's get out of here."

A Bodyguard blocked their exit. "Stop!" the Bodyguard commanded.

Damon pushed Alessa back, forcing her the other way. "Run!"

Reaching down into his belt, Damon withdrew his gun and squeezed the trigger as they sprinted away from the guard. Running backward, he intentionally fell to the floor, and landing on his back, he slid with his weapon raised.

At the opposite end of the catwalk, another Bodyguard blocked Alessa, and as bullets exploded from his gun chamber, her eyes blazed emerald green.

Four bullets flew toward her as if in slow motion, and she bent to the left, gracefully dodging them.

Damon shot the Bodyguard in his right shoulder and left kneecap as Alessa squatted down.

Hitting the floor, Alessa plucked the knife from her right leather boot and flicked her wrist, releasing the blade. The knife spun through the air before it sunk deep into the guard's open left eye.

Sliding beside her, Damon fired his last bullet into the silver suit's throat. The Bodyguard hit his knees as blood poured from his mouth.

Damon and Alessa looked at one another, and as a faint smile played on Damon's lips, a small grenade with its pin removed rolled noisily around the catwalk.

"Oh shit!" Alessa grabbed Damon's arm. She yanked him up, and as they ran for the exit, the grenade detonated.

The entire catwalk convulsed as its metal tore away from the far wall.

Alessa screamed as Damon shouted, "Hang on!"

Falling to the catwalk's floor, they wrapped their fingers between the metal pieces and held on tight. The right side of the catwalk swung down and to the left, smashing up against the wall.

"You still back there?" Damon hollered down to Alessa from above the smoke and fire.

"Yeah, I'm still here," Alessa answered, clinging to the twisted metal.

"Well, that was unexpected." He laughed nervously.

Alessa panicked as she peered around. "Uh, Damon, what do we do?"

He eyed the railing. "I want you to jump onto that railing."

She blinked dramatically. "What was that?"

"Like this." Damon reached for the railing and placed his foot on the metallic spindles between the bars. "Got it?"

"Uh, sure." Alessa scrunched her eyes in concentration. She swallowed the lump in the back of her throat before inhaling a deep breath of hot aftershock from the blast. With a silent prayer to the gods, she leaped into the air and landed on the handrail.

Alessa exhaled, clinging to the silver bars.

"You did good. Just listen to my voice and do not look down. I need you to follow me," Damon instructed.

Reaching for the next bar, Alessa pulled herself up, and they climbed their way to the top as the fire melted the factory's machinery. After hauling himself over the edge, he extended his arm for Alessa's hand and plucked her from the vertical catwalk.

Lifting her onto solid ground, he grasped her hand tightly and pulled her toward the exit door.

Rushing down the stairwell, his lungs burned with an intense need to cough.

As they passed the third floor's entrance, Alessa paused before the stairwell's door. "Camden," she mumbled under her breath.

"Come on! What are you doing?" Damon stopped reluctantly.

"I have a feeling—"

"Alessa!" he begged. "We don't have time for this."

She glared at Damon with her bright green eyes. "Do you trust me?"

Clearing his throat, he scratched the nagging tickle and rolled his eyes. "You know I do."

"Then shut up and follow me." She bolted for the closed door near the end of the hallway, and Damon followed close behind with his gun raised.

"This idea of yours better not get us killed," he warned.

She burst through the door and hit an invisible wall, horrified by the interrogation room's contents.

Torture devices were strewn up all over the left side of the room. Knives, swords, containers full of unknown chemicals, various cutting instruments, yards of rope, matches, zip ties, bear traps, tape, whips covered in spikes, and a blowtorch were a handful of what was on display.

Dirt and dust polluted the air, producing an orange haze-like cloud that encircled the dim room. The sunlight's rays struggled through several grimy windows lining the far wall, illuminating three people strapped in chairs.

Alessa snatched a knife from the metal table and ran to the first girl. She fell to her knees in front of the chair.

The young woman was held upright by the ropes tied around her shoulders. Her chin rested against her chest, and the woman's orange hair was a sticky mess of congealed blood, sweat, and dirt as it hung in front of her blank face.

"No..." Alessa reached forward and pressed her shaking fingers into the stiff girl's neck.

No pulse.

The woman's hands were bound behind her back with a zip tie that dug deep into her wrists, exposing cream-colored bone.

Swallowing the hot bile that threatened to make its way up the back of her throat, Alessa shook her head in disgust. "There's no pulse. She's gone."

Damon crouched down in front of the second fallen chair. The woman was also strapped with her arms bound behind her.

After pressing his fingers into the second girl's neck, Damon glanced at Alessa and shook his head.

He moved on to the third person, a man, as Alessa walked over to the second body.

Even in death, the woman's faded blue-grey eyes remained open, and her jaw hung slightly ajar with dried blood crusted on her lower lip.

Thinking of Kai, Alessa stood, nauseated, before the blonde woman.

Could Kai have survived what I barely did?

Overwhelmed with emotion, she turned away from the gruesome scene.

Damon pulled his fingers away from the man's neck. "Shit, Alessa, he's alive."

The injured man's blond hair was streaked red and matted to the side of his face, and his arms were stretched painfully behind his back, held together by three hand ties.

As his head hung limp down onto his chest, his muscular shoulders pulled his body forward, putting more strain on his bound wrists. Jagged cuts had been made deep in his flesh, staining his torso the color of rust.

Damon glanced over at Alessa. "Are you sure about this? There's no turning back once it's done."

"If this is who I suspect it is, the guy they were talking about back in the plant, I think it would greatly benefit us to have him on our side. Besides, we can't leave him here. Not like this."

Damon ran to the wall of torture tools and plucked a knife and scissors from a standing tray.

"I mean, I would have no problem doing just that." Damon handed Alessa the scissors. "But if you want to..." He cut the rope, releasing the bound man's feet from the chair; meanwhile, Alessa reached behind his back and snipped the zip ties securing his wrists.

No longer restrained, the large man's weakened body fell forward into Alessa.

"Oh!" she yelped.

Grabbing his shoulders, Damon shoved the man back into the chair and held him upright.

Slamming down onto the metal seat, the gravely injured man moaned and struggled to open his eyes. His head bobbed as he looked down in disbelief at his unbound wrists. He attempted to lift his hands but hissed in pain before grabbing his left bicep.

Drawing attention to her presence, Alessa asked, "May I take a look?"

Narrowing his eyes, he jerked away.

"It looks like it may be out of place," she nodded toward his shoulder.

Letting go of his left arm, he shook his head, and as she examined the man, he mumbled, "Who are you?"

He cursed in Russian as Alessa pressed into his shoulder.

"Yeah, your shoulder is dislocated. Damon," she called out. "I need your help."

The injured man's hazel eyes stared at her wearily.

"I'm Alessa, and this is Damon. We'll get you out of here, but first, we must get your arm back in the socket."

Rubbing his sore throat with his good hand, he croaked, "Why are you helping me?"

"Hold still," she demanded as Damon approached the man's chair.

Damon pressed his hands into the man's bare torso, extended his arm, and popped his arm back into place.

"Jerk!" the man bellowed out in Russian.

Damon arched his eyebrows. "You're welcome," he muttered sarcastically.

"Camden," the man grunted.

Alessa's eyes darted back to the seated man. "What was that?"

"My name ... is Camden," the man clarified in a deep, scratchy voice.

Appeased, she smiled. "Camden. We'll help you stand up, and then we're getting out of here."

Camden scooted forward onto the edge of the chair and pushed up.

Both Damon and Alessa caught Camden as he collapsed, and as he verbally protested the movement of his hurt arm, they draped his arms across their shoulders.

"Great," Alessa huffed. "Another stubborn man."

"Hey, now," Damon defended himself in a breathy voice.

As they wobbled about, trying to get their footing, Camden stiffened from the disjointed movement.

The room was growing hotter by the minute as they headed for the exit door.

Hitting the midway point, the doors unexpectedly burst open, banging against the wall, and armed Bodyguards stormed in.

CHAPTER THIRTY-FIVE

Five Bodyguards rushed into the room, followed by Miguel.

Damon and Alessa looked over at one another before simultaneously dropping Camden.

As the injured man hit the floor, Alessa lunged for the metal tray full of weapons, and Damon pulled a handgun from his belt and aimed at the incoming threat.

He dodged bullets while shooting, but after squeezing the trigger for a fourth time, it clicked. With an annoyed growl, he tossed his empty gun at the guards before reaching into his jacket pocket.

After plucking blades from the nearby table, Alessa fell forward into a somersault. A chorus of bullets ricocheted off the walls, and she thrust a dagger into one of the Bodyguard's thighs.

With a loud grunt, Alessa flung another knife into a second silver suit's right arm and thrust a third blade straight through another guard's hand.

She aimed at the first man's other leg and chucked a thick blade.

The blade struck his kneecap, and as it shattered, he screamed in agony. The suit grabbed his demolished leg, and he collapsed to the ground.

Emerging with shuriken, Damon flicked his wrist, chucking the ninja stars at the incoming suits before sprinting across the room and jumping onto the wall of torture. Running vertically across the concrete wall, he grabbed hold of a machete and, upon descent, sliced through the fallen guard.

As one of the silver suits turned to look at the bloody scene, Alessa drove a smaller blade through his right ear before she turned her focus on Miguel.

Alessa threw a knife in his direction, but the scarred Hispanic darted to the side and strategically placed a guard in front of his chest.

As the blade impaled the silver suit, Miguel fired his weapon at Alessa, nicking her left bicep.

Damon ripped the machete from the dead man's body, then sliced it straight up in the air, hacking off the second guard's right arm. He then chopped through the same man's neck, disconnecting his head from his body.

As the decapitated guard slumped to the ground, Damon skirted around the bodies toward the one remaining guard. Glancing to the right, Damon read 'Acid' on the front of a glass container.

Gripping the bottle, he balanced the liquid while exchanging blows between himself and the Bodyguard until he finally smashed it down onto the man's head.

The guard shrieked as his features contorted into a gruesome, liquified mess and melted away.

The silver suit flopped around on the floor, and Damon winced as he took a bullet in his right shoulder.

Enraged, Damon roared as he rushed forward toward Miguel.

Alessa held her breath as Miguel aimed his gun at Damon's head and squeezed the trigger.

"No!" she cried out as the gun's empty chamber clicked.

The sound of the Spanish man's skull cracking beneath Damon's fist echoed throughout the room, and Miguel collapsed to the ground as Alessa clumsily scrambled to Damon.

"How bad is it?" she panicked.

He brushed her hands aside. "I'll be fine."

Alessa grabbed his injured arm. "But he shot you!"

"Woman!" Damon hissed as she ripped his shirt down the back.

"There's no exit wound."

"Shit," Damon cursed. "Guess you'll have to dig it out."

"What?" She shook her head. "You can't be serious."

"As serious as a gunshot wound." He grinned. "Now, go grab a knife."

Alessa uneasily peered over at the table. "Oh, hell no."

"Look at me," Damon urged.

She nervously bit her lower lip as he placed his uninjured hand on her shoulder.

"Believe it or not, you've done this hundreds of times. Even though your mind doesn't remember how to do it, your body will. Trust me."

"There you go with the 'trust me' crap again," Alessa grumbled.

She stomped to the nearest metal tray littered with knives, where she chose a thin, narrow blade.

He was lying on his back, examining the hole in his flesh.

"Great choice," Damon complimented Alessa, examining the blade. "Okay, so you need to draw a cross in my wound."

Alessa licked her lips and shook her head. "Damon, I don't know if I can do this..."

"We don't have time for that mentality. The longer you take, the more I heal, and I don't like the idea of having a bullet permanently lodged in my shoulder deciding to cause further damage whenever it damn well pleases."

Alessa exhaled loudly in frustration. "Don't I need to sterilize this or something?"

"I'll be fine. I heal fast, remember?" Damon reminded Alessa.

She rolled her eyes and bent over him, pressing the sharp metal into his skin.

His hands balled into fists as he pressed his lips together. "Good. Now, place the tip of the blade in my wound until you hit resistance. It'll be the bullet."

"But how do I know if it's the bullet and not bone?"

"You'll have to trust your judgment. Like I said, you've done this plenty of times; just let your muscle memory take control," Damon encouraged.

"Ugh. That's not exactly reassuring." Alessa held the knife above his bleeding wound.

With shaking hands, she tilted the sharp knife downward and exhaled before driving the tip of the blade into his flesh.

Squeezing his eyes shut, Damon's jaw clenched as she dug deep inside his shoulder.

Striking a solid object, she jumped in excitement. "Okay, now what?"

"You have to get it out," Damon said through gritted teeth.

Pressing further into his shoulder, she pursed her lips

together in concentration, and, bending the knife backward, Alessa dug up under the bullet.

The extracted bullet made a *ding* as it hit the floor.

As Damon's muscles relaxed, blood poured from his shoulder. "That feels better." He sighed. "You see that blowtorch over there?"

Alessa peered over her shoulder. "Yeah?"

He swallowed and took a deep breath. "You need to heat the blade."

Alessa glanced nervously between the blowtorch and Damon. "Is this necessary? I thought we healed quickly."

"Quickly, yes. Instantaneously? No. This kind of injury will take a couple of hours, and I would lose quite a bit of blood by that point. Germs are easy to combat. Excessive blood loss, not so much. It would just take me more time to recover than we have. We've got fifteen, maybe twenty, minutes before the building collapses."

"Ugh!" Alessa jumped up and hurried over to the blowtorch. Balancing the knife on its handle, she heated the metal, and once the silver blade was glowing blue, Alessa rushed back to Damon.

After wiping away the blood pooling inside his wound, she positioned herself over the puncture point and jammed the knife into Damon's shoulder.

He bellowed a slur of curse words in a language foreign to Alessa as smoke drifted up from his searing skin.

"I'm sorry, I'm sorry, I'm sorry," Alessa extracted the blade and pressed it against the wound's opening before tossing it off to the side. "Did I do okay?"

Damon grabbed his arm and sucked air in between his parted lips. Grimacing, he nodded his head.

"Here, let me help you." Alessa stood up, hunched over Damon.

"Getting shot does not make me an invalid." He shooed her away.

Standing upright, Damon directed Alessa's attention toward Miguel. "Isn't that our third target?"

"In the flesh," Alessa agreed. "Hey, grab one of those chairs and some zip ties."

"We don't have time for that." Damon flashed a seductive grin.

"Seriously? It's to tie him up." Alessa laughed sheepishly as she bent down to help Camden. "Sorry I dropped you."

The corner of his lips turned up weakly. "I think you mean *threw* me down. But from what I saw, I did not want to be in your way, so it's all good."

Alessa rolled her eyes. "You're not wrong. Here, let me help you up."

She wrapped her arm around him and placed his uninjured arm atop her shoulders.

He groaned upon standing and hunched over, holding his stomach.

Alessa nearly buckled under his weight. "Are you—?"

"Just give me a minute," he begged, closing his eyes.

As Alessa supported Camden, Damon slammed Miguel's limp body down into the seat of a metal chair, walked behind him, and wrapped a zip tie around each wrist before pulling it tight.

"Whew. I'm ready," Camden huffed.

Damon pulled some white rope off the wall and wrapped it around the unconscious man's chest, forcing him to sit upright in the chair as Alessa and Camden limped across the room.

She sat the gravely injured Bodyguard in an empty chair before approaching the Hispanic man.

Once Miguel's feet were secured to the chair legs, Damon clapped his hands together. "That'll do."

As he glared at Miguel, Alessa ripped a set of brass knuckles off the wall and slid them down over her fingers. She stared at the ugly scar carved up the right side of his tanned face until an unwanted memory entrapped her.

Surrounded by men, Alessa sat strapped to a chair in a dimly lit room.

Across from Craig and Henry sat a larger man sporting a crisp white suit puffing away on his cigar. They all watched as Miguel balled his hand into a fist and punched Alessa in her jaw.

Her vision swam with newly formed tears as her head bounced around. Refusing to let the tears fall, she blinked them away and used the pain to fuel her anger.

The scarred man jabbed his fingers beneath Alessa's jaw and tilted her head, forcing her to look at his eyes. "Still not talking, mi amor?"

Miguel snickered over at the man in the white suit, leaning out of the shadows.

Alessa's eyes widened in recognition.

It was Eric Lansing.

Without uttering a word, Eric nodded yes in response to Miguel's unspoken question.

Strolling over to a table full of various tools and weapons, Miguel ripped off a lengthy piece of silver tape. He grinned sadistically, grabbed Alessa's hair, and slapped the tape over her mouth.

Alessa struggled against his hold but could not fight back with her hands restrained. Her nostrils flared in anger as she breathed heavily.

Miguel strolled back over to the table and picked up an extravagant knife. "This is one of my favorites," he taunted, sliding his palm up and down the flat edge of the sharp blade. "You see this edge? This one, right here," he said, pointing it out to Alessa.

Her chest bounced up and down with her frantic breathing.

"This," he continued, "allows me to cut at several different angles, and depending on how much pressure I apply..."

Petrified whimpers escaped from behind Alessa's taped lips as he inched closer.

Miguel's sexual arousal pressed visibly up against his grease and blood-stained pants. Disgusted and horrified, she turned her head to the side, away from him.

Stopping before her, Miguel flipped the blade around and meticulously plucked the top two buttons off her shirt. Miguel licked his lips, staring down at the top of Alessa's breasts, bobbing up and down with her muffled cries. "Oh, mi amor," he whispered. "Do you know why I refuse to cut your long hair?"

Alessa whimpered and shook uncontrollably.

Miguel reached behind her head. "I like to have something to grab ahold of."

Her breathing quickened as the scarred man grabbed a fistful of her thick, dark hair. After forcibly yanking her head back, Miguel bit into the side of her neck.

CHAPTER THIRTY-SIX

Alessa's consciousness returned to the present, and as she came to, she was kneeling on the floor, gasping for breath.

Damon was crouched over her, his forehead wrinkled in concern. "Alessa. What just—?"

Hatred dripped from her pores and her eyes burned a fierce green as Alessa pushed up off the ground. Balling her right hand into a fist, she charged Miguel with a warrior cry and bashed the side of his face with her metal knuckles.

Miguel's head lolled to the side, and his eyes sluggishly blinked.

"Why, good morning, *mi amor*," Alessa spat.

Ignoring his cries, she strolled to the wall and plucked a smaller knife from its hold. "I wish I had more time to enjoy this."

Alessa walked in front of Miguel and stabbed the blade deep in his left thigh. She twisted the hilt maliciously, worsening his shrieks of agony.

The metallic structure of the building groaned under the intensity of the heat caused by the spreading fire.

"Alessa, we need to hurry this along," Damon warned.

She held up her hand. "This won't take long."

Leaving the knife in Miguel with its handle protruding from his leg, she glared down at him.

"But *estás muerto*," Miguel panted.

"Been there, done that. Death didn't stick."

"That's impossible," Miguel grunted as spit flew between his lips.

"Maybe you should've thought twice about having your assholes dump me in public," Alessa shrugged. "Now, I will ask you some questions, and I highly suggest you answer them. I'm exhausted after killing two of your colleagues, and at this point, my patience is non-existent."

Grabbing a pair of pliers, she strode behind Miguel's back and leaned forward, wrapping the silver tool around his right pinky finger.

"Where can we find Eric?"

Miguel snickered. "Even if I told you, you'd never get past his Bodyguards."

Damon rushed to shove anything he could in the crack as smoke seeped under the door.

With a snip of the tool, Miguel's finger was cut off at the knuckle.

Unintelligible curse words were strung together as he objected loudly.

"I don't have time for your games. Where's Eric?" Alessa demanded.

Once again, he refused to answer and pressed his lips firmly together.

Out of nowhere, Damon's fist slammed into the side of Miguel's face.

With his head bobbing unsteadily, Miguel glared up at Alessa and smiled lazily through bloodied teeth.

Frantic for answers, Alessa grabbed a clear container labeled 'Dry Ice'.

Panic flashed across Miguel's face briefly, but he quickly recovered and sported a sadistic grin.

"What the fuck could you possibly be so happy about?" she demanded.

"I was just thinking about how good your sister looked bound and gagged." He chuckled.

Alessa nearly dropped the container of dry ice. "You're lying!"

"Am I?" His eyes narrowed. "How else would I know she has a tattoo of two black birds on her left shoulder blade?"

Frozen in place, Alessa stared down at the man. "Is she—?"

"Dead? She wasn't the last time I saw her. But knowing Mr. Lansing, he took what she could provide and disposed of her like the rest."

Alessa's eyes flared.

She tore both of his pant legs at the thigh, uncapped the bottle, and poured dry ice pellets onto his legs.

He screamed in agony, and Alessa slammed the container down before pacing back and forth.

She stilled but for a moment before snatching up a hooked blade and rushing toward the bound man.

"*Un momento!*" he begged. "*Un momento!*"

Alessa stilled and listened to his leg sizzle under the intense cold as she pressed the metal against his skin.

"Eric is throwing a party," Miguel spat, his voice shaking.

Trying to satiate the tickle that had worked its way into his lungs, Damon aggressively cleared his throat.

Alessa scowled. "When?"

"In two nights," Miguel grumbled.

Alessa cocked her head to the side. "And where, might I ask, is this event being held?"

Sweat gathered across the scarred Spanish man's forehead as his eyebrows furrowed. "Chicago. At his chateau."

"Is this the only location where the pills are being manufactured?" Damon asked breathily.

Miguel nodded his head. "*Sí*, they're awaiting the first shipment in the attached warehouse. It is scheduled for tonight."

Damon turned away from Miguel and Alessa, his abs flexing against the overwhelming urge to cough.

Alessa pushed the knife further into Miguel's skin, drawing bright red blood from the side of his neck. "Where can I find the cure? The actual cure."

"Eric's the only one who knows where the few doses we've already made are being kept," he answered in a thick Spanish accent.

Unable to contain his breath any longer, Damon hunched over as his throat spasmed.

Alessa pulled the sharp edge away from Miguel as her attention fell upon Damon. Concern was etched upon her face.

"He isn't lookin' too *bueno*," said Miguel.

"Shut the hell up," Alessa barked over Damon's hacking.

"Touchy." Miguel squinted as his gaze darted back and forth between Damon and Alessa. His eyes widened in comprehension. "He was given the TB pill, wasn't he?"

"You don't know what the hell you're talking about," Alessa denied.

With a smug look on his face, Miguel nodded his head. "Oh, *señora*, I think I do."

Smoke seeped in through the cracks in the wall and under the door.

Enraged, Alessa snatched up a canister from the side of the room, filled with gasoline, and dumped it over Miguel's head.

He coughed and gagged as the liquid saturated his skin and clothes.

Through violent retching, Miguel smirked wickedly. "You ... can't ... save ... him."

A spark ignited behind her green irises, and she struck a match, scowling at the doomed man. "You're mistaken. It's you who can't be saved."

Rotating on her heel, Alessa threw the lit match over her shoulder.

It landed at Miguel's feet, and he shrieked as flames consumed his body.

"What did he say?" a winded Damon asked.

"Nothing worth repeating," Alessa replied. "Do you need—?"

"I'm good," he dismissed Alessa with a wave.

Moving in unison, Damon and Alessa reached down and balanced Camden between the two of them before heading out a second door.

After hobbling down the stairs, they spilled into the chaotic lobby, blending in with the crowd as the plant's workers ran for the front door.

Bursting through the exit, they emerged from the fire-engulfed building, coughing the smoke from their lungs.

Alessa leaned Camden against their car as Damon took the keys out of his pocket and unlocked the doors.

Noticing the key around Alessa's neck, Camden lifted a shaking finger. "The key..."

She glanced down at the silver key and then back at him. "What about it? I found it on a Bodyguard."

"It ... goes ... to an .... old ... barn out ... back," he panted, slumping against the car.

Damon held onto Camden as Alessa opened the back passenger car door, and Camden collapsed, barely conscious, into the seat. "It's where ... we ... kept the ... subjects," he breathed.

"Subjects?" Damon asked.

Camden weakly nodded. "When I ... tried to stop them," he gasped. "They ... were ... terminating..." His eyes rolled into the back of his head as he was rendered unconscious.

Damon and Alessa gaped at one another, and as if reading each other's minds, they sprinted behind the burning manufacturing plant.

CHAPTER THIRTY-SEVEN

Nearly a full mile behind the burning building stood an old white barn.

As Damon and Alessa ran up to the large barn door, they were slammed with a foul odor.

Alessa's nose scrunched up in disgust, and she covered her face with her hand. "Ugh, what is that smell?"

Damon stiffened. "Alessa, you don't need to come in."

"What do you mean? Of course, I'm coming in." Alessa fumbled with the clasp behind her neck before dropping the key from the chain into her palm.

Recognizing the unforgettable scent of death, Damon warned Alessa, "You need to prepare yourself."

Alessa handed him the key. "For what, exactly?"

Damon unlocked the deadbolt and pushed the wooden door open, releasing the stench of decaying bodies.

Alessa gagged. "What the f—?"

Damon shook his head and entered the building. Scanning the perimeter for Bodyguards, he quickly realized none were necessary.

Cages lined the barn's perimeter, from the front to the back, each containing a single corpse.

Every person's chest was covered in blood, with a puddle of bodily fluids beneath their body.

Alessa's eyes landed upon a group of smaller cages in which young children were being kept, and she ran back out the door, leaned over the porch, and vomited into the dried grass.

She wiped the side of her mouth with her shaking hand. "All those people ... the kids—" Alessa's voice cracked.

Damon walked up behind her, struggling to keep his anger in check. "If we don't stop Erebos, this is just the beginning." He took Alessa's hand in his own. "Let's get out of here."

"What if—?"

"No," he shook his head. "We can't help anyone in there. Not now."

In a somber mood, they went back to the car, and as Alessa dove into the passenger seat, she peered over her shoulder at the man lying awkwardly in the back.

Damon started the car. "If we find out he had anything to do with that, back there ... I will kill him."

Unable to open her mouth in fear of vomiting again, Alessa stared out the window in silence.

"Also," he shifted into first gear, "he's damn lucky this isn't my car, or I'd kill him for bleeding all over the interior."

Every so often, Alessa glanced back at Camden, and as the minutes slipped by, she grew increasingly worried about the amount of blood pooling beneath his torso.

Alessa spoke up as the last bit of color drained from Camden's face, leaving him ashen. "Um ... Damon?" Alessa reached into the back seat and touched Camden's cool, grey face. "I think we need to stop."

"What, why?"

"If we don't treat his wounds now, he's not going to make it," Alessa pleaded.

Damon grumbled and looked into the rearview mirror. "Why do I care if he lives or dies? What's so special about this guy?"

"I think he can help us."

"What?" Damon yelled. "Are you crazy? He works for those assholes. Bodyguards don't change sides. They can't."

"I need to find out for myself."

He rolled his eyes at Alessa before peering at the man in the backseat, and with an angry sigh, he returned his attention to the road before him. "Fine. I'll stop."

A few minutes later, Damon pulled into the parking lot of an older motel. "Stay here. I'll get us a room."

As he walked away, Alessa pushed her car door open.

Reaching up toward the sky, she stretched her sore muscles. After pulling her seat forward, she wedged her body in between the fabric and the gravely injured man. "Don't tell Damon this, but I don't know what to do with you. All I know is I couldn't leave you there. If someone had found me when I was—well—I would've given anything to have been saved."

Beads of sweat covered Camden's face, and his upper lip glistened. With a quiet moan, his eyebrows pressed together as his eyes darted back and forth beneath closed lids.

"Shh ... It's okay. I've got you," Alessa cooed.

Damon snuck up behind Alessa. "You ready?"

She jumped in surprise before climbing out of the car. "Yeah, I'll go open the door for you."

He handed Alessa the key to their room and helped the

Bodyguard out of the car. "I need you to stay awake. You aren't exactly light," he instructed Camden while pulling him off the back seat.

Alessa raced for their door and opened it to find two queen-sized beds positioned side by side on the left wall, a television sitting directly across from the beds, a table with one fabric chair on either side and a small bathroom illuminated with yellow light, tucked away in the far-right corner.

Alessa fingered the lamp's switch, and its light flickered, casting a dim yellow glow across the beige carpet.

The two men shuffled in, and Alessa propped open the bathroom door, directing Damon toward the bathtub. "In here."

He kicked the front door shut and lumbered with the large man across the room. "Ugh." He tossed him into the tub.

Alessa hissed as Camden's head hit the side of the tub. "Be careful."

Standing upright, Damon stretched his back.

She repositioned Camden. "Where exactly are we?"

Damon rubbed his right shoulder. "I saw a sign for Alvin a few miles back."

"Okay, then," Alessa said while trying to figure out what to do next for the injured man. She grabbed a hand towel and wadded it before handing it to Damon. "Help me. I need you to hold pressure right here," she directed him toward Camden's flank.

Crouching beside the bathtub, Damon pressed the white towel into the man's wound while Alessa left the bathroom to look for supplies. As her eyes wandered around the motel room, she saw a silver ice bucket propped up beside the television and grabbed it.

After filling the container with hot water, Alessa plucked a bar of soap from the counter and brought it to Camden. "Thanks, I've got it from here."

Damon removed his hand and headed for the door. "I'm making a supply run. What do you need?"

She glanced around. "Whatever I need to fix him."

"I think I can figure it out." He nodded. "Hey..."

Alessa peered up at him, unable to hide her exhaustion. "Yeah?"

Damon handed her a knife. "Take this, just in case he tries anything."

Her eyes scrunched up in disbelief as she peered down at the man who was barely holding on. "Uh ... thanks?"

Damon marched out of the motel room and locked Alessa in with the unconscious Bodyguard.

Inspecting the man's wounds, she grew concerned with the extent of the damage he'd obtained. Even though she couldn't recall every bit of medical knowledge from her schooling just yet, from what she could tell, it wasn't looking good.

Letting go of the towel, she grabbed the bottom of his torn jeans, and while holding the fabric away from his skin, Alessa carefully dragged the sharp blade toward his belt.

Peeling the fabric back, dark green boxer briefs remained the only article of clothing left on Camden's body.

Burns, bruises, and jagged lines had been carved into his flesh.

Closing her eyes tight, Alessa fought to rid herself of the images of her own torture.

"I understand how you're feeling. Much more than I'd like to admit," Alessa mumbled aloud.

With a steadying breath, she wedged two towels in between the side of the tub and Camden's gaping wound to slow the bleeding. Alessa then dipped a white washcloth into the hot water, and while holding it above Camden, she squeezed the clean liquid onto his chest.

Filthy water ran down his abdomen and sides, staining the white bathtub beneath him.

After washing the loose dirt and grime from his skin, Alessa rubbed soap onto the saturated cloth and massaged the suds into Camden's wounds.

Alessa cleansed until she could no longer see through the murky water in the ice bucket. After rinsing out the silver container in the bathroom sink, she refilled it with fresh water before returning to Camden's side.

The bottom of the tub was caked in bloodied, dirty, odorous water as Alessa kneeled and eased her hands up under his body. Grunting aloud, she rolled him onto his side as far as she could.

Her arms trembled as she struggled to hold up his body weight. Examining the gaping wound forged deep into the far-left side of his back, she also found three jagged lines resembling claw marks down the man's spine.

"Dammit, Damon, where are you?"

After dropping Camden down onto his back, she wadded up the remaining towels and shoved them beneath his body to prevent additional blood loss.

With his body weight applying pressure to the wounds, Alessa sat back on her heels, consumed by helplessness. Unable to do much more without the supplies, she spoke to the man and waited impatiently for Damon to return.

"I'm sorry, but this has been a crazy week." She glanced at the unconscious man. "I've gone from being an ordinary, or at least what I thought was an ordinary, waitress, to a member of a secret society who is believed to no longer exist. Trippy, I know."

The man whimpered in his sleep, and his breathing faltered.

"Shit. Where's Damon? He needs to get back with those supplies." Alessa twirled the crisscrossed band on her finger while pacing back and forth.

The motel door opened, and Damon carried several plastic bags into the room. "He still alive?"

Alessa hurriedly took the bags and rushed toward the bathroom. "For now," she huffed, spilling the bag's contents onto the floor.

Damon eyed Camden, unmoving, in the tub. "Anything I can do?"

Alessa shook her head as she sifted through the supplies.

"You're remembering," Damon observed.

"What do you mean?"

"Just a little over two hours ago, you were shaking in your boots when you had to dig a bullet out of my shoulder. Now, look at you, practically prepping for surgery."

Her movements slowed as she realized the truth in his words. "Huh. I didn't even think about it."

"It's not a conscious decision to become your past self. It's more or less a reflex." He pointed toward the supplies strewn across the floor.

Alessa's eyes darted up toward Damon, and as an intense jolt of electricity passed between them, both sucked in a deep breath.

Damon looked away. "Okay, then. I'm gonna, uh, go grab us some food."

Alessa arched her eyebrow at Damon incredulously.

He shrugged before walking away. "What? I'm hungry."

"Just go," Alessa grumbled, picking up the orange and green T-shirts.

Texas was printed on the front of each one. She ripped the shirts down the middle and wrapped the strips of fabric around Camden's more minor lacerations.

As Alessa secured the last piece of T-shirt around his left bicep, Camden's eyes fluttered.

His dark green and brown irises pierced into her, startling Alessa.

With her heart racing, she firmly placed her hand on the man's naked shoulder. "I'm here to help. Do you remember me?"

CHAPTER THIRTY-EIGHT

Camden's eyebrows furrowed together in confusion.

"My friend and I found you back at the plant. You were tied to a chair," Alessa explained.

Looking off into the distance, his face relaxed. "Oh. That I remember. Some of it, at least."

She smiled in encouragement. "That's good."

"What's your name?" he asked.

She tied the ends of the fabric together. "Alessa."

"Alessa ... that's unique."

She bit her lip nervously and peered at the red pooling beneath his torso. "Camden, I need you to roll over."

"Why?"

"There's a wound on your back that needs to be cauterized. You've lost a lot of blood, and I'm not sure how much more you have to lose. Honestly, I'm surprised you're even conscious right now." Alessa arched an eyebrow.

"Are you a doctor?"

"Mmm. Not exactly," Alessa mumbled.

His smile disappeared. "A nurse?"

Alessa cocked her head to the side, scrunching up the left side of her face. "I'm not sure."

"Wait, what? How do you not know?" Camden stared at her, his expression one of doubt. "You're either a nurse or not; there isn't a kind-of-sort-of option."

Frustrated, she glared down at him. "Let me ask you this: do you have another choice?"

Camden's eyes wandered around the bathroom. "I guess not," he conceded with a nervous laugh.

"Okay, then." Alessa turned to the side and finished setting up.

She placed two bottles of whiskey, three packs of unflavored dental floss, a mini sewing kit, and a lighter beside her. Unscrewing the lid from a bottle of alcohol, Alessa held it out to Camden. "Here, drink some of this."

"If you're trying to get me drunk, you'll need more than one bottle." The Bodyguard's laughter ceased as he grabbed his abdomen in pain.

"This is going to hurt, and I don't have strong enough painkillers. Ibuprofen isn't going to cut it."

Camden took a swig from the bottle of whiskey. "I think I can handle a little bit of pain."

"Hurry up, you're wasting time," Alessa urged.

Dropping the bottle from his lips, Camden chortled. "Has anyone ever told you you're kind of bossy?"

Ignoring him, she stole the whiskey from his grasp. "Good?"

He grinned weakly. "Not even close."

"Well, it has to be good enough."

"Yes, mother," he quipped sarcastically.

Her eyes narrowed, and she stopped moving. "How can you possibly be joking, being this close to death?"

"I've always been a bit off. Huh. Maybe that's why I did it, why I could defy my orders." Camden stared into the distance.

Only half listening, Alessa set the bottle on the ground and sat on her knees. She shoved her hands underneath his body and paused. "You ready?"

Camden braced himself and nodded.

With a loud grunt, she rolled Camden up on his side, and as he fell onto his stomach, blood poured from the gaping wound.

His body spasmed as she pulled back the blood-soaked towel and poured the whiskey onto him.

Sucking in the air between pursed lips, he hissed and yelled, "Fuck!" into the white tub.

Dropping the glass bottle, Alessa scrambled to ignite the lighter. As she held the blade above the flame, Camden's cuts overflowed with blood.

"Come on," she urged the flame.

As the steel turned blue from the heat, Alessa tossed the lighter off to the side and pressed a clean cloth into the wound. She positioned the searing hot blade over Camden. "No matter how much this hurts, you cannot move."

His body tensed, and Alessa buried the hot weapon deep into his back.

Camden's strangled cries echoed off the bathtub, and as his fingernails scratched against the porcelain, his tendons and veins bulged from beneath his golden skin.

Choking on the smoke rising from the wound, she extracted the knife and was relieved to find the bleeding had stopped.

Camden relaxed as exhaustion took hold, and Alessa picked up the needle and dental floss. "You still with me?"

Slowly, he turned his head to the side. "Unfortunately," he grumbled.

"I thought you could handle a bit of pain," Alessa mocked as she threaded the floss through the needle. "I have to stitch you up now, so hold still," she instructed, tying a knot.

Camden grimaced as Alessa pulled his skin together on either side of the wound.

She shoved the needle into his flesh and pierced the opposite side. Tugging on the floss, she pulled the needle up before bringing the two sides together.

Camden interrupted the silence. "Where are we?"

Alessa threaded the needle and floss into his flesh yet again. "At a motel somewhere near Alvin, Texas."

"And how did I get here?"

She pulled the dental floss taut. "We drove."

"But why?"

Alessa stilled and looked in Camden's hazel eyes. "Excuse me?"

"Why did you save me? You could've easily left me to burn."

She hesitated for a moment. "For one, I heard Miguel talking about you, how you went against them. That caught my attention since that goes against everything Damon's told me: once a Bodyguard is given orders, they are to be followed, end of story."

"He's not wrong," Camden agreed.

"Interesting." Alessa paused. "So, what's your story, Camden? What made you turn?"

Before he could answer, Damon burst through the door and yelled across the motel room, "How are things coming along?"

He entered the bathroom and glanced at Alessa and Camden, raising his eyebrows in surprise. "I see Frankenstein's monster is awake."

Damon marched back into the main room, and with an

exasperated sigh, he tossed several plastic bags onto the table. "Got us some clothes and beach towels, seeing as the motel's once-white towels are pretty much shot to shit."

Damon went back over to the bathroom and leaned against the doorway. "Also, in this paper bag," he gestured to one of the two sacks he held within his grasp, "are two bottles of whiskey not to be used on that guy, but for me to consume." He handed her a greasy paper bag. "Your bacon cheeseburgers. I ate mine on the way back."

Juggling the needle and floss, Alessa placed the brown bag on the ground.

Damon flopped down on the bed closest to the bathroom before kicking off his shoes with a loud sigh. Digging into his paper bag, he pulled out a bottle and loosened its lid. *I hate drinking alcohol, but I need to numb myself before I do something stupid.*

"Thanks," Alessa said as Damon took a decent swig of whiskey.

"Anytime." He held the bottle up to his lips and sunk into the bed.

"What's with him?" Camden asked.

Alessa redirected her attention back to Camden. "Don't mind him. He's—well, from what I can tell, that's just Damon being Damon."

"What you're saying is, he's always that much of a dick? Got it."

Holding back laughter, Alessa smiled. "Is it alright with you if I continue?"

Camden nodded, wincing as she stuck the needle and floss back into his skin.

"Before Damon walked in, we were discussing why you turned on Erebos," Alessa said.

"We were?" Camden joked.

"Yes, we were."

"You're not going to let this go, are you?"

Alessa stared into his hazel eyes. "I saved your life. The least you could do is tell me it was worth the risk."

Camden conceded with a nod. "I'll give you that. Well, where should I start?"

"The beginning, I suppose."

CHAPTER THIRTY-NINE

"The beginning ... Um, well, I guess my story began when I was discovered on the doorsteps of an orphanage in Russia when I was three days old," said Camden.

He sucked in a breath of air as Alessa dug into his flesh once again.

She gave him an apologetic smile. "Sorry."

"Nothing I can't handle. Do you know who Bodyguards work for?"

"Honestly, I don't know much about them at all."

"Yet you chose to take on an entire building full of us?" Camden asked in disbelief.

"I was following Damon's lead. Now, please continue with your back story."

"From what I saw, I'm not sure if I believe that," he mumbled. "But okay. The Elite Organization trains boys from infancy to work for them as Bodyguards. Bodyguards are vigorously trained and programmed to serve and protect whoever the Elite instructs us to, no questions asked.

"Honestly, I enjoyed the life. I would've had it much worse

if the Elite hadn't taken me out of that orphanage. I was raised with a bunch of other boys who became my family.

"In the Elite, if we pass a test at seventeen, we become Brethren of the Official Bodyguards. Our entire life's work is to do as instructed without question, and we put our lives on the line for those who hire our services.

"I admit, I've had some questionable assignments in the past, but never to the extent I had when working for Erebos Industries."

Alessa realized she had stopped stitching. "Oh, sorry. Please continue."

"I am the head of security for Miguel. At least I was," Camden snickered.

"If you don't mind me asking, why are all of you dressed like models in those matching silver suits?" Alessa smirked.

"I never questioned it. It's just a uniform."

Alessa tied a double knot and pulled the floss tight. "Done." She leaned over and picked up the super glue. "I'm going to seal up the smaller cuts."

"Sounds good to me."

"That doesn't mean you stop talking," Alessa pressed.

Camden licked his lips before continuing. "It was not an easy decision to turn against my men. They're all the family I know. But Eric, that man—"

"Is evil," Alessa interrupted.

Camden huffed. "You have no idea."

"Oh, I have a pretty good one," Alessa grumbled.

"When we were instructed to collect the subjects, I tried to resist. I fought hard not to follow the orders, but it's not that simple. And then, when he gave the orders to exterminate them, I couldn't do it; wouldn't do it. The men and women were begging to be freed. And the kids, they were crying." He pushed the heel of his hands into his eyelids and trembled. "I'll never forget it. Never."

Listening to his heart-wrenching story, Alessa paused.

"I tried to stop them, and that's when I was taken down. It took at least ten experienced guards." He peered over his naked shoulder at Alessa. "I know I'm no angel, and there is probably no amount of good I can do in this world to make up for the terrible things I've done, but I need to try. I can't keep living like this."

She held his separated flesh together and applied a thin strip of glue. "Do you really want to take down Erebos?"

"Absolutely."

Alessa swallowed before she continued speaking. "Then come with us to Chicago and help us stop Eric."

Camden sighed aloud. "I'm sorry, I can't."

"Camden, please, think about it."

He shook his head slowly back and forth. "Alessa, you don't understand—"

"You deserve a fresh start, a new beginning. I, of all people, can't judge you by your past. I mean, I can't even remember all the fucked-up things I've done." She glanced over at Damon, asleep on the bed with the bottle of whiskey balanced against his arm.

"What do you mean you can't remember?"

Alessa tossed the empty tube of glue into the trash can. "I've got amnesia or something," she said casually. "You need to flip over so I can get to the rest."

Pressing his lips together, Camden pushed up off the slick tub and flopped ungracefully onto his back.

Digging through the paper bag, Alessa grabbed a burger and a water bottle. "Here," she handed him the food and drink.

As Camden took the burger and water from Alessa, he also snatched the open glass bottle.

"Before you do that..." Camden said before he tilted his head back and downed the remaining caramel liquid.

She rolled her eyes and grabbed the second, full bottle of whiskey. "You ready now?"

His body tensed. "Go for it."

Alessa sat up on her knees, and as she poured the alcohol onto his chest and stomach, it dripped down to his ankles.

Camden yelped, and a slew of curse words fell out of his mouth as the alcohol disinfected his wounds.

Alessa recapped the bottle, grabbed a new tube of adhesive, and popped the lid. Pressing the sides of the wound together, she applied the glue.

"How did you lose your memory?" Camden asked with a full mouth.

Unsure of how to respond, Alessa exhaled in frustration before peering up at the Bodyguard.

Damn, he is handsome.

Camden's hair remained red-tinged and dirty, but the water had styled his strands into a sexy mess. His face was no longer caked in dirt or blood, revealing a sharp jawline and tiny creases embedded on each side of his light pink lips. The Bodyguard's eyes were a deep, forest green with flakes of yellow and brown scattered throughout.

Alessa's insides twisted as her breathing faltered, and she licked her lips before staring down at the glue bottle as though it were suddenly the most interesting thing in the room.

"Uh..." Alessa squeezed her eyes shut and gathered her thoughts. "I worked undercover for Vindico and downloaded information Erebos wanted to keep quiet. When Eric discovered I was going to expose him, I was tortured. And then killed."

"So, you're a Spartan. Wait, you were dead? As in, your heart stopped beating?"

Alessa handed Camden another bottle of water with a shrug. "That's the story."

Eyeing her, he slowly twisted the lid off the bottle. "Then, how are you alive right now?"

"The place where Eric's men chose to dump my body was next to a busy riverfront. The truth is, I got lucky," Alessa confessed.

Camden took a long drink of water. "And how'd you lose your memory?"

"The jury is still out on that one. We aren't exactly sure how my memory was erased. Possibly a disruption in the connection to Vindico's database because of the number of times an AED was used on me, or Henry Penway mentioned something about a serum I was injected with—" She poured additional whiskey over his wounds. "Regardless, everyone at home thinks I'm dead."

Alessa reached into the paper bag for the second cheeseburger.

"You know Henry?"

"Well," Alessa choked on her saliva. "I *knew* him..."

Camden's right eyebrow arched in disbelief. "And you can't remember a single thing?"

She handed Camden the other burger. "Right after I woke up in the hospital, I could only remember my first name. After that, moments in time have slowly returned in visions and dreams—or nightmares." She stared out the bathroom door at Damon and shivered. "Some memories are coming back slower than others."

"Did Damon say when he expects you to remember everything?" Camden bit into the burger.

Alessa watched Damon breathe slowly as he slept. "There's no guarantee my memory will ever fully return."

She chuckled nervously before placing the adhesive tube against Camden's skin. Dragging a thin glue strip across a small wound, Alessa pinched his skin together and closed another gap.

Camden jerked his head in Damon's direction. "What's with that guy?" he said with his mouth full of meat.

"Who, Damon? We supposedly lived together in Colorado. He's the only one who came back for me." Alessa's stomach clenched as she was once more consumed with guilt over him being forced to take the bioengineered tuberculosis pill.

Camden's eyebrows rose as he tilted his chin down suggestively. "You lived together?"

"Oh." Alessa's eyes widened in embarrassment. "Um, no. We didn't live together, like *together*, together. Just in the same community," she rambled.

He cocked his head to the side. "Okay. So, what was that sad look about?"

Alessa watched Damon's chest move slowly up and down. "I'm not sure how much Damon wants you to know ... but ... screw it. We need your help."

CHAPTER FORTY

Alessa scooted in closer to Camden and lowered her voice. "You already know we're trying to take down Eric and his company, but we're also going to try to find my sister, who went missing at the same time as I did."

"Alessa—" Camden started.

She held her hands up to silence him. "I don't want to hear it. I know it's damn near impossible to survive being caught. Trust me, I know that all too well, but I can't accept the fact that my sister might be dead. I won't stop until I find her."

Camden exhaled loudly and closed his eyes. "Okay, okay. Being an orphan, I never had a blood family, so I can't say I get it, but—"

Her gaze pierced Camden. "There's one more thing, but you cannot tell Damon."

Camden's eyes scrunched up in concern. "Okay...?"

Alessa exhaled loudly, rubbing her palms up and down her thighs. "Damon took the red pill."

"What?" Camden exclaimed, nearly choking on his meal.

Alessa's arms flailed. "Shh! He doesn't know, and we can't

tell him. I didn't tell him after it happened because I didn't know how to tell someone they were dying. Especially since the only reason he got dosed was because he came back to help me. Plus, I don't know how he'll react. And I can't take down Eric on my own."

"The guy swallowed a death pill, and you're not going to say a thing?"

"What am I supposed to say? Thanks for being the only one from my past to come looking for me, but you came down with a super strain of tuberculosis, and I'm sorry for that, but keep your head in the game?" Alessa huffed.

Camden glanced out the bathroom door. "How much time does he have?"

She bowed her head in defeat. "At this point, we only have two nights to find the antidote."

Camden gasped. "Alessa ... that's barely enough time to make it to Chicago, let alone find and administer the cure."

"You think I don't realize that?" Alessa spat angrily as Camden lay back and sank into the hard tub.

"Please, help us," she pleaded.

"Gimme a minute to think about it." He looked up at the bathroom ceiling.

"What's there to think about? You want to stop Eric; we want to stop Eric. Why can't we work together?"

Camden sat up with a grunt. "Look, Alessa," his hazel eyes bore into her, "I'm only considering going with you because you saved my life. And well, I hate Eric Lansing, and if we don't take him down ... I guess ... Ugh ... Dammit." He paused. "Besides," Camden grinned. "You are easy on the eyes."

Her lips twisted up in embarrassment as she wiped her hands off on a towel. "Wow, you really need to get some sleep.

You are clearly delusional. Come on, let's get you out of that tub and into bed."

Alessa wrapped her arms around Camden's waist and slowly helped him out of the tub. With an arm draped across her shoulder, he shuffled across the tiles and stumbled over to the bed.

Releasing the Bodyguard, Alessa stood upright and yawned, stretching her arms upward. Being stuck in the same position working on Camden for so long had made her body ache everywhere.

Camden snored loudly within a minute of hitting the bed.

Alessa chuckled while grabbing the ice bucket on her way back to the bathroom.

After washing down the shower walls, tiled floor, and bathtub, she unzipped her filthy black combat boots and dropped each one with a thud before stretching her neck to the side.

Damon's wet cough interrupted her moment of peace, and she rushed out of the bathroom.

He was lying half naked, his shirt having been tossed off to the side. She placed her hand on his cheek and was alarmed by the temperature of his skin.

Rushing back into the bathroom, Alessa filled the ice bucket with cool water, and on her way back to the bed, she snatched one of the last remaining clean cloths from beside the sink.

Placing the bucket on the side table, she sat on the bed next to Damon and leaned against him. Her exposed thigh brushed against his searing hot skin, and she jumped at the electricity that sparked with the touch.

Alessa readjusted herself so her skin no longer touched Damon and dunked the cloth into the cool water. Pressing the white washcloth against his red-tinged forehead, she worked down his upper body, splashing cool water onto his cheeks, neck, and chest.

His eyebrows moved up and down as she re-wet the cloth and continued further down his chiseled abs. Alessa reassured Damon as his lips moved. "Shh. It's alright. I'm right here."

"Alessa?" he moaned.

Surprised by his sexual tone, she dropped the cloth into the silver bucket. "Yeah, it's me."

"Mmm ..." Damon wrapped his arms around her in a fiery embrace. Crushing their bodies against one another, he placed one hand behind Alessa's neck and pressed her lips against his own.

As they touched, an electric shock surged between their bodies, and as Alessa straddled Damon's erect cock, an unexpected moan escaped her lips.

Alessa's eyes popped open in surprise.

His thickness pressed against her, barely contained by the zipper on his jeans, and as Alessa's wetness soaked through her thin swimsuit, she left her mark on his pants.

Through shallow breaths, Damon forced Alessa's head to the side and hungrily kissed up the side of her neck while she instinctively rocked her hips back and forth.

Her eyes squeezed shut as he nipped at her exposed collarbone.

Damon's tongue and lips burned their marks into Alessa's milky skin, and his silver irises were looking into hers, setting her heart aflame with desire.

In one fluid motion, he flipped Alessa onto her back and rolled on top, pressing her into the mattress. Damon worked his knee between Alessa's legs, pushing them apart before sinking further into her.

Damon ground his hips against her own, and then he took her hands within his own and pressed them into the pillow on either side of her head.

With each stroke of his fingertips, every kiss down her neck and chest, Alessa held back her moans so they didn't wake Camden.

He released his grip on her hands, and Damon's fingers trailed down Alessa's sides as he licked between her breasts. He kissed along the middle of her yellow sundress, all the way down to her exposed black swimsuit, which barely covered her mound.

Alessa bit her lower lip seductively as Damon's silver irises pierced through her.

His fingers dug deep into her hip bones, holding her in place as he nuzzled her, smelling and licking the sweet juices that seeped through the swimsuit's fabric.

"Damon..." she moaned breathily as her hips writhed reflexively beneath his touch.

With a guttural growl, Damon wiped his mouth with the back of his hand, and propping her upright, he crashed into Alessa's red, swollen lips.

She eagerly ran her fingers through his soft hair, grabbing short brown tufts every time Damon gasped, vocalizing his pleasure.

In between kisses, he moaned her name. "Alessa..."

Damon slid his hands under her backside, lifting her up off the bed, and set her down on top of him.

He pressed his swollen cock up against Alessa, and she trembled with the intense need for him to fill her.

Lightheaded with desire, Alessa unbuttoned Damon's pants, and as she pulled down his zipper, Damon's eyes burst open, and his bright blue irises glared at Alessa's working hand.

"What the fuck?" He jumped up from the bed.

Damon turned away from Alessa and tried to coax his erection back into his pants.

Both alarmed and confused, Alessa crossed her arms in front of her chest, feeling exposed. "Damon, you—"

"Fuck ... just ... no," he grunted before putting his hand up to silence Alessa. *I can't focus like this. Is that her scent on my face? Fucking Hades.*

"I don't want to hear it," Damon barked.

He stormed to the bathroom and slammed the door behind him.

Alessa stared at the closed door in shock. "What in the hell just happened?"

Damon turned the shower on and stepped into the ice-cold water. With his arms outstretched, he leaned against the tiled wall and gritted his teeth as the water hit his erect cock.

How could I let myself go like that? If anything had happened—if I had forced a memory on her—I'd never forgive myself.

Damon fell inside a memory of him sitting on his bed, looking down at a small black box.

He lifted the lid and stared at his mother's wedding ring. A center stone made of alexandrite sat in the middle of a thin black band.

Damon erased the image from his mind with a shake of his head.

Eventually, he turned the shower off and got out of the tub. Glancing around the empty bathroom, he realized he had left the bag of new clothes out on the table near the entry door. "Fuck the gods," he cursed.

Left upset and vulnerable, Alessa fell back on the bed and stared at the stained ceiling with tear-filled eyes.

What happened? Was it something I did? Something I didn't do?

Camden's snoring interrupted her thoughts, and she peered over at the sleeping giant, thankful he hadn't witnessed the embarrassing scene.

Suddenly, very much aware of how alone in the world she was, Alessa dove under the covers and curled up on her side. As her body trembled from the adrenaline withdrawal, Alessa forced her eyes shut in a vain attempt to stop tears from tumbling down.

The pillow soon became saturated with her salty tears, and her body stiffened in response to the bathroom door creaking open.

Damon stomped across the carpet toward the table before dropping the beach towel from around his waist.

As Alessa lay perfectly still, pretending to be asleep, Damon pulled on a pair of black boxer briefs.

He ripped the price tag from a pair of blue jeans, tugged them on, and grabbed a black T-shirt and a pair of combat boots.

Marching out of the motel room, he locked the door behind him without a glance back at Alessa.

Within minutes of Damon leaving, an emotionally and physically exhausted Alessa was once again consumed by her dreams.

CHAPTER FORTY-ONE

A seven-year-old Alessa held a hand over her eyes to block the bright sun as her elder explained the rules of engagement to all the Spartan children.

"If your opponent raises their hand like this," he demonstrated, "and holds up the first two fingers at any point during the match, they are announcing their defeat, and it is over. No additional attacks will be tolerated, and you are expected to respect their decision to 'give' as it is not easy for our people to accept defeat. Your opponent is essentially deciding it is better to die, in theory, than be killed during an exercise.

"You are highly encouraged to use all your learned skills during each match; we must ensure you live to continue our bloodline in a real-life scenario."

Alessa's elder eyed her specifically. "If you are chosen to join us at your ceremony."

The memory jumped back in time, and Alessa peeked around the side of the mountain at a young, blonde-haired Kai. She was playing in the tall grass with their elder's wife, so carefree and full of life.

Watching her sister play without a care in the world, she knew that although their spirits were linked by blood, Alessa's heart would never allow her to be quite so open to love after what she had endured in the cabin.

Then, the dream fast-forwarded a few years later.

Alessa was hugging her sister before bed.

"Lessie, please don't leave me," Kai whined while being tucked in.

"Shh. You know no one is supposed to know about me sneaking out," she hushed.

"What do you do?" Kai crossed her arms and rested them upon the covers.

Alessa sighed. "I need some time by myself to clear my mind. You know we are never alone during the day, so I seek the peace the moon and stars grant me at night."

Kai rolled her eyes. "Sometimes I don't understand you."

"You and me both. Now, get to sleep. You've got a busy day ahead of you."

She kissed Kai on the forehead and quietly snuck out their bedroom door. Looking both ways down the hallway, Alessa darted into the nearest room with a hidden passage leading outside.

Emerging into the cool night air, Alessa cursed herself for not grabbing a jacket. Mumbling under her breath, she headed for the horse barn to borrow a wool blanket from the stables.

Opening the large wooden door, Alessa met a teenage boy brushing a white mare in the middle of the stalls.

She was taken by surprise. "Uh—"

A boy was looking right at Alessa with a playful slant to his lips. "Can I help you?"

"Um, yeah. I mean..." She stepped toward him, unsure of what to say.

He pointed the brush at Alessa. "I'm not going to rat on you if that's what you're worried about."

She sighed in relief. "Thank you. I wanted some time by myself, and it is much colder than I thought it would be, so I figured—"

"You could steal one from a horse? Dang, that's low." The teenager grinned.

"I've never seen you around before."

"What you're saying, without saying, is—hey, you look Asian. Why are you a Spartan? Let alone a Spartan at the Colorado base?" he said, continuing to brush the horse.

Impressed with his ability to be so direct, Alessa tilted her head. "I mean, you aren't wrong. You are quite different from the typical demographic."

He held his hand out. "I'm Quade, nice to meet you."

Unsure of what to think, Alessa laughed nervously and placed her hand within his. "Alessa."

They shook hands.

"Alessa. Alessa ... Where have I heard that name before? Oh, wait. Are you one of the girls they brought back from the woods?"

Her cheeks blushed bright pink, and she pushed her hair behind her ear. "Yep, yeah. That's me and my sister, Kai. We aren't descendants."

"Huh." He stopped brushing the horse and looked Alessa up and down. "Cool, cool. Technically speaking, neither am I. My father was among the few outsiders during his generation that the elders approved of and brought into the Spartan community. Once they faked his death, he came to live at the East Asia base, where he met my mother."

Alessa's eyes widened. "I've never met a chosen one's child."

"Yep, I am indeed one of those, but it's not as impressive as it sounds. It means my father was deemed more important than those in the oblivious general population, and the Spartans acquired his life." Quade shrugged nonchalantly. "It's not like I reap any of the benefits."

"Since you're only half a biological Spartan," Alessa clarified.

He pointed a finger at her. "Exactly, but hey, you're probably in the same situation I am, if not worse, aren't you?"

Alessa grasped her hands together and stepped forward. "Kind of, but I also don't feel a need to become a mother or have a family other than my sister. So, I'm not a threat to the Spartan community. I won't be mixing my genes with that of a pure Spartan."

Quade scoffed. "How could you possibly know that? You're what, twelve?"

"I'm fourteen, thank you very much."

"Oh." He put his hands up defensively. "I'm sorry. Those two whole years make a world of difference."

She scowled. "You have no idea what I've been through to feel like I do."

Realizing his error in judgment, Quade apologized. "You're right. I had no right to say that. I'm having a hard time adjusting. Colorado is quite different to my home base."

Alessa exhaled. "No, it's fine. I tend to get defensive quickly. I'm trying to work on it." She continued walking forward toward the snow-white horse. "Shh. It's okay," Alessa cooed as it whinnied.

Quade's features relaxed, watching Alessa interact with the mare.

"About the blanket..." Quade directed her attention to the far wall where a pile of large wool blankets was stacked upon one another.

"Oh, perfect. Thanks!" Alessa ran to the pile and snatched the heavy top blanket from the mass. "So, Quade, do you have any plans for the rest of the night?"

He arched an eyebrow in surprise, and she laughed. "I don't mean romantically. It'll be completely platonic, I swear."

"A friend," Quade breathed. "I could use one of those." He set the brush down before guiding the horse back to its stall.

Alessa threw her wool blanket at Quade as he jogged toward her, and she plucked a dark blue one from the pile to take instead.

"Me too," she agreed as they exited the barn.

As Alessa stepped onto the wet grass, her breath was expelled from her lungs by a man's fist punching her in the stomach.

Gagging and gasping for air, Alessa fought against the restraints binding her to a metal chair.

The safety of her home was gone, and her dream had transported her from what was a beautiful memory into her room of torture.

Her body ached from head to toe, but thanks to the powerful abdominal blow, she was also wracked by nausea.

Somehow, she mustered the energy to lift her head and found herself looking into her torturer's beady black eyes, altogether devoid of emotion.

Lunging forward, he wrapped his thick fingers around Alessa's pale throat. Holding her by the neck, he tilted her chair backward, and it balanced precariously on two legs.

"Stop holding out on us!" he demanded.

Releasing Alessa, the front legs slammed hard onto the concrete, and she gasped for breath.

Her lungs burned as she fought the overwhelming urge to vomit.

"You could save yourself from all this pain. Tell us where you stored the information you discovered," Eric Lansing demanded while Alessa hungrily gulped air.

She glared at him with pure hatred emanating from her soul.

An enraged Eric Lansing grabbed a nearby clear plastic bag, leaned into her, and slammed it down over her head.

Alessa screamed, and her body flailed as she struggled against the restraints. Digging further into her wrists, they cut deep lines into her flesh.

Black dots appeared in her vision as she convulsed, and her energy waned with every failed inhale.

The room and Eric Lansing in his white tailored suit disappeared as her head lolled forward.

Gasping aloud, Alessa sprang upright in bed with tears streaking down the sides of her face. Her hands frantically grabbed at her neck to release herself from the imaginary plastic bag.

With the realization she had been reliving an awful memory, Alessa welcomed the pulsating migraine that had begun.

Wiping the tears from her face, she ran to the bathroom.

She slammed the door and turned on the water to mask the sound of her cries. Stripping out of her torn dress and swimsuit, Alessa jumped in the shower. Unable to hold her sobs back any longer, she broke down as the hot water sprayed against her bruised skin.

She collapsed into the bottom of the tub and cried into the crook of her arm as waves of terror wracked her body.

Scrunching her legs up, Alessa rocked back and forth beneath the stream of clean water as she finally allowed herself to feel everything she had been holding back. All the fear, the excitement, the love, and the hate rose to the surface.

Ten minutes into her breakdown, Alessa finally mustered the strength to stand up and clean herself.

Massaging the shampoo onto her scalp, she found peace in humming a hauntingly familiar melody.

———

From out of a deep sleep, Damon's eyes sprang open, and he stared at the closed bathroom door, listening to Alessa hum the melody he had taught her years ago—the one his mom used to sing to him.

Interrupting Damon's concentration, Camden asked, "Is she for real?"

Damon jumped in alarm. "Shit! I forgot you were here." He shook his head. "What do you mean?"

"Is everything she told me the truth?"

"Great," Damon grumbled. Sitting upright, he rubbed the sleep from his eyes. "What all did she tell you?"

"You both are Spartans, and she returned from the dead to find her sister and destroy Erebos."

"Dammit." Damon huffed. "Leave that woman alone for two minutes, and she tells some stranger her life story. Or at least as much as she remembers."

"Don't blame Alessa. I'm extremely easy to talk to, and I have one hell of a likable personality. Some might call it a curse." Camden flashed a sideways grin.

Unamused, Damon glared at Camden. "She may deem you trustworthy for reasons unknown, but I do not like you. I'm honestly not even sure why we saved your life."

"She wants my help in taking down Eric."

Chuckling to himself, Damon stood upright. "Absolutely not. Hell no. What was she thinking?"

Sitting on the edge of his bed, Camden leaned over onto his knees. "If you stop and think about it, it's not that bad of an idea—for me to go with you and help in Chicago."

"No. You are not coming with us. You work for those bastards. I know what they do to you to keep you loyal. Even if you have consciously changed your mind regarding working for them, you couldn't possibly ever completely—"

Anger surged through Camden, and his eyes flickered gold.

Damon jumped back and put his fists up. "You're not just any Bodyguard. You're part of Rogue Command." He jabbed a finger at the Bodyguard.

Camden's irises returned to their original hazel hue as he lifted his hands in peace. "Hear me out—"

"We're done here," Damon growled and took a threatening step toward Camden. "If Spartan elders were ever to find out Alessa and I saved you, we could be put to death. No questions asked. Rogue Command was once partners with our people. We trusted your creator until you all began using our technology for personal gain rather than what was best for humanity. What you do, it's the lowest of low."

Sporting a smirk, Camden cocked his head. "I mean, when you say it like that ... Okay, you know our history and what being a member of Rogue Command entails, so I won't go into the details of the dangers you'd be exposing yourself to by having me tag along. But it isn't just for the vengeance I so desperately crave."

Damon's eyes narrowed in disbelief as he held steadfast in his conviction. "The fact is, you're technically controlled by the person you're employed to protect, and as soon as they flip the switch on your 'control me' remote, it doesn't matter what your intentions are; you'll be forced to fight whoever's trying to kill them."

Camden pressed his lips together.

"Which, in this case, is Eric Lansing, the guy we're trying to take down. Don't you think that might be a conflict of interest?"

Camden sarcastically rolled his eyes. "Thank you for that detailed explanation of what we both already knew."

"This isn't a game." Damon's irises blazed silver. "If you go with us and Eric recognizes you—"

"I can get us inside his home before the party to plant the weapons we need to take him down. I know the home's layout by heart, the security personnel, exactly where the cameras are located, and what portion of the house they monitor." Camden inhaled. "I can get Alessa into the party without putting her in harm's way. All I have to do is avoid Eric, which should be easy enough with the amount of people expected to attend. He can't flip the switch if he doesn't know it's me."

Considering Camden's argument, Damon rubbed his jaw. "But if he does see you?"

"He could be looking right at me and not even realize it. It's a masked party," Camden insisted. "Damon, let me help you. I need to do this. They can't succeed with what they're doing to people—with what they plan on doing."

Realizing that Camden may be their only way into Eric's party, Damon exhaled in defeat. "Alright, you can come with us. But," Damon raised his finger and pointed at Camden, "I still don't like you, and if you get in my way, I'll take you out without hesitation."

Camden laughed in amusement. "You can try."

Damon's eyes faded back to blue as he sat on the edge of the second bed.

"Hey, one last thing. What is Alessa to you?" asked Camden.

Damon's entire body stiffened, and he glared at the Bodyguard. "What are you asking?"

Camden tilted his head toward the bathroom as he clarified his question. "What I mean is, is she single?"

Damon's eyes flickered icy grey. "She's taken."

CHAPTER FORTY-TWO

Alessa exited the bathroom with her long brown hair dripping wet, wearing only a beach towel. Her eyes darted back and forth between them as she realized both men had stopped talking and were staring at her. Embarrassed by her lack of clothing, her eyes dropped to the floor, and she nervously tucked strands of hair behind her ear.

"Uh. What were you two talking about? Wait." Alessa held her hand up and stepped toward the Bodyguard. "Cam, what are you still doing here? Earlier, you weren't sure you were going to help us."

"I've been wondering the same thing," Damon agreed. "And when did you start calling him 'Cam'?" Damon's words dripped with disdain.

"Hey, Damon, your jealousy is showing." Camden winked before he smirked at Alessa. "I have decided to join you on your quest."

Hugging her towel tight, she beamed. "That's great!"

"And where any additional services are needed." Camden eyed Alessa up and down.

Grabbing a small pillow behind him, Damon chucked it hard at Camden.

Alessa rolled her eyes as the pillow smacked Camden in the side of the head.

"Leave her alone," Damon barked.

"Ah, well. Looks like it's my turn." Camden pointed to the bathroom. Before closing the door, he stuck his head out and winked at Alessa. "If you get lonely, you know where to find me."

Alessa giggled nervously. "Uh, thanks? But I'm good."

"Suit yourself." Camden shrugged before closing the door. Switching the shower on, he whistled as the water cleansed the remaining blood and soot from his skin.

Damon silently watched Alessa dig through the plastic bags for a change of clothes. As she bent over, the towel lifted, exposing the bottom of her round ass, and Damon hissed in response to the tightening in his jeans.

Closing his eyes, he pressed his fingertips deep into his eyelids.

Finally, Alessa pulled out a jersey fabric, above-the-knee, form-fitting dark green dress, and a faded blue men's long-sleeved button-up.

She glanced back at Damon uncomfortably before stammering. "Um ... Can you?"

Damon opened his eyes and nodded in understanding. "Yeah, yeah, I'm sorry. Let me just..." He turned away.

Alessa dropped her towel to the floor before wiggling into the soft dress.

"Okay, I'm good." She pulled the men's shirt on, one arm at a time, before rolling each of the sleeves up to her elbows.

Steam bellowed into the small motel room as Camden stepped out of the bathroom. His damp arms and chest were exposed, as the only thing he had on was the pink flowered beach towel wrapped tight around his waist.

Alessa couldn't help but stare at his dark pink lips that stood out against his tanned skin and sandy blond hair.

With the return of her senses, Alessa grabbed Camden's muscular arm. "How are you feeling?" she asked, pressing her fingertips into his forearm.

Unable to find any visible wounds on his flawless skin, Alessa flipped Camden's arm over. "How can this be?"

"I'm feeling much better, thanks to you." Camden grinned.

"Where are they?" she demanded, searching his body for evidence of the wounds.

"I heal rather quickly." He laughed as Alessa lifted his arm and touched his ribcage. "Wow, your fingers are cold!" he exclaimed.

Awaiting an answer, she glared up at him.

"Bodyguards heal quickly."

He strolled over to the table.

"So, you heal like we do."

"I heal even faster. I'm a special type of Bodyguard."

"Where'd the floss go if you healed?"

He shrugged his bare shoulders. "My body must've absorbed it."

"You're joking..." Her eyes fell to the towel wrapped around his hip bones, and she turned away. "Think you could maybe put some clothes on?"

"You're all feeling me up until suddenly you're shy?" Camden chortled. "What? Never seen a naked man before?" He untied the towel from his hips, and it fell to the floor.

"Oh!" Alessa gasped and turned around.

"Man, seriously?" Damon complained as he turned away.

Alessa's eyes twitched toward Damon, and she huffed. "I'm sure I have."

"Oh, yeah. You can't remember," Camden teased before picking a pair of red briefs, a plaid short-sleeved button-up, and blue jeans.

"I guess these will have to do," he grumbled.

Hearing the jingle of his pants, Alessa chanced a look back. "You good?"

"Always," Camden replied with a smug grin.

"If this is how it's going to be the entire time, you can forget about coming," Damon snapped while packing his backpack.

Ignoring the men, Alessa rummaged through one of the plastic bags on top of the table. She pulled out a pair of cute black flats and a large black belt. Alessa slipped into the shoes after looping and fastening the belt around her waist.

"Ready to get out of here?" Damon nodded in her direction.

"So ready," she agreed.

They all walked out of the motel room, leaving behind the bloody mess of towels and supplies.

Damon led the way toward a striking, sapphire blue 1970 Buick GSX.

"What happened to the other car?" Alessa asked as Damon got into the driver's seat.

"I didn't think it was the best idea to be driving around in a vehicle with his blood all over it." He tilted his head toward Camden.

Camden rolled his eyes and pushed the passenger seat forward so he could crawl into the back.

Damon started the car and handed Alessa a bag of candy, a bottle of water, and a ham sandwich wrapped in plastic as she plopped down in the front passenger seat.

Popping a chocolate in her mouth, she smiled gratefully. "Thanks."

While turning on the radio, they were greeted with an urgent announcement.

"The CDC announced today that the deadly disease originating in New York is the once-eradicated smallpox virus. Government officials are urging citizens to wear masks as schools and businesses throughout the country are being forced to shut down as the death toll rises. The borders between states are closing in two days in hopes of containing the virus. The American government is in constant contact with Erebos Industries, and we have been told they are rushing to manufacture the cure by the end of this week."

Enraged, Alessa turned off the radio. "I need a minute not to be consumed by Eric."

Pulling onto TX-6N and headed for Houston's Amtrak station, they all sat silently.

"What's wrong with flying to Chicago? Aren't we on a bit of a time crunch?" Camden complained as they parked in front of the train station.

Ignoring the Bodyguard, Damon parked the car, and while grabbing his pack, he glared into the rearview mirror.

Alessa shrugged as Damon exited the car. "Besides the restriction on flights right now, Damon hates flying."

"And why's that?"

"I'm not completely sure. I do remember his mom was killed in an airplane crash, so it's probably best not to probe," Alessa said as she opened the car door and stepped out.

As Damon bought three tickets, their train's boarding call was announced, and they marched straight onto the train.

Everyone aboard, except for the three warriors, wore masks. The civilians hurried away from them as they walked down the aisles. Finding seats near the back, Alessa slid into the chair nearest the window, and Camden dove in front of Damon, stealing the seat next to her.

Damon glowered at Camden as he sat down behind the table across from them, and while grumbling under his breath, he shoved his backpack beneath the seat.

A few minutes of awkward silence passed before he reached into the front pocket of his pack and pulled out a pair of earphones. Damon plugged them into his phone port and leaned against the window's cool glass.

Listening to the electric guitar solo, Damon slumped down in his chair and closed his eyes.

"That guy needs to take some classes on social etiquette," Camden joked with a playful grin.

Alessa fingered the moonstone around her neck. "He's been through a lot."

"And who hasn't?" Camden scoffed "So, anyway..."

Alessa chuckled at Camden's blasé attitude.

"I've been dying to do this." Camden reached across and touched her face, turning Alessa toward him.

"What are you—"

Camden silenced Alessa with a forceful kiss.

He pressed his soft lips against Alessa's, and her eyes opened wide in shock as Camden's tongue brushed against her lower lip.

With his heart threatening to jump from his chest, Damon forced himself to keep a calm exterior as he sat across from

Camden and Alessa. His insides burned with the desire to rip out the man's throat as he struggled to feign sleep.

Instinctively, Alessa lifted her right arm and clocked him in his face.

"Oh!" Alessa gasped as her hands flew up to her mouth in shock.

Camden blinked away the pain as he massaged his cheekbone. "Ow. Guess I deserved that."

She looked down at her hands, horrified. "I don't know what came over me. But yeah, I think you did."

"I believe that was your subconscious's way of telling me not to touch you without your permission," Camden chortled.

A faint smile played on Damon's lips as he had difficulty pretending to sleep after Alessa decked Camden in the side of his face.

"What's our main objective once we arrive in Chicago?" Camden's voice dropped a few octaves. "I know you want to search for your sister and the cure, but you have to decide which is more important right now—Kai or Damon."

"Why would Alessa have to choose between me or her sister? I thought our main objective was to take down Eric," Damon interjected.

Camden and Alessa stared at Damon, their eyes wide in surprise.

"How in the hell did you hear that?" Camden questioned.

Damon plucked his earphones out and leaned forward. "Tell me. Now."

Alessa pressed her back into the seat, and her eyes darted over to Camden in a silent cry for help. "Uh..."

"Well?" Damon demanded, growing impatient.

Alessa bit her lower lip. "Well ... you..."

"What about me?"

"Back when we were at Brielle's apartment, she shot you up with that neuron transfuse—"

"Yeah. And?" Damon pressed.

Alessa swallowed the lump that had formed in the back of her throat. "And while you were out of it—"

Damon gritted his teeth. "Spit it out."

"—Brielle forced you to take the tuberculosis pill." Her heart raced as she confessed the truth.

Damon squinted incredulously at Alessa.

"I tried to stop her, but I—" She licked her lips nervously, and he fervently shook his head back and forth.

"No. No, Brielle wouldn't do that to me. Not after everything—"

Alessa's chest clenched. "Damon, I watched you swallow it."

He fell back into his seat as if in slow motion.

"By the time I activated and ran to help—" Alessa reached out to him.

He held up his hand to stop her. "So, what you're saying is, I'm dying."

"No, Damon, you are not going to die. There's a cure," Alessa said, frantically reassuring him.

He closed his eyes despairingly. "That only works if you take it in time. How much time do I have?"

"Don't worry," she pleaded.

Furious, his eyes popped open, and he slammed his fist on the table. "Dammit, Alessa, how many days?"

Alessa jumped in reaction to his violent outburst. "Two, at the most."

"Huh." Damon slumped back in his seat and looked up at her despairingly. "How could you keep this from me?"

Alessa sat up straight. "What was I supposed to say? Hey,

thanks for being the only one to come back for me, but now you're going to die?"

Damon laughed humorlessly to himself as he grabbed his bag and stood up. "You could've said something, Alessa. Anything."

"Damon..." She reached for him as he stomped away, but Camden held her back. "Give him a minute to process."

"But he—" Alessa protested.

"No, seriously, the man needs a moment to himself. Being told you're dying is a lot to take in."

Damon found an empty seat five rows back, and Alessa plopped back down in her seat, deflated.

Camden placed his hand on top of Alessa's. "He'll be fine."

"As long as we get our hands on the cure." Alessa squeezed Camden's hand reassuringly.

"And who have we made the priority? Your sister or Damon?"

Alessa's eyes fell on Damon. "We'll get the cure for Damon, expose Eric, and then search for Kai."

"Alright, then. Once we arrive, we'll have less than a day to prepare."

Alessa nodded in agreement. "What do I need to do?"

"Your main priority is to find a ballgown, a masquerade mask, and shoes, while Damon and I plant the weapons."

"Seriously?" Her voice dropped an octave in disgust. "I get dolled up while you guys do all the work?"

"I'm sorry, but do you have a better plan? Their prep crew is all men. You would stick out like a sore thumb," Camden explained.

"Ugh. Being a woman sucks sometimes. So, where is Eric's château?"

"About twenty minutes north of the train station. When we

first arrive, I'll meet up with a private supplier for our weapons while Damon takes you to find a dress. Then, Damon and I will pose as workers and stash our weapons throughout Eric's house. You'll need to rent a motel room and let me know where it is so I can swing by and pick you up for the party. All this needs to happen by seven p.m."

"But won't the Bodyguards at the party recognize you?"

"It's a masquerade party, but if they do, it'll be fine." Camden shrugged.

"Wait, why—?"

"Don't worry about it. I've got time to think of something."

"What about everyone at the manufacturing plant? The Bodyguards, the workers ... Wouldn't they have contacted Eric by now?" Alessa's eyebrows furrowed in worry.

"We didn't have anyone trailing us back in Texas, so I'm assuming you and Damon took care of the guards. And as far as the workers, they're likely too frightened to call Eric themselves. He is not known for being a forgiving man."

Alessa ran her fingers through her hair. "You sure are using a lot of 'what ifs' in this scenario. What if the guards know what happened in Texas, and they realize you escaped punishment?"

"We'll more than likely be killed on the spot," he responded calmly.

"Oh. That's good." Alessa shakily exhaled.

"Good day to everyone aboard this train's final crossing of state lines," the conductor announced. "Please maintain a safe distance from others and keep your mask in place. Otherwise, I hope for this to be a rather uneventful trip."

Camden leaned back and crossed his arms, sinking into his seat. "But you can't think about all the 'what ifs' in our plan. It'll drive you crazy. Now, if you don't mind, I'm going to take a nap, seeing as I probably won't be sleeping much tomorrow night."

Pivoting in her seat, Alessa stared a hole into Damon's back.

His left elbow hung lazily out into the aisle as his head bounced left and right with the train's jerky movement.

Alessa's insides churned as she resisted the overwhelming urge to hold Damon, and with the bobbing of her head, Alessa's eyelids grew heavy.

CHAPTER FORTY-THREE

The loud bang of a gunshot echoed in Alessa's memory, and her father pointed under the bed.

"Hide. Now," he said in a hushed whisper.

Alessa's heart skipped a beat as she and Kai crawled underneath the bed frame.

Kai let out a muffled whimper, and Alessa put her finger against her lips. "Shh."

Tears fell from the scared toddler's eyes, and Alessa held her tight.

"Flora?" Alessa's dad called out for their mother.

A tall man wearing an army green balaclava stepped into the room, aimed his weapon straight at their dad's face, and, without a moment's hesitation, squeezed the trigger.

Kai cried out at the same time the gun was fired, but fortunately for the young girls, Kai's yell was masked by their mother screaming for them to stay hidden.

"Stay where you are, my loves!" Flora begged. "I love you so much. Know that!" She continued making as much noise as possible to keep her girls from being discovered.

Alessa watched her father's lifeless body fall to the ground. His head bobbed up and down after smacking the wooden floor, and his empty gaze pierced through her. She choked down the vomit threatening to force its way up the back of her throat while she attempted to keep Kai quiet.

"What is that woman screaming about?" their father's murderer hollered as he marched out of the room toward the living room.

Alessa opened her eyes wide to keep from passing out. She noticed her father's gun holster lying open, unlatched on the side of his belt. He had clearly meant to use the firearm but was unable to do so before he was killed.

Without wasting another second, Alessa scrambled out from under the bed and fell to her knees before her dad's still form.

She yanked the weapon out from her father's belt, and blood spurted out from his head wound as his limp body rocked back and forth.

"Shut her up!" the murderer yelled before he turned back around, unknowingly, toward the young girls.

Several more gunshots sounded from the living room as Alessa stood tall, feet planted shoulder-width apart, and held the gun in front of her.

As the disguised man peered down, he found a little brown-haired girl pointing a gun at his chest, and his smug grin turned to horror as Alessa squeezed the trigger.

With a fatal shot to the chest, the man collapsed to the floor, and she immediately turned her attention to her family's second and third attackers. Alessa rapidly fired several bullets into each man before they crumpled down to the floor.

Unable to fully comprehend the day's turn of events, Alessa fell to her knees, where she remained unmoving and numb.

Her ears rang from the gunshots, and she heard the muffled

sound of her sister crying when, unexpectedly, a middle-aged man rushed in through the front door of their cabin, his eyes wide and breathing labored.

Quickly assessing the scene, he grabbed the door frame for support. As his eyes landed on young Alessa sitting in the doorway holding a gun, he put his hands up in a gesture of peace.

"Hi." He peered around Alessa at the hysterically crying two-year-old. "I heard the gunshots and—" The older man surveyed the room and discovered the two little girls were the only survivors. "Are you okay?"

Unable to respond, Alessa stared at the man, still wielding the weapon.

"I'm here to help," the gentleman said, cautiously approaching her. "May I?" he asked, holding his hands out for the gun.

Alessa glanced down and eyed the weapon. She had completely forgotten she was even holding it, and with no real other option than to trust the stranger, she handed him the gun.

Engaging the safety, he tucked the gun into an empty holster around his calf and hurried around Alessa to get to Kai. Reaching down under the bed, he scooped the terrified toddler up into his arms.

While the man carried the younger of the two girls, he grasped Alessa's hand within his own and walked them toward the cabin's front door. "I've got you. You're safe now."

Alessa peered back at her father's body as he lay in a pool of blood before sneaking a peek over at her mom. Her mother's body was sprawled out on the floor, and the bottom of her bright orange shoes were facing them.

The pink and grey swirls on the underside of her mom's

sneakers were the last thing she saw before leaving their family cabin forever.

Alessa and the man holding Kai silently jogged through the woods for hours before approaching an overly abundant treed section of the forest. After he found the girls a soft bed of moss to rest on, the man started to walk away. "I'll be right back."

Alessa grabbed his hand, tugging him back toward her and the sleeping toddler.

"I need to grab something. I will return. You have my word," the man promised.

Loosening her grip, Alessa nodded and allowed him to jog away. She watched her rescuer from behind until his form shimmered and disappeared amongst the greenery.

Alessa sat on the mossy ground next to her sleeping sister. She listened to the sounds of the forest: the squirrels chittering amongst themselves, rushing water from a nearby creek, wind blowing leaves across the rocks.

Exhausted as her soul felt, she couldn't allow herself the luxury of rest without knowing whether she and Kai were truly safe.

Nearly half an hour passed before the man's blurry figure appeared behind the trees.

Overcome with relief, Alessa's eyes teared up as she inhaled a giant breath of air. "You came back," she squeaked.

"I would never abandon you. Now here, take this." He handed her a small, circular device about the size of a dime. "And place it here," he pointed directly behind her ear, near the mastoid bone.

With a furrowing of her eyebrows, Alessa did as she was told and placed the device behind her left ear.

The circle latched onto Alessa's skin, and she nearly hit the ground as it burrowed deep into her bone. Settling in place, it emanated an ear-piercing, high-pitched squeal.

Within a few seconds, the discomfort subsided for the most part, and Alessa stood upright, shaking her head back and forth.

The forest directly in front of them was no longer filled with overgrowth but was instead an obscure city off in the distance.

"Now, I also need to put the device on your sister. As you know, it hurts a bit, so she may cry," the man said.

Alessa grabbed her sister's hand as he pressed the circular device behind Kai's ear. She woke up screaming but calmed down upon seeing her sister.

"Come with me. I'll keep you safe." He extended a hand toward Alessa.

Hesitantly, Alessa slowly placed her hand within the man's and hiked alongside him toward the hazy city.

Stepping over the mysterious city's threshold, Alessa gasped as the blurry figures transformed.

The structures no longer appeared wavy as if they were a mirage but were instead detailed outlines of buildings and statues.

At the entrance to the main road, two statues depicting men stood tall, as well as an oversized fountain with a smaller statue of a woman sitting on the edge, leaning into the cascading water.

All sizes of buildings, ranging from big to small, lined the street on either side: schools, housing, the mess hall, and many smaller houses were scattered in the distance.

"Welcome to Sparta—the Colorado division," the man nodded toward the busy center of the street.

A few days after the girls' arrival, Alessa's rescuer exited the auditorium, and the large doors slammed shut behind him.

Alessa and Kai stood up and fidgeted while their elder rushed toward them.

He grabbed hold of Alessa's shoulders and took a knee. "It's not going to be easy. But you and your sister can stay and live with us. You are, as of this point, a Spartan in training. You'll have to prove yourself worthy at age twenty, but we have plenty of time to prepare for your initiation ceremony.

"I want you to realize that not everyone will accept you and Kai. This has never happened before—outsiders your age being accepted. You may need to prove yourself more or work harder than the other Spartan children, but so be it. At least you'll be safe, and I can teach you to harness the darkness that has undoubtedly crept into a corner of your soul after what you had to endure in that cabin. And I want you to know anyone who has been through something that traumatic has the same darkness within them, too. You are not alone.

"Within these city walls, you will be surrounded by those who can help you find an outlet for these emotions. We can teach you how to use them for good rather than self-destruction.

"Alessa, you and your sister may stay as long as you'd like, and if you'd have me, I'd like to be your elder. I vow to protect you from this day forth until you can protect yourself."

Unable to form coherent words in response to his proclamation, Alessa broke down before she wrapped her tiny arms tightly around the man's waist.

"I'd like that very much," Alessa squeaked as tears fell down her cheeks.

Years later, Kai and Alessa were running through a field of wildflowers.

Kai's light blue dress flowed freely around her as she spun in circles with her arms outstretched.

Scrambling behind her sister, Alessa laughed as her pale yellow dress with black accents floated above the vibrant green grass. She closed her eyes and tilted her head to the sky, listening to the birds sing.

The bright sun shone through Alessa's eyelids, and she fell back into a patch of faded violet wild geraniums.

Reliving the next memory, Alessa was fourteen years old. During the midday meal, she and her sister sat at one of the long tables in the main hall.

A thick glob of mashed potatoes smacked Kai in the back of the head.

Alessa's younger sister let out a tiny squeak before a single tear rolled down her cheek.

Enraged, Alessa picked up her tray full of food and slammed it down on the table.

The room stilled, and everyone stared at the two girls as Alessa challenged every person with a deadly glare.

Grabbing Kai's hand, Alessa dragged her outside, and the sisters trudged down the side of the mountain until they hit the valley.

Kai sniffled the entire way down, trying unsuccessfully to hold back tears.

"Bend down," Alessa said as they approached a small lake.

Kai did as she was told and bent a knee. Hanging her dirtied blonde hair over the water, Alessa washed away the sticky white starch.

"It won't always be like this. After our initiations, we will

finally be one of them. They'll have to accept us," Alessa said in determination.

Kai flipped her wet hair up, the back of it smacking against her yellow shirt. "Don't you get it, Lessie? We are not of Spartan blood. The gods did not choose us to be here. We are only in Sparta due to unforeseen events."

Alessa reached to touch Kai's shoulder, but her sister angrily swatted it away.

"No!" Kai darted upright. "I am grateful for our elder finding you and me in the woods and protecting us, but this is not our home." She paced back and forth, pressing her fingertips into her temples. "This is not my home."

Alessa panicked. "Shh. You can't speak like that. I know it must be hard for you. At times, it is for me, too. But if anyone, and I mean anyone, heard you—we could both be discarded."

Kai's breath shuddered, and she closed her eyes. "I know, I know. That was stupid. I'm sorry." She breathed. "Sometimes, I wish so hard that what happened to us—that Mom and Dad weren't dead."

"I know, I know. I wake up at night suffering from terrible nightmares," Alessa nodded and sat down, her back against a boulder.

"I pretend not to hear you, to respect your privacy." Kai walked up to Alessa and sat down beside her.

"What would I do without you?" Alessa pulled her sister in for a hug.

Kai smiled sweetly behind her sister's back. "Let's hope you never have to find out."

A few months later, Alessa was sparring against a fellow Spartan outside in the rain. Her classmates laughed as she was pushed face-first down in the thick mud. Her opponent held her down, and she struggled, squishing further into the ground.

"Enough!" Alessa's elder commanded.

The crowd hushed as Alessa struggled to get up, her legs threatening to slip from beneath her.

"Everyone, find a partner and practice the moves taught today. Alessa, come with me." He jabbed his finger toward the side of a nearby building.

Her gaze dropped to the ground, knowing she had disappointed her elder once again.

They turned the corner, and his gaze held no sympathy as he berated Alessa.

"What I witnessed cannot continue. You need to do better to earn a place within this community. You know the consequences of failing your initiation."

"I don't want to die." Alessa wiped the mud from her face with fierce determination.

"Then start acting like it," her elder demanded.

A teenage Alessa sat hunched over, surrounded by books in an elaborate, oversized library.

She didn't desire friends, meaning Alessa had a good chunk of free time she dedicated to studying the history of Sparta. This included the buildings and their forgotten passageways.

Alessa spent most nights exploring secret passageways leading from interior rooms to the outside so she could easily escape the shared housing compounds for some time to herself.

Time jumped forward yet again, and sweat flew from their elder's skin as he brutally trained Alessa in the art of sparring.

Of all his students, she must earn her place, for Alessa and Kai were his, not by blood, but by fate.

Alessa kicked him in the abdomen, and he grunted as the air was forced from his lungs.

Rotating his hips, her elder kicked Alessa's feet out from underneath her. As her back hit the ground, he stood tall above her.

Jabbing Alessa in the neck with his wooden pole, his chest heaved with deep breaths, and a smile played upon his lips.

"Good spar." Stepping back, he held out his hand.

Reaching up, she grabbed his forearm and gripped it tight.

Alessa's entire body burned from their half-hour-long continuous fight. "Yes, but you still won."

Her elder laughed jovially. "You do know how old I am. I've been doing this for quite some time. Give yourself some credit."

Limping from the meadow, he wrapped his arm around her shoulders.

Her memories continued jumping haphazardly through time.

"Hey, Quade!" Alessa bellowed down the hall, running to catch up to her friend.

"Oh, hey, Alessa." Quade waved, standing beside a beautiful dark-skinned woman.

"Seraphine, this is Alessa." He tilted his head. "She's my best friend."

"Aw, Quade, stop with the feelings; you're gonna make me blush," Alessa chuckled before turning her attention to the woman. "Welcome to the Colorado compound. When did you arrive?"

"Last night. My father was assigned as lead general surgeon

at this compound, so I figured I'd tag along. And you can call me Sera."

Alessa bowed down. "Well, we welcome you with open arms."

"At least Alessa and I do," Quade winked.

On her twentieth birthday, Alessa was slammed down to the floor by her Spartan opponent.

Both of their bodies burned and ached as they performed their violent dance.

Alessa's ribs cracked with the last kick, but she didn't react other than allowing a slightly longer-than-normal exhalation.

Her skin glistened with sweat, and Damon traced the outline of her biceps as she extended her arms.

The battle wasn't an act of desperation but was a form of art brought to life.

She took her opponent down with a powerful kick. Standing victorious above the woman, Alessa's lungs burned, and her legs shook as they threatened to give out beneath her.

Her elder beamed with pride from the audience of council members. "It is done. You are Champion and are warmly accepted into our family. Let it be marked in the Book of Blood that Alessa will forever be known as a Spartan citizen, a Coepi. You, my dear girl, have earned the title. Congratulations."

Without a word, she bowed her head and stepped back through the large doors. With the echoes of the closing doors and the knowledge that she was now officially a part of the Spartan family, Alessa allowed her emotions to wash over her, and she collapsed against a nearby wall, breaking down.

Later that same day, Alessa shared the great news with her good friend. "Sera, wait up!" Alessa beckoned from down the hall.

Seraphine smiled and waved before extending her arms out toward Alessa. "I know you're not much of a hugger, but I don't care. Congratulations are in order!"

Alessa rolled her eyes and allowed Sera's arms to embrace her. "Okay, okay. Thank you."

"Welcome to the family." Her friend beamed.

"So, about that. I chose you to be my mentor. I want to learn the trade of being a medical practitioner."

Seraphine stared at Alessa in shock.

"Um, is that okay? Your father is the region's best, and you've been training since you were ten. I hope it's okay because I'd love to learn everything you know." Alessa nervously bit her lip, awaiting her friend's response.

"Absolutely! I'm honored and humbled you chose me to study under. I'm not the most experienced and was only recently approved to mentor."

Alessa smiled. "You are the most intelligent person I know, and age has nothing to do with experience. You've seen a lot working beside your father. I have always been intrigued by everything about the human body, and science is my passion. How could I not choose you?"

Seraphine pulled Alessa in for another hug.

"Thank you, Alessa."

One year later, Seraphine stood before Alessa, holding a syringe in her hand. "Are you sure you want to do this?"

"Yes, Sera. I've considered getting the birth control implant for a long time. I don't want to risk having children, even if I'm

not in an actual relationship. Besides, it's not permanent. The hormones only last for a few years."

"You aren't wrong. I want to make sure you know what using birth control means at your age. There could be terrible consequences if the Council discovers you did this before you asked their permission," Sera hesitated.

"Thanks, Doc. I am well aware of my age. I want to improve my medical skills and give everything to my assignments. Besides, the Council should celebrate my not wanting to dilute the Spartan bloodline. Children have no place in my life. For that matter, neither does a man," she laughed. "Ow!"

"And done." Seraphine withdrew the needle from Alessa's upper arm. "You're good for the next six years."

"Great, thanks, Sera." Alessa rubbed her bicep.

"Do me a favor, and don't utter a word of this to anyone." Seraphine pointed at her friend.

Alessa held her first two fingers up. "You have my word."

"Repeat after me, six years." Sera eyed Alessa, sternly.

"Six years," Alessa repeated.

Two years later, while listening to the angelic voice of Enya through her implant, Alessa raised her bow to aim at the target.

With the rising sun illuminating the bright pink and orange sky, she opened her eyes and released the arrow.

Damon was jogging in the woods when he spotted the woman from his first initiation ceremony practicing archery in an open field. Slowing to a walk, he paused the rock music blaring in his ears.

Placing the quiver full of arrows over her shoulder and onto her back, she froze in concentration.

He hid behind a tree, watching the woman from afar.

As Enya's song ended, Our Last Night's cover of 'Total Eclipse of the Heart' began, and Alessa's eyes blazed bright green.

The music played aloud as she pressed the button on her earpiece.

She danced in place as she repeatedly grabbed an arrow and aimed at new targets on various trees throughout the wooded forest.

Damon stepped to the side, and a twig cracked beneath his foot. Without hesitation, Alessa pulled back on the string and released the arrow toward the unexpected noise.

The sharp arrow tip struck the tree trunk mere inches from Damon's ear, and he sprang upright in alarm.

Alessa stood stoically still. "What are you doing here?"

"I'm fine, thanks." Damon stepped out of the overgrowth.

"I wasn't worried," Alessa smirked. "If I had wanted to hit you, I would've. It's been a while, Damon."

Damon narrowed his eyes. "You remember me?"

"You left quite the impression." Alessa raised her eyebrows and cocked her head to the side.

"That's right," he feigned ignorance. "Your elder introduced us, didn't he?"

"Why are you watching me from behind the bushes?" Alessa kept an eye on Damon as she repositioned her bow and arrow.

"I went on a run in between classes. This isn't far from my cabin," Damon explained.

She turned toward him. "I hadn't realized you had taken the position permanently. You don't live with the other single men in the barracks?"

Damon chuckled. "That's not my style." His lips separated

into a genuine smile, and he flashed his white teeth, glancing down at the moss growing across the forest's path.

Alessa's heart unexpectedly stilled for a moment.

What was that about? Get your act together, Alessa silently scolded herself.

CHAPTER FORTY-FOUR

As her memories continued to resurface, she went back a few years, remembering when Damon found her the day after their first sparring match.

Alessa was throwing hatchets at a target wrapped around the thick tree trunk, still furious that she had lost.

"You did good yesterday," Damon projected from the tree line.

Recognizing the deep voice, Alessa whipped around to find Damon strolling toward her across the field overrun by yellow flowers. She rolled her eyes and pressed her lips firmly together. "If you call losing good, then yep, I did great," she quipped sarcastically.

Laughing to himself, Damon stepped up beside her. "You're too hard on yourself. I'm older than you. I have more experience."

"And you are a blood-born Spartan and a Wellborn," she interjected before throwing another hatchet.

"That's not where I was going with that, but okay. The point is, you need to give yourself some credit for taking me on when

no one else was willing. You are on your way to being one of the best, if not the best, female Custos, and everyone here knows it."

Inhaling a jagged breath, she looked at Damon from the side of her eyes.

He picked up a spare hatchet and flipped it into the air before catching it by the handle. "And you aren't wrong about the strength of my blood. I am a direct descendent of the original king of Sparta. This means I am next in line to take over my father's position on the Council once he steps down. The higher position of king will go to my older brother. Thank the gods," he explained.

Alessa's jaw dropped, and she stared at Damon as he chucked the weapon. It smacked the tree trunk and embedded itself deep within the target.

Alessa gulped and rubbed her hands together. "I had no idea you were that pure of a Wellborn. Were you named after—?"

Damon chuckled. "Yep. Lacedaemon. Since birth, I was expected to live up to the literal son of a god."

Alessa grimaced. "Well, shit. I'm sorry. That's got to be tough."

Handling another hatchet, he stopped mid-throw to look at Alessa. "That's the first time I've had someone feel bad for me for being a High-Borne Wellborn."

"Psh." Alessa adamantly shook her head from side to side. "I wouldn't wish that amount of responsibility on anyone. Your entire life must be—"

"Out of my control and in the hands of the gods? That sounds about right." He threw the hatchet, and it struck the bullseye again. "I'm not exactly sure why I'm telling you any of this."

"I'm not sure, either. Not many Wellborn converse with me since I'm an outsider."

He stepped toward Alessa. "Your elder would not have brought you into our community had he not thought you a Spartan at heart."

Not sure how to respond, Alessa blinked unexpected tears away.

Turning her back to Damon, she plucked a hatchet from the pile of weapons and nailed the target.

Watching her, Damon muttered under his breath. "Beautiful."

Reality blurred as her memories jumped back and forth in time. The next one was a few years after Damon and Alessa's first meeting after they had gotten to know one another.

"Hey!" Alessa hollered at Damon as he stood outside his classroom, conversing with students.

Peering down the hall, his smile relaxed as Alessa hurried toward him.

Returning to his student, he continued, "Yeah, that's right. James, you need to watch your left side. You leave it undefended too often, and your opponent will figure that out quickly and take advantage of your weakness. Don't allow yourself to be killed on your first assignment."

"Damon!" Alessa demanded his attention.

Alarmed, he excused himself from his students and faced an irate Alessa. "What's the matter?"

She nearly barreled into him. "I heard what you said today, what you did."

"What are you referring to?" His eyebrows scrunched in alarm.

Damon pulled her into his classroom and closed the door behind them.

"*You came here to learn the ways of Councilmen, and somehow you end up putting one of your students in a chokehold over something they said about me? Why would you do that?*"

Damon stepped behind the podium at the front of the room and gripped the sides of the wood.

She marched up to the podium angrily. "*You know I can handle the terrible things they say about me. I couldn't care less. I've never wanted any of them.*"

Confused by her anger, Damon stared at Alessa in bewilderment. "*My intention wasn't to offend you.*"

"*Now the others think I need you to stand up for me. Well, Damon, I don't need you to defend my honor. I can handle myself.*" She crossed her arms.

Stepping out from behind the podium, he looked down at Alessa. "*I realize you think you don't need anyone on your side, but Alessa, you're wrong. It's not weak to need friends, nor is it frowned upon to ask for help.*"

Surprised by his defensive response, she stumbled over her words. "*I-I have Kai. And Quade and Seraphine...*"

He inched closer. "*Yes, you do, and that's great. But what's so bad about having one more person willing to fight for you? Are you so jaded you refuse to accept another friend?*"

She narrowed her eyes as he slowly moved toward her. "*You want to be friends?*"

Damon shrugged. "*Why not? There's nothing in the laws that say we can't be.*"

Alessa exhaled slowly in contemplation. "*Okay, but can you stop hurting my classmates? It makes me look weak and creates bigger issues.*"

Towering above her, Damon conceded. "*I'll try. But know I*

*will always do what I feel is right. Whether or not you agree
with it."*

Holding Alessa in his arms, Damon panicked. "Alessa,
wake up!"

Her memories threatened to consume her as her body
burned with fever.

"Dammit, Damon, what's happening to her?" Camden
crouched down over her tense body.

"You ready?" Quade asked Alessa in her next memory.

*Unable to hide her excitement, she grinned wide before
biting her lower lip. "You better believe it. I'll meet you by the
basketball court in thirty so we can walk together. Will Sera be
partaking in the fun?"*

*"Unfortunately, no. She's part of the med team in place for
all the injuries we're sure to rack up." He grinned mischievously.*

*Tugging on her black combat boots, Alessa laughed. "No
doubt."*

"Alright, then. I'll see you in a bit."

*Once her boots were laced, she grabbed a few choice
weapons, tucked them into the straps around her thigh, and
grabbed the door handle.*

Throwing open the door, she crashed into Damon.

*"Ah, shit!" Alessa threw her hands up to her injured nose
and whimpered, blinking the tears away.*

"Damn, Alessa, where are you going in such a hurry?"

*"Damon!" Alessa gasped. "When did you get back from your
assignment?"*

"Just a few hours ago. I came right here after our debriefing."
She sniffed. "Well, tonight is Capture the Flag."

He rubbed a finger against his bottom lip, highlighting his full pink lips.

She forced her eyes shut and pushed her fingertips into her eyelids. "Did you not have field days at the other compounds?" Alessa closed her and Kai's apartment door before heading down the hall.

He fell into step beside her. "Yeah, just not Capture the Flag. Sounds fun."

She stopped in the middle of the hallway to face him. "You wanna join our team?"

"Are you inviting me to game night with your friends?" Damon jested.

She remained silent and continued to stare at him, awaiting his answer.

"Yeah, I'll come along." Damon laughed and rubbed his hands together in excitement.

Sporting a playful grin, Alessa nodded. "Great! We gotta go, Quade's waiting."

"Hey, Damon. Wasn't expecting to see you here." Quade's eyebrows rose in surprise.

"That makes two of us. But how can I turn down Capture the Flag?" Damon chuckled as they marched to the battlefield.

Before the woods, there were stations where each participant was marked in illuminated paint with a lambda (Λ), the official sign for Laconia or Lacedaemon, on both of their upper arms.

"Welp. Being marked with the symbol I was named after seems about right." Damon sneered at his blue lambda glowing in the dark.

The sun set behind the tall trees, and a loud horn sounded. The start of the game was announced.

"Welcome, everyone, to the two thousand, three-hundred-and-ninety-fourth anniversary of Capture the Flag."

The crowd erupted, whooping and hollering.

"Yes, yes, settle down." The announcer waved his hands. "The rules are as follows: violence is allowed, and the use of weapons is encouraged; however, the taking of life is greatly frowned upon. Only hand-to-hand combat weapons and arrows with blunt rubber tips are permitted. Please do your best to maim your comrades so they will recover within the week. There is no time limit, as many of you may recall from 2010's three-day-long game. Your glow-in-the-dark lambda must be visible at all times. This is so others know which team you are fighting for, and if your Laconia symbol is covered at any point, you will be disqualified."

Alessa's weapons were strategically strapped to her inner thighs and the inside of her boots. The container of quills was on her back, and she held the bow tight.

She touched Damon's arm as the announcer continued listing the rules. "Why haven't you taken a single weapon they've handed out?"

His hot breath caressed Alessa's skin, and a shiver ran down her back as he whispered in her ear. "You'll see."

"You have one hour to reach your designated side and take position. And with that, let the game begin!"

The horn sounded the official start to the games, and grinning wildly, they sprinted into the forest.

Sprinting as a group, they went for the left side of the tree line, away from their opponents marked with yellow paint.

Quade, Sera, Kai, and Damon stood around Alessa, laughing while handing her wrapped gifts.

"*Guys, you didn't need to,*" smiled Alessa.

"*Yeah, yeah, open them up. I wanna see if my birthday gift was the best.*" Quade waved her annoyance away.

The moving train jolted Damon and Alessa as he held her in the aisle. "I don't know, exactly. I assume she's remembering something. Something big, from the looks of it."

Alessa's body convulsed violently as she lay in Damon's arms. A small crowd had gathered a few rows back, keeping their distance from the unmasked.

"Come back to me, Alessa," Damon begged quietly.

"Nothing to see here, people; she's got a condition. It happens all the time. We got this." Camden shooed the nosy travelers away.

Alessa's body went limp, and her eyes fluttered.

Damon, Kai, Sera, Quade, and Alessa were sneaking into the night. They crept along the buildings until they reached the compound's brand-new swimming pool.

The women stripped off their long T-shirts and kicked their shoes to the side as the men jumped head over heels into the warm water.

Kai squealed as water splashed her in the face. "Watch it. Hey, Sera, where's Soren tonight?"

"He went to bed easily, for once, so we pawned toddler duty off on my father." Sera laughed.

"Having a three-year-old is exhausting," Quade huffed. Jumping out of the water, he grabbed Kai and wrapped her in a big bear hug.

"Ah, Qua–!" Kai screeched as they fell into the water.

They surfaced, laughing, and Kai splashed Quade in the face as Alessa dove into the pool headfirst.

From the far side of the room, Sera turned a key in the wall, and the ceiling retracted, exposing the bright stars up above.

With everything but her neck and head submerged, Alessa trod the water while gazing at the night sky.

"Beautiful," Damon whispered into Alessa's ear.

Alessa gasped. "Damon! Yeah, the stars ... They are beautiful."

"Oh, yeah, the stars..." he murmured.

Her missions blurred together in a montage of different colored hair in various lengths, crazy outfit changes, fake names—she played a new person in every memory.

Alessa had fought in full-blown battles human civilians had never witnessed. Thanks to the Spartans' advanced technology, they masked themselves in an invisible forcefield and muddled the minds of those nearby.

Finally, Alessa said goodbye to her sister before leaving to go undercover in Erebos Industries.

Alessa had packed the one bag of luggage she was allowed to take on the assignment, and Kai bit her nails while she sat on the bed before her.

"You're sure you can't tell me where they're sending you?" Kai asked with her fingernail between her teeth.

"You know I'm not supposed to." Alessa tossed a thin, cream-colored blouse beside her sister.

"Ugh," Kai exhaled. "How come you never fold a thing? It drives me insane!" She picked up the soft fabric and carefully folded the shirt before tucking it into Alessa's bag.

"Hey, is everything okay? You're acting more nervous than usual." Alessa tossed a black pencil skirt at her sister.

Kai glanced down at what remained of her fingernail and dropped her hand. "Oh, you know, just worried about my initiation ceremony. It's coming up soon."

Alessa's eyes widened. "That's right. I completely forgot, what with everything going on. I'm so sorry I haven't checked on you. How are you dealing? You've been practicing with our elder, right?"

Kai nodded. "Every day. Even when I'm needed in the lab, which is exhausting."

Alessa grabbed her sister's hand and sat on the bed beside her. "Good, that's good. I'm sure you'll do great."

Kai's eyes filled with tears, and Alessa pulled her sister into her arms. "Oh, Kai, I have no doubt you'll pass."

Kai sniffled.

"Okay, if I tell you where I'm going, you swear to keep it to yourself?" Alessa stared into her sister's hazel eyes.

"Really?" Kai stopped crying and stared.

Alessa exhaled loudly.

"Erebos Industries," she whispered.

"Now," she tilted Kai's chin so they were eye to eye. "You are as worthy as any other Spartan. We may not have been born here, but the gods ensured we'd find our way to this life. Don't screw it up." Alessa smiled in encouragement.

Kai's chin bounced up and down as she lunged for her sister, pulling Alessa into a tight embrace. "As long as I live, you'll be in my heart, Lessie," she cried.

"As will you be in mine," Alessa promised.

. . .

Blood trickled down from Alessa's nostrils, and her teeth clenched together.

Damon was rendered helpless as he watched Alessa. "No, no, no!"

"Isn't there anything you can do?" Camden demanded.

Damon's jaw flexed as he lifted Alessa's chest to his and held her close. "Come back to me," he pleaded.

CHAPTER FORTY-FIVE

Nearly all of Alessa's memories came rushing back to her in a bombardment of bright images, feelings, smells, tastes, and sounds.

"Muy bien," the sweaty man congratulated his colleague on his method of torture.

Alessa whimpered after the treatment she'd endured over the last few hours at the hands of the exhausted Englishman.

"Now, go get some rest. Es me turno." He grinned madly at the bound woman.

Unable to look him in the eye because of her facial swelling, Alessa recognized the most brutal of all the men by his thick Hispanic accent.

He didn't hesitate before driving a long nail down through the top of Alessa's right foot. Rather than please him with her pain, Alessa bit her lower lip to hold back her screams.

"Still won't talk, eh? Let's see how far we must go." A sadistic grin spread across his scarred face.

Alessa's body trembled as her eyes glowed bright green.

"Oh, bueno, you've still got some fight left in you," he purred.

Her memory fast-forwarded to the end of her torture, where the large blade dug into her stomach.

Alessa's head jerked back, and she looked up at the bright ceiling.

The searing pain spread throughout her entire body as the man yanked the tool from her gut.

Alessa was then dumped near the river, and as she lay on the cool ground, the Spartan warrior gasped for air as darkness consumed her.

Her vision was cloudy as she heard the deep, melodic, disembodied voice of Hades, king of the underworld.

"I expect my payment in full, or I will bring you back—four souls in exchange for your one. Our deal is done," the god declared.

"Clear!" someone hollered in the distance.

A painful electric shock struck Alessa's chest before it spread through her body.

Her mouth opened wide, and Alessa gasped as her heart beat once more.

"Alessa, babe," Damon whispered in her ear, trying to coax her back from the depths of her subconscious.

Her erratic breathing calmed, and a single person in the small crowd stepped forward, handing Damon a clean tissue.

He thanked the stranger as he wiped the crimson from her upper lip.

Camden reassured the people surrounding them. "See? She's resting. Now, please leave us alone."

Alessa's eyelids fluttered open, and she looked up, with eyes half open, into Damon's deep blue eyes.

He exhaled a sigh of relief. "Thank the gods. I thought I'd lost you." Damon caressed the side of her cheek. "How are you feeling?"

"I remember..." she croaked.

Damon stilled. "What? What do you remember?"

She grabbed the sides of her head. "A lot."

"Here, let me help you." Camden pulled her up off Damon and sat her down in the seat.

"Ugh. My entire body hurts." She arched her back.

Damon squatted in front of her and clasped her hands in his own. "Alessa, can you tell me who gave you that ring?"

"What?" She blinked in confusion.

"Where did you get your ring?" He nodded toward the crisscrossed black zirconium band.

"Uh," she rubbed the back of her neck. "That I can't tell you. I wish I didn't have to remember the cabin." She choked back tears, anxiously rubbing her hands up and down her thighs.

Damon looked down at the ground in defeat. "With the way you were—I could've sworn you were remembering everything."

Feeling attacked, Alessa scowled. "Well, I'm sorry I didn't remember what you wanted me to. I feel like I got hit by a train. Can I get a minute?"

Camden scooted into the seat beside her. "Here, lean on me and rest for a few. We're almost there."

Unable to hide his disappointment, Damon's expression grew weary.

Maybe that was it. Perhaps she'll never remember everything.

The overhead speakers announced their imminent arrival.

Camden cleared his throat. "So, Damon and I talked while you slept and convulsed."

Damon glared at Camden. "You have no tact."

Camden cast a sideways glance at Damon. "And you are an asshole."

"Seriously, that's your comeback?" Damon demanded. "You're the one cracking jokes at Alessa's expense."

Alessa held her hand up before digging her fingertips into the right side of her head. "Cool it, guys. Grab your stuff. We're here."

Camden walked out in front of Alessa while Damon trailed behind her, and they all stepped down onto the platform before pushing their way through the crowded train station.

Reaching his arm above his head, Camden flagged a cab from the mass of cars awaiting travelers.

One of the cars pulled up in front of them, and Alessa scooted into the middle of the back seat, with Camden and Damon sitting protectively on either side of her.

Noticing Alessa's nervous habit of twirling her ring around her finger, Damon placed his hand on hers. "Just breathe," he encouraged as Camden shouted an address to the driver.

An electric jolt shot up Alessa's arm with the touch of Damon's hot fingertips. She glanced down at his hand, holding her own, and squeezed his fingertips in response to the caring gesture.

Driving through several traffic lights, the taxi parked in front of a small collection of stores.

Camden pointed out the window. "This is it. We're here."

Letting go of Alessa's hand, Damon opened the door, stood tall, and turned around, extending his hand toward her.

"You remember where we're meeting?" Camden asked as Damon slammed the door shut.

"I do." Damon rolled his eyes.

Entering the store, Alessa was immediately overwhelmed by the shiny, glittery, and colorful fabrics.

"Dear gods," Damon groaned as he took in the sheer number of dresses on display.

"Jeez. Where do I begin?" Alessa's eyes widened.

She started sifting through the dresses on the closest rack, and after flipping past several gowns adorned in brightly dyed feathers, she chose a light pink dress, a deep red one, and a creamy white dress to try on.

Alessa entered the dressing room, and Damon plopped down on a cushioned bench, resting his ankle on his knee.

Hanging the gowns on the wall, she pulled the thick curtain to the side, unintentionally leaving the hanging fabric unsecured. Peering up, Damon did a double take, realizing he could see around the drape.

Out of nowhere, an older woman stepped before Damon, interrupting his view. "Do you require any assistance?"

Taken by surprise, Damon uncrossed his legs and cleared his throat. "Uh, nope. I think I'm good."

The employee eyed him suspiciously before shuffling away.

Damon brought his fingertips up to his lips and leaned forward. "Shit," he cursed, chuckling to himself.

With the curtain's opening, Damon looked at the dressing room.

Alessa was wearing the medium-length pink gown. It was strapless and hugged all the right places, but the fabric was all wrong, pooling outward to her knees.

"What do you think?" She twirled around in a circle.

"You look like you're going to prom ... in the 1950s," Damon smirked.

She stopped spinning and shrugged. "I guess I can see that," she conceded before shuffling back inside the dressing stall.

"Try the red one," Damon suggested as he relaxed again.

A few minutes later, Alessa threw the curtain to the side, and as she popped the entirety of her left leg out through the slit in the skirt, Damon licked his lips.

The sultry red dress's beaded neckline plunged deep and was connected by two horizontal strings while the halter top wrapped around her neck, accentuating her breasts.

Every inch of fabric clung to Alessa's body, highlighting her womanly curves. It even gathered on the floor in a pool of seductiveness.

"Well?" She placed her hands on her hips, awaiting Damon's opinion.

"Oh. Yeah, that one's too, uh ... revealing. We want them to imagine what's underneath, not actually see it."

"Come on!" she exclaimed, throwing her hands up and turning around.

As Alessa disappeared behind the curtain once more, Damon rotated his hips. "Damn," he mumbled under his breath, trying to talk down his erection.

Finally, Alessa pulled the curtain to the side. "What about this one?"

The cream-colored dress had an extravagant arrangement of silver crystals upon the silky fabric. Its sweetheart neckline dipped down, exposing the top of her breasts, and the front of the skirt stopped mid-thigh while the back extended down to the floor.

"That one's much better, but—"

Alessa popped a hip in frustration. "But it's still not the *right* one?" she asked, her voice dripping with annoyance.

"You got it."

"Ugh!" Alessa stomped back into the changing room. "I'm still buying it!" she hollered from behind the closed curtain.

Damon rolled his eyes. "Of course you are."

Changing back into her clothes, Alessa emerged with the cream gown draped over her arm.

"What now?" he asked.

Alessa pointed toward the exit. "You leave."

He stood up and raised his hands. "What are you talking about? Why?"

"Because you have better things to do than stick around here and help me pick out a dress. Or should I say help me *not* pick out a dress?" Alessa walked up to the cashier and set the gown on the counter. "Can I leave this here while I keep looking?"

"Absolutely, dear." The white-haired cashier grabbed the hanger.

Damon shrugged in defeat. "Guess I'll go meet up with Camden."

"Don't forget, you need to find a tux," Alessa reminded him.

Damon rolled his eyes. "Yeah, yeah. Is there anything you need before I go?"

"Well, I need cash for that dress, plus whatever dress I wear tonight. Oh, and I guess I'll also need some money for cab fare and to rent a motel room."

"This is the last of our money. I'm going to make a withdrawal from my personal account. At this point, it doesn't matter if anyone from home knows where we are. If things don't go as planned, we're screwed anyway." Digging in his pocket, Damon opened his wallet and handed Alessa two thousand dollars in twenty-dollar bills.

As she fingered the money, Damon grasped her hand and leaned into her. "Don't get into trouble while I'm gone, do you hear me? You cannot disappear on me again."

Alessa gulped like a chastised child. "Okay."

Damon nodded and released her hand. "Good. Be careful." He turned on his heel. "And make sure you don't look like a two-bit whore!" Damon hollered over his shoulder as he exited the store.

"Damon!" Alessa gasped. She glanced over at the cashier apologetically. "I am so sorry about him. He had a troubled childhood."

The older lady glared at Alessa with pursed lips. "Mm-hmm."

CHAPTER FORTY-SIX

With her cheeks flushed red in embarrassment, Alessa returned to the sea of fabric. She pushed dress after dress aside, flipping through them like pages of a book until, finally, a gown made of shiny black material caught her eye from across the store.

Alessa hurried over to the far wall, sifted through the hangers, and plucked the dress from the rack.

The silky, raven-black gown was adorned with rhinestones cascading elegantly down the bodice. Its sweetheart neckline would plunge between her breasts and be supported on either side by inch-thick straps that would run up and over her shoulders.

The soft fabric swirled together in the middle of the gown, twisting around itself before extending out to the sides and back. The dress was revealing on both sides and would expose Alessa's skin from the far underside of her breasts down to her hips. Her back would only be covered by two-inch-thick straps coming down from her shoulders, the two straps on either side and two more holding the dress skirt up. All the pieces would intertwine just below her shoulder blades.

Alessa's jaw dropped in awe, and she held it up. "This is it."

Heading for the counter, she placed it down for the cashier to ring up.

"Oh, how beautiful," the grey-haired woman complimented.

"I agree," Alessa smiled. "Oh, I also need a masquerade ball eye mask. Do you sell any?"

The woman behind the counter smiled mischievously and reached into the cabinet before her. Unlocking the door, she withdrew an entire shelf decorated with ornate eye masks. "Only the best."

Alessa plucked a black lace one from the velvet backing and placed it with the rest of her purchases.

"You know, if you're looking, there's a perfect pair of shoes to go with this dress. Right over," the woman pointed, "there."

"Oh, great, thank you." Alessa turned away.

She shrieked excitedly when she found a pair of strappy silver heels.

"That'll do." Alessa beamed, returning to the register.

"The total is eight hundred and sixty dollars," the cashier announced.

"Fuck me!" Alessa exclaimed.

The cashier's wrinkled eyes opened wide as she stood behind the counter with her hand over her heart.

"Uh," Alessa stuttered as she handed over the cash. "Sorry. What I meant was, golly, gee whiz."

Eyeing Alessa disapprovingly, the woman took the money and placed the two gowns inside separate white zippered bags. Then, she slipped the shoes into a smaller, clear plastic bag.

"Thanks." Alessa grabbed the shoes and dress, eager to get off the judgmental woman's radar.

Rushing out to the street, Alessa jumped into the back seat

of the first taxi that pulled over, and she sat down with the bundle of clothing in her lap.

"Where to?" the driver asked.

"Please take me to the nearest, cheapest motel."

"Excuse me?"

"Look, I don't have a lot of money, and I need a place to spend the night, hence a cheap motel," Alessa barked.

Looking in the rearview mirror, the driver eyed her suspiciously. "Uh-huh."

"Just shut up and drive," Alessa replied.

On their way to the motel, she caught sight of a makeup store. "Wait! Stop here."

As the man slammed on the brakes, he and Alessa jerked forward.

"What is it?" the driver panicked.

"I need to go in there." She pointed to the large window in front of the makeup store. "I'll only be a few minutes."

The man exhaled loudly. "Woman, you shrieked like I had run someone over."

Alessa handed the man one hundred dollars. "If you stay here and wait for me, I'll give you another hundred on top of your normal fee."

The driver eyeballed the cash. "I thought you said you didn't have a lot of—"

Alessa tilted her head down and glared at the man, silencing him.

"Got it. No more questions." He nodded in understanding.

"That'd be swell." She faked a smile. "I'll be right back."

Alessa threw her dresses and shoes off her lap into the seat beside her before jogging into the store.

Rushing up and down the aisles, she was awestruck by all the bright eyeshadows and fluorescent lip colors. "How hard is it to find normal ... Aha!" she declared, discovering a shimmery black compact with four shades of brown eye shadow.

In the next aisle, Alessa found jet-black gel eyeliner, rosy blush, and a bright red lipstick guaranteed not to smudge.

Approaching the checkout line, she passed a curling iron, stopped, walked backward, and peered at it while biting her lower lip in contemplation.

"Didn't even think about that."

Picking up the iron, she paid for the items and ran for the cab.

Shutting the back door, Alessa handed the man five more twenty-dollar bills, and a few minutes later, they pulled into an aged motel's parking lot with a weathered sign displaying its multiple vacancies in neon green lights.

Juggling her bags, she stumbled into the motel lobby where a big-bellied man was camped out behind the front desk, sporting a stained white T-shirt and overalls.

He was watching a small television with his feet propped up on a chair beside him.

Alessa fell forward. "Uh, hi. I'm looking for a room."

"How many beds you needin'?" The man sucked on his teeth.

"Two, please." She pressed her lips together in a forced, tight-lipped smile.

The greasy man remained seated and grabbed keys dangling from the back wall. "Room nine. How many nights you plannin' on being here?"

"Hopefully, just one." Alessa set her dresses and shoes up on the counter.

"That'll be seventy dollars." The man licked his lips, watching her pull the cash out from the inside of her bra. "You meetin' up with anyone later?" He bent his head down and raised his eyebrows above the frames of his glasses.

Alessa chortled. "Why? You think you could handle this?" She leaned in toward him, flashing the top of her breasts.

The man's jaw dropped, and his eyes grew wide.

"No? I didn't think so," she snapped, throwing the cash on the counter. "Be careful who you make sexual advances toward. Women don't typically appreciate it, and you never know when one will go crazy on you." A sadistic grin spread across her face, and she picked up her bags.

The man's face blushed scarlet, and he slowly backed away from the counter.

Snatching the keys from the countertop, she stormed out the door toward room number nine.

———

"Get over here!" Camden hissed at Damon. "What are you doing, digging in that plant?"

Damon swatted a giant leaf away from his face. "What do you think I'm doing? I'm hidin' our shit."

Camden grumbled. "Not in a plant, you're not. That's too obvious. Are you an amateur?"

Suppressing the urge to cough, Damon picked up his box, heavy with ammunition and weapons.

The men walked around Eric's château using the cardboard boxes to hide their faces. Not one person glanced in their direction as the men blended perfectly with the busy workers prepping for that night's party.

Camden turned to the right, and Damon followed close behind.

They jogged up a flight of stairs to the second floor, and Camden stopped beside the staircase.

"Stay here. I'll be right back." He strutted away with the box propped atop his shoulder.

Damon dropped his box on the ground and grabbed the nearest pile of lights. While he pretended to work, a worker shouted down from up above.

Damon tilted his head back. "Dammit," he muttered under his breath.

A man, suspended in a black harness, descended from the ceiling. "Hey! You a part of the new crew?" the guy asked as his feet hit the ground.

Damon extended his hand. "Yeah. And you would be...?"

The worker shook Damon's hand. "Sal. I've been setting up parties for Mr. Lansing for what seems like forever. I'm sorry, I didn't catch your name."

Suddenly feverish, Damon's face reddened. "Oh, uh .... Rick ... Porter."

Camden walked up behind Damon with his empty cardboard box. "That should do it."

Sal's face scrunched up in recognition as his eyes locked on Camden.

"We'd best be movin'. Got orders from the boss," Camden drawled in an indistinguishable accent, and he pulled the front of his cap further down on his head.

As Sal was about to holler at the men to stop, he was interrupted by a fellow worker who needed his help.

"Damn, that was close." Camden cursed as they exited the front door, and he headed for his car. "You get your suit yet?"

"I've still got time." Damon shrugged dismissively.

Camden opened his car door. "Man, you have got to be kidding. The party's only two hours away."

"What are you, my mother? I'll find a damn suit." Damon rolled his eyes, standing next to his stolen motorcycle.

Camden started his stolen car and rolled down the window. "Need a ride?"

"No, I'm good." Damon swung his leg over his motorcycle and sat on its seat.

"Alright, then. See you later," Camden nodded before speeding away.

Admiring her transformation, Alessa stood before the bathroom mirror.

Her dark, romantic curls fell loose halfway down her back. The black eyeliner emphasized her upper lashes, and her lips were painted into a seductive blood-red pout. Her eyes fell upon the moonstone necklace, and she fingered the glowing gem.

A knock echoed on the motel room door, and she jumped. "Who is it?" she called out, her hands pressed against her fast-beating heart.

A muffled voice yelled from behind the closed door. "It's Camden!"

"Oh, good. Okay. Come on in. It's open!"

"Seriously, Alessa, you didn't lock the door?" Camden reprimanded.

"Oh, would you relax? If Bodyguards wanted to get in this little haven, do you think that dinky lock on the door could keep them out?"

Camden marched into the motel room in an expensive, grey, three-piece suit.

Alessa emerged from the bathroom, and he froze in place.

"Wow. You look—" He shoved his hands deep in his pants pockets.

Alessa panicked. "What? Is it too much?" She looked down at herself and rotated. "I knew I should've stuck with the cream dress." She pressed her hands nervously against her stomach.

"Alessa," Camden held his hand up for her to stop and stepped forward, "you look amazing."

Her cheeks burned with embarrassment. "Oh. Uh, thank you."

He reached into his inner jacket pocket. "I almost forgot." Camden extracted a small burgundy box and handed it to Alessa.

"What is it?" She pried the box apart.

"I saw them and thought you could make them work."

Alessa stared transfixed at two diamond oval rainbow moonstone earrings. "I couldn't possibly accept—"

"You can and you will."

Alessa shook her head back and forth. "But these must've cost—"

"Stop worrying. Damon's not the only one with tricks. Now, put them on so we can get out of here." He pointed to the bathroom.

Alessa wrapped her arms around his neck. "Thanks, Cam."

She carefully looped the diamonds into each of her earlobes, and then, after she beamed at her reflection, Alessa exited the bathroom with a satisfied sigh.

Rushing out of the room, she scooped her shoes, shawl, and lace mask from the bed before Cam slammed the motel door behind her.

Tiptoeing through the parking lot, Alessa held her heels and squealed excitedly as she jumped into the silver Dodge Challenger Camden had directed her toward.

Camden shifted into first gear as she put on her heels.

"So, where's Damon?" Alessa inquired, securing her left shoe strap.

"He's ensuring we have the means to hijack the broadcast tonight so the entire world will see the truth."

"What are we broadcasting?"

"The information you downloaded to your microchip. We don't have time to waste waiting for the information to pass through the right hands. We need to stop Eric now. Besides, state lines are closing at midnight. This time-sensitive information needs to be addressed immediately. Damon explained how your downloading works. It's quite fascinating."

She sat dumbfounded, with one foot propped up on the dashboard. "Of course. It'll be the quickest way to get the truth out to the public. Why didn't I think of that?"

"Don't be too hard on yourself; you've been through quite a lot. By the way, Damon didn't have time to explain the plan to me. He said you'd know what needed to be done." Camden turned the steering wheel as they headed down a back road.

Alessa secured her right shoe strap and nodded. "Yeah, um, we'll have to find a way to transfer the files directly onto a computer. Our best bet would be a news station."

"What about a news station's van?"

"That could work," she agreed, dropping her foot on the floorboard. "What made you think of that?"

"There's bound to be plenty of reporters at the party." Camden adjusted Alessa's shoulder strap. "Explain how you can download information from your brain to a computer?"

Embarrassed by Camden's intimate gesture, Alessa blushed and nervously ran her hands down her skirt, smoothing the fabric. "The best way to describe it is I have a form of wireless built into my brain, but not. It's hard to put into words."

Camden chuckled in amusement. "Wait. Are you serious?"

Insulted, she stared him down.

His eyebrows lifted in surprise. "Huh. You are serious."

Peering out the front window, Alessa twirled the alexandrite and diamond band around her finger. "Just get us to the party," she said, suddenly feeling quite ill.

CHAPTER FORTY-SEVEN

Camden turned down a long gravel drive and pulled up beside a line of parked cars. "And here we are."

Camera crews and their vans were lined up before the main gate, interviewing partygoers upon their arrival.

Two armed Bodyguards stood watch before the large gate, and two additional guards held onto a clipboard.

Camden extended his arm toward Alessa. "You ready?"

She placed her hand on his. "Do I have another choice?"

"Not unless you want to turn a blind eye to the damn near extinction of humankind." Cam helped Alessa out of the car.

Struggling to get her footing on the uneven gravel, she flashed a sarcastic grin. "Thanks for that, Cam."

Approaching the camera crews, she pointed out a female reporter leaning back against a van with the red number seven painted on its side. The reporter brought an electronic cigarette up to her ruby-red lips.

"Her."

Camden demanded the reporter's attention. "Excuse me, ma'am!" he hollered.

The woman's leg dropped from the van behind her, and she stood up straight, exhaling white smoke. "Me?" she pointed to herself.

Alessa nodded as they continued forward. "If you want to get your hands on the story of the century, then yes."

"Story of the century..." the reporter chuckled, crossing her arms. Looking away from them, she inhaled from the e-cigarette once more.

They silently stood before the reporter. "You're not going away, are you?" She rolled her eyes and blew a ring of white smoke. "What's the catch?"

"You are to play the footage at precisely ten o'clock tonight. Not six, not nine—ten o'clock."

The reporter tilted her head before licking her lips. "Okay, what's the reasoning?"

"The president is holed up somewhere secret due to this sickness, and she is planning an announcement to the American people at that time. Am I correct?" Camden asked.

The reporter planted a hand on her hip. "You're not wrong. Which is why I am asking, why, at the exact time all eyes will be on the television to hear the President of the United States, would I play your footage?"

Alessa stepped forward. "Because we're going to hijack every television in the country at that very moment."

The reporter returned her vape pen to the pocket of her pencil skirt. "Okay, you've got my attention. What's the story?"

"We have proof that Eric Lansing, the man hosting this lavish get-together, isn't the saint he's made himself out to be," said Camden.

The reporter's eyes narrowed. "What kind of proof?"

"Footage taken directly from Eric's files containing

classified information; information never intended to be released to the public," explained Alessa.

The woman popped her right hip, straining the skirt's fabric. "And what exactly would this footage contain?"

Camden's voice dropped an octave. "First, it explains how Eric was the one who ordered the initial release of the smallpox virus."

The woman laughed incredulously. "Yeah, sure. Erebos Industries is the only company even to attempt to create a cure—"

"And why do you think that is?" Alessa demanded. "He's monopolizing the market."

The reporter shook her head in denial. "That cure is going to save millions—"

"Give me a minute to download the files so you can see it all for yourself. Then you can decide whether to believe us or take the so-called cure," Alessa pleaded.

The reporter looked back and forth between them. "Fine, you can use our equipment. It's right in there." She pointed inside their news van.

Camden helped Alessa into the vehicle, where, staring at the screen, she connected to the computer's database with a simple blink.

Activating her microchip, Alessa's memory was unlocked, and she accessed the download using the encrypted password she had established before losing her memory.

Her eyes darted back and forth as the data unloaded from her mind. The damning information was transferred onto the news van's computer, coinciding with flashes of images and fragments of conversations appearing on the monitor.

Upon completion of the download, the screen turned black.

"There," Alessa announced, her eyes fading from green to blue.

The reporter stared at Alessa in awe. "How did you do that?"

Alessa jumped out of the van and into Camden's arms. "Do what?"

Setting Alessa down on the ground, Camden stared the woman down. "You didn't see anything, got it?"

The reporter nodded in understanding, with her arms up in surrender. "Not a thing."

"You need to watch this now. The airtime is ten o'clock, no sooner. Oh, and if you screw us over," Alessa's eyes flashed emerald green, "I'll find you."

Alessa hooked her arm around Camden's, and they headed for the party.

"How are you so confident she'll air the footage?" he asked.

"She's a reporter with the best story of her career. Plus, I'd like to think I scared the shit out of her." Alessa smiled wickedly. "Hey, we should call Damon to let him know we chose Station Seven."

Guiding Alessa toward the closed gates, Camden slipped on a silver Columbia mask before pulling out a phone.

Alessa plucked her black lace mask from his other jacket pocket as he spoke.

"Hey, Damon ... Station Seven ... Right ... Yeah, she's right here. We're about to go inside." He peered at the stationed Bodyguards. "You too." He bluntly ended the call.

Camden tucked his phone back into his pocket before extending his arm around Alessa's shoulders, pulling her to his side as they approached the gate.

The first Bodyguard addressed them. "Names, please?"

They stopped walking, and Camden lifted his mask, exposing his face.

The second guard leaned forward and squinted. "Camden, is that you?"

Camden answered the man with a cocky grin and lifted his free hand in salute.

"Hey, man. I thought you were supposed to guard Miguel down in Texas?" The guard held out his hand, grinning wide.

Cam firmly gripped the man's hand. "I was sent here to watch Eric from the sidelines. You know, as extra eyes on the main man."

The first guard glared at Camden in disbelief.

Camden held his hands up defensively. "Why else would I be here tonight? I'm not here for the ladies. I mean, I've already got mine." He wrapped his arm around Alessa's waist and pulled her in tight.

Alessa smiled and forced a giggle.

"I mean, if you were here under pretenses, that would be pretty stupid," the second guard pointed out.

The first man relaxed and huffed a breath of air. "Even for you."

With a nod, Camden flashed a tight-lipped smile. "I'm glad we're all in agreement."

"Who's she?" inquired the guard while he wrote Camden's name on the guest list.

As Alessa opened her mouth to respond, Camden interceded.

"Amelia, and she's with me tonight. I'm sure she'd appreciate it if you let us in already." Camden tilted his head toward Alessa.

Every guard looked her up and down before one directed them through the tall gate. "Stay out of trouble."

Camden and Alessa peered over at one another. "I'll try my best," Camden yelled over his shoulder as they walked through the gates.

The large, two-story home was built on acreage, and in the middle of its circular drive sat a large fountain adorned with colored lights. An elegant balcony protruded off the front of the house, hovering atop the front steps, and an extravagant crystal-beaded chandelier dangled from the front porch's ceiling.

Alessa's heels clicked up the poured concrete drive as they fell in line behind the other guests heading toward the château.

Camden escorted Alessa into the oversized foyer after they filed in through the home's double doors.

One of the working men extended his hand toward Alessa. "May I take your shawl?"

She hugged her shawl tight. "Oh, no. No, thank you."

A large staircase leading up to the second floor was directly ahead. Her eyes followed the notched woodwork adorning the walls to the intricately carved ceiling, where a beautiful, circular skylight was cut out of stained glass.

Hanging down from the skylight was a golden chandelier comprised of three tiers of burning candles.

Camden and Alessa strolled through the main hall before exiting the back doors into the elaborately decorated backyard.

Hundreds of masked guests were gathered amidst colorful hanging lanterns, scantily dressed servers, and glasses filled with various types of alcohol. There were at least twenty projectors set up around the backyard, all facing a single podium.

"Oh, joy. We're attending a party with half-naked men and women, everyone drinking alcohol, and masked killers. Nothing could go wrong here," Alessa half-heartedly joked.

"I'll take two of those." Camden plucked two full wine glasses from a nearly naked waitress passing by.

He gave a glass to Alessa and placed his free hand upon her lower back before speaking quietly into her ear. "I'll start by pointing out the people I'm familiar with."

CHAPTER FORTY-EIGHT

Camden discreetly pointed to the farthest pillar on the right. "The tall man by that column, over there, is Todd. The woman standing next to him is Suzanne, and the skinny man attached to her plump hip is her husband, Bill. They're in research and development."

Camden directed Alessa's attention toward a group to their left. "That is Brian, Jason, Humphries, Alexander, Alice, and Tris. They make up the sales and marketing department."

A middle-aged man and woman burst out in laughter.

"Those two are some benefactors of the so-called cure. His name is Steven, and that's his wife, um, Margaret; yes, Margaret. They've donated a lot of money to Eric's *cause*. Of course, only after being tested for every genetic abnormality. I mean, you have to make sure you'll be included in the future of humankind before pouring all of your money into that future," Camden grumbled. "Those individuals over there," he pointed at a large group of people laughing as they sat by the pool, "are benefactors that have flown in from Russia."

"Do you know them?"

Cam side-eyed her. "Yes, Alessa. I am great friends with everyone from Russia," he sarcastically quipped.

"Jeez. Sorry I asked." She scrunched her shoulders up defensively. "And all these people, the benefactors, don't possibly understand the extent to which Eric is willing to go. Do they?"

Camden licked his lips before responding. "They know everything. Or mostly everything." Stepping onto the grass, he continued naming partygoers. "You see that tall man wearing the top hat?"

"Yeah." Alessa sipped her red drink.

"His name is Xander Mack, and he's Erebos's chief physician. He's in charge of choosing the subjects to test the product's efficacy."

"Subjects?"

Cam took a swig of alcohol. "You remember the barn in Texas?"

She recalled the stench of corpses in cages lining its walls and shivered.

"He's otherwise known as Doctor Death."

Tears stung Alessa's eyes as she stared daggers at the physician.

"Come on." Camden placed his hands on her shoulders and guided her toward the middle of the lawn.

"It's ridiculous for these people to think their identities are obscured thanks to a mask that covers only half of their faces," Alessa scoffed.

Camden shrugged. "They think they're invincible. Couldn't you say the same thing about you and me? We're hoping this thin piece of fabric conceals our identities enough to get by undetected." He tilted his head. "In their dysfunctional minds, the mask is simply a decorative status symbol."

Over the next half hour, Camden and Alessa discussed the people and whether they had a direct role within Erebos Industries or were contributors hoping to buy their way into the genetically pure future. Alessa recognized those from her time undercover at Erebos Industries, but just as many were financial contributors.

They casually strolled around the yard, Alessa's arm wrapped around Camden's until their discussion was interrupted by a finger tapping on a microphone.

"Excuse me. Welcome, and thank you for joining us on this beautiful evening." An eye-masked woman beamed. "Erebos Industries would like to thank you for participating in this wonderful journey. Eric's vision would not have been possible without you, and we look forward to working together to establish—"

"If I have to hear these people brag about themselves the entire night, I will gladly put a bullet in my brain," Camden grumbled.

Setting her empty wine glass on a server's tray, Alessa quietly giggled.

"Now, it is my pleasure to introduce the man of the hour, Mr. Eric Lansing." The female speaker extended the microphone toward the open patio doors.

Alessa's breathing hitched as a middle-aged man dressed in a white tux strutted out of the house with a young, gorgeous brunette clinging to his left arm. His dark hair was slicked to the side, and the man's thin lips separated into a ghastly smile as he reached for the microphone.

Eric was the only person at the party not wearing an eye mask.

Overcome with rage, Alessa's insides quivered.

As Eric began his speech, his muddy brown eyes scanned the crowd.

A memory of Alessa falling to her knees with blood dripping from her lower lip forced its way into her consciousness.

"What did you do with the information?" Eric demanded.

Alessa choked. "I didn't ... see ... anything."

Eric shoved a hunter's knife from his weathered leather strap before her nose.

After a brief pause, he lifted the blade above his head and sliced it across Alessa's forearm.

"Tell us what you know! Tell us, now!" another man shouted.

Alessa spat onto the concrete as blood dripped down her arm. "Fuck. You."

Eric raised his left hand menacingly up in the air.

With her hands restrained tightly behind her back, Alessa's body tensed for the impending hit.

Her cheekbone cracked as his fist connected with her face, and Alessa's head lolled to the side.

Eric squatted down in front of her, rubbing his bloodied knuckles.

"We will continue to ask where the download is, and until you tell us, my men and I will allow your wounds to heal." He grabbed her jaw and tilted her chin. "Then I will take this knife and drive it in through your flesh and muscle, again, and again, and again."

Eric's rancid breath burned Alessa's nostrils as his lips hovered before hers.

"If somehow you hold out and do not tell me what I want to know, I will show no mercy. These concrete walls, splattered with your blood, will be the last thing you ever see. I promise you that."

The vile memory disappeared as a nearly naked woman balancing a tray of glasses full of champagne passed in front of Alessa and Camden.

He squeezed her arm, noticing her muscles tense. "Are you okay?"

Alessa was glad she wasn't holding the glass anymore, as it would've shattered beneath her clenched fingers. She glared at Eric and dug her fingertips into Camden's arm.

He steadied himself as she took out her rage on his appendage, and once Alessa relaxed, he took a deep breath. "We good now?"

Regaining control of her emotions, Alessa exhaled loudly.

Camden reached for a glass of champagne from another waitress's tray. "I'm going to need this."

"You have no idea." Alessa grasped a glass in each hand and downed them as if they were shots.

"That's what I'm talking about." Holding a glass in each of his hands, Camden tilted his head back, downing each, just as Alessa had done.

"To our health!" he exclaimed in Russian.

They placed their empty glasses on the server's tray, and Camden snatched up two more full glasses, winking at the beautiful server.

Before beginning his speech, Eric stretched his neck up and to the left, a quirk Alessa got the chills recalling him do, repeatedly, while in the room of torture.

"I do hope you all are enjoying yourselves. In a few days, this,' he dug into his inner coat pocket and emerged holding a small, elongated glass vial containing a pearly canary yellow liquid, "cure will end the smallpox pandemic, and it will ensure a brighter future for all of mankind."

Alessa gasped. *The cure. Damon's cure.* It was only a couple hundred feet in front of them.

All the guests in attendance raised their glasses, and Eric uncapped the vial. "To the future." He toasted and downed the liquid.

Alessa nearly lunged forward, but Camden held her back.

"To the future," the crowd echoed.

"Cam..." she begged.

"If he has one dose, I guarantee you he has more. Be patient."

"Please follow me inside for music and dancing." Eric pranced into his château with the young brunette clinging to his arm.

Alessa leaned against Camden. "I need a break. Where is the bathroom?"

Camden held his arm out. "I'll escort you."

"Thanks," Alessa said as she looped her arm through his.

They wove through the crowd of partygoers and approached the staircase. As they climbed the stairs, Alessa peered down at the foyer's elaborate marble flooring while Camden turned his face away from the guests, hoping to avoid Eric's wandering gaze.

Camden stepped up onto the second floor and pointed down the long hallway. "That closed door at the end is the restroom. I'll wait for you here."

Walking down the hall, she glanced nervously at every closed door.

Once at the double doors, Alessa tugged on the knobs and stood stunned in front of the enormous washroom.

A skylight was carved into the center of the ceiling, and an old-fashioned wooden fireplace sat against the far wall. An elaborate vanity took up the entire left side of the room, and a chandelier hung above the deep bathtub.

"Jeez. All I need is a toilet." She closed the door and threw her shawl onto the counter.

After using the facilities, Alessa washed her hands under the gold faucet and popped her knee up. Balancing on the ball of her foot, she lifted her skirt and adjusted the thin black strap that was pressing her gun up against her inner thigh.

Dropping her heel down to the floor, Alessa draped her gown's black fabric over her leg and returned to the top of the staircase.

Camden was draped over the railing, watching the guests dance down below.

Gazing over at Alessa as she approached, Camden grinned handsomely. "I thought maybe you'd fallen in."

Alessa rolled her eyes and stepped down a stair with a smile. "You are so weird."

Looking at the bottom of the stairs, Camden panicked.

Eric was standing on the landing.

As he turned toward them, Camden whipped around and rushed back up to the second floor, abandoning Alessa.

CHAPTER FORTY-NINE

Pacing the foyer, Damon dodged the people congregating in the main hall.

"Where are they?" he grunted.

The tickle in the back of his throat worsened, and his eyes watered uncontrollably as he fought the urge to cough.

Rushing to a secluded corner of the room, Damon pulled a white handkerchief from his inner jacket pocket.

Air rushed from his lungs as he hacked painfully into the palm of his hand, and he closed his eyes tightly as searing heat spread upward from his chest.

Gripping the wall to steady himself, Damon's knuckles blanched white, and he gasped for air.

His dark blue eyes opened beneath his black mask, and his heart raced as he stared at the handkerchief.

In the middle of the white cloth was a circular splatter stained red with his blood.

Looking into the mirror hanging from the wall, an unfamiliar face stared back at Damon. His blue eyes stood out against his pale skin, and his lips were smeared with crimson.

He folded the cloth with trembling hands and wiped the deep red from around his mouth. With a shaky exhale, he left the alcove and froze, watching Alessa descend the stairs.

———

Her dark hair bounced up and down against her breasts, and the gown's black fabric clung to her hips. The silver gems scattered throughout the dress reflected the light cast down by the hanging chandelier, and the skirt lightly caressed the floor, barely exposing her silver heels.

From behind her ebony lace mask, Alessa's bright blue eyes locked with Damon's, and her heart fluttered.

He was devastatingly handsome in his black tux.

As if in a trance, Damon tossed his handkerchief into the nearest trash can and walked toward the bottom of the staircase, never taking his eyes off Alessa.

Her heart pounded as Damon flashed a provocative smile, the same one in her memories.

As her cheeks reddened, Alessa tore her gaze away from Damon's, and she watched her silver heels hit each stair.

A shadow unexpectedly appeared before her, and with a gasp, she jolted to a stop. Alessa's head jerked upright, and her heart ceased beating as she looked into Eric's deep brown eyes.

He took her hand into his own. "Good evening. I couldn't help but notice you." His eyes drifted down her body.

Alessa's mouth went dry with the return of her erratic heartbeat, and her hand fell limp within Eric's grasp.

"Uh..." Alessa stalled, looking back for Camden.

Of course, she knew she'd be confronting Eric tonight, but not like this.

The feeling of terror threatened to consume Alessa. It was as though she was a fly caught in a spider's web.

"I'm Eric, president of Erebos Industries." He bent down and kissed the back of her hand. Eric remained bent over as his gaze darted up. "And you would be?"

Alessa swallowed the impulse to vomit, forced herself to take a steadying breath, and recalled the name Camden had told the front guards. "Amelia."

Eric mistook Alessa's shaking voice for her being intimidated and smiled.

"Amelia." He placed his other hand on top of hers, holding Alessa in place. "Dance with me."

He pulled Alessa behind him down the final few stairs as Damon stepped to the side, blending in with the crowd.

From behind his black mask, Damon's eyes bore into Eric as he entered the dancefloor with Alessa.

Eric positioned Alessa in front of him and grabbed her right hand. "So, Amelia, what brings you to my home this evening?"

Alessa forced herself to keep eye contact with Eric even though every fiber of her being demanded she get away. "I was invited. By a friend," she lied.

"And who would this friend be?" Eric pulled Alessa in close.

Alessa nervously looked away. "Patricia." Her eyes landed on Damon's glowing silver irises, and, for a moment, she forgot about their awkward interaction in the motel room and resisted the urge to run into his arms.

"Ah," Eric said. "Patricia's been very supportive of our cause."

Alessa closed her eyes and nodded. Feeding off Damon's intense energy and the realization Eric had no idea who she was, Alessa leaned back into Eric's arms. "Mr. Lansing—"

He flashed his pearly whites. "Call me Eric."

"Alright, Eric. Could you please explain to me when the exact moment was that you became interested in developing a cure for the smallpox pandemic?"

"I'm sorry?" He chuckled in amusement.

Eric turned her around, and they promenaded in a circle.

Alessa pushed further. "I researched your company, and Erebos Industries appeared out of the blue within the last three years. Your company's first medication is the cure for smallpox, which happens to be perfectly timed with an outbreak."

Grasping her fingers, Eric spun Alessa in a circle, and his eyes widened as they fell upon her distinctive tattoo.

Swaying her hips back and forth, she dragged her hand across his back. Stepping before Eric, Alessa thrust her hand into his and forced him to step back.

Eric's eyes narrowed. "What are you implying?"

"I'm just saying, do you honestly think no one will figure it out? You're this mystery billionaire who's never donated a cent toward medical research. Then, you become president of the only pharmaceutical company to successfully create a cure for the smallpox pandemic that somehow, no one but you saw coming."

Eric's grip tightened on Alessa. "Some would say it's a miracle."

"Or a conspiracy," she retorted without missing a beat. "And clearly, I am well aware of the future we are celebrating this evening, but I'm honestly surprised not a single soul has discovered the truth."

Forcing Alessa up against his swollen belly, Eric pressed his hand into her lower back and looked deep into her eyes. "Oh, Amelia, you're a feisty one." He licked his lips. "Is Patricia the only one you came with tonight?"

Alessa peered down at Eric's lips, hovering mere inches before her own. "Uh, yes..."

He grinned. "Good."

Alessa's eyes darted to the side of the room where Damon was standing. His gunmetal grey irises seared through Eric as he glowered at them.

She gasped aloud as Eric threw her back into a low dip, nearly hitting her head on the marble floor.

Her lips parted in shock, and her body stiffened as Eric held her precariously upside down.

"I'd like you to come to my room later," he growled.

Alessa pressed her red lips together and silently nodded in submission. "Oh, okay."

Eric slowly stood her upright. "Nine-thirty? It'll be the only room upstairs with guards positioned in front of the door."

Alessa swallowed the lump in the back of her throat before responding. "Nine-thirty." She smiled faintly and nodded.

Eric released her waist and kissed the back of her hand. "Now, if you'll excuse me, I have some business to attend to."

Rotating on his heels, Eric was escorted down the hall by two Bodyguards on either side.

Alessa was suddenly alone in the middle of the dancefloor, rubbing feverishly at the back of her hand, attempting to scrub away the sensation of Eric's lips from her skin.

"I thought he'd never leave."

Alessa jumped and turned around.

"Cam!" she shrieked before hitting his shoulder.

Wrapping his other arm around her waist, he took her hand and held Alessa's arm to the side.

Alessa's heart pounded against her chest. "You nearly gave me a heart attack."

Their bodies twisted around to the fast-paced music. "That

would've been a damn shame. I had no idea you were so timid. I'll have to be more careful next time." He grinned wickedly.

Alessa laughed as she lay her head on Cam's shoulder. "Where'd you go earlier? You took off and left me alone."

"I, uh, had to check something," Camden lied. He couldn't tell Alessa the truth behind his need to evade Eric. "How'd the dancing go with Eric?"

"Good, I guess." Alessa lifted her head. "He invited me to his room."

"Not bad." Camden wiggled his eyebrows up and down.

"Ew, gross. But wasn't that the point of me dressing up like this? To get him to notice me?"

Camden peered down at her. "He's not the only one who can't keep his eyes off you."

Alessa's lips parted as Cam spun her in a circle.

He extended his arm. "Eric seemed agitated towards the end of the conversation. What'd you say to him?"

Alessa bit her lower lip. "Nothing."

Camden pulled Alessa in closer. "That sounds like you. So quiet and demure."

As their bodies pressed together, Alessa blushed.

"Thanks again for helping us tonight."

Cam's fingers on Alessa's lower back gently rubbed against the soft gown. "It's not like I had anything better to do."

Alessa smiled and gazed into his hazel eyes. "You are one hell of a friend."

Camden smiled as if he were laughing at a private joke. "Just you wait and see. We're going to raise hell together. You're stuck with me. At least 'til my life debt is repaid."

His body stiffened as fingers tapped his upper back.

"May I cut in?" Damon asked.

Camden glanced over his shoulder. "Do I have a choice?"

Damon shook his head. "No, you don't."

With a loud sigh, Camden released Alessa and stepped beside her.

"Let me know if he tries anything," he whispered before kissing her on the cheek.

Camden walked away, and Damon growled, "He'd better watch himself."

"Oh, stop it, Damon. He was kidding."

Sweeping her up into his arms, Damon spun Alessa around and placed her before him.

"Sure, he was." Damon glanced sideways at Camden's back as he left the room.

Alessa's skin burned where Damon's fingers wrapped around her hand. "Damon, you're on fire."

Closing his eyes tightly, Damon turned toward Alessa and inhaled deeply.

"Hey, are you feeling okay?"

"I'm good." Damon opened his eyes, and his entire demeanor softened. "You look stunning."

She placed her free hand on the side of his face, beneath his mask, and was alarmed by the intense heat radiating from his body. "You're not okay. You're burning up. You shouldn't be—"

Damon dipped Alessa to the side. "I'll be fine."

"Damon, you are *not* fine—"

"Tell me what happened with Eric," he interjected.

Alessa exhaled loudly in defeat. "I'm meeting him at nine-thirty. Upstairs, in his quarters."

Looking off in the distance, Damon nodded. "That's perfect. We'll have everything ready to ambush him."

The music slowed as a cover of Rihanna's song, 'Stay,' played from the speakers, and they danced amidst the crowded room.

"So, what's the plan once I enter his room?"

"Camden and I will take down the guards stationed in the hallway while you kill the ones inside. Then, we rush the room. We don't have a shot in Hades at taking down Eric until we destroy his Bodyguards."

Damon caressed the skin between her shoulder blades, and Alessa closed her eyes before tilting her head slightly to the left.

After a moment, she opened her eyes. "How many Bodyguards are we expecting there to be?"

Damon swallowed. "Plenty."

Pulling her close, his hot breath burned a trail down Alessa's neck as his lips grazed the top of her shoulder. Heat flowed from Damon's fingertips, and he massaged down her spine, stopping just above her tailbone.

He flattened his palm on Alessa's lower back, and while loosening his grip, Damon spun Alessa. Their arms stretched out between their bodies before he twirled her back into him.

Alessa folded her hand into his chest, and as her body crashed into Damon's, she inhaled sharply.

His breathing was ragged as their bodies pressed against one another. Damon's eyes opened wide as the hot, searing pain forced its way up from his chest once more.

Gripping Alessa's hand tightly, he turned to the side, and his abdominal muscles flexed as he resisted coughing.

"Damon, what's wrong?" Alessa placed her hand on his pale face and turned him toward her.

Damon fell forward and pressed his forehead against hers. "Alessa, if I don't make it, I need you to know something."

Pulling away, Alessa whimpered. "Damon—"

"Dammit, woman, let me finish," he said breathily.

Damon held Alessa tightly, gazing deep into her eyes as she stood in surprised silence. "I need you to know that whatever we had, whatever we were to each other ... it was real."

Her eyebrows scrunched up in anguish. "Why does it feel like you're saying goodbye?" Alessa's eyes widened, and she inched closer. "Wait, wait. What was real, Damon?"

"I"—he shook his head back and forth—"can't tell you."

Alessa's insides boiled. "Why can't you tell me?"

As Damon unexpectedly bent Alessa back into a dip, she put one hand around the nape of his neck and gripped his hand tight.

His lips hovered mere inches above hers as he confessed, "You were my everything."

Standing her upright, Damon pulled free from Alessa and pushed through the crowd toward the back door.

Regaining her wits, Alessa chased after him. "Damon! Damon, please stop!"

Her heels clicked loudly against the tile as she fell into the cool night air, nearly colliding with a man walking inside.

"Watch where you're going!" the man chastised as Alessa turned.

Ignoring the angry man, she ran after Damon.

"Damon, please! You can't say something like that and then walk away—"

Rounding a corner, Damon whipped around to face Alessa, and as she continued forward, he placed a hand on either side of her face and pulled her lips against his.

An electric current spread throughout her body as Damon's lips melted into Alessa's.

He wrapped his arms around her, and she fell into Damon as he lifted her off the ground.

Alessa's arms wrapped around his neck, demanding his touch as her lips swelled against his. Her body was set aflame as his heat transferred through his lips into hers, and as their kiss deepened, Damon set Alessa back on the ground and pushed her backward toward a secluded corner of the house. Reaching out behind Alessa, Damon touched the wall before pressing her back against the cool surface.

Alessa's fingers plunged deep into Damon's tufts of hair while his tongue rhythmically stroked her own.

A whisper of a moan escaped her lips, and upon hearing her say his name, Damon activated, and his eyes blazed silver.

"Alessa..." he exhaled.

Damon's hands gripped Alessa's curves as he inhaled her high-pitched moans. He lifted her left leg, and as she held it against him, Damon caressed her upper thigh.

Alessa drew a sharp breath, and the ground gave out from beneath her as she disappeared within an onslaught of memories.

CHAPTER FIFTY

In the first of her memories, it was late morning, and Alessa was walking beside Kai when they heard the strumming of a guitar. Intrigued, the young women rounded the corner and discovered a group of Coepi gathered around several musicians, giving an impromptu acoustic cover of "Grow as We Go" by Ben Platt.

Alessa and her sister weaved through the bodies, inching closer to the performers.

Recognizing the man's voice, Alessa's breathing faltered. She peered over the shoulder of the person sitting down in front of her, and Alessa's eyes widened.

Both the guitarist and singer was Damon.

He licked his lips before singing the pre-chorus and chorus of the song, explaining how the woman he was falling for was not the only one who needed to learn and how he'd like to stay by her side through their time of growth.

A musician sat beside Damon, strumming away on his instrument as he sang harmoniously. A relaxed smile played upon Damon's lips, and as he scanned the crowd, he locked eyes with Alessa.

Through the crowd, he sang the bridge directly to her.

The lyrics described two people making a future they wanted for themselves, not necessarily one expected of them, and how they could be their authentic selves with one another without repercussions.

Feeling oddly exposed amidst the sea of bodies, Alessa broke eye contact and nervously rubbed her arms.

The small crowd applauded at the song's ending, and those close to Damon patted him on the back.

"What was that about?" Kai questioned Alessa after witnessing the intensity between Damon and her sister.

Alessa pursed her lips together in an awkward smile and turned to walk away. After taking a few steps, she glanced back to find Damon watching her leave.

She then remembered the night of the pool house in its entirety.

Alessa, her sister, and their friends played games in the pool and splashed around for a couple of hours before Quade and Sera escaped to the seclusion of the hot tub. Kai jumped out and towel-dried herself before laying on a large blanket outside beneath the moon.

Floating on her back in the calm water, Alessa admired the bright moon and the stars scattered throughout the night sky through the skylight.

"Were you taught the constellations?" Damon interrupted the silence.

"All Spartans are taught the constellations."

"And how many of us can recall their stories?" He floated beside Alessa and pointed up at a specific collection of stars. "Such as the Legend of Lyra?"

Alessa remained silent, awaiting Damon's story.

"*I'll take your silence as you do not.*" He chuckled. "*Well, the celestial harp, Lyra, was invented by Hermes and given to Orpheus by Apollo. Orpheus played such beautiful love songs to his bride, Eurydice, that both people and animals would stop and listen.*

"*One day, his young wife unexpectedly died, breaking Orpheus's heart. In a desperate attempt to bring her soul back from the dead, Orpheus played his lyre for Hades and made a deal with the ruler of the underworld in which he would continue playing his lyre as long as Eurydice would be released to him as soon as his song was complete. Hades agreed under one condition: While leaving the underworld, Orpheus could not look behind him, not even once, to ensure his wife was following.*

"*Without hesitation, Orpheus agreed and continued to play his harp with newfound hope and enthusiasm. As the song neared its end, Orpheus began his ascent from the underworld. Soon after, his beloved's footsteps echoed behind him, and tears welled in his eyes as his heart skipped a beat. Nearing the end of the trail, the two lovers must pass through a pine grove, which deadens the sound of her footsteps. Unable to endure the quiet any longer, Orpheus cheated a glance from the corner of his eye, only to witness Eurydice's fading form reach out for him. Hades returned the man's wife to the underworld for betraying their deal.*

"*On the eve of Orpheus's death, Zeus placed the constellation Lyra into the heavens to honor the man's beautiful music and the great love Orpheus had for Eurydice.*"

Alessa's eyebrows furrowed as she silently glared at Damon.

Damon chuckled. "What? It's my favorite of all the constellations' legends. There's something tragically beautiful about the story."

"You think two people being kept apart is beautiful?" she asked.

Damon sighed before explaining himself. *"The concept of a man loving another so much he is willing to go to the underworld to save her soul is inspiring."*

Alessa's facial features softened as Damon made his heartfelt confession.

"And the fact he was so concerned with his wife making it out by his side, Orpheus couldn't even make it a few more minutes without checking on her safety is—"

"Heartbreaking?" Alessa interjected.

"Yes, it is, but it's also something I hope to experience someday." He eyed Quade and Sera snuggled over in the far corner of the pool house. *"Not all of us get the chance to fall in love. What about you?"*

"What about me?" She swam toward the stairs, having grown uneasy with the direction of the conversation.

"Have your views changed since our first talk at the coffee shop?"

She climbed the steps out of the pool and shook her head back and forth. *"No, they have not. I don't foresee children or a husband in my future."* Alessa plucked her towel from a nearby chair and wrapped it around her torso.

"Huh..." Damon followed her out of the pool and grabbed a towel beside her.

She shook out her long, wet hair. *"What?"*

He dried his wet hair with a navy blue towel. *"You work so well with the children. I assumed, maybe, you had changed your mind."*

"No, I simply love children's innocence. I also appreciate their uncanny ability to call out anyone on their bullshit. And

they don't hide what they're feeling," Alessa explained before she grabbed dry clothes and headed outside.

Finding Kai fast asleep, Alessa bent down, swept a stray piece of blonde hair out of Kai's face, and kissed her forehead. "Love you, Kitty Kat," she whispered.

Damon watched from the doorway, giving the sisters their space. "I think you'd make a great mom," he confessed, standing against the doorframe with his arms crossed over his chest.

Alessa eyed Damon and stood awkwardly, unsure of how to respond. "Thanks?" She carried her clothes over to the far side of a thick tree trunk. "Can you...?" she asked, motioning for him to turn around.

"Oh, yeah. Sorry," he apologized as he turned his back. "I guess I should get dressed as well."

Walking to the side of the pool house, Damon stripped out of his wet swim trunks and dried off before putting on dry clothes.

By the time Damon got his shirt on and walked back over to Alessa, she was fully dressed and lying beside her sister.

He quietly lay down beside Alessa.

She looked at him and licked her lips. "You know, you were stationed here nearly three years ago, and I feel like there's still so much to learn about you."

"I'm an open book," he admitted as he gazed at the sky. "Ask me anything. I won't lie to you." Damon propped himself on his elbow.

"Why is that? Why won't you lie to me?"

"I guess I'm so closed off to everyone else because I don't care for them to know me. But with you, I care." He slowly reached out and caressed the side of her cheek. "About how you see me, what you think of me. I've grown to care about you."

Alessa's insides lit aflame, and her cheeks blushed red as Damon validated her feelings.

For a few brief moments, Alessa and Damon looked into one another's eyes, awaiting the other's reaction.

Unable to hold back his need to kiss her, Damon scooted over and bent down. Their lips touched, and a searing heat passed between them. Their tongues played as their mouths moved against one another, daring the other to take things one step further.

Alessa's fingers wrapped eagerly behind Damon's head, and she ran her fingers through his dark brown hair, pulling him closer.

He propped himself above Alessa, and his free hand reached beneath her shirt and pressed firmly on the side of her hip.

After pulling apart, they were both left panting.

Damon glanced at Kai and practically growled in frustration at her proximity.

Unexpectedly, the door to the pool house opened and shut with a loud bang. Damon jumped off Alessa, and she instantaneously pulled the bottom of her shirt down.

"Hey, guys!" Quade called out as he and Sera headed over to their group, hand in hand.

"Hey..." Damon said through gritted teeth.

Alessa smiled sheepishly and sat up to grab an oversized blanket. "Was the hot tub nice?"

Sera exhaled. "It was. Tonight was just what I needed to recharge. Now, I'm ready to pass out. We have a busy day today."

Looking at Kai, Quade addressed Alessa. "How is she doing with her sparring?"

"Our elder is practicing with her every day. But honestly, I worry about her. Kai's heart doesn't seem to be in it, which concerns me," Alessa confessed in a hushed whisper.

Quade attempted to reassure her with a half-smile. "I'm sure she'll work it out, and it will all be fine. She's got you by her side, and your elder is the best."

"Thanks, Quade." Alessa lay back, and with a heavy heart, she looked up at the stars.

Damon reached beneath Alessa's blanket, grasped her hand, and gently squeezed it.

She closed her eyes tight, and a tear rolled down her cheek as she silently worried about her sister's future.

CHAPTER FIFTY-ONE

The next thing Alessa knew, she and Damon were running, bloodied and dirty, through the woods.

An excited smile was plastered on both their faces as they played Capture the Flag for the first time together.

The Spartan's rendition of Capture the Flag wasn't the same as the subdued traditional game. It had been transformed into an intense sporting event involving arrows, spears, knives, and whips.

This was the most hardcore version of the game Damon had ever played, and he was loving it.

Alessa's pulse increased due to the excitement of the game and because Damon licked his lips seductively every time he anticipated their opponent's next move.

Approaching the other team's final defense, Quade snuck up from behind. "Are we ready?"

"Oh, wait, hold on a sec." Damon disappeared around a large boulder. The sound of a body hitting the ground was heard, as well as a guttural groan, before he returned with a newly obtained weapon in hand. "Okay, you're good."

"*Go win us the game!*" *Alessa cheered as Quade ran up the hill toward the trees surrounding the neon yellow flag.*

Alessa and the other archers stood guard and shot their arrows into the darkness, creating a protective barrier around Quade as he sprinted for the flag.

Scaling two trees, he kicked back and forth from one to the other until he reached his hand up and grabbed the flag.

A bright white floodlight split the dark sky, and the blue team was announced as the victors.

The area surrounding Damon and Alessa erupted into chaos with both curses of despair and shouts of joy.

Damon and Alessa smiled widely and bellowed Spartan warrior cries as they lifted their weapons.

Everyone who wasn't seriously injured, on both the losing and winning sides of the game, ran toward the lake. The air was crisp in the early hours of the fall morning, but even so, all members of Spartan society who had participated in the game jumped into the lake, hollering as their bodies struck the cold water.

Watching the mass of bodies splash one another, Damon and Alessa laughed from the shoreline before he extended his arm toward her.

"*Come with me.*"

Eyeing him suspiciously, she placed her hand in his, and they jogged further into the woods.

Damon maintained a steady pace, only slowing once he heard water rushing.

Alessa's lungs burned, and she rested against a tree as Damon walked out of view behind several large bushes.

"*Damon?*" *she called out, attempting to stand up straight. Her sore muscles burned as she forced them to move her body forward.*

A splash echoed through the trees as she rounded the corner.

Damon was fully dressed as he swam in the large pond. "Come on! Get cleaned off. Your clothes stink." He splashed Alessa again.

The cold water hit her sticky skin, and Alessa gasped. After stripping out of her archery gear, she jumped up and tucked her feet under her rear into a cannonball.

Damon yelled as the water struck him in the face and laughed as Alessa came up for air, gasping.

"Shit, that's cold! Ah," she cursed, swimming for the shoreline.

Laughing hysterically, Damon followed close behind. "Oh, come on, it's not that bad."

Alessa stepped onto the shoreline and stood with her arms crossed in front of her chest, looking back toward the city. "What do we do now? I'm so far from my room."

Running his hands through his wet hair, Damon wrung out his shirt and eyed Alessa.

Her wet clothes clung tight to the curves of her body, and as his eyes fell to Alessa's backside, Damon was overcome with the need to feel her against him.

With his eyes piercing hers, he closed the distance between them, reached behind her neck, and bent down, pressing his warm lips against her cold ones.

Her mouth opened, and her tongue playfully flicked Damon's. He released an unintentional moan before pulling back to utter one simple sentence.

"To answer your question, my place is right over there." He turned his head and pointed out his cabin with a glance.

He looked down at Alessa, silently awaiting her answer.

Wrapping her hands behind his neck, she jumped up and wrapped her legs around his waist, pulling his lips to hers.

After a passionate embrace that left them both breathing heavily, Alessa jumped down, and they quickly closed the distance between the body of water and Damon's cabin.

Facing one another outside Damon's door, Alessa wet her lower lip in anticipation.

Damon's voice dropped an octave. "I want you. I want all of you."

Jumping into his muscular arms, Alessa's eyes glowed a fiery green, and as their bodies crashed into one another, she moaned into Damon's open mouth.

Carrying her in through the front door, his lips explored the curves of her neck and chest. Damon's guttural moans echoed Alessa's, and while holding her, he dug his fingertips into the sides of her buttocks.

Kicking the door closed, Damon pinned Alessa's wet body against the door and pressed his hard cock into her mound.

With a gasp and a moan, her head thrust back against the wooden doorframe, and he growled into her ear. "That's what you have to look forward to, but first..."

Damon kissed and nipped his way down her neck before backing up. He yanked his drenched shirt off and slapped it onto the hardwood floor.

Mimicking Damon, Alessa stripped, exposing her red lace bra.

An animalistic growl escaped Damon's throat, and he kicked off his combat boots.

Sweeping his arm across the top of a nearby table, he knocked its contents down to the ground before picking Alessa up and setting her atop its slick surface.

Feeling the deep ache of her sore muscles, Alessa whimpered, but as Damon seductively bit the side of her neck, her pain turned to pleasure.

Nibbling down her torso, Damon looked up into her eyes.

Alessa licked her lips, and as adrenaline pumped through his veins, Damon wrapped his hand around her neck and pulled her in for an impassioned kiss, chasing Alessa's tongue with his own.

Pushing her back onto the table, Damon hungrily explored every inch of her exposed skin.

He held Alessa firmly in place as she writhed beneath him, and as Damon flicked his tongue across her breasts and down her stomach, Alessa's breathing became erratic.

Reaching the top of her black leather pants, Damon bit down on the button, yanking it apart with his teeth. Grabbing her pants, he peeled off the tight fabric, exposing her smooth legs and matching red lace panties, which were already soaked through.

Damon dropped to his knees and knelt before Alessa's spread legs. He exhaled hot breaths of air onto her, building her anticipation, and then hungrily pressed his lips against the cool skin of her inner thigh.

Kissing up Alessa's left leg, Damon inhaled her sweet scent before nipping the outside of her panties.

Alessa trembled from head to toe with a 'fuck me' whimper.

Alessa inhaled sharply and bit her lower lip as Damon eagerly unbuckled his belt. As she arched her back, he placed his hands behind Alessa, sitting her upright.

Reaching behind her, Damon grabbed Alessa's ass, forcing a moan from her parted lips as he rammed her into his bulge.

She dug her fingernails into his back, thickening his erection.

Holding Alessa tight, Damon carried her over to his bed, their lips never leaving one another's bruised and battered skin.

Plopping down on the edge of the bed, Alessa fingered his

pants, unbuttoning and working the zipper to his jeans. She tugged down, and they pooled around his ankles.

Before Damon had time to react, Alessa shoved her hand down his undershorts and grasped his thick shaft.

His breathing hitched as she tightened her grip and stroked his length, up and down. Damon's eyes rolled back with a deep growl, and his lips separated in ecstasy as his growing cock twitched within the palm of her hand.

Alessa licked her lips. She was throbbing in response to Damon's arousal, and as he opened his silver eyes, Damon stared down at her, transfixed.

Pulling her hand away, Damon pushed Alessa onto the bed.

Reaching behind Alessa, he unhooked her bra, and each side of the fabric broke free. He peeled the red lace from her chest before flinging it carelessly off to the side of the room.

Wrapping his arms around Alessa, Damon lifted her atop him and touched his lips to her right breast. His tongue swirled around her supple, pink nipple, and with the arching of her back, her breathing paused.

Unwilling to restrain himself any longer, Damon dipped his fingertips into Alessa's panties.

Her breathing resumed as Damon rubbed his fingertips back and forth. She panted uncontrollably, and Damon inhaled her sweet scent as her head tilted toward the ceiling.

Sinking into her warmth, he pressed the length of his fingers, slowly at first—increasing the rhythm of her gyrating hips.

As she rode his fingers, he felt the walls of her pussy tighten.

"Damon, uh!" she gasped as he made her cum.

Withdrawing his fingers, Damon licked each one slowly, tasting Alessa for the first time. Then he peeled Alessa's soaked lace panties from her mound and dropped his black undershorts.

Reaching over to his nightstand, he pulled open the drawer, revealing a box of condoms.

Alessa grabbed Damon's neck and pulled him in. "You don't have to worry about children with me. I've taken care of it."

Damon narrowed his eyes and tilted his head in confusion.

Alessa pressed her lips against his and bit his bottom lip. "Trust me. I want you for you. Not for your bloodline."

"Fuck," Damon moaned and climbed onto the mattress. Lying beside her, he lifted Alessa off the bed and positioned her above his arousal.

While they locked eyes, Damon lowered Alessa down onto himself, and she gasped as she slowly took in every inch of him.

His hand pressed firmly on the back of her neck so he could watch her reaction as she felt every ridge.

Alessa's eyes rolled back in ecstasy, and Damon moaned as Alessa's hips moved rhythmically up and down.

Alessa writhed in agony as blood poured from her nostrils, and her body violently convulsed as Damon forced his way back into existence via Alessa's memories.

"Fuck. Oh, fuck. Alessa ... Babe..." Damon cursed in Italian. Scooping her up in his arms, Damon carried her unconscious form through a doorway into a storage room and set her down on an older chaise.

"What have I done? I knew I shouldn't have ... I-I didn't mean to. I've killed her ... fuck! Alessa, come back to me. Please don't die," Damon begged as Alessa's eyelids fluttered. "I'll never forgive myself—"

. . .

After they climaxed together for the second time that night, Alessa fell to the side. Unable to fight the exhaustion any longer, she slipped peacefully into the darkness as Damon's calloused hand wrapped around her midsection and pulled her back against his chest.

"Mmm..." he moaned gently in her ear, and as she drifted off to sleep, Damon whispered into her messy dark hair, "Sydämen liekki, my heart's flame."

Alessa gasped as her skull threatened to split in half.

"Alessa?" Damon pleaded.

As her body went limp, he clutched Alessa against his chest. Tears streamed down his face, and he nearly screamed in frustration. "What can I do? I don't know what to do."

The day following Capture the Flag flooded back into its original place in Alessa's mind as if it had never been missing.

She woke up in Damon's bed, naked and happy.

Smiling, she pressed her face into his soft pillow and inhaled Damon's musky scent. Rolling out of bed, Alessa stretched her arms up and allowed the bedsheets to fall, exposing her breasts.

Feeling the chill of the small cabin, Alessa tiptoed barefoot to the bathroom and joined Damon in the steamy shower.

She stepped into the hot water, wrapped her arms around his torso, and rested her hands on his chest.

He turned around and grinned. "Good morning. You're still able to stand upright?" His smile turned seductive. "Let's remedy that."

Damon leaned down into Alessa and licked the side of her neck as his hands explored her wet, naked body.

. . .

Alessa heard Damon calling to her from somewhere far away, but she could not focus on his words as the sights and sounds from the past continued to bombard her.

Images flowed from one scene to another, connecting the dots and filling the gaps previously missing from her memory.

"It's breathtaking," said Alessa as Damon held the ring before her.

Damon took the ring out of the box. "It was my mother's."

Alessa shook her head back and forth as she stared at the gift. "I can't accept this. Your mother, she meant everything to you."

"You can and you will." Damon slid the ring onto her finger.

She threw her arms around Damon's muscular neck. "I love you," she mumbled into the warmth of his skin.

Damon responded with a heartfelt kiss before he pressed his forehead against Alessa's. "And I, you."

"Da-Damon?"

"Alessa? Oh gods. Baby..." Damon cried. "Hold on."

He found a box of cloth napkins to clean the blood from her cheek.

When her vision cleared, Alessa focused on Damon's face, which was etched with concern.

"Are you—" Damon began but was interrupted by Alessa springing upright and tearing the mask from his eyes.

She stared at Damon for a few intense moments before placing her hands on either side of his face. As Alessa pulled him down to her, they sank into the chaise, and her lips moved frantically against Damon's.

Pulling away, Alessa cried, "I remember everything. I remember us."

CHAPTER FIFTY-TWO

Relief washed across Damon's face as he wiped away Alessa's tears.

Pressing his forehead against hers, he choked back tears. "I've missed you so much, sydämen liekki."

"You should've told me," Alessa demanded. "Why didn't you tell me?"

"I didn't even know if you would make it when you remembered things on your own time. You didn't see how your body fought against it." He caressed the side of her face. "But you came back to me."

Alessa placed her hand on Damon's and noticed, for the first time, the longing in his eyes.

Grasping her hand, Damon slid his mask back over his eyes and hurried them out of the room.

"Damon, where are we going?"

"There are too many people that'll hear," he growled as he guided her toward the guesthouse on the edge of Eric's backyard. Approaching the small house, Damon didn't hesitate before kicking open the front door.

"Hello?" he shouted, slamming the door shut and flicking on the light.

"Damon, what are we—?"

He wrapped his arms around Alessa and pressed his lips, hard and desperate, against hers.

Pressing her back up against the door, Damon unbuttoned his suit and shrugged out of the jacket.

Her fingers instinctively unbuttoned his shirt, and as she reached his waist, Alessa tugged the bottom of his shirt up, exposing his toned abdomen.

As her fingers caressed his stomach, she jumped in alarm at the heat radiating off his body. "Babe, you're on fire—"

Ignoring her concern, Damon distracted Alessa by kissing in between her breasts, and as his lips met the dress's fabric, Alessa pressed her fingertips into the bottom of Damon's chin, lifting his lips back up to hers.

Tearing off his mask, she then threw it onto the floor before doing the same with her own. Unbuttoning his pants, Alessa kissed him frantically, making up for lost time.

Damon forced himself to remain patient and nearly splintered the wood as he pressed his hands into the front door on either side of her.

Unzipping Damon's pants, Alessa thrust her hand down his undershorts and grasped his engorged cock.

Damon released a guttural moan as her hand stroked his stiff, smooth shaft, and as her pace quickened, he pressed further into Alessa, rocking his hips while licking and biting her neck.

"Oh, sydämen liekki," he moaned into her ear.

Alessa bit her lower lip as Damon grasped her dress between his fingers, lifting the fabric inch by inch. Finally, the bottom of her skirt reached Alessa's pale upper thighs, and

Damon unclasped the gun and holster from her leg before dropping it onto the floor.

Keeping hold of the dress with one hand, Damon removed Alessa's hand from his erection with the other, and he peeled her gown up over her head.

Damon stopped breathing altogether, and he stood unmoving, staring at her scarred midsection.

Dropping Alessa's dress onto the floor, he fell to his knees, devastated.

Gripping her hips, he held Alessa in place as he tried to remember what her abdomen looked like before.

"Baby, don't—" Alessa started.

He released her left hip and gently traced the scar's puffy edge, lightly caressing the elevated tissue.

"I'm sorry I wasn't there to protect you. I'm so sorry," he apologized in between kisses up her torso.

"Shh..." Alessa shivered, and goosebumps spread from her head to her toes as Damon reached her breasts.

Alessa's back arched, and Damon guided her into his mouth. Wrapping his reddened lips around her hardened nipple, Damon tweaked the sensitive skin with the tip of his tongue.

"Uh! Damon!" Alessa moaned, plunging her fingers into his thick, dark hair.

Moving from Alessa's left breast to her right, Damon slipped his fingers down into her black panties. He bent down and inhaled her breath. "Say my name again," he implored.

"Dam—uh!" she exclaimed as he slipped two fingers inside her.

He grinned devilishly. "My name is not Da-uh. Alessa, my goddess. Say my name," he growled.

Through rapid breaths, Alessa tried again. "Da—uh!" she exclaimed as he slid another finger inside her.

Her mouth opened further as she rocked back and forth on Damon's hand.

He moved his fingers rhythmically in and out, up and down, before pulling out slowly.

Alessa bit Damon's bottom lip, and he thrust his fingers back into her. Her back arched, and she moaned loudly as he held her in place.

Damon massaged, faster and faster, until Alessa's breathing hitched, and a restrained whimper escaped her throat as she came.

Reclaiming her lips with his own, Damon inhaled every unintelligible sound she made, and withdrawing, he left Alessa aching to be filled.

Bringing his slick fingers to his lips, he sucked her juices from them as she leaned into Damon, recovering from her orgasm. Dipping his thumbs into the top of her black lace panties, Damon slid them down her legs as she lifted her right foot and then the other.

She stood before Damon in nothing but her silver heels.

He ran his tongue up the inside of her calf before kissing the entirety of her leg. His tongue swirled in circles upon reaching Alessa's inner thigh, and he gave a single kiss and a lick just below her groin.

His gunmetal grey eyes pierced up into her own activated irises before he lifted one of her thighs onto his shoulder and plunged his tongue deep inside her. His tongue ran up her center before flicking her clit.

He growled in frustration. "I wish we had more time."

Jumping up, Damon turned his head to the side and

coughed. He planted his hands on the wooden door behind Alessa to avoid falling.

She placed her hands on either side of Damon's face while he struggled to catch his breath. "Damon, we don't have to—"

Damon stood tall, and in one swift movement, he dropped both his pants and undershorts. Pulling her into him, Damon silenced Alessa by picking her up with one arm and, with the other hand, pulled her in for an impassioned kiss.

She wrapped her legs around his waist as Damon carried her to the nearest wall.

With Alessa's back against the woodwork, he lowered her hips and thrust inside her.

She moaned loudly in ecstasy, and as Damon withdrew himself, his cock twitched as Alessa tightened around his girth.

Gripping her wrists, Damon pinned Alessa's arms back against the wall as he thrust inside her again and again.

"Damon! Fuck, babe! Oh my gods," she panted.

He plucked Alessa from the wall, laid her down on the rug, and thrust deep inside her.

They both dissolved into a chorus of whimpers, moans and gasps as their bodies moved as one.

"Alessa, baby, say my name."

Unable to think coherently, Alessa panted.

"I want to hear you say it. Say my name, baby. Scream it for me."

"Damon!" she pleaded.

"Cum for me. Cum for me, now," Damon commanded.

Climaxing, Alessa cried out while Damon's body stiffened with his release.

Her body trembled beneath Damon's muscular form before she fell limp onto the floor.

Damon brushed away several stray hairs that had fallen onto her face. "Now, how are you feeling?"

Her eyes remained closed as she responded dreamily, with a hint of a smile. "Mmm ... I missed this. I missed you."

Damon chuckled and stroked her face, but was hit with the terrible realization their reunion had to end.

When she finally opened her eyes, Alessa smiled lazily up at Damon. "I love you. Thank you for not giving up on me."

He leaned forward and rested on his elbow. "Oh, I came close." Damon chuckled. "But know this: I will always find you in this life and the next. You are mine, sydämen liekki."

Damon lifted her chin and kissed Alessa with all the passion he could muster in his weakened state before he reluctantly pulled away. "I wish we could pretend like the world isn't about to end, but we don't have that luxury," he grunted as he grabbed his pants.

Alessa begrudgingly stood up beside him, and after she pulled her panties up, Damon held her dress out for her to slide back into.

She lifted her hands above her head, and he slowly pulled the fabric down over Alessa's shoulders, breasts, stomach, and then hips. His feverish hands burned a path upon her skin as he helped adjust the material over her womanly curves.

Damon finished dressing while Alessa quickly fastened the gun and strapped it around her leg.

She sighed in despair. "Do you think there's any scenario in which we both make it out alive?"

Damon's smile didn't quite reach his eyes as he placed a hot hand on the side of her face.

For what may have been the last time, Damon and Alessa held each other tight, and he lowered his lips onto hers.

Finally, Damon pulled back and slipped the ebony lace

mask back into place on Alessa before putting his mask over his eyes.

Somehow, Damon mustered the strength to let Alessa go, and as he stepped back, he pressed his lips against his mother's ring on Alessa's finger before looking into her eyes. "Be safe, sydämen liekki."

Damon's hand fell away as he held back the urge to cough again and hurried out the door.

Fighting the overwhelming urge to run after him, Alessa's fists clenched and unclenched as she stood alone in front of the guest house's door.

As she focused on the near-impossible task of saving Damon's life, Alessa twisted the band around her finger.

After a few deep breaths, she tilted her chin in determination and left the guest house behind. Stepping out into the chilly night air, she marched across the grass toward Eric's château.

When Alessa re-entered the house, most guests were pumped full of liquor, laughing loudly, and dancing. As she hurried past the dancefloor, Alessa scanned the room for both Damon and Camden.

Unable to find either one, she ascended the main staircase to join Eric in his quarters.

Alessa quickly found the room, thanks to the large men stationed outside Eric's doors. She nervously cleared her throat as she approached the large Bodyguards. "I'm, uh, here to see Eric."

One of the three men mumbled into a radio attached to his upper jacket sleeve, and with a curt nod of his head, one of the other men opened the door.

Alessa took a steadying breath and stepped forward into the room.

CHAPTER FIFTY-THREE

Inside the doorway was a small circular table with a white cloth draped over the top, displaying a bottle of red wine, meat, cheese, and crackers.

Against the left wall was a large bed adorned with animal hides, and on the right side of the room stood a tall shelf stacked high with books.

Alessa walked apprehensively into the bedchamber, scanning the room for possible threats.

Eric was standing alone on the dark balcony behind a billowing curtain; the tip of his cigar glowing bright orange in the dark as he took a puff.

With her heels clicking loudly against the tiled floor, Alessa swallowed the bile creeping up the back of her throat and crossed the room.

The bloated man turned around, extended his free hand toward her, and blew white smoke directly into Alessa's face.

Fighting back an intense wave of nausea, she closed her eyes and hesitated for a moment before placing her hand within his.

She plastered a fake smile and stepped onto the balcony, joining him in the darkness.

He puffed on his cigar as he wrapped his arm around her waist. "Isn't this a beautiful view?"

White smoke swirled out of his mouth and nose as they looked across his expansive yard toward the dense treeline outlined by the city's lights.

Alessa stood frozen in silence as the tips of his fingers ran up and down her exposed, tattooed side.

Eric stared at her smooth, pale skin. "You want to know something I've never told anyone?"

She remained in his arms, rigid and unmoving.

"Every reporter eventually asks me about my childhood. For some reason, having a lot of money means people like to ask about your upbringing. And do you know what I always tell them? My parents cherished me, and I became the product of a loving home." He cocked his head to the side and laughed maniacally. "Of course, none of that is true."

Eric puffed on his cigar before continuing.

"When I was a child," he exhaled, "my parents were members of a religious cult. We lived on a self-sustaining farm with little access to modern conveniences. We were taught from infancy that our only purpose in life was to breed and follow the word of God."

Eric snickered.

"My parents taught us children to fear the outside world, that the heathens would be the end of us. My mom and dad were nothing special; they were ignorant people who let some idea of who they were supposed to be consume their lives. They were weak."

Eric directed Alessa inside. "Walk with me."

She anxiously spun Damon's ring around her finger as they returned inside.

Following her, Eric placed his hand on her lower back, ushering her toward the small circular table. "There was a leader on this farm. One who claimed God spoke through him, instructing him to do heinous things to us children, for that was the only way to purify our souls for entry into heaven."

As he approached the food and wine, Eric extended his head to the left and pulled his shirt collar down, exposing a circular scar on his neck.

"Pressing a lit cigar into a helpless child's flesh was one of the lesser punishments for misbehaving."

As Eric uncorked the wine and poured the red liquid into two glasses, Alessa remained stoic and emotionless. *What is he hoping to accomplish by telling me this?*

He held a full glass out to Alessa. "Over time, I found myself growing hateful toward the community until finally, after many years of abuse, all I had left in my heart was disdain." Eric scowled and extinguished his cigar on a plate.

"When I was sixteen years old, our community's leader killed my little sister because she didn't want to become his tenth wife. Our leader bludgeoned her to death with his metal dinner plate." He shook his head back and forth in disgust. "The next morning, I found that old bastard sitting at his kitchen table, eating breakfast." Eric grinned wickedly.

"And as he sat there eating his eggs benedict, I smashed a tire iron into the back of his skull, again and again, until I was confident he'd never lay his hands on another human being. At least not in this life," He chuckled.

Alessa nearly choked on a mouthful of wine as she listened to his confession.

"Please, do try the cheese. It's imported from Italy," he

suggested casually. Picking up his glass, Eric chugged half of the red wine as his large frame shuffled to the bookcase.

"Of course, after killing the commune's leader, I had no choice but to flee. But not before my six-year-old nephew and I trapped my parents in their home and set it on fire. As the flames rose into the sky, I realized something." He placed his fingertips on a crimson book's spine on the fourth shelf. "I was looking at humanity's future. If ignorant, weak-minded, and ill-genetically structured people are allowed to continue procreating, our species won't stand a chance."

Eric's eyes burned into Alessa's, and he tilted the top of the book toward him.

The shelves made a mechanical clicking noise, and the large bookcase swung away from the wall, revealing a hidden room.

Two women were restrained to metallic chairs with thick yellow straps.

The blonde woman sitting on the left's head was hanging unnaturally, resting upon her right shoulder, with a pool of congealed blood encircling her bare feet.

The other woman's curly, dark brown hair bobbed back and forth as her head wobbled.

Alessa froze, and her jaw dropped as she looked at the woman's badly beaten face. Her left eye was swollen shut, and the whites of her right eye were stained red with broken blood vessels.

As Alessa recognized the tanned woman, she gasped.

"Reagan, no!" Alessa cried out, darting across the room.

She fell before her friend and placed her shaking hand upon Reagan's bruised cheek. Tears streaked down Reagan's filthy face onto her pale, cracked lips.

"Reagan. I am so sorry." Tears fell from Alessa's eyes as her body trembled with rage.

Her heart dropped as her eyes darted toward McKenzie. "Kenzie!" Alessa cried.

Her friend's stiff body sat at an unnatural angle as she stared expressionless at the floor, unblinking.

Alessa whipped around, and her eyes flared green. "How could you do this? They didn't know anything!" Alessa yelled.

Several guards rushed into the room behind Eric, pointing guns at Alessa and her friends.

"Well, *Alessa* ... Is it okay to call you by your real name, or are we still pretending you're this Amelia character?" Eric glared. "We couldn't have known that when we first picked them up. You did live with these girls; you were supposedly best friends. I thought girls told each other everything?" he guffawed sarcastically.

Alessa stood protectively before Reagan.

"I had assumed they would know something, anything, about who you truly were, but clearly, I was wrong." Eric shrugged.

Alessa scowled.

"Hey, it takes a real man to admit he's wrong. Besides, it was fun while it lasted." Eric puckered his lips and blew Reagan a kiss.

Alessa's friend whimpered and turned away.

"You know, I didn't even know who you were until we were dancing. I saw your distinctive tattoo, and then you threatened to out me. No one has ever dared speak to me like that. But you look so different now." Eric licked his lips.

Stepping further in front of Reagan, Alessa prepared for battle by sticking her pale thigh out to the side so she could free her pistol from her inner thigh strap.

More guards filtered in behind Eric as he stepped closer. "Unfortunately, this cannot be a fair fight, as I need to ensure you are put down for good."

As Alessa's fingers dug into the opening of her skirt's slit, loud gunshots echoed from outside the bedroom.

Eric and his men redirected their attention toward the main room's entrance as Damon and Camden burst in.

With the Bodyguards distracted, Alessa whipped her gun out from her thigh strap and flipped the small blade strategically placed on top of the barrel. She sawed through each of Reagan's restraints while Damon and Camden worked on reducing the number of Eric's Bodyguards.

"I'm so sorry, Rae. We're going to get you out of here," Alessa promised. "Stay down and out of the way."

Cutting through the final strap, Alessa draped Reagan's arm over her shoulders and helped her limp to the black couch, up against the secret room's entry wall.

Setting Reagan down on the couch, Alessa fired a kill shot into the nearest guard's ear. She then executed a second guard before the man realized what was happening.

Alessa fired four more shots but failed to fatally wound any additional Bodyguards before running out of bullets.

As the shoot-out in the next room took precedence once more, Alessa crawled to the nearest fallen Bodyguard and dug through his uniform for additional firearms.

She tucked a small gun into her thigh strap before withdrawing a few throwing stars and a knife from his inner jacket pocket. Alessa stood upright, holding a larger gun, and she swiftly executed the group of Bodyguards facing away from her. As their bodies hit the floor, she marched into Eric's bedroom, where a full-blown battle was taking place.

Camden was stationed near the room's entrance, taking

down men left and right while three Bodyguards cornered Damon.

Additional guards continued to filter in through the entryway, threatening to overpower the Spartans and Camden.

Alessa aimed and shot at an approaching Bodyguard, striking him between the eyes. Another guard charged her, and Alessa scooped a nightstick up off the floor and tilted it to the side, blocking the man's fist. Using her elbow, she pushed the metal into his stomach.

As the guard doubled over, Alessa threw the second baton in Damon's direction. "Damon, catch!"

The baton flew while two men rushed Camden. Alessa withdrew two throwing stars from her thigh strap and chucked one into the back of Eric's men.

Grabbing the stick in mid-air, Damon blocked a powerful punch.

Surprised, the man hesitated, allowing Damon enough time to kick his heel into his attacker's abdomen. As he was propelled backward, the second guard, positioned on Damon's right side, threw a punch as the third man, wielding a sharp blade, lunged for Damon.

Damon twirled the ebony baton up and down before flipping the stick sideways, blocking the men's every attempt. He dodged the second Bodyguard's dagger while grabbing the first one's necktie.

Twisting the fabric around the man's throat, Damon pulled down hard and fast, snapping his attacker's neck. Jumping up, Damon swung the baton and lunged to the right, forcefully jabbing the other guard in the diaphragm. As the man bent in half, Damon whipped the stick around one last time, crushing his skull.

Alessa ducked to the right and rolled to the ground to avoid a stray bullet. Propping on one knee, she tossed her remaining star into the shooter's chest.

While Alessa and Damon took on the guards inside the chamber, Camden remained posted near the bedroom's door, taking on the additional guards entering the room.

Camden grabbed an attacking guard and pulled the man to his chest.

As the man flailed about, Camden reached into the Bodyguard's open jacket and withdrew his pistol.

"No! Don't!" The guard's grip on Camden's arm intensified as he pressed the tip of the barrel up into the man's lower jaw. Without a second thought, Camden pulled the trigger, demolishing his ex-colleague's face.

As the bullet passed through the man's skull, up toward the ceiling, he dropped the limp body and aimed at another attacking guard.

He shot the man in the shoulder, and the guard's body jerked back with the twisting of his torso.

Stomping over to the fallen guard in his shiny black dress shoes, Camden lifted the gun and aimed at the man's face. At the precise moment the injured Bodyguard recognized him, Camden shot him.

Glancing up from his dead comrade, Camden locked eyes with Eric.

"Oh shit," Camden grumbled.

A kick to the back pushed Alessa forward into the arms of a sadistically smiling guard, who grabbed both her wrists and squeezed.

She grunted painfully and dropped the nightstick.

The guard restraining Alessa spun her around to face a second attacker, and after raising his fist, the guard punched her square in the jaw.

Her neck jerked to the side, and a high-pitched squeal reverberated throughout her head.

After collecting her thoughts, Alessa used her body's momentum and went limp in the man's arms, forcing them down to the ground.

She reached for the new gun strapped to the inside of her thigh, wrapped her fingers around the grip, and pulled out the pistol, shooting the man standing directly before her.

The guard behind Alessa regained control of her once more and dug his fingers deep into her wrists.

He picked the baton up from the ground as she dropped the gun.

Alessa fought back while the guard rammed the black stick into her throat and pressed it against her trachea, depriving her of oxygen. With her eyes bulging, she grabbed the baton and pressed forward, pushing further into the stick.

Alessa then charged toward the wall in front of them. As she hit the drywall, she placed one foot in front of the other and ran up the golden wallpaper. Pushing outward on the nightstick, she relieved the pressure against her throat and inhaled a much-needed breath.

Gripping the baton, Alessa flipped over her attacker and landed behind him. Releasing the baton, she sprinted for the gun lying on the floor.

She hit the ground, slid on the skirt of her dress, grabbed the firearm, and fired. The bullet struck the Bodyguard's chest, and with a thud, his body was sent flying backward.

Another guard charged from the side, and Alessa turned, aimed the gun, and squeezed the trigger, only to hear the faint click of an empty chamber.

"Shit," she cursed, tossing the pistol aside.

Alessa whipped out her knife, unfolded the blade, and threw it into the middle of the sprinting man's chest.

The guard fell to his knees with a grunt, grasping clumsily at the fatal wound.

Camden rushed Eric, trying to stop him from obtaining the remote he needed to control Camden, but the Bodyguards dove in front of Eric, sacrificing their lives as he bolted for his portrait hanging on the wall.

Tilting the frame, Eric revealed a safe hidden within the drywall.

Camden's face contorted in fiery determination as he took down guard after guard before he grabbed a blade from within a fallen guard's jacket.

Rushing to get the remote before Camden got to him, Eric sloppily punched in a six-digit code, and with a mechanical whir, he whipped the door open and grabbed the silver remote inside the wall.

As Camden raised his arm to chuck the blade at the president, Eric pressed the remote's button, and its circle glowed red.

"Fuck," Camden cursed.

His irises flickered gold as he was forced to activate in Eric's favor.

Alessa watched helplessly as Camden turned toward them with the blade in his hand and brought his arm back, aiming at Damon.

"Cam, no!" she shrieked with outstretched arms. Alessa's eyes flickered red before returning to their emerald green hue.

Camden yelled, "Damon, get down!" just before he released the blade.

CHAPTER FIFTY-FOUR

The knife flipped through the air as Damon hit the floor.

Alessa collided with Camden and pushed him to the side.

"What the hell are you doing?" she demanded.

"Watch out!" Camden warned as his fist swung at her. "I can't stop!"

Alessa ducked, bounced back, and kicked him in the side.

As Alessa's foot connected with Cam's ribs, he grabbed her foot and twisted her leg. His eyebrows scrunched up apologetically. "I'm sorry. He's controlling me!"

Alessa landed hard, smacking her cheek against the cold floor.

Sprinting across the room, Damon jumped before Alessa and blocked Camden's kick, meant for her head.

Damon punched Camden. "I fucking knew this would happen!"

Camden fought back with fists flying. "Oh, shut the hell up. I'm just as pissed as you are."

"I warned you—" Damon threatened.

"Oh, I recall that empty promise," Camden remarked

sarcastically as he punched Damon in the side of his face. "Aw, shit. Sorry, man," he apologized with a satisfied smirk.

Rubbing her bruised face, Alessa stood up and watched the men in confusion. "Would someone please explain what the hell is going on?"

"He's Rogue Command," Damon explained in between punches. "Eric's controlling his microchip."

"Go right!" Camden shouted.

Damon dove to the right as Camden brought his fist down into space.

"Cam?" Alessa hollered, jumping back in defense.

As Alessa, Damon, and Camden fought in the center of the bedroom, Eric's guards backed away, filing in front of the president to protect him.

"Let Camden handle the two of them. They'll never make it out alive," Eric told his Bodyguards with a sadistic grin.

"Left!" Camden shouted as he jabbed at Alessa's right side.

Alessa blocked the hit but was pushed backward.

"He's telling the truth, Alessa," Camden confessed.

"Why didn't you—"

"Back up!" Camden shouted, hitting Damon in the abdomen. "You wouldn't have known what Rogue Command was at the time. Besides," Camden threw an uppercut into Damon's lower jaw and grunted, "I had to risk it to help you."

"Well, this," Alessa panted, "is *not* helping."

"Knock me out already, so I stop fighting you," Camden insisted.

"We're trying!" Damon and Alessa shouted in unison.

With a bloodied lip, Damon stepped forward and jabbed toward Camden.

As Cam focused all his energy on Damon, Alessa hit the tiled floor and fell forward into a somersault. Sitting up next to the small table, she picked up an empty gun lying on the floor and aimed the weapon at Eric, intentionally distracting Camden.

Camden sprinted toward Alessa to stop her, and just before he reached Alessa, Damon picked up a metal chair and slammed it down hard on the back of Camden's head.

Knocked out cold, Camden dropped to the floor as Damon fell to his knees, coughing and gasping for air.

"Damon?" Alessa crawled before him and placed her hands on either side of his face. "Baby, listen to my voice. Take slow, deep breaths."

As exhaustion took hold, Damon collapsed in Alessa's arms.

"We're so close. Please don't give up."

Unable to fight back the infection any longer, Damon's body convulsed. Tilting his head to the side, Damon choked up dark crimson blood on the cold floor.

Alessa panicked. "No, no, no," she cried as she helped him onto his side.

"Well, what do we have here?" Eric stepped forward, his voice dripping with intrigue. "Did your beloved happen to consume one of our red pills?"

Consumed by rage, Alessa's green irises flickered red once more.

"Aw. He did, didn't he?" Eric grinned with satisfaction.

Turning Damon onto his back, Alessa scooped him into her arms and held him tight.

"I think it's safe to assume," Eric reached into his jacket pocket, "you came here tonight looking for this?" His hand emerged, holding a vial filled with a pearly, canary yellow liquid.

Alessa's eyes widened in desperation as Eric confidently stepped before the guards, rolling the vial between his fingers.

Eric's entourage inched toward Alessa and Damon while Eric strolled across the room.

Holding Damon close, Alessa's lips moved silently as she counted the increasing seconds between his shallow breaths. Unsure of what to do, Alessa used her ebony skirt to wipe the blood from his lips.

Eric stopped in front of the open bookcase. "How does it feel knowing the cure is a mere twenty feet in front of you?" He smirked. "Don't worry, Alessa. I'll ensure you don't live long enough to miss him too much."

Tears streamed down her face as Damon's breathing hitched.

Somehow, he found the energy to lift his shaking hand to wipe away her tears. "Shh. Don't be sad, sydämen liekki. I'm so glad ... the gods brought you ... into my life." Damon closed his eyes, and a sad smile played upon his lips. "Maybe ... you can learn to play the harp ... and make a deal with Hades ... to bring me back."

His forced laugh turned into an uncontrollable coughing fit.

A piercing familiarity struck Alessa as Damon mentioned her striking a deal with Hades.

Standing in the background, Eric watched Damon and Alessa's interaction.

"Alright, enough of this."

As Damon's breathing hitched again, Alessa leaned down and pressed her lips against his, mixing his blood with her salty tears. "I'm so sorry. I failed you."

She pulled back, and Damon caressed her cheek.

He inhaled shakily. "You know the moment ... I realized I ... was falling for ... the one ... woman ... I couldn't have?"

Alessa's tears fell freely from her eyes as she shook her head.

He smiled weakly. "When I ... woke up ... to you asleep ... on my chest ... the morning after ... our first ... kiss." Blood seeped out from the corner of his mouth as he continued his confession. "With the rising of ... the new day's sun ... I knew I would ... forever be yours."

Unable to hold back her anguish, she choked on her overwhelming grief as Damon forced a smile.

"You ... must live ... for the both of us, now. I'll ... always ... love—" His eyelids closed, and with a loud exhale, his hand dropped, heavy, to the floor.

"No, Damon!" Alessa grabbed his limp hand and pressed it against her cheek. "Stay with me. No, no, no. You can't leave me," she sobbed. "Please don't leave me. Damon, please. No!"

Camden stirred with a groan, and sitting upright, he grabbed his head.

Eric pointed at Damon. "As soon as that man's chest stops moving, fire at will," he instructed the Bodyguards.

Pressing Damon against her chest, Alessa's hope dissipated as she curled herself into him, and as Eric turned on his heel to exit the room, he released a blood-curdling scream.

CHAPTER FIFTY-FIVE

Reagan stood behind him, holding the knife's handle protruding from his side.

She twisted the blade further, and Eric dropped the vial containing Damon's lifesaving serum and Camden's silver controller.

"That's for McKenzie," Reagan growled. "And this is for me." Stomping on Camden's controller, she crunched it beneath her bare foot.

"Reagan, no!" Alessa yelled as the armed Bodyguards unloaded a round into her.

Alessa violently shook as Reagan's limp body fell amongst the dead.

Her friend's eyes remained open as her head lolled, lifeless, to the side.

Leaving Alessa and Damon unattended, Eric's Bodyguards rushed to his side.

"We need an evac chopper at Eric's balcony, now!" one of the Bodyguards shouted into his radio.

Eyeing the serum lying in the middle of the floor, Alessa dropped Damon and scrambled across the tile.

Camden ran up behind Alessa, but she kept going. Knowing Damon didn't stand a chance if the cure wasn't administered quickly, she braced herself for the hit, accepting the pain Camden was about to inflict upon her.

But instead of tackling Alessa, Camden flew past her.

Bellowing out a warrior's war cry, he lunged at the room full of Bodyguards, taking them all on at once.

Thanks to Reagan destroying the remote, Eric no longer controlled Camden and he could fight for himself again.

Returning to Damon's side, Alessa lifted him under his arms and propped his torso against her chest. "Open your mouth, Damon."

When he failed to comply, Alessa pried his jaw open and poured the cure into his mouth.

"Come on ... come on," she begged. "This has to work; it can't be too late. Please, work."

Seconds turned to minutes as Alessa willed Damon to open his eyes. "Please, please don't leave me. I can't do this on my own. You have no idea how much I love you. I-I don't know how to live without you."

Alessa's hope dwindled as his lips turned a shade of light blue. "Damon?" she cried.

Snuggling him into her neck, Alessa screamed. "This isn't fair! I just got you back. It isn't supposed to end like this!"

She rocked back and forth, holding the love of her life against her chest.

"I'm sorry. I'm so sorry," Alessa sobbed into his dark tufts of hair.

In the background, Camden grunted, swore, and shouted

obscenities as he took on all the Bodyguards, but there were too many for one man.

Bending down, Alessa kissed Damon's lips in one last act of desperation. "Come back to me, Damon. Please come back. Don't do this."

Through blurry vision, Alessa looked up at Camden, losing the fight. She trembled with every hit Camden received, and as she watched her friend fight in her honor, Alessa's insides burned.

She gently set Damon down on the ground before slowly rising. Her hatred toward the men flowed through her veins, and in Alessa's mind, nothing was more important than making the Bodyguards suffer.

Her rage intensified, and soon she was consumed by hate.

As something deep inside of Alessa snapped, her microchip glitched.

She glared at the fighting men with blood-red irises, and one at a time, the electronics around the room exploded in a fiery blaze.

Everyone jumped in surprise as the electronics burst into flames.

Alessa stared down one of the guards, focusing all her energy on his implanted microchip. As she imagined the tiny device exploding inside his skull, the man's face contorted, and he grabbed the sides of his head.

Hitting his knees, the guard let out an ear-piercing scream, and his eyes seeped red as he fell forward, flat onto his face.

Turning to the next guard, Alessa pictured his microchip exploding into a thousand pieces, its shrapnel ripping through him.

He, too, collapsed in a matter of seconds.

The flames spread quickly, setting the room ablaze while

Alessa expended all her energy on killing every single Bodyguard.

Camden stood, stunned, as the men around him fell like rag dolls.

With Alessa distracted, Eric limped toward the balcony doors. Leaving behind a trail of blood, he grabbed the ladder dangling from a helicopter hovering above his balcony.

Her attention returned to Eric as she glared at him through tear-streaked vision. Unable to pursue him, Alessa watched Eric's outline disappear into the night sky as his helicopter flew away.

Her adrenaline dwindled, and her energy wavered until Alessa's irises turned back to blue.

Collapsing to the floor, Alessa's face scrunched up in determination as she crawled over to Damon.

"Well, that was a neat trick." Camden slowly shook his head, breathing heavily. "You didn't tell me you were a technopath. Either that or your microchip suffered the worst glitch I've ever seen."

Realizing Alessa was clinging tightly to Damon's lifeless body, Camden dropped down beside her. "Oh, Alessa. I'm so sorry." His eyebrows furrowed.

A chunk of the large window valance broke off, crashing down to the floor, and Camden threw himself on top of Alessa.

"Alessa, we've got to get out of here." He placed his hand on her shoulder.

She jerked her arm away. "I'm not leaving him."

Cam desperately unpeeled Alessa's arms from Damon's body. "There's nothing we can do for him now."

The flames licked the bedroom's wooden door frame, threatening to consume their exit.

"Cam, I—" she begged.

"Alessa, listen to me. We have to get out of the house before it burns down with us in it," Camden pleaded. "Or else Damon lost his life for nothing."

Refusing to budge, Alessa vehemently shook her head as she pushed Camden away.

"Forgive me," Camden apologized as he ripped Alessa's hands away from Damon and flung her over his shoulder.

"Cam, no! Stop! Damon!" Alessa begged, reaching out for Damon's still form.

Camden carried Alessa through the doorway, dodging smoke and fire as she yelled for him to stop.

"No!" She kicked her legs and flailed her arms. "Damon!" she screamed. "Cam, you can't do this! Damon, no! Damon!"

As they rounded the corner, Damon disappeared from Alessa's view, and she smacked Camden's back. "Cam, stop! We have to go back for him!"

Reaching the top of the staircase, Camden set Alessa down. His forehead scrunched up as he held her in place while she tried pushing him away.

"Listen to me, Alessa. Listen!" Cam demanded. "He's gone. Damon's gone."

As the truth of his words sunk in, Alessa's heart clenched.

"Come on, we gotta move!"

With the falling of the elaborate chandelier, they both dashed down the staircase, joining the rest of the partygoers escaping the burning house.

The château burned in the background as they ran down the drive, away from the tragic night.

As Alessa's knees gave out beneath her, Camden scooped her up into his arms and pressed her against his chest.

The well-dressed guests panicked around the manicured yard as Eric's château was engulfed in bright flames.

Unable to comprehend the scene before her, Alessa watched the fire dance up the side of the home before she closed her eyes.

Television reporters scrambled about, trying to get the best angle of the fiery scene.

As Camden placed Alessa in the car, she slumped into the passenger seat and glanced back into the back seat, where four duffel bags and Damon's laptop bag were stashed.

Nauseated by the sight of Damon's things, Alessa glanced out her window as Camden threw the car into reverse and gunned it, barely missing a man and woman frantically running and crying.

Tall red, orange, and yellow flames reached up to the dark heavens toward the flickering stars.

Alessa's breath was taken away as she remembered Damon teaching her about the constellation Lyra and the reason behind its formation: lovers separated by death. Unable to keep the image of Damon lying upstairs in Eric's bedchamber, waiting for the fire to consume him out of her mind, Alessa broke down.

With a guttural moan, Alessa tried to keep her unsurmountable pain beneath the surface, and she curled up into as tiny a ball as she could manage.

As they passed electronic billboards posted on either side of the road, Alessa gasped as they all flickered simultaneously to the same man's picture: Eric Lansing.

His smug face lit up on every screen as the boards played her downloaded footage.

It must be ten o'clock.

As pictures flashed before her, a man's voice echoed from every billboard's speaker.

"The golden-flaked serum will be marketed as the

ultimate cure for smallpox, the vaccine and treatment all-in-one. However, for the world to need either a vaccine or treatment, the disease has to be reintroduced to the world population.

"We plan on releasing the infected mist into the New York subway. A single mist spray on just one train will ensure everyone on board has the highly contagious disease. The infection rate is approximately thirty people, meaning every infected individual can potentially infect thirty more.

"We have secured connections with the one lab within the United States capable of producing a cure and a vaccine. Erebos Industries will be the only company with the ability to make the much-needed medication, and the CDC will be so desperate for a cure that they won't stop to question us.

"No one will suspect the outbreak started with us. It will be advertised as a wonder drug created to eradicate the smallpox virus.

"Once the liquid is ingested, the smallpox virus will successfully be eliminated. However, if there are any life ending genetic anomalies within their DNA, the individual will then contract an accelerated, mutated version of tuberculosis.

"This ensures our ability to control the future's genetic pool."

Eric's smiling face was plastered on the screen with the words 'future president of the world' displayed beneath his picture.

As another voice described Eric Lansing's vision of the new world, Alessa closed her eyes and collapsed back against the seat as tears cascaded down her flushed cheeks.

"Thank you, Damon," she whispered.

In response to the news, citizens swarmed the streets in a

violent uproar. Cars were set on fire, and buildings defiled as men and women threw bricks through panes of glass.

The enraged citizens marched up and down the streets, bellowing, "Death to Erebos! Death to Lansing!"

Camden honked his horn and pushed through the mass of people.

Parking outside their motel, Camden jumped out of the car, lifted Alessa into his arms, and carried her inside their room. Before hurrying into the bathroom, he laid her on the bed's lumpy comforter.

The shower turned on, and Alessa rolled onto her side. Reliving the memories of Damon, she lost all composure.

His scent of musk and cinnamon surrounding her.

Damon smiling up at Alessa after kissing her stomach.

His arms wrapped around her waist.

Damon confessing his love.

The touch of his hand on Alessa's lower back as they moved together across the dancefloor.

Camden gently placed his hand upon Alessa's shoulder, and her heart shattered as she realized she would never again feel Damon's touch.

Alessa's breath escaped her lungs as she burst into tears and curled up helplessly in Camden's arms as he rolled her into his chest.

Lifting Alessa off the bed, Camden carried her to the shower and stepped into the tub while holding her trembling figure.

He stood Alessa beside himself before ripping her skirt up to her thighs. Comforting her beneath the water, Camden sat

Alessa on his lap and held her beneath the warm running water.

"He's gone, Cam," Alessa gasped between sobs as the water soaked her dress. "Damon's gone! Please, Damon," Alessa whimpered, grasping onto Camden's arms.

Not knowing how else to comfort her, Camden held Alessa tightly as she cried beneath the running water.

"Come back, Damon. Please, come back..."

CHAPTER FIFTY-SIX

The guest's screams echoed throughout the château as vibrant flames licked its walls.

Waiting to be consumed by the fire, Damon lay in the smoke-filled bedroom as orange embers flew haphazardly above.

As his love's voice faded away down the hall, Damon's chest rose imperceptibly.

Unbeknownst to Alessa, with the final beat of his heart, the cure had spread throughout his body, and as color returned to his cheeks, Damon awoke with a gasp.

READY FOR MORE?

Keep a look out for book two in the Glitched Series.

ABOUT THE AUTHOR

Eisley Rose is the author of the debut novel *Glitched*. She is also a registered nurse, a stay-at-home mom, and an entrepreneur who lives in the greater Kansas City area. She loves reading, writing, painting, attending concerts, playing tennis, watching movies, and playing board games with her family. Her love for science formed the backbone of this story, but she also adores anything creative and openly embraces the unique.

"If you choose to be one thing in this world, choose to be unequivocally, unapologetically, you."
— Eisley Rose

Social Media Accounts:

facebook.com/eisleyrosebooks

instagram.com/eisleyrosebooks

goodreads.com/eisleyrosebooks

youtube.com/@EisleyRoseBooks

tiktok.com/@eisleyrosebooks

REVIEWS APPRECIATED

Please feel free to leave a review online.